# A STRANGE INTRUSION

# A STRANGE INTRUSION

## A DETECTIVE INSPECTOR ROLAND BENITO THRILLER

## INGER GAMMELGAARD MADSEN

Translated from Danish by Sinéad Quirke Køngerskov

Podium

SAGA
EGMONT

This is a work of fiction. Names, characters, places, and incidents are either products of the author's imagination or used fictitiously. Any resemblance to actual events, locales, or persons, living, dead, or undead, is entirely coincidental.



English translation copyright © 2023 by Saga Egmont

Cover design by Podium Publishing

ISBN: 978-1-0394-3656-5

Published in 2023 by Podium Publishing, ULC
www.podiumaudio.com

Podium

# A STRANGE INTRUSION

# 1

---

The freezing temperatures had dropped further as darkness fell. He felt it as soon as he came out of the hot, damp stables. The hairs in his nostrils froze, and the snow splintered under his boots as he walked up to the farmhouse. His breath hung in the air as petrified white mist. Minus thirteen degrees Celsius said the thermometer on the wall.

Gunda was still up even though she had done the milking at five o'clock that morning. Now she was making the evening coffee. The ceiling lamp illuminated the darkness in front of the kitchen window, casting a golden glow onto the snow.

The car was still there. Now he could see that it hadn't just been abandoned by a motorist stuck in a snowdrift as he had first assumed. A glow from a cigarette lit up briefly in the darkness. Or had he imagined it? Would he even be able to see that from this distance? The car was parked between the trees by the road that connected the four closest-lying farms. He stamped the snow off on the mat and looked at the car again before going inside. It had been there for a long time. When he'd gone out to the stable, it hadn't been completely dark. Still, the white car hadn't been easy to spot in the snowy landscape. He'd only noticed it because it wasn't normal for anyone to park there. He had been about to go up and ask if there were any problems but stopped himself. What did that car have to do with him? A couple in love, maybe, even if it was a chilly pleasure, and if so, they were taking their time about it.

The heat inside hit just as hard as the cold had done. The hairs in his nose thawed, making it run. He wiped his nose on a Kleenex. Gunda looked at him from the kitchen.

"You're not getting sick, are you, Thorkild?"

"No. It's just the frost."

He took off his cap and coat in the utility room, where there was already a smell of cow from wellies and outerwear, and he stroked his hand over his head as if to comb his hair in place, but it had started to fall out before he'd even turned forty. His head was like an egg now. What could you expect when you were in your mid-fifties? Gunda wiped the oil cloth and placed the coffee pot on a trivet. He sat down on the bench and poured coffee for himself. The farm was a real family farm like in good old Morten Korch films. But life in the country had not been all rosy. Agriculture didn't count for anything nowadays. The environment, shops, and homes were more important, so many farmers were forced to surrender and sell their land to meet those needs. They were also severely criticised for helping to pollute nature. And yet people couldn't do without milk, butter, and cheese as if they thought it grew on trees or that the big supermarket chains had cows out in their back rooms. He snorted at the thought.

"What did you spot up by the road?" asked Gunda, putting cakes on the table.

"Oh, it's just a car that's been up there for a while."

"Strange place to park. Who can it be?"

She stared out the window, but it was impossible to see the car from there in the dark.

"It's nothing to do with us."

She sat down, too, poured coffee, and put a piece of the Danish butter-ring and a biscuit on her plate. Afterwards, she pushed the dish towards him.

"Maybe it's someone visiting the Hovgaards again. They seem to have guests all the time," she said with her mouth full of cake.

"Then it definitely doesn't have anything to do with us!" he said firmly.

They consumed their evening coffee in silence, but he kept thinking about the car. Who would sit out in that cold for so long?

*The lights in the farmhouse windows of the few scattered yards in the landscape had long since been extinguished, one by one. It had begun to snow again.*

*The flakes dropped like glittering crystals, settled on shrubs and trees, forming a protective white blanket against the harsh frost. They lit up in the stillness of the night, broken only by the eerie screeches of a tawny owl and the quiet creaking of car doors as they were slowly opened. Three dark figures stepped out and began to walk along the road. They melted into the grey shadows of the trees, walking silently in the snow in white wellies, slowly and purposefully and with black balaclavas to protect against the cold. They had waited a long time, and the time had now come.*

# 2

Detective Inspector Roland Benito froze even more as he stepped out of the car's warmth. He pulled the collar of his coat well up around his ears. Very bloody funny to be ordered out of his warm bed at three o'clock in the morning by Chief Superintendent Kurt Olsen's hoarse, sleepy voice on the phone. He had been short-tempered and given only a few vital details, such as an address and what little he knew about the crime for now. It hadn't sounded as violent as it had looked at first glance when Roland was greeted by the police barricade that contrasted with the snow-white surroundings. Fluttering proof that a crime had taken place. A fact that was reconfirmed by the forensic technicians in the yard. In the dark, their white suits merged with the snow that was falling quietly, reminiscent of a peaceful Christmas night. Discouraged, he walked across the yard.

The technicians only glanced at him and said a brief hello as he walked past them. The officer in front of the door handed him a white overall, latex gloves, a face mask, a blue plastic hat, and shoe covers. As he put the suit on, he fleetingly noticed that the front door had been broken open at the lock. Forensics were working inside the house, too, taking fingerprints and collecting evidence.

Kurt Olsen had arrived and was talking to an excited woman in a darkened bedroom. He wasn't recognisable, either, in the white suit that was mandatory at a crime scene. Another woman was sitting on the bed. Her nose and upper lip were bleeding, and one eye was red and swollen shut.

Yet another home robbery in an otherwise quiet and peaceful area far out in the country, where, in days gone by, you never had to lock your door. After banks and businesses had become impregnable forts with improved security, expensive alarm systems, and surveillance, burglars were now seeking other targets: mostly the elderly, the innocent, and the defenceless, who never dreamed of something like this happening in their peaceful neighbourhoods and certainly not in their own safe homes. According to the myth, it was foreign gangs. Eastern Europeans, in particular, were blamed. But an analysis from the Danish National Police resulted in completely different figures. Most crimes were actually committed by young Danes. Quite often *very* young Danes.

Roland thought it must be the crime scene he was looking at from the doorway. A lamp had fallen from the bedside table, and he glimpsed blood on the pillow behind the woman on the bed. She sat like a white plaster figure, petrified, staring into thin air. He judged her to be in her late fifties. The woman who spoke to Kurt Olsen appeared a little younger and had a sturdy appearance and rough features. A wide nose, glasses with oval lenses and mouse-brown hair. Wisps stuck out of a messy hairdo—probably tousled from sleep. Her voice was deep and hoarse, but that could have been due to anxiety or nervousness. He looked around the house and found forensic pathologist Henry Leander in the kitchen with a couple of technicians. They were taking pictures of a lifeless man lying on the floor in a distorted position. Yet another crime scene. Roland nodded a greeting that was silently answered by Leander, who rose from his kneeling position and looked at him with a serious expression.

"What would you do if you were assaulted in the middle of the night in your own home? Go on the defence and protect your valuables or stand there?"

Roland shrugged. It wasn't exactly a situation he had considered.

"Maybe there are no valuables worth fighting for." Leander sighed, looking down at the man on the floor. Roland tried not to. Leander was right; nothing material was worth enough to make a person look like that.

"What's the cause of death?"

"Internal bleeding after seemingly random blunt force trauma to the head and body. He tried to defend himself with his hands; his fingers are broken. The kneecaps are busted, too." Henry Leander pulled off his white gloves with a swipe. "The autopsy may show more."

Kurt Olsen had spotted Roland and came towards him along with the sturdy-looking woman. Henry Leander quickly closed the door to the kitchen after the woman stretched her neck to see into the room. She looked nervously at the window when they heard ambulance sirens out in the dark. Shortly afterwards, two emergency responders with a stretcher knocked on the door. Olsen showed them into the bedroom and then turned to face Roland again.

"I'm going to the hospital. Ella Geisler here is the nearest neighbour. Signe Hovgaard ran over to them to get help. See what you can get out of her," Olsen whispered and disappeared through the open door and into the cold. Freezing temperatures filled the hallway as the battered woman was carried out to the waiting ambulance. Ella Geisler stood in the doorway, watching her neighbour, horror painted all over her face. The emergency responders quickly closed the doors once they'd pushed the stretcher into place and the ambulance took off at high speed down the road. Ella Geisler was wearing only a turquoise velour dressing gown, which she had quickly put on over her nightdress when she had been awakened in the middle of the night. But she didn't seem to care about the cold. Maybe the slightly too-thick padding helped to keep her warm; Roland was freezing despite the coat and the extra kilos that many lunches and dinners had gifted him over Christmas and New Year's. Gently, he pulled Ella Geisler inside, closed the door, and spoke softly to a technician about where they could sit without destroying evidence. The technician pointed to a room where they had finished but hadn't found anything.

"Imagine that this kind of thing happens?" mumbled Ella Geisler as she sat obediently in a leather chair after he asked her. He gave her a chequered wool blanket that lay over the armrest of the chair he sat in. She pulled the blanket around her with automatic movements as she continued to mumble incomprehensibly. In the living room next door were overturned chairs, pieces of broken glass, and shattered flowerpots—the soil had spilled out over a perhaps genuine Persian rug. A forensic technician was erecting little signs with numbers and taking pictures from several angles. There were obvious signs that Albert Hovgaard had fought for his life. Maybe they both had. Was it worth it? Roland asked himself again, getting up to close the door so they could talk undisturbed.

"Can you tell me what happened here last night? Calmly."

She stopped mumbling, looked at him, and started shaking. "Signe woke us up. She was very scared. There was blood all over her face. It took a while for her to tell us what had happened. As you can see, she is completely distraught," she began. Her eyes were large and startled, yet with a little glow of eagerness that most people display when revealing something sensational. There was sure to be a lot of talk over hedges for the next while.

"What did she say happened?"

"She was awakened by some commotion in the house, and when she opened her eyes, she was looking into the eyes of a man wearing a mask."

"A mask?"

"Yes, only the eyes were visible. It may have been a balaclava. Isn't that what they use?"

"Who?"

"Eastern Europeans."

"Did she say it was Eastern Europeans?"

"Isn't that always the case? They spoke a language Signe didn't understand anyway. Russian maybe? There were three of them apparently—maybe four." She pulled the blanket more closely around her and scowled at the closed door. Roland noticed through a south-facing window that an ambulance with tinted windows had arrived. Leander had probably ordered it to the back door so the body could be driven to the morgue without attracting too much attention. But unrest clearly could be heard from behind the door.

"Then what happened?"

She looked at him again and shook her head. "Seemingly, Albert got into a fight, and Signe ran over to us. We live right over there."

She turned and pointed to the window.

"We? You and your husband?"

"Yes, and our twins, Sam and Dorthe. They're thirteen."

"Where are they now?"

"They went out to look for the criminals; they may have left tracks in the snow."

Roland frowned. That wasn't exactly what they needed at this point in the investigation.

"You don't have a way to get hold of them, do you? It's not good that they are running around playing detectives."

"Sam and Dorthe have phones, but I don't, so . . ."

He took his mobile out of his pocket. "Do you remember their numbers?"

"Not at the moment; I can't even remember my own name."

Roland gave up. It was only a hope that enough evidence had been gathered inside the house. There usually was in these cases. And if there had been three or four burglars, it would be strange if none of them had left something.

"Did Signe Hovgaard take part in the fight, too?"

Ella wrung her hands under the blanket. "The man with the mask punched her in the face with his fist. If they'd discovered her running through the hedge and along the field road over to us, they probably would have followed and killed her. But they must have thought she had fainted . . . or was dead."

"So, you came over here immediately? Did you see the perpetrators?"

"No, they were gone. We had to understand what Signe was shouting about first. When we came to help Albert, he was lying dead on the floor." Ella Geisler hiccupped but held back the tears.

"You didn't notice anything unusual tonight? Parked cars or anything?" If it was Eastern Europeans, they usually operated with different tactics than Danish thieves. They often kept the chosen dwelling under observation for a long time, and it all proceeded without haste. Gangs were known to monitor their chosen targets for several days before striking when they thought the opportunity was best. They ate and slept in the vehicle all the while.

"No, I didn't notice anything. But we can't see the road from our windows, so if they were parked there . . ."

"Do you know if any items were taken? Was anything of value here?"

"No, I don't think so. We're only poor farmers." She forced a superficial smile.

"It doesn't look so poor out here!" He had noticed that everything was as new, from furniture to walls, windows, and the ceiling.

"Their farm burned down a few years ago. The living room and kitchen almost burned to the ground. It was horrible. We feared for those who lived nearby. Fortunately, no one came to harm, and they rebuilt it with the insurance money. There was talk that they set fire to the farm themselves, and . . ." She fell silent. "Do you have more questions? I . . ."

Roland shook his head. It had been an unusual night for everyone. He probably wouldn't get more out of her now anyway. He hoped Olsen would have better luck at the hospital—that is, if he was even able to talk to Signe Hovgaard at all. When he was alone, he went out into the kitchen to the working technician. Henry Leander had gone back to the Institute of Forensic Medicine to examine the body more thoroughly under better conditions.

The kitchen floor resembled the floor of a slaughterhouse. A forensic technician squatted down to gather small white lumps from a pool of blood with a pair of tweezers and carefully placed them in a bag. He lifted it up towards Roland and shook it. "One of them might be from the perp," he said as if to explain the situation. Roland swallowed an extra time when he realised the white lumps were teeth. He quickly learned he was only a nuisance in the kitchen and looked around the other rooms instead. It was impossible to know whether anything had been stolen. Only Signe Hovgaard could determine that, but when he came to the office, which could be Albert Hovgaard's study, he saw that the door to a solid metal cabinet was open. On the wall next to it hung a medal on a red-and-white-striped ribbon. He studied it more closely. Albert Hovgaard apparently had been a shooter. A pistol shooter. One of the tough ones who won gold medals. It wasn't a safe, as Roland had first thought—it was a gun safe, in which such guns were legally required to be stored. It was empty. There was no ammunition, either. Had the thieves managed to find the key, or had they forced the owner to hand it over or unlock it? The standard pistol in most gun clubs was a .22 calibre, he knew, but perhaps Albert Hovgaard had other and maybe even more powerful weapons. Was that the burglars' target? Did they know about the safe? So, there were armed killers on the run. He suddenly felt absolutely exhausted. In three hours, he was due to be at the police station; it was hardly worth leaving and going back to bed again.

# 3

Anne Larsen angrily shut down the laptop by slamming it with a bang. Even today there was nothing. It was hopeless! She had dreamed of a weekday without work and obligations for so long, like in her teenage years when she spent her time on demonstrations, occupying empty houses, and on being a left-wing activist in Nørrebro in the fight for justice. Now she was bored because she couldn't take the bike and ride into the office. My, how times had changed. Completely changed!

Really, she knew full well that it couldn't keep going like this. When the financial crisis warning hit on top of an already challenging time for the newspaper industry, there wasn't much to do. The crisis came rolling across the Atlantic from the United States without anyone or anything being able to stop it—like everything else—McDonald's, hip-hop, roller skates, and skateboards. When it went bad "across the pond," it certainly contaminated Europe, too. At least, that's how it sounded in the media according to journalists, financiers, economists, futurists, and other doomsday soothsayers. In the aftermath, they were blamed for writing the agenda of the financial crisis with a self-reinforcing lack of confidence in the future. But it was a hot topic. It sold newspapers. Everyone wanted to know how tomorrow would look. With the housing market, the banks, the stock markets—the labour market. Maybe they did inflate the crisis, maybe they didn't. But how many places of work had been lost? Banks had foreclosed on people and many employees had been made redundant. Had they been so exaggerated? And the worst was yet to come, they predicted.

Editor Ivan Thygesen's voice had shaken when he informed them that the paper was closing. He was very moved; she had never seen him like that before. He was planning to take early retirement, but he had worked in the newspaper business all his life—day and night—hours of writing and disseminating the news, barely taking a holiday or finding time to nurture a hobby for his retirement. So, what would he do when his work life was over?

Kamilla was the luckiest. She hadn't been herself after her mother's funeral last October. She'd suddenly resigned because she had got a job as an advertising photographer in a photo studio on Nørregade. That was what she was trained as—not as a press photographer, she had argued against all their protests. She would be working with two other photographers, and Anne could well understand her choice, though she was disappointed that Kamilla was leaving. Leaving her. They had become friends who stuck together and supported each other in everything. But there was something that Kamilla hadn't been open about. Something had happened at that funeral in autumn that had changed her and that she wouldn't talk about. Not even with her. It hurt that Kamilla didn't reciprocate, considering how much Anne had confided in her. But maybe it was due to everything Kamilla had been through. It naturally made you afraid of trusting and opening up too much. So, she had left before the financial crisis and the tumult really took hold. But they would have been separated from each other anyway, given how things were. It had only been a few months. The *Daily News* was shut down and she was out of work. For the next six months, she would be on her own and had to find another job herself; that's what they had told her at the unemployment insurance fund, which she was fortunate to be a member of through the Danish Union of Journalists. After the six months, she would receive an activation offer from the Jobcentre. But if she was unlucky enough not to find work—and she now strongly doubted she would—she would consider retraining or further education. For what, she didn't know, but it would certainly be something to do with communication, even though the powers that be warned that the coming years would be even harsher for the traditional media—almost brutal—and that the media industry would be halved within four years. Many laid-off journalists had switched to completely different industries to avoid the uncertainty. Some had become taxi drivers, others were consultants in companies, and a few even had changed fields completely—but where could anyone feel safe?

She had gone down to the kiosk around the corner to buy a few newspapers. Some of those still remained after all. Newspaper corporations had acquired each other. Unfortunately, no one had bought the *Daily News*. A small local rag full of ads. As far as she knew, Thygesen had been to a few meetings, but it had never led to a sale that might have saved them. Soon, probably only one printed newspaper would be left to cover the entire country—until it, too, succumbed to the digital world.

She flipped slowly through the newspaper as she skimmed the columns. Christenings, weddings, anniversaries, and obituaries on the same page. An overview of life's phases. She cast a quick glance at the stack of old copies of the *Daily News* on the floor. Suddenly, she found the layout very old-fashioned in comparison to the newspapers on the table. Other editors had redesigned their newspapers during the crisis in the battle for readers. Was that the only thing they had done wrong? That they hadn't gone for a revamp? Should she have suggested that Thygesen contact Danny Cramer's advertising agency and ask for help with new, young designs and a more modern colour palette? Would it have helped? Probably not, and how would it have affected Kamilla that Danny was involved—she would definitely have resigned as soon as she'd heard. But the *Daily News was* old-fashioned. With time, newspapers would be a piece of nostalgia for her. She had kept the ones with her greatest journalistic triumphs. Like the Gitte murder in the Doll Child Case and the Bog Case last autumn. Creepy murder cases she still hadn't shaken off. *But how can I live without crime?* Should she become a private detective? She smiled at the thought of the job postings she'd found on the East Jutland Police website when she'd been nosing around. They were looking for students specialising in public administration or finance. Unfortunately, she specialised in nothing other than journalism, otherwise she would have applied for the positions. Roland Benito would surely have raised an eyebrow if she was hired. They were also looking for police officers—maybe that was a better job for her. Unfortunately, it would take her too long to be trained up and ready to work at the police station in Aarhus. Benito would tear his hair out! He must feel relieved now that she could no longer interfere in his work. She swallowed a lump when she realised she was actually going to miss him. How was she supposed to be able to manage without her job?

When the day's job opportunities had been researched in vain both online and in the printed newspapers, Anne made a pot of coffee and lit a cigarette. She sat down on the sofa and stared out the window. The frost had adorned a pane with pretty ice flowers that the sun was beginning to melt. Shouldn't she just be happy that she didn't have to be wrapped in a thick coat, mittens, scarf, and hat and be out in the cold to get to work? The bike paths probably weren't cleared, either, and the snowplough had most likely just thrown the snow from the road into them so cars and buses could get past. So, she'd have to take the car, and the old yellow Lada was down in the yard covered in ice and snow and was guaranteed not to start. Such hassle to get work—if she hadn't been made redundant. She smiled sarcastically and tapped ash off the cigarette. And there were probably those from the paper who felt worse than her. Mads Dam, for example, their ineffective sports journalist, who spent more time at the pub than at the football pitch. Would he end up drinking? Her colleague Britt would probably find work given the bosom she was equipped with. She could easily get a job at a nightclub or in a bar. She could get beers for Mads Dam. Anne smiled bitterly again. And Thygesen—what would become of him when he could no longer get upset over little things at the office and scold her to high heaven? Would it hurt his wife, so a divorce would be the next tragedy? Such a fate! She wanted to call Kamilla and hear how things were going in the new job. They hadn't seen each other since she'd left. So much had happened. They hadn't actually talked very much since Kamilla's mother's funeral, which had taken a heavy toll on her, despite her saying she hadn't been overly attached to her mum. Just as Anne wasn't to her own mother. Maybe she was no longer alive, either. Who would tell her if she wasn't? *I don't care either way.* She put out the cigarette butt hard in the ashtray and took a sip of the hot coffee. She couldn't bring herself to call Kamilla. It could wait until she had found a job, so she had some good news, and so she wouldn't have to admit that she was still unemployed. She was lost in her thoughts and heard only a faint chime, as if someone didn't dare to press the button on the doorbell all the way. But when the bell rang again, she heard it and almost spilled the coffee in fright. Her thoughts had wandered to her stepfather, Torsten. He always set her nerves on edge.

"Yes, yes, yes!" she mumbled, annoyed, and got up when the doorbell rang again. When she finally opened it, she saw a small woman who had apparently given up and was on her way down the stairs. She immediately turned around when she heard the door open. She had shoulder-length wavy grey hair gathered in a ponytail with a bobbin. Her shoulders hung, one more than the other due to a huge bag with a worn strap that was weighing it down further. Her mouth was surrounded by fine lines that revealed the habits of a heavy smoker. The bags and the dark shadows under her eyes could also indicate a penchant for alcohol—maybe even drugs. But she was in a beautiful coat with a fur collar, and you could see she cared for her appearance, as best she could. A layer of blush was just a shade too red, so it looked like someone had given her a few slaps rather than natural rosy cheeks, and the lipstick leaked out into the wrinkles around her mouth. The blue eye shadow wasn't applied too well, either. But when Anne looked into the tired grey eyes, a strange sensation hit her chest. They reminded her of something she couldn't put into words.

"Yes?" Anne said dismissively, expecting a copy of *The Watchtower* to be handed to her. But the woman turned around with a cautious smile and seemed to want to embrace her as she made her way back up the stairs. She stopped herself, but her voice was mushy. "Anne?"

Anne nodded, perplexed. It was on the nameplate on the door, so why ask? But there was also too much emotion in the word to be just a question.

"I hardly recognised you. Only the scar, that . . ." The woman reached out, wanting to touch her eyebrows, and as if in a flashback, Anne saw Torsten's hand that night, when he had surprised her here in the apartment. He had also wanted to touch the scar. It was thanks to Roland Benito that she had survived. She grabbed the woman's slender wrist hard before the hand managed to touch her.

"Who are you?" Anne's voice sounded like a hiss, for deep down she knew well who the woman had to be. She recognised the eyes, so the feeling she had in her chest had to be hatred.

"Can I come in for a moment, little Annie? It's been so long . . ."

Now, she was sure. She was the only one who called her Annie, and it was said as if she couldn't bear to pronounce her actual name. The very distinctive Nørrebro accent wasn't to be mistaken, either.

"So long that it's too late," Anne interrupted, her voice cold as ice. "Why are you here? What do you want?"

"I can answer all that if you let me in. Is that coffee I smell?" She inhaled the scent from the kitchen, her nostrils dilating.

"We don't have anything to talk about!"

The grey eyes bore into her. His eyes were full of remorse and despair. It was like looking in the mirror. The same grey-blue colour and the same slightly sleepy expression due to large eyelids that were made beautiful with eye shadow—if you knew how to apply it correctly, that is.

"Okay then, come in for a moment," she said reluctantly. "But I'm busy," she hastened to add, trying to make her voice sound authoritative. What was she doing here? Why was she seeking her out after all these years? She could enter as long as Torsten wasn't with her. Just to be sure, Anne looked down the stairs before closing and locking the door. No, he was still behind bars. Unless he'd been released on probation again.

Nervous, the woman looked around the apartment. She didn't seem to dare to sit on the furniture.

"Just sit down, Mum," Anne said, putting another mug on the table. Her mother looked at her quickly—even she was startled to hear the word come out of Anne's mouth. So surprisingly easy to say it again, but it was hard to say it without anger. She had just never called her anything else; Rose Teresa Larsen didn't suit her. Mum didn't really, either.

Rose sat down while her eyes kept inspecting all of Anne's things.

"You've done so well, Annie. Became a well-known journalist with a permanent job and a good salary. Your own apartment. Furniture and lots of nice things." Her gaze stopped abruptly at a picture on the bookshelf. She gave a faint smile. "You still have a picture of Dad out, I see."

"What do you want? I haven't seen or heard from you in what—yeah, it must be—thirteen, fourteen years? And then you suddenly show up here one morning—unannounced!"

Rose looked at her daughter for a long time. "You were only fourteen years old, yes. I remember it so clearly." Her gaze flickered, and she hurried to take out a crumpled packet of cigarettes from her pocket. "I'm sorry for what happened between you and Torsten; I wanted to . . ."

"To what? What did you want to? Would you have helped me? No, you bloody well wouldn't. You only thought of the four boys—his offspring. They meant more to you than your own daughter!"

"No, Annie. That's not true! Of course you were most important. But you were so . . ." She scrutinised her daughter. "You have changed a lot. In fact, it's only your unruly black hair that looks like itself. Back then you were a wandering pin cushion with studs everywhere and heavy black make-up and clothes; you looked awful." She laughed hoarsely and concentrated on lighting the cigarette. The lighter clicked a few times before she succeeded.

Anne stared at her in anger.

"And no one understood us! You understood fuck all!" She lit a cigarette, too, her hand shaking. "We fought for justice. But how could *I* demand justice in the world when my stepfather turned out to be a mean drug dealer and murderer, and my mother supported him in that!"

Rose fidgeted nervously with her sleeve; her eyes turned to the almost melted ice crystals on the window. She hadn't taken off her coat, and Anne didn't ask her to—she would be going again soon.

"You've probably been following what's happening in Nørrebro nowadays, no? So, do you call *that* justice?" Her mother looked at her again. "We can barely walk on the streets without fear of being hit by a stray bullet from fighting gangs. There is something to fight for in Nørrebro nowadays if you want justice. There wasn't back then. The union vote and—a youth centre!" She snorted the words out of both nostrils along with the smoke.

That's how she knew her mother. Anne had never done anything good enough in her eyes. And she was the one who had run away from home without saying where she was staying. But had her mother ever looked for her? Had she tried to find her at all? She could have been dead. Murdered!

"How did you really find me? You didn't try to find me then!" she asked aloofly.

"It was Torsten, sweetie. He told me it was best I let you be. That you were living your own life."

"Okay—as a fourteen-year-old?" Anne raised an eyebrow reproachfully and shook her head disapprovingly. "And you've always listened to Torsten. Do you know that he found me when he was released on parole?" She looked directly at the little woman who seemed to be growing smaller under her gaze.

"No, he didn't say. I don't visit him that often anymore. I can't stand going to that prison. He didn't hurt you, did he?" She sounded genuinely worried.

"I survived, like I always have without your help—and with a few extra scars to remind me."

"You have to understand that I couldn't intervene when he hit you. He would have killed me. You know that!"

"If only he contented himself with just hitting me. You could have moved away from him, Mum! Why didn't we just move?" There were tears in the voice of the little girl from back then, who sat begging her mother to move without her listening. She wasn't listening now, either. Rose picked up an edition of the *Daily News* from the stack on the floor and flipped through it randomly. "So that's the newspaper you make," she said, motherly pride in her voice.

"I don't make it. There are a few articles in it that I wrote." The change of subject suited her. She would rather not talk about or think about the past and Torsten.

"You must earn plenty to be able to afford to live here. I've moved to a small one-bed apartment in Nørrebro. Couldn't afford anything else; the old one was renovated, and the rent increased to more than double. The other one is cheap, but it's old." She sighed and laid the cigarette on the edge of the ashtray as she flipped through the paper. Anne wondered what had become of her stepsiblings, but she didn't ask. Didn't really want to know.

"Do you have a job?" she asked instead.

"No, what can I do? Fuck all. I don't have your abilities. But, fortunately, we live in a country that takes care of 'the weak,' even though it can be hard to be in the system. They demand so much of us today; it gets worse and worse, and the money is less and less." She had reached the last page. She threw the newspaper back onto the stack indifferently. Anne sat uneasily in her chair. She was never going to end up like her mother—that was for sure. But was that where she was headed? The social inheritance—was that strongest anyway?

"You look a lot like your father. You have his jet-black hair." Rose looked at the picture of her deceased husband again. There was a small, loving smile on her wrinkled mouth; it softened her features. Suddenly, Anne could see that her mother had probably been pretty once.

"You haven't said much about him," she said reproachfully. "I don't even know how he died."

Rose kept looking at the picture as if she were talking to it and not to Anne.

"Jonas was a good person. He was a truck driver and drove to Denmark for various companies. I met him when I was working at a motorway café. He always came in and ordered a chicken sandwich and a cup of coffee from me."

"He drove *to* Denmark—from where?"

"Lithuania. His name was Jonas Maldeikis."

"Was Dad Lithuanian!?" Anne couldn't hide her amazement.

Rose nodded. "We chose not to give you his conspicuous surname. He was a true communist."

"How did he die?"

"A car accident. A solo accident at the Polish border. You had just turned two."

"Why did you never tell me?"

Rose shrugged. "What good would it have done? You were so young. The year after, I met Torsten, who was supposed to be your father instead. But you never accepted him. Then you ran away. You didn't give him a chance."

"Just stop!" Anne began to take the mugs off the table in fury. Her brain tumbled with the news that she had Lithuanian blood in her veins and unknown family over there. Would it mean something for her future? Could she use it for anything at all? She still hadn't figured out the purpose of her mother's visit, but she realised it before she made it out to the kitchen with the empty mugs.

"I don't suppose I could stay for a few days, Annie. It's so unsafe in Nørrebro, I dare not be alone, and—I only have you."

# 4

Henry Leander was right in his assumption about the cause of death. The autopsy hadn't revealed much more than the post-mortem examination. Albert Hovgaard had been brutally and ruthlessly beaten to death.

Roland leaned back in his chair. He hadn't slept for the few hours that had been available. He hadn't wanted to wake Irene by crawling into bed with her again as cold as he was, so he had lain down on the sofa in the living room where Angolo had immediately found him. Now six months old, the cute puppy-dog look was starting to leave him; you could see what a handsome German Shepherd he was becoming. Roland had fought hard against Irene's desire for him to become a dog handler, so the Canine Unit training had been abandoned. Irene still took Angolo to obedience classes, and the dog's behaviour was faultless—especially when Irene gave the commands—and he had immediately lain down on the floor next to the couch when Roland had authoritatively said *sit*! Cousin Salvatore liked Angolo, too, and he loved coming to training. He had been allowed to stay for Christmas and New Year. Aunt Giovanna was delighted to give him permission. She was the one who had insisted on Salvatore staying with them in Denmark. The aim of which, Roland tried not to think about. He hadn't got very far with that mission. Salvatore wasn't easy to talk to. Such was the way with fifteen-year-old boys who thought they were adults and knew everything. You couldn't teach them anything. But he seemed to have settled in and didn't question why he'd suddenly been sent on "holiday" to the cold North, so Roland had dropped it for the time being. Now the snow had come. Lots of snow. More than Salvatore had ever seen in Naples. He enjoyed it. Maybe they'd never get rid of him—that was often the case with family. He smiled tiredly. It was a pleasure to have him staying with them. It had refreshed his mother tongue; he spoke almost as fluent Italian as Salvatore, who resembled Roland so much. Same black eyes, same annoying curl on the right side that always made the hair fall onto his forehead. They had inherited it from Roland's paternal side. The memory of his father niggled away at the guilty conscience deep within him. It had been reduced a little by being able to help the family now. He wouldn't have been able to do that if his mother hadn't fled with him to Denmark when La Camorra killed his father. And it was Italy, and Naples especially, that Salvatore needed to get away from. "The System"—what the mafia in Naples calls itself.

His thoughts took on a life of their own that he explained away by his fatigue. He could barely concentrate on even the most basic things, despite having filled himself with tar-like coffee since getting to the station at eight o'clock. He came to abruptly when there was a loud knock on the door and DS Kim Ansager entered. He had developed an unpleasant habit of knocking and bursting in without waiting for an answer. *So why even bother to knock?* He remained standing in the doorway, hanging by his arms like a monkey. Making a monkey spectacle of himself, more like. He pushed his vintage black specs, which had gained an almost cult-like status in the fashion industry, into place on his nose with one finger and already seemed to be on his way out again. Obviously, only a brief message. There was not much time for chit-chat anymore. The financial crisis was affecting the police station, too. Times of crisis make creativity flourish among those who lose their jobs, he had read in the newspaper, but some also choose criminal creativity to get by. The number of burglaries and robberies was rising sharply.

"Forensics have matched the fingerprints with two other unsolved burglaries in East Jutland. They ran them through the Automated Fingerprint Identification System database but hadn't found a match there. The perps were apparently new to the criminal scene. Not previously suspected, or sentenced, at least."

"No, not here in Denmark. Have they tried Interpol?"

Ansager shrugged. "I assume so."

"Assume so! This is about murder. It's not *just* an insignificant home robbery. I hope you made them aware of that!"

Annoyed, Kim nodded. "Of course I did. Do you not think you should go home and get some sleep; you sound so . . ."

"Has no one got in touch about the car? The thieves must have arrived in a vehicle; they were hardly on foot in this weather."

"Maybe they skied!"

"Seriously, Kim!"

"But there was no evidence of car tyres or any other vehicles. It snowed heavily all night and this morning, and we can't send out an APB for a car that we don't know. Olsen has told the press that they are welcome to call for witnesses and people to contact us if they saw or heard anything suspicious on Monday night."

"Okay. That's good coming from Olsen."

Kim suddenly smiled. "By the way, have you heard that the *Daily News* has gone belly-up? That's one annoying journalist less." He laughed, hovering, and was gone again.

Roland closed his eyes. God, he needed to sleep. They probably shouldn't be complaining about the financial crisis. It gave *them* more work, but many others hadn't made it. Small- and medium-sized enterprises, where banks had suddenly cut off their overdraft facility despite the government's financial package that was supposed to prevent it. And now the *Daily News* had apparently also succumbed. Anne Larsen was no longer a nuisance. He had wondered where she was on the night of the murder. She used to show up before them like she could smell blood. Vampires did that. He smiled grimly at the comparison. First came the joy and relief, then another feeling. Worry? She had been bloody irritating—to put it mildly—they'd had plenty of clashes that had occasionally shed new light on the investigation and in solving it. Would he miss her? He got up and put on a jumper. No, of course he wouldn't.

The snow piled halfway up on the window, changing the light in the office to a soft, subdued glow. Winter really had arrived in Denmark. Just looking out turned his bones to ice; he put on his sheepskin coat and gloves and wrapped the scarf around his neck three times. Talking with the locals in the area couldn't be postponed any longer. Someone must have noticed a vehicle, and it was about getting to them while a detailed description was still fresh in their memory so they could move on with the search. The getaway car would be a good start. Getting out into the country would probably freshen him up a bit, too.

# 5

The man outside the door didn't seem to belong under these cold skies. He looked wrong in the white snow, but Gunda Hansen could easily see that it wasn't just a case of too much sunbed, which most city dwellers were in favour of despite all the experts warning about the danger of skin cancer. His southern European features were evident. He wasn't very tall, his hair was almost as black as his eyes, and his voice was deep and mature but pleasant and without an accent.

"Gunda Hansen?"

"Yes."

He showed her his badge; she had to come a little closer to decipher it. She hadn't brought her glasses with her when the doorbell rang. A sock got wet as she stepped out on the front steps.

"Detective Inspector Roland Benito. May I come into the warmth for a moment?" he asked with a friendly but tired smile and a quick glance at her wet sock.

"We didn't see or hear any of what happened last night, so . . ." She wanted to close the door again, but Roland managed to put a hand against it, and the look he sent her was not to be misunderstood.

"We have to talk to all the neighbours, even if they didn't see or hear anything. So, now I'm starting with you, as you live closest to the road."

Gunda opened the door and glanced around outside before closing the door again. But as usual, there was nothing to see. She took off her socks and stuffed her cold feet into a pair of sheepskin slippers.

"Is your husband in the stable?" asked Roland, taking off his coat, gloves, and scarf as if he were expecting to stay for a while. Gunda sat down at the kitchen table that was still full of used cups and plates from breakfast. The cheese stank and mixed with the smell of cow from the utility room— probably not the aroma the inspector was used to being surrounded by. How did it smell at a police station? She had no idea, but Roland Benito didn't seem to be bothered, though he did hang his coat over the chair instead of in the utility room. He sat down in front of her and nodded an affirmative to coffee. She took a clean mug from the cupboard and started pouring him a cup.

"He should be in soon for his morning coffee. Like I said, we didn't hear anything last night." Before she managed to finish pouring the coffee, the back door in the utility room slammed and the cold penetrated the kitchen. She shivered. Had it been cold at Signe and Albert's, too, when the killers broke in last night? When you sleep, you don't feel it like that, do you? She poured some coffee into Thorkild's used cup and got up to cut more bread. He was in the utility room for a while. The tap was running for a long time out there. He probably hadn't seen or heard the car in the yard and didn't know about the nice visit they were having. He was also surprised when he discovered the strange, dark man in his kitchen. The inspector stood up politely, held out his hand, and introduced himself. Thorkild reciprocated the handshake, and his grimace told Gunda that he didn't like having the police in the house, either. The neighbours would talk, and their home wasn't like on the farm at the very end of the road, where the young people lived in a collective. A couple of them came from Copenhagen, she'd heard. A patrol car had often passed by. Maybe it was them? Could one of them have killed Albert?

Thorkild sat down and spread a thick layer of butter on a slice of Vienna bread and then put an even thicker slice of cheese over that. Their guest had declined the offer of food with the apology that he'd just eaten.

"So, you didn't see or hear anything unusual last night, I understand?" Roland looked at Thorkild and took a mouthful of coffee. He also seemed to need something to refresh him. He was probably the one who had come to the area last night. Ella had mentioned something about a police officer who had questioned her hard.

"I think you should talk to them up in the collective, don't you think so, Thorkild?"

"The collective! Why?"

"Those young people don't always behave according to the law. The police have been there several times."

Roland Benito didn't seem surprised. "Yes, we know a little about them, and of course we will talk to them, too, but right now we urgently need to find a vehicle. You didn't notice any parked cars?"

"But, if it *is* them up there, then they were on foot, and there would be no car." She was absolutely convinced she was right. There were some bad apples in that bunch, though a few of the girls seemed very sweet. In fact, one of them reminded her of herself as a young woman. Flower power. Make love, not war.

Roland said, "It could be a car that was parked here for a long time." An annoyed *think carefully now* lay in his words, and suddenly Gunda looked at Thorkild.

"We haven't seen anything," he said sternly, staring back at her.

"But you saw the strange car by the road last night. Don't you remember that?" She turned to look into the inspector's friendly brown eyes. She knew well Thorkild would rather not be involved in anything that had to do with the police, but now it was about the death of a neighbour. Albert, but still. It could have been them; they lived closest to the road and were the most obvious target as such, and she had always had a good relationship with Signe. They had far more in common than she had with any of the other neighbouring wives. But it wasn't something they talked about.

"Strange how? What car was it?"

"It was hard to see," Thorkild replied measuredly.

"It was white, you said," she helped him along.

Thorkild looked at her again and then at Roland.

"Yes, it was white. An older model. Could have been an Opel Kadett Caravan, but I'm not sure. It was dark outside. And if you're going to ask for the registration, I didn't see it." He took a bite of the bread and cheese.

"But the strange thing is that it'd been there for a long time, and up there between the trees isn't a place people usually park," Gunda added.

"How long was it parked for?"

Thorkild finished chewing. "Have no idea. I noticed it in the afternoon as I was walking over to the barn. When I finished milking, it was still there."

"And what time was that?"

Bewildered, Thorkild looked at Gunda. "What time was it when I came in? You were making the evening coffee."

"It was probably nine—half past nine when I made coffee. I was listening to the late news on the radio as I was making it."

"But it was still there then?"

Thorkild nodded and took a deep breath; it looked as if he had suddenly surrendered. "I got up for a piss around midnight. I looked out the window from the bathroom. In the gable end. From there, there's a good view of the road, and the car was still there. It was difficult to see it in the dark, but there's a streetlamp, so I could clearly see the outline of the car because I knew it was parked there."

"And you didn't think to tell us that after what happened?"

"We thought it was someone who'd got stuck in the snowdrifts and left the car," muttered Thorkild.

Roland got up and put on his coat. "I would like you to come with me and show me exactly where the car was parked," he said firmly as he wrapped the scarf around his neck. Thorkild reluctantly went out into the utility room and put on his coat.

"Do you think it's one of those Eastern European gangs doing all these burglaries around here?" Gunda asked, hearing the fear in her voice.

"We're not making any assumptions or ruling anything out yet."

"So, you're going to talk to them up in the collective—and the other neighbours?"

She started clearing the table to get ready for lunch.

"Yes, we'll get to around to everyone," promised the inspector, shaking hands in farewell. He seemed to have recovered a little after being in the country.

# 6

Anne hadn't even reached the first step of the stairs when she noticed the loud voices and smell of cigarettes spreading throughout the stairwell. It sounded like a party was being held in one of the apartments. Strange, it was always so quiet and calm here. Most of the residents were elderly people whose urge for wild parties had long since come to an end. Her frightened suspicions were confirmed when she reached the next landing and the neighbour below her suddenly stepped out of her door, as if she'd been waiting for Anne.

"Someone is having a party in your apartment," she whispered. She was a skinny little lady in her seventies with white permed hair who always wore a black skirt and a blouse with a pattern of little flowers. Her eyes looked at her through thick lenses that made them unnaturally large in a comical way. Anne had had words with her before. She complained about everything. Visitors' shoes outside the door in the stairwell. If someone had forgotten their turn to mop the stairs or hadn't done it well enough. If some residents' grandchildren were playing and making noise on the stairs. Anything that could disturb the old bag's fine sense of hearing and her feelings. Initially, the old lady had annoyed Anne no end, but then she had realised that it actually was very handy to have someone who kept an eye on all the goings-on. As was always the case with herd animals. There had to be a leader, a chief. Most often it was a male, but the men in this herd didn't have the courage to stand up to this woman.

"I am very sorry, Mrs. Jansen. My mother is staying with me. I'll have a serious word with her."

"Your mother! Shouldn't she be old enough to know that such behaviour is unacceptable in our building?"

Anne took a deep breath and tried to control herself. But it was her mother she was furious with because the old bag was right. She smiled smoothly. "As far as I can tell, they're just having fun—though a little loudly." At the same time, she wondered who might be visiting, whose company would amuse her mother so much.

"Yes, now they are, but you should have heard them this morning. Clinking bottles and shouting in a language I don't know. If that's some of those *coloureds* visiting you, then . . ."

Anne was just about to remind Mrs. Jansen that the world's most powerful man was Black when there came a loud noise and roaring laughter coming down from the apartment.

"Excuse me," she mumbled, taking the last stairs two at a time.

"What the hell is going on here?" Anne shouted, slamming the door with a bang. Mrs. Jansen could certainly hear that, too; she was probably standing down in her ugly wallpapered entrance, smiling triumphantly. The coffee table was full of empty beer bottles, and a fragile glass ashtray seemed to crack under the weight of all the cigarette butts pressed into it. Ash was scattered across the table, probably because they were no longer in a state to be able to hit the target of the ashtray. There were six people in the cramped living room. On the bright two-person sofa sat Rose in a red velour lounge suit along with two young men who had squeezed in beside her. Another was sitting in the armchair with a bottle of beer balancing on one of the armrests. The last two, still wearing coats, were sitting on the floor. There was immediate silence, and Rose, in the middle of a heavy drag of a cigarette, inhaled deeply and smiled crookedly as the smoke seeped out between her lips, which had no colour today. She hadn't taken the trouble to look even just a little bit presentable. Maybe she'd still been in bed when the men had called. She was still asleep when Anne had gone to the job interview that morning, and she spotted the duvet and pillow lying on the floor behind the sofa.

"Sorry, are we making too much noise?" Rose snorted. "Do you want a beer?" She rummaged in the box on the floor next to the couch.

"No, I don't want a beer! And the party stops now! What in the world were you thinking? Who are they?" She pointed towards the young men who looked at her in horror.

"But, little Annie, we'll try to be quiet!" She said something to the boys that Anne didn't understand. They smiled and nodded at her. One of them got up from the floor and offered Anne his hand in greeting—he wanted to say something—but Anne crossed her arms and looked accusingly at her mother.

"I was just telling them who you are." She smiled uncertainly. If she hadn't been so drunk, she would probably have understood the situation better.

"Out!" shouted Anne, turning towards the door like a weathervane in a strong wind. "Pack up and get out of here!" She held the door wide open.

Her mother looked at her uneasily and said something to the young men in a serious tone. Only one of them laughed and shook his head—the most intoxicated of them—the others walked, heads down, out the door.

"Take your shit with you!" she was shouting again, pointing at the empty bottles that were lying all over the place like a hurricane had determined where they were to end up. The last young man quickly gathered up the bottles and put them in the box. He didn't look at Anne as he walked past her and out the door; she slammed it hard before he'd made it completely through, making him almost drop the beer crate down the stairwell.

Rose got up with all the dexterity of a newborn foal; she clearly wanted to protest but didn't have the strength to prevent what was happening. "Does that apply to me, too? Should I get out of here, too?" she asked in an angry, blurred voice.

"Yes, you should. But sit down first; I need to talk to you about this."

Rose obeyed and took another puff of the cigarette. Anne sat down in a chair and looked despairingly at the coffee table, where crumbs, ash, and spilled beer blended into a gruel of small stains. They had eaten rolls with the beers, it seemed. The empty ripped-open bakery bag was in the middle of the mess. Anne internally counted to ten.

"Mum," she said in a calm voice, but with even greater contempt than had always been in that word. "How could you have a party here without asking me first? My neighbours are mad, and this is not the first time. I've received warnings from the landlord before, and the last one made it clear that next time I'd be evicted."

Her mother smiled crookedly and sent her a searching look. "So, the apple doesn't fall far from the tree? You've had a few too many hard parties, and—"

"It's not the same," she interrupted. "The first time was a housewarming party, and I had put up a note in the hallway saying that there would probably be a little noise and that I hoped everyone would understand. The second time, I just happened to play the music a little too loud, but the neighbours—especially the woman who lives below me—are so . . ." She realised that her mother was still sitting and smiling as if she didn't believe a word of what Anne was saying. She gave up. "And who was here anyway? I didn't know you knew any languages other than 'Nørrebroese.'"

Rose tapped the ash off the end of the cigarette. "I speak Lithuanian. I learned a little when I lived with your father's family. Remember I told you that you were born there. Your grandparents threw me out of the house when they discovered I was pregnant. They didn't care about me at all. Imagine being like that towards your own daughter!" Rose's eyes searched in vain for sympathy from Anne.

"You're right. The apple doesn't fall far from the tree," Anne replied bitterly. "So, your visitors were from Lithuania?"

Her mother drained the bottle and set it down on the floor next to the sofa where the beer crate had stood. It looked like a regular motion, and Anne didn't want to think about the state of the apartment in Nørrebro.

"You can't behave like that, little Annie. The one who tried to shake your hand is Adomas. He's your cousin; the others are some mates he had with him."

"My cousin! Did you just invite my cousin without telling me!" exclaimed Anne with a look of reproach.

Her mother waved her hand as if chasing away a fly.

"No, no. They weren't invited, they—"

"How did they know my address?"

Rose sighed loudly. "Adomas said that he'd visit me a while ago. He was working on a building site here in Jutland, but it's stopped now because of the weather, and so he decided to visit me in the meantime. He contacted me yesterday to say he was on his way with some friends, and then I gave him your address because I was on my way here. It was stupid. They went to Copenhagen because I—"

"Okay. You didn't tell me that yesterday. What if I decided not to let you stay here?"

"But I knew you would, little darling. I'm your mother!" She laughed loudly.

Anne didn't respond.

"Anyway, they came and woke me up this morning with a crate of Tuborg Green and some bread rolls. They're sweet boys, you know."

"That may be, but you should have said something to me. It is my apartment after all, and—"

"Can't Adomas stay here, too?" she broke in. "His mates came to Denmark to find work, too. Milk and honey, and all that. It's not going so well for them. Three of them have got jobs at a garden centre somewhere, but the others have got themselves into some shit."

Anne regretted more and more opening the door to her mother yesterday.

"You're at work during the day, so you won't even know we're here. And I'll spoil you, cook dinner for when you get home, and . . ."

Anne went out into the kitchen and put a filter in the funnel of the coffee machine. It was not a desire for coffee that made her do it, rather the urge to get away from her mother's gaze. She had never been one for barefaced lying, but she wasn't about to tell her mother that she'd lost her job. Milk and honey, yes, that was in the book of Exodus. Or the construction boom a few years ago—equity and almost no unemployment. And the apple doesn't fall far from the tree, yeah, there was something to that. But she would have a job again soon, so Rose didn't need to know anything about Anne's current unemployment. That was why she had come home late—to make it look like she'd been at the paper. The job interview had only taken half an hour, and she was to get an answer later in the week. But there had been a lot of applicants, they said, so . . . She'd had lunch at McDonald's afterwards and sat in a café down in the Latin Quarter, staring at the freezing cold people passing by outside the window on their way home from work in thick winter coats and with stony faces. After eight hours, she went back to the apartment on J. P. Larsens Vej.

"There will be no such thing, I can promise you! You're not staying here anymore. There's already one too many." She fell silent as she counted spoonfuls of coffee grounds and threw them into the filter. Shortly afterwards, the machine started snoring and the fragrance spread. She started cleaning up the kitchen.

"Annie, you always wanted to help people in need. I know that well. I know you so well. And they haven't done what you accuse them of in the newspaper."

She stopped in the middle of wiping the inside of a cup with the tea towel and turned and looked at Rose. "What are we accusing them of?"

"You know that yourself. It probably wasn't *your* newspaper, but you all write roughly the same things, don't you? Great, you're making coffee. I really need some."

"What exactly are you talking about?" She didn't know what was happening in the city anymore. Without her job, she was completely ignorant. Blissful ignorance, she had heard someone call it, but ignorance didn't bring her any bliss. She should have bought a newspaper today, too, but there was the interview, and she hadn't thought about what else might be happening. As if all crime had stopped when the *Daily News* had closed its doors.

"I mean that thing about them killing the farmer. They didn't do it. They said they didn't. And Adomas knows they're telling the truth. They're his best mates. They've known each other since they were kids, went to school with each other, and . . ."

"Mates! Is my cousin a criminal?"

"No, he bloody well isn't," she snapped, sniffing. "He has a good job and earns his own money. He can pay to stay here, but he suddenly couldn't stay in the room he'd found any longer; the landlord—"

"But his mates are criminals!"

"Only some of them. What else can they do when they can't find work? After all, they've only the shirts on their backs because they spent all their money on travelling here. They stole the car, but they haven't done anything else. Oh, Annie, can't he, please? Just until he finds somewhere else to live."

"No, I don't want to help. You can say hi and tell him. I don't understand why you want to be mixed up in that kind of thing again, Mum!" She took two mugs and poured the coffee. "Drink this and sober up. You can sleep here tonight, but when I come home from work tomorrow afternoon, I would like you to have gone back to Nørrebro. Your 'friends' will probably thrive better there as well."

# 7

A snowy landscape is usually odourless. Only frost can be felt in the nostrils, but when he opened the car door, the unmistakable smell of pigs hit him, too. A large wooden sign above the driveway proclaimed that he was now on a truly organic farm. *From Farm to Fork* was written in squiggly brushstrokes. The whitewashed farm buildings looked lifeless in the white surroundings. It reminded Roland of a corpse on a white sheet. The only signs of life were some pigs walking and rummaging in the frosty ground they had dug out behind a barn. A small area of snow on the roof of the stable building had melted; it was an old grey Eternit roof with moss hiding underneath. If two gates in the gable of the barn hadn't been painted Swedish red, the yard would practically have been camouflaged. He tried to spot the road, but you wouldn't be able to see a parked car from here. He could just make out Gunda and Thorkild Hansen's gable and some of the driveway to their yard, but there was still a good distance to both the neighbour and the road.

There was nothing to see up there between the trees. New snow had covered everything, but he sent for a couple of forensic technicians anyway; they might be able to find something—a hair, chewing gum— something, despite the frost and snow probably destroying any trace of DNA. If the car had been there for a long time, it might be possible to find a tyre print in the ice. If they were lucky.

"From farm to fork," he mumbled, looking at the sign again. At first glance, it didn't sound overly appealing. Fortunately, Irene was apparently done experimenting with various diets and new lifestyles. She hadn't jumped on the organic wave—yet. The blood type diet had been the craze in the autumn, but it had stopped abruptly before Christmas. Suddenly, they had been allowed to eat everything again. Perhaps it was Salvatore's visit that had put a stop to the experiment. Italian boys were used to hearty foods like pasta with meat sauce and pizza oozing with cheese and toppings, and something Irene absolutely wouldn't have was for the boy to not feel at home with his family in Denmark.

Aggressive barking capable of starting an avalanche on the snow-covered roof made him wince. He slowly turned his head and saw he was dangerously close to a black-speckled, muscly dog that had suddenly appeared at the barn door. Fortunately, it couldn't get to him thanks to a solid steel chain that abruptly stopped and bridled it like a runaway horse. He recognised the breed as an American pit bull from cases where humans had been assaulted and bitten by that type of dog. He didn't like them. Even though it often turned out that the dog owners were unable to handle a fighting dog, it was always the dog that was killed. It was clear that the bulldog didn't like him, either. It fixed him with a pair of blood-shot brown eyes reminiscent of his own that day. The slanted posture and distance between the four legs made it look like an antique white chest of drawers over which black paint had been spilled in unfortunate places. One side of the head was black, the other white, and with the flat snout and drooping jaws, it looked more comical than dangerous. But the bared teeth and the awful snarl that told him he was unwelcome was unmistakable. What had become of the loyal and obedient German Shepherd on a leash at Danish farms?

A curtain was lifted at the kitchen window. So, the farmhouse wasn't as dead as it seemed; they were probably wondering what he was doing out here, or why he hadn't long ago withdrawn after that welcome. If they hadn't heard his car slip into the yard in the cushioning layer of snow, the dog certainly announced his arrival.

It took a long time for the door to be opened when he rang the doorbell and he was finally able to introduce himself to the man, who wasn't particularly astonished at a police visit. He must have been around fifty—maybe they were the same age. Roland had turned fifty-six in early January. Of course, in the middle of a snowstorm, none of the few invited guests had made it.

Vagn Mortensen presented himself briefly and invited Roland inside with a certain reservation in his posture. He admonished the dog calmly, and it slunk, crestfallen, into the stable again. Roland went in behind Vagn and couldn't help but stare at his thick neck. The man was heavily built, you could see on his body that he was used to hard work, which was probably done by hand rather than with machines. His hair looked like a stubble-field, in both length and colour. But his beard was like an untamed, withered pasture. His wife sat on the couch and blended in with the grey furniture like the farmhouse blended with the snow. Her voice was almost inaudible when she said her name, and her handshake was weak, but he could tell that she helped with the work—she was more muscular than you would expect for her type. Vagn sat down next to his wife. Roland sat down in a chair opposite them.

"I suppose you know what happened to your neighbour last night—I'd just like to know if you observed anything suspicious over the last few days. A parked car, for example?"

"No, nothing. Everything has been as usual out here," Vagn replied.

"How is Signe doing?" Olga Mortensen asked in a monotone.

"We haven't yet been able to talk to her, but the hospital says she's fine under the circumstances," Roland replied, looking into her flickering gaze. Something lay behind that look, as if she was hiding something and didn't dare meet his eyes.

"Albert wasn't very well-liked. He was a tyrant. Signe can confirm that. Anyone could have killed him," came the curt response from Vagn, thereby saving his wife from Roland's attempt at making eye contact; she looked at her husband in horror.

"I don't think so. Signe told Ella the intruders spoke Russian." Olga kept staring at Vagn with suspicion in her eyes, then she moved back to Roland. "Can you find a gang like that quickly? Are you going to station some officers here?"

"Unfortunately, we don't really have the capacity for that. But we will, of course, do what we can to find the culprits quickly," he promised, quietly wondering about her fear with the killer dog in the yard and the well-built man by her side. But as a rule, hardcore gangs didn't go out of their way for anything. The sight of Albert Hovgaard's bruised body was fixed in his mind's eye, and the killers were armed, too. Her fears *were* perhaps more than justified.

"So, if you can help with some information—no matter what it may be—it would be very welcome. For example, did you notice a white Opel Kadett Caravan or similar up by the road?" He looked directly at Vagn, as he assumed he knew most about car brands.

"No, we have not seen anything." Vagn looked at Olga, who confirmed this by shaking her head.

Roland drummed his fingers on his thighs. He was afraid they were telling the truth. What could they have seen when there was no view of neither the road nor Signe and Albert Hovgaard's property at all. "Do you remember when you went to bed last night?"

"We get up early, so we usually go to bed once I check the stables for the last time. I don't remember when that was last night."

Roland realised it was useless to push them more on that topic. "I can see your farm is organic. Isn't that risky in these times?"

"When is it not risky? We have the right conditions to raise our animals so that the meat is free of hormonal and pesticide residues. Like in the good old days, you could say."

It sounded like the type of spiel he was used to giving to butchers or customers in their farm shop, which Roland had noticed in one of the stable buildings before the dog had demanded his attention. He looked out the living room window and stretched his neck.

"Is it forest out there?"

"Yes, our own private one."

"Do the pigs go down there, too?"

"In the spring and summer. Right now, everything is frozen."

Roland nodded and got up. "Well, I won't take up any more of your time. But if you think of anything, then . . ." He put his business card on the table.

Vagn and Olga got up, too. She followed him to the door. He just managed to say goodbye before she slammed the door shut after him.


He stopped at the woods, got out of the car, and stepped into a snowdrift, soaking his shoes and trouser legs in the process. The snowplough hadn't been here yet, but some of the tracks that led into the woods by the barrier were only slightly covered with snow. They must have been made recently. He followed them for a while but stopped abruptly at a sign with large red letters: PRIVATE AREA! NO TRESPASSING!

# 8

Anita saw the couple from the kitchen window. They were on their way home from the Brugsen supermarket with shopping bags in their arms; they slid around in the snowdrifts in the driveway, which had only been sparsely cleared following the tyre tracks from the garage to the road and back again. Bitten laughed out loud as she almost fell. Brian had an extinguished cigarette hanging from his lips, reminding her of a young version of the actor Mads Mikkelsen, with dark hair a little too long and fluffy and dark stubble on his chin and cheeks. He closed the garage door; it didn't seem as if he intended to help with more than that. He had driven, so the day's chores were probably done from his point of view. There were always problems when it was his turn. He strolled after the others with the same indifference he had towards everything else in life. His large black down jacket made him look like the Michelin Man and gave his upper body fullness. His thin legs in worn jeans and feet in big moon boots didn't seem to be able to bear the bulk. Again, she thought about how she'd liked him when he'd moved into the collective a few months earlier. It was something about his eyes. They were brown, almost black. But his personality left something to be desired. He was coarse and rude and had brought some bad habits with him from Copenhagen. He was the one who'd introduced cannabis smoking at parties, even though both Linda and Andreas were against it. However, they had said a definite no to the Ecstasy pills that Brian had also packed in his suitcase—he called them "love drugs" and thought they blended in nicely with the collective's concept. The collective had been Linda and Andreas's idea, the goal being to share everyday life—and expenses—with other like-minded students who shared the same values as them, too—that is, to create a better way of life that wasn't only based on material things. Andreas had inherited the farm from his parents; he was the oldest resident at twenty-eight. The alternative had been to sell it, but since his greatest strength—and perhaps also his greatest weakness—was to think of others, his mission had turned to helping other students in need of housing. That is, for those who wanted to live far out on the farm and didn't want discos, nightclubs, and cafés within easy reach. But in Anita's eyes, he wasn't tough enough to weed out and reject new, unsuitable applicants. The same ad was submitted to the newspaper every time they were looking for new residents. The one she herself had fallen for because living cheaply in the countryside in a community sounded like a lovely life, and the location couldn't have been more perfect for her, even though her parents were very much against both the place and the collective. But Brian had been a mistake. She didn't understand how he could keep up with the studies at Aarhus Tech. His level of absence was quite high. And then his girlfriend, Bitten, had suddenly come to Aarhus and moved in. She'd got an apprenticeship at a hairdressing salon in the city centre and so wasn't a student, but Andreas hadn't seen that as a problem given that she was Brian's girlfriend, and after all, Brian had been approved. But she was no better than him. Just the sound of that mangy Copenhagen voice gave Anita goosebumps. They behaved like they owned the farm. But Andreas didn't do anything about it. Nor did Linda, who usually had plenty to say. They seemed to be almost fascinated by the two Copenhageners.

There was a commotion in the utility room. The sound of people talking came in waves along with the cold and the noise of shoes being stomped free of snow on the mat and thrown onto the tiled floor. There was always a pile of junk, so it was hard to find your own shoes and boots when you had to leave in the morning, but the mess wasn't worth cleaning up.

Bitten entered the kitchen first with a shopping bag in her arms. "Hey, Fatso!" She put the bag on the kitchen table. Suddenly, they all came in together, each with a bag, except Brian, who stood in the doorway with his hands in his pockets, looking at them lazily. Anita busied herself putting items in the fridge and freezer. She had kitchen duty today and had just finished the dishes. She hated that job, but it was part of living in a community, and she didn't complain. The rent was cheap so they could all get by on their scholarships or student salaries. Being called Fatso didn't hurt her. She saw it as a compliment, as everything good, from clothes to events, was described as fat in Danish, a word the Copenhageners had also introduced into their vocabulary.

"Close the bloody door!" shouted Bitten to Brian, who instead of obeying, went into the living room and threw himself onto the couch without taking off either his puffy coat or moon boots. Anita shook her head, unnoticed. He was just *trouble*. Bitten had taken a cucumber out of the shopping bag and took a bite of it before handing it to her, smiling provocatively, to put in the fridge. And so was she. Big trouble, both of them. Why couldn't Andreas see it? Or could he? Andreas closed the door and helped her with the shopping, even though it was not his job today. His face was serious, but it almost always was. When he occasionally smiled, it was more reminiscent of a spasm, and it quickly disappeared again. He looked like so many others you saw on the street, so it was rare that anyone noticed him. He blended in with the crowd. Red-blond hair, slightly lighter stubble with a weak moustache, which seemed to run down the corners of his mouth and mingle with the other few hairs on his chin and cheeks—it didn't equate to the full beard he imagined it did. His intelligent expression came from a pair of glasses with thin black frames that sat a little too far down on the narrow bridge of his nose. The rust-coloured knitted jumper he almost always wore matched his hair and beard and completed the picture. He studied history at university and was obsessed with everything that happened from the year AD 700 to AD 1050. Anita smiled at him. He was a weird nerd, but she liked him and Linda, who had also started to help unpack the items. Linda found a packet of biscuits and threatened to make coffee. Her coffee was always so strong that no one could sleep at night if she made the evening coffee. Brian had fallen asleep on the couch, and Bitten sat next to him, watching him dreamily while she gently played with his long fringe. Anita was always afraid they would go too far with their public displays of affection. They sometimes laid out almost everything before Bitten would drag him into their room, which was adjacent to the living room, and thankfully close the door. She wasn't as quite of an exhibitionist as he was.

Linda acted on her threat and made coffee. Anita and Andreas put mugs and plates on the coffee table, where they usually drank tea and coffee—and beer if it were a Friday night.

Brian woke up to the smell of coffee and sat down comfortably with an arm around Bitten's shoulders and a hand on her thigh. That was what they were both best at—being waited on—and it was starting to annoy her. Sometimes she felt like she was doing the lion's share.

"Coffee's ready!" shouted Linda, putting the insulated coffee pot on the table. Shortly afterwards, they heard a door open upstairs and Bjørn came running down. Anita smiled. Coffee always lured him out of his cave. Even more so because he'd managed to convince them that they should always buy organic fair trade coffee. Bjørn was finishing the second year of his master's degree in biology, so he was immersed in studies in his room for most of the day when he wasn't in the reading room in the Biology Department at Aarhus University; they really only saw him at dinner and when he came down to do his chores. He was just as big a nerd as Andreas. Those two had such intellectual conversations that the others couldn't join in. Bjørn was a big man. Not in height, but in width. Anita was glad she wasn't the only one whose BMI was less than perfect. He was in a crumpled khaki check Fjällräven shirt that hung halfway out over brown trousers. Natural colours. He sat down heavily on the couch next to Bitten and Brian and looked grateful for the break. "I'll do the shopping next time," he promised, taking a biscuit. "Was it cold out there?" A twinkle in his eye; he had apparently tricked Bitten.

"Funny question from a biologist. What the hell do you think?"

Bjørn blinked a few times with small eyes under bushy eyebrows, his face ruddy. His hair was a tangle of frizzy light blond curls. He had the hardest time getting used to the two new ones in "the family," maybe because he wasn't with them that often.

"Do you know that the police are going around the neighbourhood, trying to find witnesses? They haven't been here yet, have they?" he said quickly.

It gave Brian a little start.

"How do you know that?" Andreas asked in his calm and sober manner.

"I saw him from the window. He's definitely a cop; he's driving from farm to farm."

The collective was on a hill somewhat higher than the other neighbouring farms, so Bjørn had a fairly unobstructed view of the area from his room in the attic.

"So what?" Bitten chewed a chocolate biscuit. "Why should he come here? We live so far out of the way that we can't possibly have seen or heard anything. You're the only one who could have seen or heard something."

"Except that it was pitch-black," muttered Bjørn.

"I really hope they find a lead. It's awful what happened," said Linda. Anita tried to avoid looking at Brian. He'd only made a sick comment about Eastern Europeans when they'd discussed the subject at breakfast. When she walked down to the bus stop by the road this morning, she had peeked in at the farm as she walked past. She'd felt nauseated and had begun to shake, to freeze all the way to the bone. There were red-and-white stripes of tape hung around the farm with POLICE printed on the white parts, and the door to the main building was sealed with a yellow sign. At the college, not much had been said about the murder, but she'd had difficulty concentrating on the lectures. It had all been too close. It had happened the night before while they were lying asleep just a few kilometres away. Whoever did it could have broken into their house. The newspaper said the police suspected that the farm had been under observation for a long time. If that were the case, they would have quickly realised that there was nothing of value from a group of poor students. But she shuddered at the thought of perhaps having been watched by killers.

"People can bloody well just stop advertising that they have weapons," said Brian, throwing a leg up over the armrest of the sofa and taking a mouthful of coffee.

"How do you know they have weapons?" asked Bitten.

Brian straightened up on the couch. "It's only been a few days since he was in the paper, bragging that he'd won a gold medal in pistol shooting; idiot." He shook his head scornfully.

"It's a sport. What's wrong with that? I can understand that he's proud," said Linda. It was her first time to reproach Brian, even though Anita thought there had been plenty of other more justifiable occasions.

"Still," Bitten defended her boyfriend. "It's a bloody stupid thing to do." She looked disapprovingly at Linda.

"It's not certain that's the reason. Robberies have taken place throughout the history of humankind," Andreas soothed. He always intervened diplomatically when a quarrel was brewing.

"Oh yeah, it was fine for 'your' Vikings," teased Bjørn. They often challenged each other on a friendly level—history versus biology and vice versa. "They pillaged, raped, and sacrificed to their gods."

"'Your' animal kingdom is no better. They don't always settle for just stealing food from each other, they eat each other if they're hungry enough."

"Don't forget that we also belong to the animal kingdom." Bjørn smiled, gnashing his teeth.

Linda laughed and shook her head. "Andreas knows that well. He's always talking about going back to a more primitive time—we were probably nothing more than apes back then."

Andreas looked at her seriously. "Yes, and I mean it. Our brains aren't geared to live the way we do. Parts of the human brain haven't evolved since then. Just look at Bjørn."

They all stared at Bjørn, who was leaning back on the sofa so that his stomach strutted up over his belt. He yawned loudly. He was also the one who had eaten the most biscuits.

"Now his brain is saying he needs to sleep. It's an ancient instinct. Early peoples had to rest between meals so they were ready for the next hunt with bows and arrows."

Anita laughed at the thought of Bjørn with an animal skin around his waist and a bow in his hand to catch a rabbit for dinner. It was unlikely he had the stamina to run three metres, big and sluggish as he was—like her.

"And the fact that we can't multitask also dates back to prehistoric times. Our brains are only created for us to get food, sleep, and multiply—not to talk on a mobile phone, control a car in traffic, eat a hot dog, and listen to music at the same time," Andreas continued.

"Ah, it's only men who can't multitask," teased Linda.

"Yes, but women also had to do more in prehistory—give birth, look after their many children, cook, and protect the settlement while the men went hunting. That's what our brains are wired for. The primordial instinct is also one of the things that comes alive when you go running."

Linda was the only one who exercised, evident from her long, slender limbs, which Anita sometimes jealously scowled at.

"The brain enjoys being stressed in a natural way, like when prehistoric man ran away from wild animals or was hunting, and endorphins were released. The substance released in the brain is the same as—"

"Fucking nonsense," Brian interrupted gruffly. He got up from the couch and pulled up Bitten, who almost spilled her coffee. "Come on, we're not interested in listening to their prehistoric debate; we can go and propagate." He spat the last word into Andreas's face. "Bring the coffee," he commanded, as Bitten seemed to want to protest. They disappeared into their room.

There was silence around the table.

"There is something to what you say," Bjørn admitted, embarrassed about the episode. "We don't live right. I can feel how my brain can't really keep up sometimes. And we're living in the countryside, away from the noise, stress, and pollution of the city. Think about what those two have been exposed to in the capital." He nodded towards the closed door. You could hear it wasn't said to excuse the Copenhageners' rude departure. Anita seized her chance, now that the opportunity was there, to vent her scepticism towards the two new ones.

"I don't think they belong here, either. They don't fit in at all," she said softly. "We're not popular with the neighbours, and the police know our address. What happened last night was unlucky." She looked around at all of them but found no eye contact.

Andreas pulled thoughtfully at the thin down on his chin. Finally, he looked at her. "They're fine, Anita. They're young. I'm sure it will be all right when they fall into our rhythm."

"Fall into our rhythm! They'll never do that!" She shouted a little too loudly and looked nervously at the closed door.

"I agree with Anita a little," Linda said hesitantly. "Do you know that Brian goes out at night? What does he do?"

Andreas looked at her with both a worried and reproachful look. "Are you sure? How do you know that?"

"Because I've been reading the last couple of nights. My brain works best at night; maybe that's from prehistoric times, too," she replied sarcastically.

"I haven't heard you get up. Have you seen Brian out at night? Why haven't you said anything before now?"

"He's gone out after midnight several nights, and he only comes back a few hours later."

"Has he seen you, too?" Anita asked, wondering.

Linda shook her head. "I was sitting in the conservatory with a little lamp; he couldn't see it from the outside."

"Did he take the car?" whispered Bjørn.

"No, he walks in those big moon boots. Towards the road. He went out last night, too."

# 9

The wind was beginning to strengthen, and a blizzard heralded its arrival out over the fields by the menacing approach of dark clouds. Roland shuffled from foot to foot on the steps while he waited. It might seem like impatience, but it was the cold that was forcing him to move. It went through his thick sheepskin coat, jumper, shirt, and vest despite the many promising sales arguments about the vest's extra-warm quality cotton from the young clerk in the shop.

From the stairs, he could see the field road that Signe Hovgaard had run down last night to seek help from the neighbour. He wondered if the intruders had spotted her, as the kitchen window offered a view of the road. It was dark, of course, but wouldn't they easily have noticed a figure in a red nightdress fleeing in the white snow? Maybe they hadn't been in the kitchen just then, or they had been occupied with beating Albert Hovgaard to death. They could also have been in his study, threatening him to unlock and hand over the guns. Thoughts swirled like snow from the hedges until suddenly something else popped into his head when Ella Geisler opened the door only slightly. The eyes belonging to the Aboriginal person in front of him grew larger with astonishment. "Is that you, Inspector?" I thought I was done being questioned."

"Yes, we're finished for now, but if your husband is home, I would very much like to talk to him a little."

"He is not."

"And the twins?"

"Dorthe and Sam? They have nothing to do with this; they're not to be involved!"

He understood well her wanting to protect them, but they were probably already involved in some way, as they'd been out with their father to find clues in the snow last night.

"Besides, they're not at home, they—" She stopped abruptly when two teenagers having a heated discussion came walking around the hedge and into the yard. They shared their mother's Indigenous facial features and wore knitted hats pulled well down over their foreheads; both carried modern school backpacks. The girl began to shrug hers off—a task made more difficult because she was wearing mittens. Their faces were red with cold; they looked frozen stiff. He guessed they had walked all the way down from the road where there was a bus stop. They stopped when they spotted the car in the yard, then their eyes turned towards their mother and him on the stairs.

"Well, they're here now!" stated Ella Geisler mockingly. "This is a police officer. He wants to talk to you." She went inside, leaving the door open. Roland let Dorthe and Sam go in first, he followed and took off his boots in the hallway. There was no stink of cow nor pig here like at the neighbours, but instead, a sweet fragrance of onion prevailed.

Dorthe and Sam didn't seem to quite know how to deal with the unexpected police visit. They looked as if they had done something illegal. But didn't everyone have something on their conscience when faced with the long arm of the law?

"Let's go into one of your rooms and don't worry, I just have a few questions I want to ask you," Roland reassured them, following them into what he could see must be Dorthe's room.

"Very tidy in here," she said, sending her brother a vicious look as she pulled off her hat. Light curls tumbled out and surrounded her round cheeks. She looked at Roland defiantly. "So, what do you want to ask us?"

He glimpsed Ella Geisler in the doorway; she clearly didn't like their conversation but could do nothing to prevent it. She looked at him resignedly as he closed the door behind him with an apologetic smile. He sat down on a black sofa-bed and took in the room. It looked like something out of *House Beautiful*. Completely different from his daughter's room when she'd been that age. This was probably what was considered trendy today, even when you lived in the country, or maybe *especially* when you lived in the country. One wall was lined with Marimekko's iconic brightly coloured flowers, screaming pink and orange. The pillows on the sofa-bed matched, though they were broken up by a pair in bright red. In one corner stood a black office chair in front of a desk with a smart laptop—even that was pink. On the wall hung a flat-screen TV. No dolls, no teddy bears. That time was long gone. Now there were so-called teens who controlled the lives of the families. Poor Mr. and Mrs. Geisler had two of that kind. Roland turned his gaze to the girl whose face had taken on the reluctant expression typical of a teen.

"What type of farm is this? There are no animals that I noticed," he said.

That surprised Dorthe; she quickly looked at Sam. He answered. "Just boring stuff: wheat, rye, barley, onions, and corn in between. But we have a cat."

Roland smiled. "Of course. I would also like to know if you saw or heard anything last night when there was a burglary at your neighbour's."

"No, I didn't hear anything." Sam deferred to Dorthe.

"No, not until there was trouble downstairs when Signe came and woke up the whole house," she continued. They practically talked over each other about the events of the night, but the explanation was the same as their mother's, so there was nothing to suggest that any of them were lying about anything.

"You went out with your father looking for clues; where did you look?"

"All the way down to the road, but there was nothing to see. It had snowed a lot."

Roland nodded. "You didn't go into the woods?"

"The Troll Forest?" Sam's eyes were startled.

"Well, is that what's it called? Why is that?" Roland tried to keep his face straight and looked seriously at the boy.

Dorthe sat down on the corner of the desk and crossed her arms. "You mean the little forest, not Trige Forest, right?"

"No, I mean the small forest that Olga and Vagn Mortensen own. It's close by, so it was obvious to head there?"

Dorthe stared at him as if he were mad.

"Or maybe it's too dangerous to go in there—into the Troll Forest?" Roland asked, struggling to hide a teasing tone.

"We're not allowed to go in there. It's really dangerous; we've always been told that. There's a lake in there, and once a boy drowned in it. It's creepy. That's why we call it the Troll Forest. Once, I saw—"

"Shut up, Sam!" Dorthe interrupted harshly. The look she gave him made him obey immediately.

"What did you see, Sam?"

"Nothing."

"So, you weren't in there last night?"

"No. Why do you want to know?"

Roland got up and walked closer to a picture of a bunch of teenage girls, Dorthe standing in the middle. She was obviously a handball player. "I just want to know where you were, so we don't have to look there. But we'll have to look in the forest. Which team do you play for?" He looked at Dorthe again, his rough face softened by an admiring smile.

"Skovbakken. I hope to get on the national team someday."

Roland's eyes discreetly took in the slightly too full-bodied shape of the young girl, but handball players weren't usually on the small side.

Sam skimmed a little over the amount of attention paid to his sister and spoke. "If you want to search in that forest, you have to get hold of Vagn, because you can only get in there if he is with you," he said authoritatively.

"What do you mean?"

"He has the key."

"The key? A key to a forest?"

"Yeah," Dorthe agreed. "There are fences around most of the forest and the lake. It was put up after what happened to the boy, so that no one else falls in. There's a padlock on the fence, and only Vagn has a key."

"Why is the forest fenced and not just the lake? To keep the trolls in?"

A smile tugged at Dorthe's lips despite everything. She was the hardest of the two to fool. But it was Sam who answered.

"No, it's because of the game. There's red deer in there, and Vagn doesn't want them to run out onto the road and be hit. Sometimes people go hunting, and so it's dangerous to walk in the woods then. I don't think anyone would hide in there, either. You can't see anything when it's dark," he added.

Roland nodded. He didn't believe so, either, not after all he'd heard. If a car couldn't drive in there, then it ruled it out as a hiding place. He was just about to ask more when the door burst open. A man entered the girl's room menacingly. He didn't match the brightly coloured floral surroundings.

"I want to know what you're asking my kids about," Finn Geisler said menacingly. "Shouldn't adults be present during a child interrogation?" He was wearing a thick coat and a deerstalker hat with the flaps pulled down over his ears. His face was red, and his moustache vibrated slightly because he was breathing heavily, as if he'd run. There was frost on it, and his eyes were watering. Either he had just come home, or his wife had gone to get him. She stood behind him, craning her neck.

"Dad!" exclaimed Dorthe. She looked crushed again, probably at being called a child.

"I'm done talking to them. But good you're home. If you have a moment, I would like to talk to you, too." Roland smiled at the children. He would have liked to have asked them more, but the man's threatening face almost half a metre above his own made him wait.

"I understand that you didn't find anything when you searched last night," he said as they entered a living room with dark furniture.

The Geislers didn't ask him to sit down, and they didn't sit down themselves. "Unfortunately, no. There were no footprints. It was snowing a lot. Or the psychopaths walked in the footsteps on the road. Maybe they had the car parked nearby."

Roland chose not to reproach them for wading through the crime scene. It was futile now. Here, in the country, it was probably only natural for neighbours to help each other, and Finn Geisler probably wouldn't understand his point anyway.

"So, you were the first at the scene?"

The man sat down heavily on the sofa and took off the thick sheepskin gloves. "It was horrible to find him like that. Had we arrived just a little earlier . . . but I immediately called the police."

Roland nodded appreciatively.

"So, you haven't found them yet?"

"Unfortunately, not. You didn't notice a car parked by the road, either?"

"No, we can't see the road."

Ella sat down next to her husband. "I think I told everything we know last night, so . . ."

Roland put his business card on the table. "In case you think of something," he said, pointing to the card.

Ella Geisler followed him out into the hallway and politely said good-bye before showing him out in the cold and quickly closing the door behind him. He rubbed his gloves against each other, pulled his collar up around his ears and looked up at the snow swirling around until he became completely dizzy. The car was almost covered, so he had to use the scraper before he could drive. He could just make out the forest's treetops over the ridge of Vagn and Olga Mortensen's farm.

"The Troll Forest," he mumbled with a small smile. Who was the boy who had drowned? If he existed at all, that is? Or was it the fabrication of some desperate parents who didn't want to lose their twins in a forest lake?

# 10

The blizzard raged outside behind the blackout curtains, but it was hot under the lamps. Her feet had started throbbing after being squeezed inside tight boots all day, and now that she was alone in the studio, she sat down on a small stool they used for seated photo shoots. She unzipped her boots as she looked at the line of jewellery and watches she was working on, wiggling her toes in the wool socks as soon as they were freed from the tight black leather.

The Rolex watch on the left had to be moved a smidgen to the right, she judged with her trained eye and sense of graphic composition. The cold from the stone floor penetrated her socks, but it felt liberating to her tormented hot feet. Her concentration was again directed at the camera and the line-up; she took a series of pictures from different angles. Only two more shoots and they'd be ready for the watch and jewellery catalogue. She got a cup of coffee in the modest kitchen before moving on to the next shoot. The smell of coffee and photo equipment, the darkness around her, lamps that only illuminated the products on the photo table brightly, and the rush of the storm outside the window put her in a comfortable mood. There was nothing like being alone here and feeling that it was her own studio she was working in. But the room she'd used as a study as a freelance photographer in the old house on Mejlbyvej had long since become storage space for everything that she now had no room for, and she couldn't understand how she'd been able to do without it before.

The fear of regretting her resignation from the paper last autumn had been completely unfounded. It had been a far better decision than she had initially thought. No more photos of creepy finds and acts and dead people to give her sleepless nights. She'd never be a press photographer again, at least not with a crime reporter. She had read about the paper closing, causing her to think about Anne, Thygesen, Britt, Mads Dam, and Nicolaj, who wouldn't have even finished his internship. She had wanted to call Anne many times to hear what had really happened, but there had been so much to do with the new job, and there was probably a reason why Anne hadn't contacted her, either . . .

After the last shot, she cleaned up, put the expensive watches and jewellery in the safe, and then sat down in a black leather chaise-longue, which the super-thin lingerie models often posed on. Pierre-Louis was an expert in seeing to them; he was the model photographer. He was also the boss. She was better at lifeless things—as long as they weren't in body bags—so she and Oliver were the product photographers.

She took out her hairclip and shook her head; blond hair cascaded around her face like a silk cloud and fell into place around her shoulders. She felt dry-eyed from standing and focusing in the bright light all day. A headache throbbed at her temples. She massaged them and lay back on the chaise-longue with her eyes closed. It was well past finishing time. When it came to that, working here was no better than at the paper, where she had often finished late, but it didn't matter to her. She didn't have anything to go home to anyway—only Tarzan, who remained faithful despite his cat flap in the utility room door and being able to go wherever he wanted. She stretched and heard the door slam down on the ground floor. Immediately afterwards, footsteps could be heard on the stairs. Pierre-Louis didn't notice her stretched out on the chaise-longue. He cursed quietly in a French accent. His father was French, and his mother was Danish, but he'd lived in Denmark for many years and had opened his photo studio on Nørregade six years ago. Things were going well; customers were loyal. Despite the crisis, ads had to go out—actually, for some, *because of* the crisis.

"Kamilla!" he exclaimed loudly, almost dropping his camera bag. "God, you scared me. I didn't see you. Why are you lying here in the dark?" He placed his bag on the floor and turned on the ceiling light. It wasn't sharp, but it still made her squint. She sat up, suddenly embarrassed to be lying there in her socks in front of the boss, even though it was late, and even though she had finished her work.

"Hey, Pierre. Sorry. I just have a little headache."

"Not at all—stay there." He disappeared into the kitchen and came back with a large glass of water. "If I know you right, you've been drinking coffee by the bucketload. Here, drink this."

There was no arguing with Pierre when he issued commands, so she drank the water while he looked at her with his dark eyes, as if she were a child having to take cod liver oil. She handed him the empty glass. He smiled contentedly and put the glass on the floor, then he lightly pushed her back down onto the chaise-longue and sat down on the edge.

"Sometimes I worry about you. You push yourself too hard; isn't there someone you should be going home to?"

She hadn't told him anything about herself apart from the essentials, and she was glad of that. No one looked at her sympathetically or treated her like fragile glass because they knew what she'd been through. And Pierre and Oliver didn't need to know anything, either; it made everyday life much easier and actually helped her keep it all at more of a distance, too.

"Yes, I have a cat," she replied with a small smile, unconsciously withdrawing a little when he reached out to her and gently stroked a lock of hair away from her forehead.

"I don't understand how you are single! Were you married? Did someone cheat on you . . . or maybe someone—"

"What made you curse just now?"

Pierre shrugged and abandoned trying to get more out of her again. "Oh, it was from the meeting about the new assignment. They want the fish photographed at a port. It's perfect with the snow and ice now—that's what they want for the ad, but they want a 'real' fisherman to present the fucking flatfish on his cutter." Tired, he ran a hand down his face. "I called all the fishermen in the port of Aarhus and finally found someone willing to do it, but then the customer didn't want it shot in Aarhus with all the people there. It has to be a large beach in the background. Grant me patience!" He got up and started unpacking the camera bag.

"Beach? So, what are you going to do?"

"I rang some fishermen at Bønnerup Strand—that would be ideal," he said as he rolled a cable up in quick movements. "But no one wanted to join that galley. The fishermen there seem shyer and more embarrassed somehow. When they heard that they themselves would be acting, they all backed out."

"So, what are you going to do?" Kamilla couldn't help but smile a little at the episode. All that hassle for a couple of measly plaice for an ad campaign. It was definitely a special industry. But fishermen and Bønnerup Strand had other ideas. Her biological father was a fisherman at Bønnerup Strand. She had decided not to contact him again when she heard his wife's voice and the children's laughter in the background that time she had called last autumn. She wasn't about to ruin his life. If she had known him, he might have helped Pierre, but she didn't dare to call again. There was no room for more defeats in her life.

Pierre put the tightly coiled cord back in the camera bag and zipped it up. He straightened up, ran his hand through his dark, fashionably styled hair that was a little too long at the nape of his neck, and smiled triumphantly. "I actually managed to find a willing victim. I'm going out there tomorrow, and you know what, Kamilla, as it's about product shots—because the fish are dead and not living models—I was thinking you should take them. What do you think?"

Her headache intensified. What did she think of that? Would she go near the area where her father lived with another family, perhaps unaware that he had a daughter—a fact that had been concealed due to a tragic accident in his youth. She looked at Pierre, who was anxiously awaiting an answer.

"Yeah, of course I'll take them."

There was no arguing with Pierre when he issued a command.

# 11

The utility room was littered with muddy boots and shoes with white edges of road salt. The mat lay in a lake of filthy meltwater. The young woman who opened the door looked at him apologetically when he introduced himself. She wore a loose-fitting tunic in orange, red, and yellow, which didn't hide the extra kilos on her lower body despite the cut. A wide brown velour skirt did nothing to conceal her large buttocks, either, when she turned around and led him into a living room that was a tad more orderly. She had a sweet face. Sweet was the right word—round cheeks, plump lips that didn't need lipstick to be highlighted, a cute little stub nose, and green eyes that played with life, all surrounded by long dark blond hair that tumbled down around her face like a curtain divided by a distinct white centre parting. "Anita Andersen," she introduced herself. She stood, a little embarrassed, pulling down the sleeves of her tunic. "Would you like some tea? Or a cup of coffee, maybe? There's more in the pot."

Roland politely accepted the coffee for the warmth. Tea had never been his thing. He put his coat, scarf, and gloves on the back of a chair, which he sat in while she was in the kitchen. From behind a closed door came the bass of a rock song. Probably one of the many new bands that had emerged from obscurity. It was a bit heavy, though. Not his taste.

Anita returned quickly with the coffee on a tray along with large mugs and two packets of chocolate biscuits. Apparently, no one used regular coffee cups anymore. He asked her to stop pouring when the mug was half full. She sat down and filled her own almost to the brim.

"I told the others that you were coming and wanted to talk to us"—she looked demonstratively at her watch—"but you said in twenty minutes, and it's only been ten minutes since you rang."

"I was close by, but the two of us can start. It's about the robbery at your neighbour's. Did you observe anything unusual last night?"

She drank from the mug before answering. "We live a little far away from it all, so I don't think any of us saw or heard anything." She hesitated and picked up her mug even though she had just set it down. She sat with it between her hands, her thumbs running up and down the porcelain.

"How many of you live here?"

"There's six of us. We're students. Linda and Andreas started the collective together. Andreas is studying history at the university, and Linda is at sports college. Bjørn is studying biology. The last two are Brian and Bitten—they're both from Copenhagen. Brian is at technical college, and Bitten is a trainee hairdresser. I go to Aarhus Seminarium, or VIA University College, as it's called now." She drank from the mug again.

Just then a young man came down the stairs. He was almost as stocky as the young woman and reminded Roland of an oversized green olive thanks to his clothes. He shook hands and said cheerfully, "Thorbjørn Møller." Roland reciprocated the firm handshake, and Anita explained that Thorbjørn was the biology student and that she called him Bjørn—he was like a cuddly teddy bear. Bjørn sat down next to her, and then the others suddenly swarmed from their rooms like ants from an anthill. Roland glanced at his watch—it was exactly twenty minutes since he'd first called.

He cleared his throat and was ready to start, but Anita got up and went to the closed door from where the rock music was still thumping through the wall. "We're not all here yet," she said, knocking on the door. First gently, then a little more aggressively.

There was a snarl. "Yes, yes, for fuck's sake." And the music stopped. Anita sat down again on the couch and looked down resignedly at her mug. Only the girl came out after a few minutes. There was something punk about her, but not in an extreme way. It was the heavy black eye makeup that gave that impression; the spiked hair that changed from traffic-light red to black and purple; the short, black leather jacket; and, not least, the studded collar that reminded him of what he had seen on Olga and Vagn

Mortensen's muscly black-speckled dog. The man—or boy—as he was tempted to say, who indifferently followed her, wasn't one of the nicer-looking boys, either. He stroked his long hair back, and a pimpled forehead came into view. He sat lazily in a chair with his eyes absently focused on the packet of biscuits. His eyes were dark brown, and again Roland thought of the American pit bull.

He cleared his throat once more. "So, are we all here?" Anita nodded and introduced the two last arrivals who hadn't presented themselves to their guest. The atmosphere was heavy. He wondered if he would get more out of them by talking to them individually. He could do that later if he felt there was more to talk to them about. He wasn't too much in doubt as to who was to blame for the police's many visits to the collective. Brian Kjeldsen's eyes were blurry in a hash daze, and the unmistakable smell lingered on his black Metallica T-shirt with *Metal Up Your Ass* emblazoned on it. But he couldn't deal with that right now.

"Do you farm, or has all that stopped?" he asked to loosen the tense atmosphere a bit.

Andreas replied, "I inherited my parents' farm. It was originally a stud farm, but the stables are empty now. We're using them for storage at the moment. But I've been thinking about renting the boxes out to horse own-ers." He looked tensely at the others, as if it was something he hadn't yet discussed with them. He seemed to be the oldest of the inhabitants, some-where between his early and mid-twenties, from what Roland could tell.

Only Linda Carlsen nodded in the affirmative. "It would give us some extra income, so we're definitely working towards it," she said, backing her boyfriend. She was slim and toned. Her blond hair was cut in a short, sporty hairstyle that seemed to just sit by itself. She was a pretty and natu-ral young woman, who dressed in colours that matched her light skin and hair. She was in direct contrast to Bitten Mørk, who stared at him with her black-framed eyes and provocatively chewed gum. None of the others said anything. Roland drank his coffee while he considered them. It was undeniably a motley bunch sitting around the low oak coffee table. He wondered what they could have in common that allowed them to endure living under the same roof.

"As it's your parents' farm, you must have grown up here and know the neighbours well?"

Anita suddenly got up, interrupting him. "Oh, sorry, Brian. I forgot the sugar." She quickly slipped into the kitchen. Roland watched her; apparently, she was the one who looked after the household.

Andreas both nodded and shook his head at the same time.

"Yes and no. When I met Linda five years ago, I moved in with her—"

"I lived in Herning back then," Linda interjected with a cautious smile.

Andreas looked at her and nodded. "My parents both died in a car accident, and then the question was what should happen with the farm. As for the neighbours, I've only known Olga and Vagn Mortensen and those who lived on the farm next door at the time since I was a child."

Roland nodded. "I've spoken to Dorthe and Sam Geisler, the twins. They talked about a boy who drowned in the lake down in the private forest. Do you know anything about that?"

Andreas frowned and nodded slowly. "Yes, I remember a little about it. But it happened when I lived in Herning. Can you remember it?" He turned to Linda, who nodded seriously.

"My parents were shocked. Marcus used to visit them a lot—a sweet boy—and . . . my parents and the other neighbours demanded that fences be put up around the lake." He scratched the almost invisible beard on his chin that reminded Roland of the hair on a pig. "It was spring four years ago that it happened, as far as I can remember."

"Who was the boy?" Roland didn't really feel it mattered, but he was curious to hear about the accident that could cause the landowners to fence off an entire forest.

"He was the son of the people who lived on the farm where Signe and Albert Hovgaard live now actually," Andreas replied with a frightened look in his eyes. "I never really thought about that until now."

He stared into the air in front of him.

Anita came back and put a flowery sugar bowl on the table. "I think we can say we didn't see or hear anything last night, can't we?" she said, looking at Brian as if she were urging him to say something. Roland tried to catch his dark gaze, too, but Brian was suddenly preoccupied with stirring sugar into his coffee.

"The one who may have seen something is Bjørn," said Bitten, looking at the green olive curled up in the corner of the sofa.

He straightened up. "It's true, I can see part of the yard where it happened, but I was asleep at that time of night!" He directed the last words at Bitten.

"Of course," said Roland, "but it's also important for us to know whether you observed anything in the days leading up to last night. Parked cars or anything suspicious?"

"It's those fucking Eastern Europeans." Brian's dull eyes turned from the coffee in the mug towards Roland.

"We don't know yet, so it's important that you give us any information you may have."

"We don't know shit!"

"And that applies to all of you?" Roland looked at them one by one. Bjørn took a biscuit from the packet when he got to him, thereby avoiding looking him in the eye.

"So, you haven't found the weapons?" Brian leaned back in his chair and crossed his arms so that only the *Metal Up Your Ass* text was visible. There was a scornful expression in his black eyes.

"No, we haven't found the weapons. What do you know about them?"

"Nothing. I just saw Hovgaard boasting about them in the paper."

"When was that?"

"A couple of days ago. Such an idiot! He should have been able to bloody well figure out that someone would come to them."

"Did you save that paper?" Roland looked directly at Anita, who seemed to be the one in charge of everything.

"I don't actually know; it might not have been thrown out yet, as it wasn't that long ago." She went out into the kitchen, returning shortly afterwards with the newspaper and handing it to Roland. He flipped through to the article with the picture of a widely smiling Albert Hovgaard with the gold medal around his neck, photographed in front of the open weapons cabinet, where the guns hung side by side.

"May I take the newspaper with me?"

"Of course. We're only going to throw it out anyway."

"Yeah, it gives you an overview of what weapons were in the locker. He's serving them up there like it's help-yourself." Brian laughed.

Linda snarled. "Only if some criminals think that. It shouldn't matter if other people know what you own, should it!"

Roland folded up the newspaper. There were always criminals who had ideas. He tended to agree with Brian there. Displaying his weapons collection like that, with his full name and address, wasn't a smart move. Of course, not much worse than estate agents' websites displaying tantalising flat screens and other technical equipment. But were the weapons alone the reason for the burglary and murder? He got up, put on his coat and hat, and thanked them for their help. Unfortunately, he sensed that there was nothing more to glean here. Most of the day had been spent talking, so now he needed to go back to the police station and enter everything into the system. It was getting dark, and he was anxious to see if any more leads had appeared. He was afraid that wasn't the case—they would have contacted him if it were.

Anita followed him to the door. "Is there any chance that you'll find them?" she asked.

"Not much has come forward, but we hope to find the car that was seen by the road." He opened the door, and an icy wind blew through the utility room, causing the coats on the coat-rack to flutter. Snowdrifts were systematically building up in the yard with each gust of wind. Anita put her arms around herself to protect against the cold. Roland put on his gloves and thanked her for the coffee. He had the feeling she wanted to say more, but the words on her lips took the form of a smile. Then she closed the door.

# 12

The only sound faintly getting through to him was a quiet hiss. The wind was swirling little snow crystals over a frozen surface. He had lost his sense of time and slipped back and forth between frightening reality and a trance-like dream state. That is, if he wasn't still unconscious. Or was he dead? He tried to open his eyes, but his eyelids were as heavy as lead and didn't immediately obey. When they finally slowly opened as narrow cracks, he only saw darkness. Now he could feel the cold. It had begun to penetrate him wherever he was. So, he wasn't dead. He could hear and feel. But he couldn't move. When he tried to turn around, he bumped into an obstacle, and when he lifted his head, it hit something, too. It sounded like wood. A wooden box. Was he lying in a wooden box? His hand wasn't only shaking from the cold as it searched towards his pocket. It was empty. The schnapps! The bottle was gone. That scared him more than lying in a cramped wooden box. He turned his head. He felt something tighten and cut deep into his throat. His frozen fingers groped their way to his neck and felt the roughness around it. He remembered only fragments of what had happened. What he thought had happened. Had it been a dream? A nightmare in a drunken stupor? His fingertips, which were dirty and yellow with nicotine and protruded from the knitted gloves, felt his body. It hadn't been a nightmare. The rope was still there. That was what was tightening, choking him. He loosened it gently as if it were an expensive tie. An item of clothing he hadn't worn in a lifetime, not since his heyday when everything had been different.

He lay on his back, and as his eyes adjusted to the darkness; he began to see contours. The lid was only a few centimetres above his nose. The others had always teased him about that. Rudolf, they'd called him, because it was always red. Red from alcohol. He shook even more. This is how abstinence began. How long had it been since he'd had anything to drink: a day, two, longer? Maybe it was due to all the booze in his blood that he hadn't died of hypothermia yet. But why hadn't they finished it? Or did they think they had? Was that why he was lying in a wooden box—a coffin? He stared up into the darkness, and his life played like a movie in his mind's eye. It began with a childhood that had been fine in a middle-class home in a quiet neighbourhood of detached houses. A successful company that nobody believed would work. The first employees. The money that flowed in. The car. A Mercedes. White. Not brand new of course. Bodil. Their wedding. Happiness. He wanted to dry his eyes but couldn't get life into his arms, so he let the tears run, tasted the salt. Johan, Simon, and Trille. Where were they now? The same place where he would soon end up? They disappeared that summer night. It was that Mercedes again. If only he'd never bought it. He sobbed loudly. A wailing sound in a wooden box. Cursed sobriety! Questions to be drowned. Questions that went on and on and drove him crazy; why hadn't he listened to Bodil? Why hadn't he let her drive? But he was a man of the world who wasn't going to let a woman take control. Stubborn as he always was. And she had given in, like she'd always done. Had helped Simon and Johan with their seat belts in the back and checked the belt on Trille's car seat. Closed his own belt. As though it would help. As if it would save lives. Now it was all gone—Bodil, the children, the company, the Mercedes, his life—all transformed into a miserable existence in the gutter. But his comrades were still somewhere out there. True friends who didn't judge because they themselves were judged. Society no longer needed them when they were unable to contribute. Yet, without his friends, he wouldn't have lived this long. Kept alive by them, alcohol, and cigarettes, and what he could find in bins, which luckily was not so little. As a rule, people at bus stops pretended not to see him rummaging late at night. Embarrassed on his behalf. Or on their own—who knew?

When these thoughts stopped, the sound of the wind had become louder. It sounded like a blizzard swirling the snow around out there. Ice crystals hit a nearby window, sounding like sand and pebbles on a car window on a sweltering summer night. If he stayed lying down, he was going to freeze to death. Again, he tried to get up and hit his head against the lid. He put his knees against it and pushed upwards. The lid gave way, it fell to the floor with a rattling sound; finally, he could sit up. Everything spun and he had to throw up. He remained sitting in the box for a moment. Gradually, a little more strength returned to his arms and legs. The room he was in was dark, too, but the snow shone bright through a window that faced into the night, so he could see the outline of the items around him. He was in a shed with lots of storage boxes in assorted sizes. Mostly wood. They looked like fruit boxes. Where was he, and why was he here? This was the worst hangover he'd ever had. Unsure, he rose to his feet, leaned against the sides of the box, and crawled out like a child from a playpen. His bare feet hit an icy-cold cement floor. Where were his old worn shoes? The box looked homemade; planks unprofessionally nailed together. There was another one, almost a match, not far from him. What was in it? Something edible? His intestines screamed and writhed like hissing snakes in his stomach. He staggered on numb feet towards it, pushed the lid off, but he couldn't see anything in the darkness. He reached down and felt around. It was cold and felt like clothes on the line on a frosty day. Fabric? His hands slid further up and hit something rough. With trembling fingers, he slid along the roughness and felt a neck, a chin with prickly stubble, a mouth. Cold and stiff. He pulled his hand away with a jerk. A human! A dead man with a rope around his neck like his own. He tried to pull it off, but the more he heaved it, the tighter it got. He let it hang. The anxiety and cold froze his muscles. His legs were stiff; they carried him like stilts as he moved towards the door, where the snow pressed through between the planks and flew across the cement floor and over the two wooden boxes. He pulled the door open. It wasn't locked, either. What was the point if the man was dead? He couldn't escape. Could he? Was he dead, too? Was he now a ghost that had risen from the dead body? Or was he a soul that would soon disappear to heaven, up to Bodil, Johan, Simon, and Trille? To apologise. To receive forgiveness. He looked at his own wooden box, but it was empty. There was no thin, dirty, hollow-cheeked man with a red nose, grey hair, and a beard, wearing worn clothes that his soul had risen from. How could it—it had long since left him, and without a soul, you were nothing more than an empty shell. He went out into the storm. Cold and sweeping snow hit him in the dark. He gasped. His feet moved only by sliding through the snow, as if they were on skis or in snowshoes. What could happen to a shell? It couldn't even die.

# 13

Anne stamped off the snow onto the doormat. Just when you thought there couldn't be more, then . . .

She opened the door and stepped into the heat. It was noticeably quiet, and the smell of cigarettes had disappeared. Gently, she pushed open the door to the living room and, startled, jumped back a little. It was nicer and cleaner than she had ever seen it. It had been tidied, vacuumed, and dusted. The scent of fresh frost indicated that the windows had been left open for some time to air out. In fact, it also looked like they'd been cleaned on the inside. Even the dishes in the kitchen were gone—it almost looked like the apartment was uninhabited. She swallowed a lump. It was a side of her mother that she didn't know. So, that's what it would have been like to come home from school to a nice and tidy home, but instead she'd come home to screaming stepsiblings, clutter and disorder, and an angry mother who scolded Anne with a cigarette hanging from her lips as soon as she stepped inside with her schoolbag. The gesture she had shown here must be a sign. Maybe an "apology." A hint that she could make herself useful if she was allowed to stay. Anne tossed her backpack in the corner by the desk and sat down stiffly on the couch, completely empty inside. There was no note with a greeting or information about where her mother had gone. Anne leaned back and closed her eyes. All night she had listened to the howl of the blizzard around the gable. At one point, she went to the toilet and had stood in the doorway and watched her mother lying on her back on the sofa with her mouth half open and her arms out to the sides in a grotesque position, like was she being crucified. A warm feeling had flowed through her, but she didn't quite know what it was. Care, compassion—love? She had given up trying to find out, had poured a glass of juice from the fridge, carefully so as not to make a noise, and had gone back to bed with it. She lay there for a long time, listening to the sounds outside and her mother's calm breathing from the living room that made her feel safe. Was it because that sound had calmed her when she'd been in her mother's womb? No matter what happened in your life, was there an unbreakable bond to your maternal origin—similar to the one Kamilla had talked about after she'd lost her mother? Was it wrong to have asked Rose to leave when Anne had come back from work—or her job search, as Anne should have said? Travel back to Nørrebro, from where many residents had fled due to the gang war. No one felt safe there. But earlier today, when she had walked into her living room that stank of cigarettes and had an ugly woman in a nightdress and a half-empty beer bottle in her hand, it hadn't made her change her mind.

She opened her eyes. It was so quiet. Too quiet. She missed her work, Kamilla, Britt, Nicolaj—yeah, even Thygesen. She needed to find a job soon, but at least now she didn't have to go out into the cold every day just so her secret wouldn't be revealed. She stretched her legs out from under the coffee table. An empty beer bottle rolled across the wooden floor; the sound was ear-splitting in the silence. She bent down and picked it up. So, something had slipped past the cleaning lady. She smiled bitterly as she looked at the bottle. It was to her mother what a soother was to a baby. When had it started? When her husband died in a car accident? When Torsten came into her life to plague her? She didn't remember seeing her mother drunk before that time. But where was she now? How many places could she know in Aarhus? She went out into the kitchen, put the bottle on the kitchen table, and made tea. As she was on her way back to the sofa with the hot mug, the doorbell rang. She hesitated for a long time before opening the door. Even though it was empty with her mother gone, she didn't want her back. So if it was her—

"Sorry to disturb you again, I . . . I . . ." stammered the young man outside the door in excellent Danish with a slight accent. She recognised him immediately. Adomas, her Lithuanian cousin.

"Did you forget something yesterday?"

"No, no. I just want to . . . talk to you, if—"

"Did she not tell you that you can't stay here? You can't! And she is no longer staying here, either."

"It's not that at all. But do you know where your mother is now?"

"No idea. And I don't care, either. It's my turn not to." She went to close the door, but Adomas put his hand against it and pushed it open so forcefully that she was flung towards the sofa. He approached her threateningly. She straightened up and looked him defiantly in the eyes with a beating heart, wanting to say something, but he interrupted her plan.

"Is that how you treat family here in Denmark? With total indifference! She's your mother; shouldn't you know where you've sent her?"

"Me? Where *I've* sent her!?" Anne looked away and searched in her pocket for her cigarettes, found them, and fumbled to get one out of the packet and between her lips. Her hands shook.

Adomas took out a lighter and lit it for her. "Did you really think I was going to hit you?" He clicked off the lighter and put it back in his pocket. "I know where your mother is. She's sitting in a shelter for the homeless. Is that what you want for her?"

Anne sat down on the couch and looked up at him. "Yes, you're right, we treat our family peculiarly. Rose hasn't known where I was for fourteen years. She has been as indifferent to me as I am to her."

"That's not true, Annie—"

"My name is Anne!"

"Okay, sorry, but it's not true—Anne. I've known your mother for a very long time. She really wanted to find you, but didn't dare to—"

"He's been in jail for years now, so that excuse doesn't hold anymore!" she interrupted.

"Because she was afraid to meet you . . . I was going to say."

"Afraid? To meet *me*?!"

"She knows well that she's treated you badly. Of course she was afraid of how you were going to react to her. It has been a great . . . what do you call it . . . mission to find you."

Anne looked at him intently. He resembled the man in the picture on the bookshelf a lot. It was probably what her father had looked like when his mother had fallen in love with him. Same age definitely.

"Where did you learn to speak Danish so well?"

Adomas smiled shyly. "I have lived in Denmark for many years. Your mother helped me a lot with the language. You can get a decent job here, so I took Danish lessons to get better opportunities—and meet Danish girls."

"Oh, okay. Did you need to be able to talk to the girls?"

He laughed, and there was something about his laughter that made her smile.

"Not always. They are special, the Danish girls." He grew serious again. "I mean, Anne, your mother's having a hard time. I accompanied her to the shelter because I'm worried about her. You have to help her."

"Would you like a cup of tea?"

Adomas nodded and sat down. He took off his coat.

"Which shelter is she in?" she asked, setting the mug in front of him.

"I don't know the name. I think the street is . . . Mejlgade. In the city centre." He drank and burned himself.

"Oh, I know where that is. It's the Church Shelter. How does Mum know that?"

"I saw her talking to some people down by the church, they probably told her where to go. But it's not a place for Rose. She's not homeless. She has family!" His eyes penetrated her; she looked down at the table.

"You don't understand, Adomas. It goes way back. I have never known my father, my stepfather is in prison for murder, and my mother has always supported him. She's never helped me in any way, so . . ."

"I've met your stepfather."

Anne looked at him quickly.

"Only once, but that was enough."

"What happened?"

"I got a few slaps." He smiled crookedly.

Anne smiled back and drank from her mug as she continued looking at him. To think that they were family. He was her cousin; it was a thought she would have to get used to. Plus, the fact that she was half Lithuanian.

"You might be used to being beaten up?" she asked.

"No, not at all, at least, not at home. We've ended up in fights a few times in the city, but only because we were provoked and maybe were a little too drunk."

Anne put her mug back on the table. "Mum mentioned that some of your friends had been in trouble. What happened?"

"I'm not supposed to talk to anyone about it . . ."

"I won't say anything to anyone, but maybe I can help. I understand that they've been unfairly accused." Anne felt something stir inside her. This is what she missed. Digging deep—to find out what had really happened. Bringing it to light.

"I don't know, Anne. What they did is criminal, but that's not what they're wanted for. It's much worse."

"Are they wanted? What did they do?"

Adomas looked at her long and questioningly before answering. "They couldn't get jobs, and they desperately needed money to travel back to Lithuania. You know, Eastern Europeans are always blamed for the home break-ins, so they decided to break into a farm where they knew there was money. That's all they did. But now they are wanted for murder."

"Murder?!" Anne straightened, annoyed that she hadn't bought a newspaper again, but she had been in such a hurry to get home to see if her mother had vanished that it had gone completely out of her head.

"Yeah, the police found the man beaten to death, but they weren't the ones who did it; I know they weren't. They admit that they had to punch the wife in the face to get her to shut up, but they didn't do the other thing."

"Are you sure? Maybe something went wrong?"

"I've known them since we were kids. They aren't violent. Not that violent," he added as she cleared her throat.

"A few slaps here and there, but to kill someone so brutally—they just wouldn't do that."

"Where are they now, your mates?"

"I'm not telling you that."

"Okay. But they have to go to the police. They have to tell them what happened."

"I'll never get them to do that. No one would believe them. It'd be pure suicide."

"We don't have the death penalty here in Denmark, and if they report themselves, it can only improve their case. If they are truly innocent, then the evidence will prove it. Try to talk to them, right?"

He nodded. "But then you must also promise me that you will go down and talk to your mother in the shelter. Will you?"

Anne nodded reluctantly. "Okay, okay, I will."

# 14

Roland turned up the radiator when he returned to the station, and there was a smell of hot paint.

"So, Forensics only found a cigarette butt in the snow, which may have been thrown there by anyone other than the suspects?" He took a bite of a rum ball that had tempted him in the baker's window. Isabella and Mikkel had politely declined the offer to enjoy one with their coffee.

"And there are no answers yet from the forensic investigation of the crime scene?" He chewed the confection and dried his fingers in a napkin.

"Nothing yet, but they're working on it. And we still need to find the car," Mikkel replied. He moved his arm a good distance beyond the armrest of his chair so that it rested against Isabella's elbow. Otherwise, they had managed to keep their relationship well hidden from the chief superintendent. Kurt Olsen did not tolerate office romances; it gave too many distractions, he said. But Roland had discovered the couple's secret. He shouldn't hide that kind of thing from the top superior, but he liked the two young people, they were good at their jobs. And, my God, what did a little love mean in the workplace?

"Are you listening?"

Mikkel waved a hand in front of Roland's stiff gaze and finished by snapping his fingers. Isabella smiled. Roland still loved that smile, but he had seen how it was Mikkel's prize. Perhaps also lost was the promotion that Roland had given up pursuing after Irene's many admonitions. They had enough money, she kept claiming.

"Of course I'm listening. We're still searching for the car, yes?"

"Yes, but with the sparse description, we get either nothing or loads of people contacting us with useless information."

"Did nothing come out of talking to the neighbours at all?" asked Isabella.

"No, no one saw anything unusual. Only Thorkild Hansen observed the car. But his wife had to force it out of him. They all seem pretty shy."

"I saw one of them on TV 2 East Jutland last night. It's unbelievable that she's willing to go on local television to talk about the episode when the suspects are still at large."

Mikkel took her hand and gave it a squeeze. "Sensationalism, my sweet. Most people love being in the know. Being able to share gruesome news and make others shudder."

"Who was it?" asked Roland.

"I think her name was Ella. Ella Geisler."

Roland smiled wryly. "That would make bloody sense. She looked like a light-skinned Aboriginal, didn't she?"

"A what?"

"Native Australian," Mikkel contributed.

Isabella laughed. "Yes, she did."

Roland took the newspaper he had picked up in the collective. "Albert Hovgaard himself was in the press recently." He looked up the article and handed the paper to Mikkel.

"Shit, that's quite an arsenal of weapons. Is that really what the killers now have in their possession?" Mikkel shook his head slowly. Isabella leaned in over his arm and placed her cheek against his shoulder as she read along. *If Kurt Olsen turned up now.* Roland looked nervously at the door.

"We have to assume so. Either way, they are not harmless. We have to face that."

"Is it wise to display that kind of thing?" asked Isabella, looking at him over the edge of the newspaper.

"A bit careless, to put it mildly."

"But sadly, it has become like that." Isabella read on, and Roland remained silent as he watched them. Mikkel's clean-shaven head leaned against Isabella's, her blond hair falling softly down her shoulders. Their pupils moved back and forth as they read the article. He imagined them sitting like that at the breakfast table to the aroma of coffee and bread rolls, her wearing only a slightly open dressing gown, revealing just a hint, and him—preferably fully clothed. He felt a tingling sensation in his chest. A need. But the longing was more for a time than a situation.

It was a long time since he and Irene had read the morning paper together like that. He looked up when Isabella finished reading and looked at him again.

"Could Albert Hovgaard be a victim because of the article?"

"It can't be ruled out. Have we checked surveillance cameras at petrol stations and so on in the area?"

Mikkel laid the paper on the table and nodded. "No car that matches the description. But we have patrols out there looking for it, so if they have left it somewhere, there's hope we'll find it."

"If they haven't gone back to Eastern Europe with the loot." Roland sighed.

"How much did they actually get—in addition to the weapons?" asked Isabella.

"Olsen's going to the hospital again today to try to talk to Signe Hovgaard. He wasn't able to get in to talk to her yesterday, so we don't know for sure."

The phone rang. Roland was happy to hear Gert Schmidt's overly loud voice. Mikkel and Isabella could easily listen along. A call from the head of Forensics was always welcomed.

"What do you have, Schmidt? Do you have good news for us?"

"Yes and no. I have the results of the analysis of the teeth found on the kitchen floor. Not all are from the same person. I suspect we have two of the murderers' teeth. That means we have DNA."

"Well, that's good news, but . . ."

"It is, but as long as we don't have known perps, the knowledge is of no use. They're not from people on our register, at least."

"That's a shame, but it gives us a good opportunity to trap the people when we find them. Anything else?"

"You probably heard that the fingerprints are identical to those from three other robberies in East Jutland, haven't you?"

"Yes, I heard that. We need to find the owners. Thanks for the help, Schmidt." He hung up, and Isabella and Mikkel nodded to confirm that they'd been listening.

"So, we have both DNA and fingerprints—that means we 'only' need to find three or four Eastern Europeans," Mikkel said dryly, patting Isabella on the thigh as a sign that they should move on. *Like how you pat a dog,* Roland thought, making a face. They both stood up, as if it were a movement of one and the same person. "If it takes too long, the chances of finding them reduce. Interpol has, of course, been informed, and the borders are being monitored. I don't think they'll be able to get out of the country," continued Mikkel.

"If they're not already over the mountains. Let's get this case closed. We really only need to find the perps." He watched them as they walked towards the door. Mikkel, tall and muscular, was more than a head taller than her.

"Oh, Isabella . . ." She turned immediately in the doorway. "There's something I'd like you to look at, too, if you will?"

"Which case is it?" She entered his office again and pushed the door in a little.

"In the spring four years ago—or thereabouts—a boy drowned in the lake in the forest that is part of Olga and Vagn Mortensen's property. I only know that his name was probably Marcus. Will you try to find what we have on that case?"

Isabella frowned. "Does it have anything to do with the robbery and the murder, then?"

"No, I don't think so. It's just strange that the boy lived with his family on the property where Signe and Albert Hovgaard live now."

"So, the same farm where Albert was murdered . . ."

"Exactly."

"It sounds like a coincidence. You don't remember anything about it?"

"I only vaguely remember something about a boy who drowned, but so many terrible things happen that the brain, fortunately, doesn't remember them all. Plus, it wasn't a CID case."

Isabella nodded. "Okay."

"It's probably a coincidence, but if you can find out where Marcus's family lives now, it could be interesting to hear what they have to tell us—just view it as a completely different case that we're re-investigating because of the circumstances."

# 15

Kamilla enjoyed the view as they drove along Ny Havnevej. She had a fondness for marinas. The red buildings with pointed black roofs and panoramic windows reminded her of those at Egå Marina. Even in the winter, the boats were always a beautiful sight. They lay steadfast in the ice and with snow on their decks. Everything was frozen until spring would bring life to the harbour again. The horizon faded into the blue-grey haze of winter, so you couldn't see very far out to sea. The wind turbines on the headland with its long pier turned merrily; all seven of them were blowing at a good tempo. It was nice for once to be a passenger and not to have to concentrate on driving on the slippery roads, despite Pierre driving like he was used to in France. Her feet had moved on the floorboard of the car, as if she herself were sitting behind the wheel; the foot on the would-be brake often pressed all the way down onto the car's soft carpet. They had arrived. Pierre turned onto Østre Mole and parked. Here was where they were to meet the fisherman who had agreed to the gig.

The wind was hard and biting and a harsh contrast to the car's heating system. She slammed the door shut and looked at Pierre, who was wearing a black unisex ski hat. She was annoyed that she had forgotten her own. Her ears already hurt terribly. She helped him take the photo bags out of the car and grabbed one of them. The strap cut into her shoulder; it weighed a ton. Such was the case with the outdoor shoots, where they had to bring all their equipment with them.

"Where did you agree to meet the fisherman?" she asked, almost slipping on the slush the road salt had produced. Pierre grabbed her by the arm.

"At Bønnerup Fisk. Can you see it?"

"I think it's over there."

He kept hold of her arm as they walked towards the building. A fisherman stood waiting. He wore a knitted hat with lambskin trim on his head and an orange one-piece suit with reflectors on top of what seemed to be several layers of jumpers, though only a grey jumper with a zipper could be seen at the neckline. Pierre introduced them both, and the fisherman's weather-beaten face lit up with a smile that was reflected in the blue eyes.

"Kjeld Åge Hansen. I won't shake hands." He held up his hands, which were in blue rubber gloves and covered in fish scales. "But welcome. I'm really excited about this. Taking photos of some flatfish. I always thought it was about good 'herrings' in your business." He winked at Kamilla. She tried to smile even though the cold paralysed her face.

"We need to have a little strand in the background; we don't get that here," said Pierre. Kamilla looked around. The fishing boats were lined up along both Østre and Vestre Mole, but there wasn't much strand to see.

"I think we should start by finding some suitable large plaice as photo models in here"—he pointed behind him—"then we can sail out and find a place to 'park' so we can have some of the strand in the background." The fisherman shook his head, saying without words how foolish he found the idea.

They managed to find some nice specimens of plaice in the fish-house. They sailed out to sea, where the cold was even more biting, if possible. The pain in her ears was so strong that she could have screamed, and when Pierre took off his hat and pulled it down over her head and cold, red ears, she did not protest, even though she knew he would now suffer.

She took a series of photos of the fish beautifully laid out on clear chunks of ice flanked by lemon halves and some of the snowy strand in the background, like the client's advertising agency had produced in the full-page draft ad. Pierre checked the LCD screen and nodded contentedly. Kjeld Åge watched with his arms crossed over his chest, constantly shaking his head—he'd never seen so much fuss over fish, but he was happy to participate when asked. He held the biggest fish by its tail and smiled proudly at the camera, as if it were his own catch. The world of advertising is built on illusions.

When the shoot was finished, they sailed back to the harbour. Kamilla handed Pierre his hat and thanked him for his thoughtfulness.

"Do you want to join me at Den Blå Kutter and have a bite to eat before you drive back? It's getting late," enticed Kjeld Åge. "It's just here."

Kamilla caught Pierre's eye and tried to signal that she would rather go home, but he smiled cordially at the helpful fisherman. "Of course we will. I'm getting pretty hungry, aren't you, Kamilla?"

She nodded.

The restaurant was nicely decorated in a maritime yet modern style. The fisherman told them how the building used to be the harbour's old smithy, but that in 1994, it was converted into this maritime eatery, which, naturally, primarily served fresh local fish. Kjeld Åge was enormously proud of his town—he couldn't hide it—and they got the whole story of Bønnerup Strand in detail while they waited for their food. Fishing had been its main industry for more than a hundred years, he said. There were well over eight hundred inhabitants and even more when the tourist season began. His detailed narration was interrupted by a couple who stopped at their table.

"Don't believe everything a fisherman tells you; they're full of tall tales," said the man jokingly.

Kjeld Åge smiled at the sarcasm and presented his guests as two photographers from Aarhus, who had driven all the way here in the snow to take pictures of some plaice—and a snowy strand. The man and woman stared at them without saying anything, but you could see what they were thinking.

"Won't you join us?" Kjeld Åge pulled out a chair for the woman, but the man replied that they had just eaten and were on their way home. "Mathias is home alone, so . . ."

"Well, I'll see you at Ida and Ole's wedding on Saturday," said Kjeld Åge, accepting his plate of fragrant fish that the waiter had just brought.

"Yes, you will," replied the man, looking at his companion as if he suddenly had an idea. "Didn't Ida say they need a photographer for the big day?"

His hair was a splendid mix of white and dark strands that could have been done by a hairdresser, but he didn't seem that type. His eyes were blue and intense, as if he were a curious person who was interested in others. His companion was younger than him, with shoulder-length hair that also had splashes of grey but were not as evident in her blond hair. She wasn't wearing any make-up, and her skin was very pale. Both were dressed in elegant black clothes as if coming from a party.

"Is that something you might be interested in?"

It dawned on her that he was speaking to her, and she glanced at Pierre for help. But he had a teasing twinkle in his eye again, so he wasn't about to come to the rescue.

"Kamilla is a very good photographer. I'm sure she'd love to do it." He smiled, and she would have punched him hard on the arm if no one else had been there.

"Do you have a business card that I can give to Ida?" the man asked next.

"No, I haven't got my business cards yet. I've only just started working for Pierre. Besides, I'm a product photographer—I prefer not to take pictures of people—actually, it's Pierre who normally . . ."

Pierre handed his business card to the woman, who accepted it with a smile that lit up her face. "Thank you, Ida will be delighted," she said, putting it in a delicate black clutch bag.

Kamilla breathed a sigh of relief. Pierre had accepted the job. Private shoots were not something they did a lot. Usually only for close friends.

"Nice people," said Kjeld Åge, putting a napkin in his lap when they were gone.

"Is he a local? He seemed to have an accent," asked Pierre, who always enjoyed running into other 'immigrants.'

Kjeld Åge acknowledged his observation with a nod. "You're right. Though it's not as nice as your own," he replied, winking at Kamilla again. "He came here about fifteen years ago, it must be." He impaled a piece of fish with his fork and stuffed it in his mouth.

"Where's he from?"

"Um, from Horsens, I think—he was a fisherman there, too. Why he chose to move here, I have no idea. Maybe he just wanted to get away from the city. But then he met our shopkeeper's daughter, Alice, and they had a son, Mathias. An accident, I heard," he added with a theatrical whisper, "but he settled in quickly here. Ida and Ole are mutual friends. A young couple who've decided to take the plunge on Saturday—in the cold—God only knows why they're not waiting for spring."

"A winter wedding can be beautiful, too. Is she going to be wearing white?" Pierre looked questioningly at Kjeld Åge, who nodded. "It could make for be some amazing pictures." He looked at Kamilla encouragingly.

She finished chewing and held his gaze. "It's your responsibility as a model photographer," she pointed out, but Pierre smiled craftily and toasted.

"The boss doesn't usually do private shoots, you know," he replied again. They drank, Kamilla kept an eye on him over the edge of the glass. He was up to something, she could see. He was going to keep putting her to the test, she realised. She was a student—kind of—again, but she held fast that her area was dead stuff, so he wasn't going to get far.

"I was born and raised in Horsens, too. What's his name, your friend?" she asked Kjeld Åge after they had eaten for a while in silence.

"His name is Mogens. But he didn't always live in Horsens. Apparently, he's one of the tough ones—which means he's fought against the dangerous undercurrents of the North Sea."

"West Jutland? I thought there was something strange about that accent all right," muttered Pierre between two mouthfuls.

Kamilla had finished eating and was staring down into her wine glass; the red wine had transformed into the dark waters of the North Sea in her mind, where a boy disappeared over the railing forever. Her heart pounded so violently that she became uncomfortable. "What's his surname?" she heard herself ask, even though she already knew the answer.

# 16

The warm yellow light from the windows, which his watery eyes suddenly caught like a mirage on the bluish horizon, was reminiscent of a Disney Christmas fairy tale appearing in the night. All that was missing was for a fairy to come flying by on its little fluttery, silvery wings and sprinkle magic dust over him so that his hunger and exhaustion would disappear, and he would have the strength to drag himself all the way there.

It was the first house he'd seen in the eternity he felt had passed since he'd escaped from the wooden coffin and shed. There had only been darkness and an impenetrable forest. An infinity of tree after tree and snow upon snow. He had fallen, had lain down, had got up again, and had staggered on driven only by the thought that otherwise, he would die. And what would that really matter? Who would it affect? No one. No one was left. That had gone round and round in his dizzy head, too. As well as how he missed his family, love, and life. His thoughts had become a blurred image of an unreal world that didn't exist—that had never existed.

His eyes stung and watered. His breath was frozen in his beard like stinging needles. He had feared getting lost and never finding his way out. Back to the newspapers along the wall by the church, the warm blanket, and the bag of booze. Life around him. Drunk young people on their way home from the discos; they usually had a few words for him. People rushing to bus stops. They were as cold as the frost—sent no smiles—didn't even look at him. Yet they still made him feel like he wasn't completely alone. It was probably all gone now. The bag of spirits at least. Spirits! He was so thirsty! The others had needed it. Or maybe they had sought refuge in the shelter. He would give his life to sit there with friendly people around him again. The only place in the world he felt there were still people who wanted to keep him alive.

The property in front of him looked like a small fortune had been spent on modernising it. It was just outside the forest, but what forest had he fought his way through? Marselisborg? It was the biggest he knew, and the area he traversed had to have been big. A giant Christmas tree was lit in the yard. Like in the city. The big one down by the City Hall with the little ones around it. All through January, they illuminated the little bulbs out on the balconies. Gave courage to get through the dark time. Even to him.

His legs couldn't carry him the last steps up the stone stairs that felt like an invincible pyramid. He fell on the first step and only just reached the bottom of the door, but he had no strength left to knock. It was like a dog's miserable scratch to get into the warmth. He tried to move closer. Crawled on his stomach in snow and ice up the steps. Made a fist and knocked again and again until he no longer felt his knuckles. Diagonally above him, he saw a curtain being lifted. Eyes searching the darkness. A couple more came along. He imagined what the residents were saying to each other. *It's just a beggar; he probably only wants to beg or steal. Leave him there.* Maybe they couldn't see him here on the stairs and thought it was the wind. He tried to come up onto his knees to reach the doorbell, but he slipped and fell into a snowdrift, knocking over a rubbish bin in the fall. The contents spilled out into the snow, and the familiar smell of waste food intensified his hunger. He rummaged in the litter and found a piece of meat that had only been half eaten. Potato peels and a crust of rye bread. He stuffed it all into his mouth until there was no more room in there. Only when he heard a door being gently closed did it dawn on him that the occupants had opened it and looked out. They had seen him do it. A wild beast with a rope around its neck, tearing through their rubbish. He stared at the closed door and tried to say something—to shout—but no sound came from his throat. The light was turned off in the windows, and soon afterwards the little lights on the Christmas tree in the yard went out, too. Darkness closed in around him, only the snow provided enough light to orient himself. At the gable, he glimpsed a tool-shed or a garage. He crawled towards it, his feet could no longer carry him, and soon his arms wouldn't be able to support him, either. He prayed that the shed wasn't locked, that it was dry, sheltered, and a little warm. Several times he put a hand or a knee on the stump of the rope, tightening it around his throat. A violent pain in his stomach caused him to curl up. He threw up in the snow and lay, exhausted, on his back, feeling the snowflakes hit his face like little cold, soft, gentle feathers of down. They melted and ran like tears down his cheeks. What had happened in the last twenty-four hours? How did he end up here? His eyes closed, and this time he knew he wouldn't open them again.

# 17

———

The forensic pathologist's voice was completely neutral as he described the condition of the body over the phone.

"Undoubtedly suicide. The rope is still sitting around his neck, and it looks like he almost succeeded. Given the injuries it caused, it's incredible he survived that. He was out in the cold for a long time. The frost injuries can't only be from last night. The feet are black and blue due to dry gangrene—tissue necrosis. Shit, he's been out in the snow and frost without shoes, and—"

"Without shoes?" Roland interrupted in surprise, shaking a new piece of nicotine chewing gum out of its pack. He had stopped smoking but couldn't give up the chewing gum now; one addiction had just taken over from the other.

"Yes, he was found without anything on his feet. There are many indications that the deceased is homeless. There hasn't been any dental care for years, the clothes haven't been washed—neither has the body—soiled and grungy, you know—nor the hair. It looks as if he cut it himself. A sad sight. Sad life. You can understand why he chose what he did, even though I'm not supposed to say so. I'm treating the case as suicide. Is there anything new in your murder case?"

"Not yet, unfortunately. We have DNA and fingerprints, but don't have the owners. But even if the man is homeless, it's not normal to walk around without shoes in one of the worst winters we've had in a long time. And how did he end up at the address on Trige Skovvej—wasn't that where he was found?"

"Yeah, it is suspicious. Most homeless people live in the city. He probably took the bus—for free. Maybe you'd like to look into it a little?"

The forensic pathologist was one of the young new employees. Roland missed Henry Leander, who was at a conference for the rest of the week; it was all too clear that his substitute didn't have much time for the homeless. He simply was still too green.

"Were you able to identify him?"

"He has no papers on him, but I can try to take fingerprints if . . . ?"

"I think you should. There may be relatives who need to be notified. Homeless people aren't necessarily rootless." Roland hung up, annoyed. Suicide was not uncommon. And certainly not suicide among the homeless. Nearly half of all homeless, poor, drug addicts, and other social outcasts tried to take their own lives. Some of them succeeded. But it wasn't normal for them to be found outside the front door of a nice home so far away from the city. The couple had called early in the morning when they found him lying dead under the snow amid debris from the bin, which they thought he had probably overturned when he fell. They hadn't heard any commotion last night and so didn't know how long he had been lying there, when he'd arrived, and why he had chosen to lie down to die right in front of their home. They didn't know him, and as he was covered in snow that had been falling across the country for most of the night. It was almost by chance that they had even discovered him on their way to check the letterbox. If there were relatives who wanted the case opened, they would have to do so, but otherwise, there was nothing to do but—as the enterprising forensic pathologist had said—file it as yet another tragic suicide.

He looked relieved when Chief Superintendent Olsen entered his office after a quick knock on the door that was more for the purpose of announcing his presence rather than requiring an answer. He remained standing in the doorway.

"The car has apparently been found. We think it's the one. Unfortunately, it's burned, so there won't be much evidence."

"Damn it!" Roland slapped a fist on the table angrily. "Where was it found?"

"On a remote dirt road nearby, but a neighbour reported his car stolen, so now we have a better lead to follow. A silver-grey Mitsubishi. We have the reg and everything—if it was the murderers who stole it."

"It may be too late. They're probably across the border by now."

"All patrols are looking for it, and Interpol has been informed, so if they haven't already left the country, then . . . I was also finally allowed a brief conversation with Signe Hovgaard."

"Did you get anything useful?"

Kurt Olsen came in and closed the door. He sat down on the chair in front of Roland's desk, grabbed the insulated coffee pot, and poured some coffee into a plastic mug. "She is obviously in shock," he replied as he continued pouring. "The son takes care of the pigs. I asked her if anything had been stolen, but she said it didn't matter. Only her husband had mattered, and he was no longer here." He drank from the mug and looked sadly at Roland. "My goodness! She's right. What do stolen items mean when the one you love is gone forever?"

"Stolen weapons are not entirely without significance," Roland reminded him, and Kurt Olsen shook his head gloomily.

"There's a press conference this afternoon. Are you going to participate?"

"Preferably not, but if you insist, then . . ."

"It's about to overflow with journalists. You've probably heard that your little tormentor can't bother you this time, haven't you?" His laugh was without amusement.

"So I've heard." The mixed feelings rumbled again in his abdominal region. What was she doing now? Had she gone back to Copenhagen to annoy the police over there? Returned to her old roots and become a left-wing activist? Though he couldn't really imagine that; there had been many changes in her over the years she had worked as a journalist at the *Daily News*. He thought back to when he found her on the floor of her apartment the night her stepfather had been close to killing her. Roland had saved her life. Maybe that was the episode that triggered the care and concern he couldn't completely shake off now. Who was it that said, "When you save someone else's life, you are bound to them forever"?

"You don't actually look happy, Benito. Don't tell me you're going to miss her!"

"Argh, but you have to admit that she helped us with certain cases. What would she say about a B&E and murder? Mind you, it wouldn't have surprised me if she found the car before it was burned, if she . . ."

"Stop talking nonsense! Don't dare suggest that a journalist does police work better than us."

"That's not what I meant, but she knew something that made her way of investigating more effective than ours. She wasn't subject to the strict controls of her methods like we are, where everyone watches our every movement."

"No, and who watches most, hmm? Everyone! The pressure of every-one—they'll be there if we step just a little bit over the line."

Roland nodded in agreement. Kurt Olsen was right.

"What was that case that came in this morning? A suicide?" Olsen asked.

"That's what the forensic pathologist assumes, so we must take him at his word, don't we? There are indications of suicide, even if the circum-stances are strange."

"That he was found in front of the house, you mean? I suppose he just wandered around after the failed suicide attempt. Maybe he tried to hang himself in a tree nearby. Maybe he lived at Fællesgården; it's not that far from there."

Roland nodded again. He hadn't thought of that possibility at all. Fællesgården in Trige, run by the church, embraced its mission to acti-vate the weakest groups in society and, through practical work and social events, to give them a meaningful life in a safe environment.

"That's quite possible. But why would he be walking around without any shoes? That makes no sense to me."

"Three sheets to the wind; probably didn't feel the cold. Maybe the shoes are in a snowdrift somewhere. Do you know who he is?"

"It sounded like the forensic pathologist was going to investigate the case."

"He bloody well better. When's Henry Leander back?"

"Not until Monday," Roland replied hesitantly. He knew that Julie Hermansen from the National Police's Special Operations Unit was also at the conference and staying at the same hotel, so it wouldn't surprise him if they decided to take an extended weekend in Copenhagen. But he couldn't reveal that to the superintendent, as Roland wasn't supposed to know about their relationship—not officially at least—despite it having gone on for years.

Kurt Olsen nodded, looked at his watch, and emptied the mug. He got up and straightened his tie. "Well, I better get ready for the press conference. If you deal with the car we're searching for and the burned out one, you're off the hook. Unfortunately, there's nothing much new to tell the vultures."

Roland looked wearily after him when he turned his back and walked away. He threw the empty mug in the bin and immersed himself in the report. No results had yet come from the examination of the cigarette butt found in the snow where the car had apparently been parked. If the DNA matched what was found in the teeth at the crime scene, the perp could also be placed in the car or at least near it. He called Forensics and, after a short wait, got Gert Schmidt, as requested. He couldn't cope with another clueless substitute.

"Yes, Benito, the results are a shame, but it was investigated by another department given how interesting it was . . ."

"Interesting how? Did you find DNA?"

"Unfortunately, no. Water and frost ruined it, but the analysis showed that it wasn't the butt of a genuine Marlboro cigarette."

"Fake cigarettes?" He could hear Gert presumably nodding with the phone clamped to his shoulder as usual so that his hands were free for his work. It sounded as though his chin was rubbing against the fabric of his lab coat as he moved.

"Yes, counterfeit cigarettes from Eastern Europe, where they are manufactured and sold throughout Europe as the real thing, have been seized before."

"Illegal cigarette factories have also been uncovered in Germany, and a fake cigarette isn't unequivocal evidence that Eastern Europeans committed the murder," Roland replied with some reservations in his voice, for he had to admit, too, that it was highly probable that the man who had thrown or dropped the cigarette in the snow by the parked car could be one of those Signe Hovgaard had heard speaking a Slavic language.

"Should I send the report?"

"It's not urgent, Schmidt. It was the DNA I was interested in—so we could compare it and link things."

"Okay, that's a pity. I'll send it when I have the chance."

Roland thanked him and hung up. Just then, DS Mikkel Jensen stuck his head in the doorway with an eager expression. "The Mitsubishi we've been searching for turned up abandoned at a rest stop near Vejle. It's being taken to Forensics and checked for evidence."

"Good, Mikkel. And the weapons?"

"They took them with them—of course."

# 18

───────

Anne wrestled herself out of her coat and let it fall onto the floor. You could no longer tell the apartment had been scrubbed from top to bottom the day before. When everything inside her was chaos, it was reflected in her surroundings. Empty mugs and cups covered the coffee table, the kitchen table, and in the kitchen sink; the ashtray hadn't been emptied, and the smell of old pubs lingered—just like when her mother had stayed there.

She had been around to the shelter on Mejlgade again, but like the day before, she hadn't found her mother among the other poor people sitting in all their misery and trying to find meaning in life. She didn't know her mother's new address in Nørrebro, and no one could give it to her. They couldn't even find Rose's name when she'd tried the White Pages. Adomas said she was still in Aarhus but didn't know where she was staying. Her guilty conscience wore on her; she knew well what it was like to be left in the belief that no one loved you. How you sank deeper and deeper and eventually became indifferent to what you were doing and what happened to you.

She was rummaging in her coat pocket on the floor for her mobile phone when the shrill Nokia tone broke the silence. She saw in the display that it was him.

"Yes, Adomas?"

"She has just entered the shelter. She doesn't look well, Anne."

"Shit, I'll be right there. Where are you now?"

"I've been keeping an eye on the building; I told you she'd come back. You have to talk to her."

"Why don't you do that yourself?"

"She's *your* mother!"

She just nodded despite Adomas not being able to see it. "Are you staying?"

"I can't stay. I have to meet . . ." He hesitated.

"With your mates? Remember what I said! They have to go the police to prove they haven't done what the police think they have."

"Hurry, Anne, before she leaves again. Talk soon." He hung up, and she suddenly felt completely alone. What was she going to do with her mother? Rose moving in here was out of the question. Maybe she was best in that shelter; maybe Anne should just be indifferent and let her mother take care of herself like her mother had chosen to do when she herself had disappeared into Copenhagen's underworld.

She put on her coat, hat, and scarf and found her car keys in her coat pocket. "Shit," she mumbled, walking out into the cold again and onto the pavement, which was still not cleared of snow in front of the front door. *Can't you be fined for that? Aren't you supposed to pay compensation if someone falls and injures themselves?*

There were no spaces available on Mejlgade, so she parked illegally and walked up to the shelter building. She had always found the houses here beautiful with their pastel-coloured walls, cosy lattice windows, and dormer windows in the roof.

The heat hit her when she opened the door. *Shelter* was the perfect name; the contrast to the freezing temperatures outside was sharp. There was the smell of coffee. A TV was on and switched to a channel airing an old Dirch Passer movie that a man with a white beard, who was talking to himself, was trying to drown out. Or was he talking into a mobile on a wireless headset? Hardly, he was the real deal. It was hard to tell nowadays; it was no longer unusual to meet people talking to "themselves" out in the open. A woman with bags under her eyes sat reading the newspaper without paying any attention to the man's loud talking. Two men played Ludo at a table. Being "knocked back to square one" wasn't the worst thing that could happen to a homeless person, she thought as she looked around, but she could not spot her mother any-where. An employee, though, caught sight of Anne and greeted her with a friendly smile.

"Are you looking for someone?"

"A Rose Teresa Larsen should be here. Do you know her? Do you know where she is?"

The Ludo players and the newspaper reader looked up, vaguely inter-ested, and then concentrated again on what they were doing, indifference returning.

The employee pointed to a table where three women were sitting. The woman with her back to her resembled Rose. Anne reluctantly went over, wondering what to say and what it was Adomas was expecting of her.

They seemed to be in the middle of a serious conversation, bending over the table towards each other to talk as quietly as possible among themselves. It was almost reminiscent of a sports team's pep talk before a match except that the three looked anything but sporty.

"Annie!" Her mother looked up at her. She wasn't wearing any make-up. Adomas was right about Rose sprucing herself up to give her the courage to meet her prodigal daughter. That could explain the unsuc-cessful makeover; she had no practice at that kind of thing. Now her face was pale and wrinkled, her hair ugly and dirty, and her eyes red-rimmed. She stank of a mixture of liquor and coffee, but suddenly life came to her eyes.

"This is my daughter," she said proudly to the two women who stared at her curiously. "And this is Tove and Marie." She introduced her companions as if they were old friends from a distant past.

Anne greeted them and sat down on the edge of a chair.

"Mum . . ." she began.

"Do you want a cup of coffee, my darling?" As though in her own home, Rose had already got up to get it, and Anne couldn't be bothered to pro-test. She smiled uncertainly at her mother's new friends. Marie had marks from a black eye that appeared to have arisen from a hard blow to the jaw. It made her eye hang as much as Anne's did because of the scar on her eyebrow. A loving greeting from her stepfather, Torsten. Who was Marie's greeting from? Maybe she had a little in common with the women in this room after all—unemployed and with an eternal bodily fear of running into a man who didn't hesitate to use violence.

She accepted the cup when it was handed to her with a slightly shaking hand. Her mother sat down again, offering a little smile. "What a surprise. How did you know I was here?"

"I went looking for you."

"Did you?"

"Where are you going to sleep tonight?"

"With my friends." She smiled at the two women.

"Where do you live?" asked Anne, as it didn't sound like her mother intended to elaborate.

"Here and there. We can usually find an apartment stairwell where the front door isn't locked," Tove replied. She was morbidly thin, and her fingers were stained yellow with nicotine. There were probably puncture marks from needles on her body, too.

"But when it's so cold, we usually spend the night in Nørre Allé," said Marie in a rusty voice. She coughed hollowly.

"It's the night services," explained Tove. "The only place in Aarhus city centre where we can come into the warmth at night."

Anne looked desperately at her mother but didn't have any alternatives to offer, certainly not now that she'd also have to offer a place to stay to the other two. Four people in the small apartment would definitely be too many.

"It's not that bad, Annie. There is nothing to be afraid of, except . . ." She fiddled with a button on her shirt and looked desperately at the other two as if searching for permission to tell a common secret.

"Except what?"

Tove leaned confidently across the table towards her. The smell of sweat and bad breath came closer.

"Except that people are disappearing," she whispered.

"Disappearing how?"

"No one notices when someone from the streets is suddenly no longer there."

"No, they don't. Who sees us?" Marie interjected dryly.

"That's what we were talking about when you came in. Tove and Marie say that Rudolf has disappeared."

"And—Rudolf is homeless?"

Marie nodded. "He used to stay down by the church wall, but now he's gone."

"Couldn't he just be somewhere else, gone to Herberg or something?"

"Not Rudolf. Not without telling anyone. The others always knew where he was going if he left the wall."

"And there are no relatives he could be with?"

"I don't think so. Not anyone he'd see anyway. And the strange thing is that his trolley is still by the wall. He drove around with all his things in a shopping trolley from Brugsen. Everything was left there. Rudolf would never do that."

"Especially not his booze," Tove contributed with a crooked smile that slowly died.

"Has no one reported all those who are missing?"

"Missing homeless people?" Tove rolled her eyes.

"Well, it does not matter that you are homeless. The police have to treat you like everyone else!" protested Anne.

Tove shook her head in despair. "They're nice enough, but—"

"But Annie is actually a journalist. Maybe she can help?" Rose's pleading eyes fixed on Anne and made her look guiltily down at the table.

"She works with the police on murder cases and has helped solve loads of them," her mother added excitedly.

"You can help, Annie. You *have* to!"

Anne felt her adrenaline pumping, like it always had when an exciting new case appeared at the paper.

"Marie and Rose have started researching the case themselves," Tove said with a pointed expression in her eyes while she nervously rubbed her throat. Her skin was covered in small red spots that looked like an allergic reaction.

"Missing people can't be dead and gone without anyone noticing it."

"You don't know that. A woman named Ruth fell in love with Klatte, as we called him. When he disappeared, she tried to find him, but none of the authorities knew anything about him being dead."

# 19

The snow was high on the bird feeder. Everything in the garden around the house in Højbjerg was weighed down by snow, just as everything else was weighed down by the financial crisis. Though that looked dark, according to the experts, the snow, at least was white and illuminated, and spring always returns. In two months, the blackbirds would sing again. It's about looking on the bright side of life, as Irene used to say.

Angolo and Salvatore had been playing in the snow. A snowman stood half-finished in the light from the kitchen window. He was delighted to learn about the boy's behaviour. Normal stuff. Something a teenager should spend their time on. Not on supporting his mother by working for the waste-dumping mafia in a life-threatening work environment at a job that everyone else refused because it meant certain death. But how was he supposed to talk to Salvatore about it? How could he prevent him from returning to the high-paying job when he returned to Naples?

Irene sat alone at the set table. She was pouring more red wine into her glass.

"Are you sitting here all on your own? Have you eaten?"

Irene looked up and smiled wearily. "Salvatore has."

Angolo jumped up from his blanket at the sound of Roland's voice and wagged his tail until Irene told him to go to bed. She had as much control over the dog as she had over him. He only just managed to scratch Angolo behind the ears before he dutifully went to the blanket in the nook and laid down again, but his dark, adoring eyes followed Roland.

"Where's Salvatore?"

"In his room. He's on the phone."

"On the phone? With whom? His mother?"

"No, he called a friend back home."

"A friend! I told him he's not allowed . . . Where did he get the phone from?" Roland was on his way to the stairs to the guest room where Salvatore was staying while he was living with them, but Irene got up from her chair and grabbed his sleeve.

"Leave him alone, Rolando."

"Damn it, Irene! You know what it means for him if he's in contact with his friends! Many of them work for the mafia, too; the conversation could be traced, and his 'friends' may talk about where he is." His voice was more snarling and reprimanding than intended.

"Sit down for a moment." She poured some wine into his glass. He noticed fleetingly that it was the expensive 1989 Bartolo Mascarello Barolo, which he loved, and which they only opened on special occasions. He was about to scold her again but instead sat down, tired, on the chair and stared at the stairs, thinking of Salvatore up there in the process of revealing where he was hiding. But Roland had to admit it was his own fault. He should have told Salvatore what was going on a long time ago. Why he was in Denmark. Why his mother had asked them to take him for a while—away from the streets of Naples and the crime—explained to him, in his capacity as a male role model and detective, the bad choice he was about to make. La Camorra had moved closer to his life, to him, to his family. Was it deliberate that they had chosen Salvatore, who was related to Adriano Benito—the famous Carabiniere who had dedicated and sacrificed his life to fight the ugliness of the mafia, and who the rest of the family had continued to fight against? All except *i traditori*—the traitors—who had turned their back on Italy to save their own skin. That had been his mother's choice; Roland had had no say as a four-year-old, but neither had he done anything to change it since. He had followed in his father's footsteps, but not in the right country. He was a traitor. Maybe the Camorra didn't know who Salvatore was at all? But what would happen if they found out? He had to prevent Salvatore from getting back into their clutches. Giovanna had refused to move from Naples when he'd suggested it to her as a solution. She had instead demanded that Roland return to finish his father's work. He reached for the glass and took a mouthful of the wonderful wine. Italy was full of good experiences, too.

"We have to realise that Salvatore misses his friends," Irene said in a low voice. "He's been with us for almost three months now. Teenagers hang out with people their own age. And I can feel that we . . . that . . . I'm starting to get on his nerves."

"How? Did something happen?"

"Something. I don't quite know what it is. He's stayed in his room most of the day. I went up and ordered him out to get some fresh air. It's not healthy for a boy his age to be indoors all the time. And there is a language barrier, so communication is difficult, but I'm sure he was just pretending that he didn't understand what I meant." She looked at him intently. "He should go to school; he'll fall too far behind, and . . . I know he doesn't want to go to school and wouldn't have in Naples, either, but it's wrong, Rolando."

He could not contradict her on that. "But someone's been out tumbling in the snow and built half a snowman. Angolo didn't do all that on his own." He tried to bring some humour into their conversations again—they had been so serious of late—but Irene did not smile. She stared down at her large glass as she thoughtfully swirled the wine around the bottom of it with a dull motion.

"No, he came out then. Angolo convinced him to. I sent him in to see Salvatore with his collar in his mouth. The dog communicates better with him than I do; shortly afterwards he came down fully clothed and went out. He didn't come in again until it got dark. Neither did Angolo."

"How did he get hold of his mobile phone?" After all, we agreed that he wasn't to use it. I thought he understood—he knows it's very expensive to call home."

"We got into a quarrel, or whatever you want to call it. Fisticuffs, more like it. He wanted to eat, but I said we had to wait for you. *Aspettare Rolando*, I said. Isn't that how you pronounce it?"

He nodded.

"But he wouldn't wait because he was hungry, so I had to serve the lord and master. Afterwards, I understood from his signs and gestures that he wanted his phone. *Costa troppo*, I said, but he has obviously become indifferent to what it costs. He started threatening me, so I gave him his mobile. The battery was dead—he must have had a charger in his suitcase."

"Threatening you how? Did he become violent?" Roland looked at Irene with a sense of unease; the phone call upstairs and the misuse of his expensive wine were suddenly irrelevant.

"Only verbally, fortunately. I hate it when he calls me *puttana*; it's an ugly word."

"*Puttana*! He called you a whore?" He jumped up from the chair, took the stairs with long strides, and ignored Irene's desperate pleas.

A double espresso put a full stop to both the meal and the day. The quarrel with Salvatore had dragged on. Irene had done laundry in the meantime. The food had gone cold and had to be warmed in the oven. But he had said it. It was a relief. Now he could feel it—the promise to Aunt Giovanna— that had put pressure on his chest. His guilty conscience always settled there, so he should have figured it out sooner. Had he expected the lad to take it any differently than he had? Maybe it shouldn't have come out in a quarrel, but apparently, that's what it took for him to pull himself together to say the words *La Camorra*. As if leaving it said unspoken would keep them out of his life. Salvatore made no promise to stay away from working as a young driver—far too young a driver—and the shipments of chemical waste that could one day take his life—also far too young. Salvatore had argued that life itself was dangerous, that the work paid good money, and that he couldn't *fucking* stand that his mother wouldn't accept his *denaro sporco*—blood money. Not even the reminder that the same clan had murdered his uncle could change his mind, despite the remark slowing his furious packing of his suitcase. Roland was later able to inform Irene that Salvatore was leaving for Naples the next day. He was going to drive him to the airport once he had got the tickets. It both pleased and shocked him that she seemed happy and relieved at the information.

"We mustn't part as enemies; I don't like that," she said firmly.

Roland shook his head. "He's angry right now, but it'll probably have evaporated by the morning. After all, he's been happy to be here." He looked at Angolo, who was curled up on his blanket and immediately began to wag his tail at the attention. "And he loves that dog, something he will definitely miss. I'll go in later tomorrow so we can all have breakfast together."

Irene nodded gratefully and began to clear the table. He distributed the last of the wine between their glasses and helped her put the plates in the dishwasher. Afterwards, he handed her the glass and toasted with her.

"Sorry for a chaotic night, *we* can't become enemies, either. It's a waste of my good red wine." He winked at her to show that he didn't blame her for the choice.

"I think Angolo needs to get out for a little bit. Will you?"

He didn't feel like it, but that was part of having a dog, and it was so late that a run around the garden without a lead would have to do.

"Put on a jacket, Rolando!" she shouted after him.

It was cold on the steps in only his knitted jumper, but he needed to cool down. It had been a long time since he'd had an argument with a teenager—and in Italian at that.

Angolo mooched around in the snow ahead of him, occasionally disappearing into the many dark shadows further down in the overgrown garden. Irene had a flair for that kind of thing. Each shrub, tree, and flower was carefully selected according to the season. Some bloomed in the spring to be replaced by others that bloomed in early summer, and these again were replaced by others so there were flowers in the garden all year round. Somewhere beneath the thick white layer of snow lay a bed of fully bloomed white Christmas roses, a beautiful sign that there was still life. He took a deep, icy breath and called for Angolo. The dog was sniffing at something under a bush, certainly one of his own productions. His mobile rang and vibrated against his thigh in his trouser pocket, disturbing the idyllic botanical Christmas fairy tale. He answered it and was very surprised when he heard the voice. He hadn't expected to hear it again.

# 20

I t sounds like you're freezing. Are you out in the cold?" she asked.

She didn't have to introduce herself. The Nørrebro accent would always give her away. He sounded surprised. He had, of course, heard that the *Daily News* had closed.

"Taking the dog out; it's cold." His words gave off a suspicious undertone.

She had a hard time picturing his private and family life—a man taking his dog out. In the same way, it had been difficult to picture her editor, Thygesen, in a family setting. As a result, he'd completely disappeared from her mind's eye as well, because who was the man, Ivan Thygesen, really?

"What kind of dog do you have?" It amazed her that she didn't quite know what to say now that she had finally pulled herself together to call him.

"A German Shepherd."

"Of course."

Long pause.

"How are you, Anne? I heard you lost your job." Here his suspicious undertone turned annoyed.

"It's going well. I'm trying to find another job, but it's not that easy right now. Fortunately, my mother is visiting, so I have her to take care of me—"

"And your stepfather?"

She heard ice being crushed under the soles of boots, barking, and breathing, and she figured out that the dog was nearby and that Roland was on the move. Then the sound of a door being opened and the dog's claws against tiles followed by wooden floors.

"Fortunately, he's not visiting."

"Did you ring for something specific, or did you just want to know whether I was freezing?"

She was fond of his sarcasm and felt the despair again. How could the conversation suddenly be over?

"There is actually something I'd like you to investigate for me—if you have the time?"

"Hmm?"

"I was talking to some homeless people who told me their friends are disappearing without a trace. Have the police heard of anything?"

"If we did, you know I wouldn't be able to talk about it."

"Roland, I'm not a journalist anymore. This is me as a private citizen, raising a concern. Do you know anything?"

"What do you know?"

"Not much, only that a few people have disappeared, which the authorities know nothing about, apparently dead of natural causes."

"Did nobody issue missing person's reports, so we can look for them?"

"Someone tried to go to the police once. But who wants to listen to a vagrant who stinks of booze?"

It was quiet for a long time.

"So, what do you want to do—report it?"

"Make you aware of it at least. Something weird is happening among homeless people. The last one to disappear was named Rudolf. Do you know whether you've brought him in? If he's found dead, isn't that the normal procedure to bring in the deceased? Or maybe you don't care when it's 'only' a homeless man? As indifferent about those who died as the living."

"Don't start, Anne! And speaking of procedure, I think it should be followed by everyone. First, an APB needs to be issued for the missing person."

"So, you don't want to help me?"

"Will not—or cannot. What am I to help you with? I don't know anything. When a homeless person ends up at the Institute of Forensic Medicine, it's usually death by natural causes or suicide."

"But the others on the street don't think it's that."

"Of course not."

A woman's voice asked if it was work—his wife?

"Fine, Roland. If you won't help me, I'll find out for myself. But I'm sure you won't mind that!" She herself could be sarcastic and delighted a little in being able to be so without fear of losing a good police contact.

"You tend to be pretty good at that anyway, Anne."

He paused briefly; she sensed there was something he wasn't saying, a feeling that was amplified as he continued. "If you find out anything suspicious, will you promise to inform me?"

"There's something you're not telling me. Are you stuck in a case?"

"Not one that concerns the homeless. I suppose you've heard of the B&E?"

"The one that ended in murder. Yeah, I heard about it. Do you have no suspects at all?"

"Anne, you know I can't tell you that."

"I'm just a concerned citizen."

"And certainly not to a concerned citizen."

Anne sighed. "Well, so everything is as it was before."

He laughed. "Take care of yourself, Anne." The phone went dead, and she sat back again with an empty feeling.

"Shit!" She Googled further from where she'd left off when she'd gathered herself to call him. She hadn't realised how late it was when she ran out of keywords after trying almost everything. She got up and scouted out the darkness. The streetlights shone with a faint yellowish glow because of the snow that had settled on them like little white, woolly hats. The cars parked down by the kerb were completely covered, many of them certainly wouldn't start in the morning. She'd undoubtedly be woken by the many attempts to get to work on time: the hacking, rattling engines and car doors being furiously slammed. She smiled at the knowledge that she could just turn over and pull the duvet up over her head. Maybe you could get used to being unemployed. She sat back down as she tried to think of a new keyword; impulsively, she typed *homeless found* into the search box and pressed Enter. The link to the newspaper article was at the top. Although the concept of Netavis—online newspapers—had helped to out-compete the sale of printed newspapers, being able to find articles online like this was great. She clicked on the link and read the article, which was written by a journalist from *Aarhus Stiftstidende*. She envied her. She had tried to send them an unsolicited application but received only a friendly rejection. They didn't need anyone at the moment. They *certainly* didn't need anyone at the moment. As she read, blood rose to her face, making her cheeks glow. A homeless man had been found dead in front of a farm on Trige Skovvej. The article was short and not very sensational. There was no doubt it was suicide, the article said, and the man had not yet been identified. Was that what Roland was trying to hide from her? He had mentioned something about suicide. Was he himself suspicious? She wanted to call him back but knew it would be futile. She was on her own now. Not even Thygesen could get involved—in fact, this was a rather pleasant thought that made eagerness bubble up in her. But it was late now, she could do no more today, so she shut down the computer, went out to the bathroom to brush her teeth and pull on the warm, blue-striped flannel pyjamas, knowing she wasn't going to get a wink of sleep that night.

# 21

The morning briefing was not uplifting. Not much had been found in the abandoned car. The perps had, of course, worn gloves, perhaps not so much to avoid leaving evidence, but because you couldn't be outside without them. The most important find was traces of weapon oil on the back seat, indicating that the stolen weapons had been there. The owner of the car had no weapons; he was, as he put it, only a meagre postman. As if postal workers had no need to defend themselves against people's anger over huge postage increases from year to year despite the poorer service. But where were the car thieves now? Abroad? Safely picked up by a car next to the motorway?

The staffing at the police station was weakened as several employees were ill with the flu—the so-called swine flu—which had been at its peak before Christmas. None of the staff affected were part of the vulnerable group, so they were treated as if they had ordinary flu, even though catching swine flu, according to the press, meant certain death would follow. As a result, the Danish Emergency Management Agency had been set to work. What had happened in the meantime? Roland had been spared, for now; only a sniffle had begun to creep into his nose.

DS Niels Nyborg had remained after the meeting, drumming a ballpoint pen against his thigh as he reclined in the chair with one long leg resting on another as he read the article about Albert Hovgaard's gold medal revolver prowess.

"Bloody hell, we could use a good shooter here in the department," he said. "So, the weapons were definitely the reason for the burglary and murder. That's what they were after, and Albert resisted."

"Who knows what happened? But you have to be careful nowadays about putting your private life on public display."

"Tell that to my daughter. She posts everything on Facebook so her friends can see where she's going and what she's doing. Today, you're nothing if you don't have a Facebook profile so others can follow your moves. New lifestyle."

"Dangerous lifestyle. Remember the Doll Child Case."

"The Doll Child Case, in particular, taught me to keep a close eye on what she writes about and with whom, but I can't watch her all the time. Apparently, you can make some things 'private' so only friends can see them, but can you trust it?"

"How old is Lotte now?"

"Seventeen. She's a young woman." Niels immersed himself in the newspaper again, this time it was the sports pages.

"They reach that stage at age ten nowadays." Roland clearly remembered having a teenager in the house: Rikke's first trip to the city with her friends, how she dressed that night, and how much they argued about it. Her first time getting drunk and having a hangover, the first boyfriend, the unrest, and the worry, but it had turned out well—she had found a good husband, and Roland could boast of being Marianna's grandfather. But when Marianna came of age, Rikke would also get a chance to feel the worries; he hoped she would remember and understand why he had acted as he did back then. Back in those days, he often felt she hated him.

But his concern wasn't so much for his own daughter and granddaughter right now. Salvatore had been a tad distant at their airport farewell. He'd been wearing dark sunglasses, so Roland couldn't see his eyes. The sun had been dazzling in the chalk-white snow, and he imagined that was why his own eyes were watery. Breakfast had been eaten in a tense atmosphere. Irene was undoubtedly right; it was time he returned to his own life—whatever that would turn out to be. Early that morning, Roland had called Aunt Giovanna from his study to tell her that Salvatore would be returning to Naples later in the day. She hadn't sounded entirely satisfied with Roland's summary of the conversation he'd had with her son. He hadn't even told her the entire truth; he hadn't admitted to how long the conversation had been postponed, and he hadn't said that it had been forced by an argument as late as last night. But it was out of his hands now. What more could he do? It was all up to her now—and Salvatore.

"Well, not even the sports results have anything positive to say," muttered Nyborg, throwing the paper on the table. "How do we move on? What about the fake cigarette? Is it a clue or just a coincidence, do you think?"

"We'll have to wait and see; maybe a shipment arrived that hasn't been detected." He sent a pitying thought to the poor, who hadn't yet weaned themselves off cigarettes and who would pay the price for fake cigarettes.

"I'll review all the testimony again. Maybe we overlooked something." Nyborg's long legs untangled themselves from each other, reminiscent of a giraffe rising from a supine position.

"Good idea, but, unfortunately, I think it'll be in vain, Niels."

"Inconceivable. We have DNA, fingerprints, both getaway cars, but no leads."

Roland looked up at him and couldn't help but agree that it looked hopeless.

"What about the murder weapon?"

He shook his head. "Nothing there, either."

"Do you think we need the journalist?" Nyborg smiled mischievously.

"I talked to her last night, actually. Late last night."

"Did you contact her?"

"No, no! She called me. I was out with Angolo."

Niels Nyborg crossed his arms over his chest. "What the hell did she want?"

"No idea, it was something about some missing homeless people." Roland drove the chair into position in front of the computer screen and pulled up his sleeves a little.

"The homeless! As if we have nothing else to do"—Niels snorted lightly—"but of course she doesn't."

"I don't know how seriously I should take it. The discovery yesterday could be suspicious, but—"

"The homeless man? It was suicide, wasn't it?"

"The forensic pathologist thinks so. It's not being treated as murder. But I expect to hear from him once they've identified the deceased; it would be nice to know who he was."

"You don't think you know him, do you?"

Roland looked up from the screen. "You never know. Who are the homeless in reality, and who thinks about them? There can be many different reasons for their tragic lives. No one ends up homeless of their own free will."

"Either way, it can't be a healthy life. Not at this time of year. It's bloody freezing out there. It'll be a miracle if they survive the winter. Last night, it went down to minus fifteen degrees in some places, and with the wind . . . The hostels must be full. A breeding ground for the swine flu. Have you heard any more from Jensen?"

"He called this morning to say the doctor has ordered him indoors until his fever and symptoms are gone."

"Thank God! I don't want to be infected. I'm actually surprised that it can hit a man as big and strong as Mikkel."

"We could all get it, Niels."

"Seems so. Isabella is affected, too. I wonder if they've been a little too close to each other . . ."

"What do you mean?"

"Have you not seen that Mikkel fancies her, and she him? It shines out of their eyes. In love, that's what they are. I hope Olsen doesn't spot it."

Roland felt the blow to his chest again. The reminder that not so long ago, he also had been quite fascinated by the young, fair-haired detective and had thought she felt something for him, too. To think he could sink so deep, be so naïve. It was middle-aged panic. Panic over what exactly? He had Irene; he had all the love he needed.

"Ha, in love. Do you really think so?" Roland concentrated on the keyboard.

"Absolutely, but she's not the worst to look at, either. She's *bella*. Isn't that *beautiful* in Italian?"

Roland nodded and let out a deep sigh as Niels went out and closed the door behind him. There was a lot of computer work to be done, and he hated it. He would much rather be out in the field catching criminals, even if was biting cold. He didn't know how much time had been spent on pressing keys, deleting, printing, squeezing his eyes together to see the letters on the screen, when the phone call that gave him new courage came in. An attempted armed robbery at Jyske Bank in Kolding. The Southeast Jutland Police had contacted the superintendent after three Lithuanians had been arrested and the weapons were confirmed as those being searched for in the Trige murder case. Yes! Finally, the assailants had made the wrong move he'd been waiting for. They had them now—apart from the driver, who had escaped.

# 22

Y ou're wrong, Linda. Anyone can become a murderer—you don't have to be evil—it's in all of us. A gene. In ancient times, instinct was vital to us. If we couldn't kill, we couldn't survive," argued Andreas.

They were at it again. Anita was reclining on the sofa with her legs pulled up under her, trying to concentrate on reading. Maybe it was just an excuse for not participating in the usual Friday debate, which often ended in shouting matches once the beers started affecting their brains. She herself had only drunk half of her Tuborg Christmas brew; they hadn't managed to drink them all over Christmas. The ad with the Tuborg car and reindeer on the blue background with large white snowflakes, just as she remembered from childhood, had rolled across the TV screen for most of November and December, brainwashing Andreas's primeval brain into buying several crates. They'd be drinking the Christmas brew until well into summer. She didn't like it—too bitter and strong for her taste—but she didn't want to be deemed as too much by her housemates, either.

"You're right, Andreas, that's how it is with animals. They kill to survive, too. If they're pushed into a corner, the killer instinct is immediately triggered." Bjørn drank from his glass and got foam on his upper lip. He was the only one who used a glass.

"You're all so fucking clever to listen to," said Brian, who, fortunately, had not brought hash that night. There'd been enough police visits lately.

He sat with his back to them, staring at the TV, *The X Factor* flickering across the screen. The others had no interest in watching the part where hopeful, both talented and absolutely untalented, singers were brutally deprived of their dreams. Brian found that part most entertaining, and there were several howls of laughter from his chair. Bitten had remained in their room, due to a major quarrel with Brian, or at least that's what it had sounded like.

"It's not clever, Brian. It's facts. You could commit murder, too, if you were driven far enough," Andreas replied.

Anita glanced up from the book, first at Andreas, then at Brian, who apathetically turned the swivel-foot leather chair so that he was facing Andreas. "And you mean, I would have to be driven to absolute great lengths to do that?" The twinkle in his eye made her shudder, then he laughed, showing the chalk-white teeth and that side of himself that she'd fallen for when he moved in—both whimsical and dangerous at once. Brian was certainly not boring. But was he dangerous?

Andreas laughed, too. "You never know with you 'Copenhageners'— you're a different breed."

"That we are," Brian replied, clinking beers with Andreas, Linda, and Bjørn, who had to get up slightly to reach Brian's bottle with his glass. It seemed like a huge effort, and he sank in the cushions heavily afterwards.

"What must have driven him—or them—to murder Albert?" asked Linda. Anita had given up trying to read. She didn't dare to add her two-pence, for Bitten announced her arrival by slamming the door of the room hard behind her, probably to show Brian that she still wasn't over their disagreement, whatever it had been. She came to the sofa and stood in front of Anita with her hands by her sides.

"Move, lard-arse, you're taking up room for three."

Anita moved into the corner to make room for Bitten's skinny backside, even though there was already enough room.

Brian scowled at Bitten as she sat down; the looks they sent each other certainly weren't loving.

"You've all gone so quiet. What were you talking about—*me?*"

"Not everything is about you, babe," Brian replied without putting any warmth into the term of endearment.

"So what?"

"The Hovgaard murder, of course."

"God, nothing else! I just heard on the local radio that they caught those who did it."

They all looked curiously at Bitten. She lit a cigarette and took so long that it seemed deliberately planned to increase the excitement. A ring of black lipstick remained on the filter after she took a deep drag. She let the smoke seep out slowly between her lips and directed it towards the ceiling by pushing her lower lip slightly forward.

Linda looked at her angrily but said nothing. It was impossible to keep the smoking ban with Bitten in the house.

"They tried to rob a bank in Kolding and were caught. They used the stolen weapons."

"Amateurs!" shouted Brian, slapping his forehead.

"So, was it Eastern Europeans?" asked Anita.

"Lithuanian. The one in the getaway car got away."

"Thank God they have them now! Maybe we can start sleeping soundly at night again." Linda sighed, throwing her legs up onto Andreas's lap. He patted one of her feet in its thick Icelandic sock and smiled at her.

"What have you been afraid of? You have me!"

Brian snorted scornfully.

"It could be him—the one who got away—who's the killer; no one can know for sure yet," Bitten kindly pointed out as she peeled off some black nail polish that was chipped on her thumb.

"Well, let's get some more beers to celebrate the event." Andreas pushed Linda's legs down from his lap, got up, and disappeared into the kitchen. Clinking bottles could be heard out there, and a little later, he came in with several in his arms and set them in the middle of the table next to the empty ones.

The rest of the evening and most of the night was spent sitting around the coffee table. They talked about everything, and as always, some disagreed and raised their voices. Bjørn fell asleep a little after midnight and snored—like a bear. He didn't even wake up when the music was turned up because Bitten suddenly wanted to dance. It was the couple's reconciliation. After a close slow set and French kiss, they disappeared into their room. Bjørn was helped up to his bed by Linda and Andreas, and Anita tidied up a little before she headed to bed, too. Friday night, almost exactly like it used to be.

* * *

She had a headache and couldn't fall asleep. Even brushing her teeth hadn't got rid of the taste of the strong beer; it seemed to be stuck deep down in her throat. She got up again and took a couple of paracetamol, lay back in the warm bed, and stared up at the whitewashed ceiling, where the moonlight was casting shadows. The bare branches outside the window looked like crooked fingers. She didn't know what time it was when she heard something. It was a very small sound; she probably wouldn't have heard it if she had been asleep. She got up and went to the window, where she spotted him down on the road. The Michelin Man in his big moon boots. She stared at the figure until it disappeared behind the trees. What was he doing out there at that time of night?

# 23

K amilla clenched the steering wheel through her soft black lambskin gloves and tried to focus all her attention on the slippery road. Small roads, in particular, were ice rinks. Luckily, there wasn't much traffic on a Saturday morning. She should have said no to this. Stood up to Pierre even though he was her boss. Said it like it was—that he wouldn't have sent her out to do this if he knew the truth. Her weak protest had feebly been that she wasn't a model photographer and that she thought he should take the job since he had handed out his business card. But Pierre had replied that Mogens Arnskov had explicitly requested her. And there was no arguing with Pierre when he commanded.

She drove through Nimtofte, enjoying the sight of the white fields stretching out around her until she turned off at Ramten and onto Hoved-vejen. Shortly afterwards, she turned left and continued towards Glesborg, then there were only about eight kilometres left according to her GPS. Her heart began to pound violently, and she had to take a deep breath to calm it down. He had looked at her so attentively that night. She had seen pictures of her mother at her age, and they absolutely resembled each other. Quite a lot, she had to reluctantly admit to herself. She glanced in the rear-view mirror and smiled carefully to see what it looked like. The fine wrinkles around her eyes became clearer. Smile lines, some called them. As if she had smiled a lot in her thirty-seven years of life. She'd applied just a touch of make-up. Not what she usually did when she was going to a wedding—an event that, unfortunately, didn't happen so often. She had been to more funerals than weddings. Her eyes were highlighted with black mascara that made her lashes seem longer, eyeliner, and a light eye shadow that complemented the green in her irises. No lipstick, just a dab of lip gloss that made her lips shine a little. A father might not like to look at too much make-up on his daughter, she had thought in front of the mirror. His wife, Alice, had been completely au naturel, despite them apparently having been at an event that night. And if she looked like her mother when she was young, would she also look like her when she was old? She shooed the thought away and consoled herself with the fact that her mother's harsh face and many deep wrinkles had come from all the hatred she had carried until her death from a brain haemorrhage last autumn. That was her preferred cause of death. She had repeated it so many times to herself that she now believed it. That's what had happened. She couldn't have done anything to prevent it. Hatred made people ugly, and she didn't hate anyone. Or did she? Danny. What about Danny? Was it hatred she felt when she thought of him? Was it hatred that made her have trouble breathing? Maybe it was; she no longer knew what she felt for him. Had they set a date, he and Majken? She bit her lip hard. She knew only too well what she felt now—jealousy. It bothered her that the thought of Danny and Majken's engagement evoked that feeling. People say it's a fine line between love and hate, but should it be taken literally?

She had her full focus on the road again. A snowplough had appeared in front of her, so she had to step on the brake and inch along behind it, but she had plenty of time—there was no need to panic. Actually, it was convenient, because the snow was still drifting, and new snowdrifts were quickly forming out here on the open land. The wind was due to blow off in the afternoon; she hoped the roads wouldn't close and that she could drive back as soon as the photos were taken.

"Bønnerupvej," she mumbled, keeping an eye on the house numbers. When she found it, and the monotonous voice in the GPS indicated that she had arrived, she turned it off and parked behind a large pile of snow, which the snowplough had dropped off at the bend. She stepped out. Her boot heels crunched in the ice as she walked down the pavement towards the house. It had a plastered yellow façade, window frames painted white, and a red-tiled roof. Classic "Bønnerup style." The garden was surrounded by a high hedge that seemed to be an evergreen judging by the gaps without snow cover. She spotted the boy over the hedge. He was rolling a snowball, but it wasn't going so well as it was more ice than proper snow. When he looked up and pushed his knitted hat further up his forehead with his large mitten, she stood as if frozen to the ice on the path. He looked like Rasmus. The same freckles, the same blue-green eyes that looked like hers. It had to be Mathias. Her half-brother was standing in front of her in the snow—looking like Rasmus. Tears pressed behind her eyes, and a lump formed in her throat. She almost called to him. *Rasmus!* Suddenly he looked at her. His gaze was sceptical—she had been staring—and then the tears ran. She wiped them away quickly and walked up the driveway.

"Are you the photographer?" he asked, smiling. Same smile as Rasmus.

"Yes, how could you guess that?"

"The bag." He pointed.

Same logic as Rasmus. "Yes, of course" She laughed. He laughed, too. Same laugh as Rasmus. She felt dizzy.

"Mum and Dad are getting ready for the party. Mum always takes ages, and then Dad gets impatient."

An open and talkative boy who had no reservations about strangers. Just like . . . She nodded her thanks to him, walked gently up the slippery stone steps, and rang the doorbell. It wasn't long before the door opened. Mogens Arnskov was in a tuxedo, but she noticed his eyes most.

"Kamilla Holm. Welcome." He shook her hand while at the same time gallantly helping her over a little snowdrift that had built up in front of the door. He smelled of an expensive men's aftershave. Here was the man her mother had fallen for when she was young. Very young. Way too young. Here was the man who had been complicit in her uncle's death. Premature death. Here was the man who was her father. So close that she could hear his heart beating. Or was it her own?

"Come into the heat. It's bitterly cold today. I hope the bride and groom can endure it." He quickly adjusted his butterfly bow-tie as he walked past a mirror in the hallway.

"It's due to ease off this afternoon, so . . ." she replied, putting her camera bag on the floor. She was standing in one corner of a large living room with a wood-burning stove that provided a different kind of heat than she was used to. All the chairs were black leather, including those around a large oak dining table that stood in a cold white light from the window at the end of the living room. Lime-coloured pillows and a matching blanket accented a black fabric sofa. On the glass coffee table lay some weekly magazines and a *Computerworld*. Naturally, there was a large flat-screen TV. Soon she'd be the only one left in all of Denmark with a small twenty-inch telly.

"Let me take your coat."

She stood for a moment, as if she had no intention of taking it off. Shouldn't they be leaving? Then she took it off and handed it to him. He took it out into the hallway and returned quickly.

"You met Mathias?" he said.

She nodded.

"Come and sit down for a moment. Alice always takes ages to get ready. It's her friend who's getting married today." He straightened his cuff-links and sat down on the couch.

Kamilla wondered why she could be taking so long given that she didn't wear make-up.

"Where do they want the pictures taken?" she asked, unable to think of anything else. Now that she was alone with him, she wished more and more that she had said no when Pierre had ordered her out on the job.

Meeting her father this way was a completely different experience to what she'd imagined. She had spent the whole long sleepless night preparing for it. Word for word, she had decided what she was going to say. Tell him she was his daughter without blaming him for never contacting her. How it wasn't until her mother's funeral last autumn that an unknown aunt had confided in her about what had happened in her sister's youth, and how the late Henning Holm wasn't her biological father. That she had spent time finding him, that it hadn't been too difficult at all, and that he would also have been able to find her. If he had known she existed. But now, fate had—as always—intervened and chosen for her. She was here now with no idea what to say. She sat down in the chair on the other side of the glass table that was so polished that she didn't dare touch it for fear of leaving fingerprints. How could it be so clean with a child in the house?

"They're getting married in Rimsø Church. A very beautiful and old Romanesque stone church from around 1150 and with Denmark's oldest rectory. The bride and groom know exactly where they want to be photographed nearby." Mogens squinted at his watch. "Would you like something to drink?"

Kamilla shook her head. "No, thank you."

He drummed his fingers nervously on his thighs. He probably didn't dare touch the table, either.

"I'm glad you came. It's hard to find photographers out here."

"Who are you talking to, Mogens? Me?" said a voice behind a closed door out in the hallway. The bathroom, guessed Kamilla.

"No, darling. It's just the photographer."

She clenched her fists so that her nails drilled into her palm. Could you be called anything more impersonal by your father than *just the photographer?*

"Okay, I'm ready now." Somewhere behind her, the door opened. She noticed the strong perfume before she realised that Alice was standing next to her, holding out her hand. Uncomfortable, she got up, looked at the woman, and found herself wondering. Alice Arnskov didn't look anything like the woman she'd met in Den Blå Kutter earlier that week. Her hair was in an up-do and the make-up was so perfect that you wouldn't think she'd done it herself. That's why it had taken so long, Kamilla thought and smiled. Alice was in a long, blue silk dress with a light shawl over her bare shoulders. Mogens got up from the sofa and went out into the hall. Soon it would all start, and she probably wouldn't see him again when they disappeared to attend the wedding party afterwards. She wouldn't get to tell him who she was.

"It was really sweet of you to come and help with the photos," Alice said, turning to her husband. "But we'd better get going, well?"

Mogens was already in his coat and had two others over his arm. He handed Kamilla's to her first, and then he helped his wife into a fur coat. Kamilla had no idea whether it was genuine.

"You can follow us," Mogens said. "It's not far, about ten kilometres."

As they walked past the garden, Mathias waved at them. He had managed to build a half-decent snowman from the frosty snow. His cheeks and nose were as red as tomatoes. "Have fun!" he yelled.

"Is he not coming?" Kamilla asked in astonishment. Alice walked effortlessly in the high-heeled shoes on the ice-covered paving slabs. She reached for Mogens's arm and leaned on it.

"No other children are going, and Mathias would rather stay here and enjoy the snow. A babysitter is coming soon. But he's fine on his own for the time being. He was last Saturday when we went to the funeral."

Kamilla nodded and sent Mathias an uplifting smile over the hedge. But mostly, she wanted to go in and take him in her arms, hug him hard, and say that he should take good care of himself and not go out on the road. She got into the Suzuki and pulled the camera bag around her onto the passenger seat. Mogens reversed a Bordeaux-coloured Fiat Punto out of the garage; he was arguing with Alice. Neither of them saw their son waving. Kamilla waved back to him and cast another glance back at the garden as she drove out from the kerb. He looked so small and alone behind the hedge. Reluctantly, she followed the car in front. It was rare for anyone to think that they were possibly seeing someone for the last time . . .

# 24

He began his Saturday by jumping into the icy water at the Ballehage Sea Baths. Only serious winter bathers did the cut-a-hole-in-the-ice thing with the water hovering at freezing. He had joined the Winter Bathing Club, founded in 1929, one of the country's oldest clubs, and he had been given the key to the clubhouse, a green shed that didn't look like much down by the strand—but was certainly better than the caves the first winter bathers made in the buff—so they could change clothes and seek shelter, just as the old written narratives spoke of. In the clubhouse, there was a wood-burning stove and kitchenette, but he didn't use the facilities much. Neither did he attend the events held for members, who now numbered upwards of one hundred. What he enjoyed most about these morning excursions was that he had the sea all to himself, since he was usually the first on-site. It made him feel like a real Viking. Fresher than ever, he drove to the station.

The three Lithuanians had been brought to Aarhus and interrogated. They pleaded guilty to burglary and robbery, but they vehemently denied having murdered Albert Hovgaard. The interpreter had had difficulty keeping up the simultaneous translation. Roland didn't believe them. It was rare for killers to confess at the first interrogation. They would have to wait for the DNA analyses to get them now. Evidence no one could talk their way out of and rarely tried.

When he returned to his office, he discovered a fax lying on his desk. He picked it up and looked at the information, not quite understanding at first what it was about. There was a picture of a man, or an aristocrat more like. Suit and tie. He looked like a businessman. Verner Thybo Hansen. Born in 1955 in Aarhus and trained as a mechanical engineer. Invented an injection-moulding tool for the production of thin plastic items, and in 2008, he opened Thybo Værktøjsfabrik in Viby, which ended up with fifteen employees. Two years later, he drove too fast over a slope in a newly acquired Mercedes. He was only slightly injured, but his wife, two sons, aged seven and eight, and a five-month-old daughter died. The factory closed shortly afterwards, and Verner Thybo Hansen went underground. No one had seen him since.

Slowly, it dawned on Roland that the forensic pathologist had identified the homeless man who had hanged himself. No wonder with such a terrible fate. He sat down on his office chair. Had it been Leander, he would have called Roland instead of just sending a bloody fax. He threw it on the desk. Anne Larsen had called the homeless man Rudolf, the one who was supposed to have disappeared. So, fortunately, it wasn't him they had found, and there was probably no reason to spend resources on solving such an obvious suicide. Not to mention that he had great confidence that Anne herself would solve the case, and as long as she was occupied with that case, she'd probably refrain from interfering in his.

DS Niels Nyborg gently pushed open the door.

"There doesn't seem to be any reason to wait for the DNA results. The fingerprints are identical to those found in the house, and one Lithuanian left a cigarette butt in the ashtray.

Same type as the one found where the car was parked." Niels smiled contentedly.

"So, he was in possession of illegal cigarettes—that may be a coincidence. It doesn't immediately make him a murderer."

"Of course not, but it is worth considering."

"We do also know they *were* at the scene. They've confessed to burglary. There's no doubt we can get them for that. The Institute of Forensic Medicine also revealed that the fingerprints are identical to some from other burglaries in East Jutland—perhaps we have a regular organised gang on our hands."

"And cigarette smugglers."

"Well, we don't know that yet. What about the getaway car and the driver?"

"Nothing new. We won't get any further if he was the one who murdered Albert Hovgaard." Niels leaned against the doorframe. "By the way, I talked to Isabella. She'll be back on Monday, she said."

"Already. What about Mikkel?"

"He still has a fever, so he's staying in bed a little longer."

"Okay." The case would be solved soon anyway, so it was better for the sick to stay at home until they were free of infection.

"Are you vaccinated, Roland?"

"No, I'm bloody well not. Are you?" He looked up curiously at the tall man in front of him.

"Yes, we both are. The girls, too. We don't want to risk anything. My wife is so stressed about it. The news keeps droning on about that flu every night."

Roland nodded. "Exactly—about something non-existent. It evaporated, just like during COP15, when the press got something else to talk about." But it was still nice to know that there would always be one vaccinated person to hold down the fort if they all went down with the flu. Though he'd heard of outbreaks despite the vaccination; so, what use would it have been to expose himself to the danger of the vaccine? Given that the pharmaceutical industry disclaimed any responsibility for side effects, he wouldn't be taking them up on that offer. And, in his opinion, it was better to get the disease and develop his body's own immune system against it, so he would be resistant the next time swine flu came to Denmark. He accepted this probably wouldn't be the last time. Mind you, he wasn't in the risk group, either, but neither were Niels and his wife and children.

"Let's hope the pandemic is over soon. Nature tries to exterminate us every once in a while; it's just a matter of hanging on." It was supposed to sound reassuring, but it didn't. "Right. Well, Niels, all we can do is wait for those analyses—we probably won't get any further today. It's Saturday, so . . ." He slammed his fingertips against the edge of the table and got up. "Thanks for coming. I'll walk down with you."


The steps from Ridderstræde up towards Fredensgade were closed because of the snow. He scraped ice from the car windows and was looking forward to getting home to the heat and Irene. She was much happier and more relaxed since Salvatore had gone back to Naples. Roland missed him, though. Missed speaking Italian. His mother tongue, which was usually only refreshed by the annual summer trips home to the family. Zia Giovanna had reported that her son was safely home and believed he had come up with some better ideas. Roland just knew better with boys that age. The fear gnawed still.

# 25

In Rimsø cemetery, a large burial mound and a particular rune stone from the Viking Age had been preserved. While Kamilla waited for the bride and groom, who were being congratulated after a beautiful wedding ceremony, which she'd been allowed to take a few photos of, she stood and admired it.

"Ancient memories. About a hundred Danish churches have non-Christian burial mounds by the church, but not many have a rune stone like this." Suddenly, a cemetery worker was standing next to her in green thermal clothing and a lined cap with ear warmers. He leaned on the snow shovel, clinging to the handle.

"Do they know what it says?" she asked, studying the runic characters.

"It's the Futhark alphabet and consists of sixteen characters. It dates the stone to the middle of the Viking Age, around the year 900. Some words are written backwards, and it's the only Danish rune stone where it is found—*Lønskrift*, it's called—cryptic runes. Only some of the text has been translated: THORIR, ENRÅDE'S BROTHER, RAISED THIS STONE IN MEMORY OF HIS MOTHER AND . . . well, there's apparently no more. So, it's assumed that it's his mother who is buried in the burial mound."

"Have archaeologists not excavated it?"

"No, so we still don't know what's hidden in it."

Kamilla didn't know much about the Viking Age. Rasmus had been a Viking once at a Fastelavn party, dressed in a helmet with horns and a dramatic sword. They had learned about Vikings in school, and he'd regaled her excitedly about how very harsh they were, murdering and plundering. She looked at the man and smiled. "It sounds like you know a lot about that time."

"Many people ask me about it when I'm pottering around here, tending to the graves, so I've done my homework. And my brother has now become an Asatruar. He believes in the Nordic gods. It gives you pause for thought." The man cast an apologetic glance at the church and shook his head incomprehensibly. "It should be banned!"

She didn't have time to comment. The bride and groom were ready and calling for her. The cemetery worker nodded a short goodbye and continued his work, shovelling snow. She went over to them by the church. Their plan was for the pictures to be taken in front of the beautiful old half-timbered village rectory, and when Kamilla saw it, she agreed completely with their choice. Ida was a beautiful bride. The white dress blended with the snow, and a bolero that resembled fur kept her warm. She had reddish hair that matched the colours of the bridal bouquet, and again Kamilla thought of her old friend Majken. How beautiful she would be when she soon married Danny.

It took a long time for all the pictures to be taken. Ida was starting to turn blue from the cold. Kamilla took one last picture of the bridal bouquet that she laid in the snow. The warm red colours looked like fire in the glittering ice crystals. Afterwards, she said goodbye to the happy couple and wished them a good reception. The guests had gone on to the inn where the event was to be celebrated. Her chance to talk to her father disappeared. It would be a detour, but there was something directing her the same way back. One reason was that she didn't know whether she'd ever get the chance to see Mathias again.

He was still out in the garden and had got a little further with his snowman. A stubborn little boy who didn't just give up; even on that point, there was a resemblance to her son. He looked up and spotted the car. She rolled down the side window. "All the photos are taken. I just wanted to say a proper goodbye to you. Are you still on your own?"

"Tanja isn't coming now at all. She called. She's snowed in. They live way out in the country," he added.

Kamilla got out of the car and walked into the garden. "Why did she not call your mum and dad?"

"She tried to, but they didn't answer. I promised to call once they were out of the church."

"And have you?"

"No. They so rarely get out—the last time was for a funeral—so I didn't want to ruin their party. I'm okay on my own." He started gathering snow again. It was getting dark.

"Are you not freezing? You've been out here most of the day. Your nose will fall off."

He shrugged. "Are you freezing?"

She nodded.

"Do you like hot chocolate?" Shyly, he pushed the hat further up on his forehead and looked down at his boots, which were wet with snow.

Kamilla took a deep breath, the cold hurting as much as the memory in her chest. Hot chocolate had been Rasmus's favourite, too. Made with Matilde chocolate milk.

"I love hot chocolate!"

Mathias looked up at her and smiled broadly. "So, will you stay?"

"Okay, but only if you give me a cup of hot chocolate!" She winked at him.

He took her by the hand and dragged her with him. She squeezed his cold hand inside the wet mitt as if she never wanted to let it go again.

They were playing a computer game on Mathias's laptop with two steaming mugs of hot Matilde chocolate milk in front of them when the door opened in the hall. Shortly afterwards, Mogens Arnskov was in the living room.

"Dad!" shouted Mathias, surprised. "Is the party over already?"

"No, your mother forgot the speech—of course. Where's Tanja?" He looked almost reproachfully at Kamilla, as if he thought she had chased the babysitter away.

"Tanja is snowed in. But Kamilla is here, so . . ." Mathias looked down at the table. He should have called his parents and knew it well. She should have done it, too, but Mathias had made her forget the time and where she was.

"I'll stay until you get home," she said.

Mogens sent her an ambiguous smile. "I must say, you are a photographer with many talents. But is it not too much? I'm sure you have your own family waiting for you." She shook her head and hurried to take a sip from the mug. Mathias ran to his father as he walked into a room that could have been Alice's home office. Kamilla glimpsed a sewing machine and a computer screen in there before they came out again and Mogens closed the door. He had a roll of pages in his hand.

"I can't believe Mum forgot it! She spent months writing it." Mathias laughed.

"Well, you know how forgetful your mother can be." He looked at his watch and put the speech on the table. "It's nearly your bedtime, Mathias. Go out and brush your teeth and put on your PJs." He tugged at the boy's blond hair. It wasn't red like Rasmus's, but Rasmus had that from Jan.

"Argh, Dad. Can I not stay up a little longer today?" he begged.

"You know the answer, my friend."

Pouting, Mathias shrugged in defeat, then slumped into the bathroom and closed the door. Mogens sat down next to her.

"I'm happy to stay. I mean it," she said again.

"It's very sweet of you, but I don't think I can . . ."

Suddenly, she understood what he meant. She would never have left Rasmus with a random stranger who had just turned up that day to take pictures of a wedding. But she wasn't a stranger, she was . . .

"I understand if you're insecure about leaving me with him. But I'll take good care of him as if—"

"As if he were your own son?"

She looked him in the eyes and nodded.

"Do you have children, Kamilla?"

She turned her gaze away. "No, unfortunately not . . ."

"You're not married?" He looked at her right hand.

"Not anymore."

"Divorced, so."

Now was the opportunity to tell him who she was. She took a deep breath and was about to say something, when the door to the bathroom opened and Mathias came out in his pyjamas. He smelled of toothpaste.

"Haven't you gone yet, Dad?"

Mogens Arnskov got up.

"No, I was just talking to Kamilla. She's going to stay with you until we get home. It won't be long." He gave his son's shoulder a squeeze and looked at her. "You can stay here if you want." Then he was out the door.

Mathias sat down on the sofa. "Can I please stay up a little longer? It's Sunday tomorrow." His green eyes looked pleadingly at her. Rasmus's pleading eyes. She nodded.

"Okay, but only for an hour. We better do as Dad says."

Mathias's dad. Her dad. It was all so unreal.

# 26

Anne was just about to drift into sleep when the doorbell and a persistent knock on the door mingled with what she thought was the start of an erotic dream. She turned on the light and blinked at the clock. It was only two o'clock. Who the fuck was waking her up in the middle of the night? That insane woman downstairs? Groggy, she got up and put on her dressing gown. Someone knocked very hard on the door again. If it *wasn't* Mrs. Jansen, she would undoubtedly appear soon.

Startled, she looked at Adomas, who quickly stepped inside as if there was someone after him on the stairs. She hurriedly closed the door after him.

"What do you want at this hour?" She tried to catch his eye. He looked terrified. "Is it my mother?"

"No, no! But can I not spend the night here? I beg you! It's life or death!"

"Here? Life or death! No, now you have to fucking stop!"

"You have to help me, Anne! I have nowhere else to go, and it . . . it's a fucking mess!

"What happened?"

"I tried to get my friends to go to the police, like you said, but now they're after me." He looked at her with desperation in his eyes.

"After you? How?"

"They think I'm going to report them, so they want to silence me."

"Silence you! Are they going to kill you?!"

"That's what I'm afraid of." He sat down on the couch and hid his face in his hands. Dark hair protruded between his fingers. He had a gold ring with a black onyx stone on one finger. She sat down next to him. "They're your friends. It can't be true that they want to kill you." She smiled reassuringly, though he didn't look at her, and she laid her hand on his arm. Felt the muscles and another sensation that started throbbing. For the last few years, she hadn't had the time or desire to think about men and relationships and certainly not about sex. She blamed her stepfather Torsten for that, too. But now she was feeling something that she hadn't felt for a long time. Something forbidden. He was her cousin. Could you desire your cousin? He moved his hands from his face and looked at her. His eyes were grey like hers with small dark flecks. His skin was pale with freckles. She leaned in closer to him. He didn't move, and the inevitable meeting of lips on lips, first gentle kisses, then more demanding, deeper and more demanding. She tugged at his T-shirt; he pulled it off to reveal a well-toned chest with dark hair. She kissed his stomach and fumbled with his belt buckle. He pulled her dressing gown and nightdress off her. The only sound was their rapid breathing, which was almost in unison. Outside, the city slept shrouded in soothing cotton wool. She dragged him with her into the bedroom, gasping for pleasure at the feeling of his hands touching her naked body as she clung to him. Excited and hot. He was *not* her cousin. He was a wild stranger, who had suddenly appeared in the night. A fantasy lover. She had imagined this all her life, as recently as just before she was about to fall asleep. She closed her eyes and willingly let her desire take over.

She was awakened by the sound of ice scrapers furiously grinding against the frozen car windows down on the street. Adomas's arm lay heavy and sweaty across her stomach. Her thighs were sticky with his semen. What had they done? Was it incest? Now that desire no longer had power, guilt took over. She knew it better than desire. She wriggled out from under his arm and gently rolled out of bed until her legs hit the floor. He didn't wake, only moved and grunted a little as his arm slid down on the bed. Her legs were like jelly. She staggered out into the bathroom and locked the door. How could it have happened so fast? Was it her or him who had started it? Had it just been a convenient way for him to stay the night? Maybe that was how he was used to getting his way? But then she thought of his kiss, his mouth, and his hands all over her body. He wasn't the worst lover she had had. She was twenty-six years old. Most people her age were married with children. She was hopelessly behind. But he was her cousin, for fuck's sake. But wasn't that allowed in Denmark? It was distant family, so it didn't matter. He had whispered to her that she was beautiful, that she was lovely. Words she didn't hear very often. Was she really beautiful? Now that she looked in the mirror, she could well see the Eastern European features. They were from her father. Adomas's uncle. *Was* his position in the family so distant that it really didn't matter? She took a shower, washed the guilt away, and said to herself that everything was okay. It felt okay. More than okay.

When she came out of the bathroom, Adomas was up. He was fastening the belt on his jeans, and he put on his T-shirt afterwards. She just managed to see the dark hairs on his chest that she had slept on and smelled the night before. He smiled and pulled her in to him. "Thank you for a wonderful night," he whispered into her throat, and to her annoyance, she felt the urge throbbing again.

"What are you going to do today?" she asked casually, looking for her clothes on the floor.

"Don't know. I'd better find somewhere to hide."

She sat down on the bed and put on tights while she watched him. "It can't be true that they want to kill you, Adomas. You only advised them to do what's best for them—to report themselves. Who are you really afraid of?"

"Them! You have no idea what they're like."

"Okay, okay. I was just thinking that you said they weren't criminals." She got up and pulled a jumper over her head. "You can stay here if you want. Do you have any money?"

He nodded.

"Then feel free to buy something for the fridge while I'm gone."

"Gone? What are you going to do?"

She noticed his suspicious look, smiled, and patted him on the cheek, which had small prickly stubble that she found sexy and masculine; the same stubble that she'd felt tenderly on her own cheeks, chin, and neck the night before. "I'm not going to reveal to your 'friends' where you are." She went out into the kitchen to find some bread and make coffee. He came

out and took her and hugged her hard into him while she counted spoonfuls into the coffee filter. She spilled some on the table.

"Thanks. Promise me. I'll buy some food. But what are your plans for
the day? To be with your mum?"

"In a way, yeah. I've had a couple of job interviews, too." Adomas found
mugs and sliced some bread. She could easily get used to this.

Aarhus city centre was a chaos of cars and rushing cyclists and pedestrians crossing the road as if they were still asleep. She found a vacant
parking space on Klostergade behind Our Lady's Church. It was that wall
where Rudolf had sheltered. She walked towards two younger men and
a Greenlandic-looking woman, who was standing with a beer bottle in
her hand under the trees, already having problems with her balance. They
looked at her sceptically.

"Rudolf—do you know him?" she asked, sticking her hands in her coat
pocket. She had forgotten her gloves, distracted by Adomas being with her
and kissing her eagerly before she left. She wasn't thinking clearly today.

One of the men who had to be freezing in something that looked like
a tracksuit over a pullover looked drowsily at her. His eyes were dull and
lifeless. "Rudolf isn't here anymore," he replied, no life in his voice, either.
The other two just stared at her.

"What do you want with Rudolf?" the Greenlandic woman asked
hoarsely.

"Just to talk to him for a moment. Do you know where he is?"

"Are you a copper?" asked the other man. His voice sounded as if it
came from a little boy and didn't match his big body.

"No, I'm not a copper. I'm an old friend of his family."

The sceptical facial expressions became no less sceptical. The Greenlandic woman nodded towards the wall by the church.

"He used to sit over there with his shopping trolley of booze and
blankets."

"Where's the trolley now?"

"Someone removed it. Probably drawn by the booze." The Greenlander
laughed, but it wasn't a genuine laugh.

"Who spoke to him last? Was anyone close to him?"

The fat man looked around searchingly. "Viggo, but he has not got here
yet. We haven't seen him that much since Rudolf disappeared."

Anne nodded understandingly.

"He usually sits on a bench up on Busgaden, talking to himself. At least, he was when I passed by a quarter of an hour ago," said the man in the tracksuit top as he lit a cigarette with shaking, nicotine-stained fingers.

Anne thanked them and walked up to Busgaden. The smell of diesel made her nauseated as she walked through the tunnel, where you weren't supposed to walk for fear of being run down by a bus. But it was the fastest route, and she stayed close to the wall. She caught sight of him among the waiting commuters. He was sitting alone on a bench. No one would sit next to a strange man with an inverted blue cap on his head, wild eyebrows, shoulder-length hair and untidy beard, several coloured blankets over his shoulders on top of a chequered coat, who was talking to himself as he stared down at a beer bottle at ten in the morning. People stole looks at him, probably felt a little sorry for him, but what could they do? Anne got some weird looks as she sat down next to him. He didn't look at her and seemed quite intoxicated. Maybe it was pointless to ask him anything meaningful.

"Do you miss Rudolf?"

He stopped mumbling and squinted at her without turning his head. "Who?"

"Rudolf."

"Rudolf?" He tasted the word. "Well, you mean Rudolf with the red nose?" There was a sound that was supposed to be a joking laugh but it turned into a bark. He coughed.

"No. Your friend, Rudolf. The one with the shopping trolley of booze."

He nodded, still without looking at her. "Verner? He's gone."

"Verner, you say. Is your friend's name not Rudolf?"

He closed his eyes, and it looked as if he had fallen into a deep sleep. She gave up and went to get up, but he grabbed her coat and pulled her back down onto the bench again. He leaned all the way into her ear so that his beard tickled her cheek, and she could smell that he hadn't washed for a long time. "Rudolf. I saw them take him," he whispered, slowly lifting a forefinger towards her to point. "*They* took him!"

"Who took him?"

He closed his eyes again and leaned his head against her shoulder. She watched a group of people get on the number nine bus to Lystrup and tried not to think about what they must have thought of her. She pushed him up to sitting and spoke more urgently. "Is Rudolf who you call Verner? Is his name Verner?"

He nodded with his eyes closed.

"What's his surname—Verner what?"

No answer.

"Who took him?"

"*They* took him!" He shouted it so loudly and unexpectedly that she jumped, and a few people at the stop turned around, annoyed, and looked at them. The rest pretended to be both deaf and blind. A woman in fur smiled indulgently and turned her back to them.

"Who was it, Viggo," she whispered. "What did they look like?"

He turned a pair of dull eyes towards her and tried to focus. "How do you know what my name is?"

"Your friends told me."

He shook his head violently. "I don't have any friends!" he shouted again loudly.

Anne began to find it embarrassing, but he definitely knew something. "When did you see that they took Rudolf?"

He shrugged.

"You have to tell me something more, Viggo, so we can find Rudolf. Do you want to go somewhere and have a cup of hot coffee? Something to eat, and—"

He jumped up from the bench with such force as if possessed by a completely different person. "You're one of them! That's what they said to Rudolf, too!" He flayed wildly with his arms, as though a swarm of sting-ing bees were around him, and he toppled the bottle of beer that stood between his feet as he set off running—or rather shuffling—towards Telef-ontorvet with the blankets fluttering behind him.

Anne leaned back dejectedly against the cold bench, wanting to give the finger to all the people glaring at her. Politicians had been saying for years that the homeless were to be taken off the streets. The government had set aside money for it, of which Aarhus Municipality was to receive a double-digit million kroner sum for the project. Homeless people didn't belong in a tourist city, especially not over three hundred of them, and certainly not the roughly thirty of them who routinely slept on the streets. But you couldn't just get rid of them like that if they didn't get help. She lit a cigarette, telling herself it would warm her up. Hash, alcohol, and drugs dominated among those who slept on the streets. Several of them were mentally ill, others suffered from physical illnesses. But how could a human being end up there? Couldn't they just pull themselves together and get a life? That was certainly what the woman in the rabbit fur coat, who had smiled with a red lipstick mouth must have thought. But Anne knew what it was like to live on the streets and occupy empty houses so as not to freeze to death. She had read online that most homeless people were aged between thirty and forty-nine years, and they typically had debt and lived on the lowest bracket of benefits. The cost of drugs or alcohol ate it all up. It wasn't a top priority for either the municipality or the government at national level. In Copenhagen, the number of homeless was even higher. Maybe it was the municipality quietly removing them from the street so they could use the money for something else? Who knew what was going on? The lady with the fur coat got on the number six to Højbjerg. Out there, they probably didn't have many homeless people on the street. That was where Roland Benito lived, as far as she knew. She stubbed out the cigarette against the bench and threw the butt in the bin. A man in an orange suit walked around shovelling snow. He reminded her of a Guantanamo prisoner; she smiled at him as she walked by but got none in return. *The city of smiles . . .*

Where was Rudolf?

# 27

Monday morning briefings with cakes and coffee were usually a lively affair with talk of the weekend's events before the meetings got underway. This morning, the empty chairs again testified to the pandemic that had emptied many workplaces—and not least schools and kindergartens. However, Isabella was back, though she was paler than usual. But their low numbers put a dampener on private chit-chat, so the meeting was over quickly. Roland informed them of Saturday's interrogation of the arrested Lithuanians, who had pleaded not guilty to the murder but were now in custody until the DNA analyses came back. Then he allocated his staff various tasks and went back to his office. That case should soon be closed.

He called Leander at Forensics and was delighted to hear that his old friend was back.

"Thank you, Roland. It was a good seminar. We've come back a little wiser. New technology is being developed all the time—we'll be able to find the criminals before they even know they want to do something criminal," he said in response to Roland's polite introductory question.

"I bloody well hope not, otherwise I'll soon have to join the queue of unemployed," Roland replied theatrically.

"Ah, it was hypothetical, of course. But we can do a lot nowadays."

"Now that you can do so much, can you tell me when the results of the DNA analyses will be in? The three Lithuanians."

"Unfortunately, no, that may take some time. The technicians are sick, too."

"Of course they are," Roland replied, annoyed.

"Is there any doubt that it *is* them?"

"There's always doubt—even though you are so good," he replied sarcastically, "but the matter won't be settled until we get that answer and can compare DNA samples."

"I heard on the radio that you're looking for a getaway car from the attempted bank robbery in Kolding and one from a gang member. So you're missing one?"

"Yes, unfortunately, one of them got away. He's probably changed cars."

They chatted a little. Roland wanted to ask about Julie but didn't. He hoped Leander would open up and tell him about his romance soon. Maybe Leander didn't dare to because both Roland and Irene had liked Mary, but years had passed since she died of lung cancer, and of course Henry had to move on with his life. A man in his early sixties shouldn't be alone. Definitely not *him*. He would become a strange old codger whose only interest would be the dead and the insect collection in his basement. A tank crawling with ants.

After Roland had hung up, the phone rang. It was Isabella. Her voice was still a little hoarse, sexy like Bonnie Tyler's. She had been Rikke's favourite singer. The music of her idol had filled the house back then. Stanzas of the songs "Total Eclipse of the Heart" and "It's a Heartache" resounded in his head. Both suited Isabella perfectly, it seemed to him.

"The boy's parents have moved to Sweden," she said as though he understood the reference. "The one who drowned," she elaborated, as Roland's silence could also be interpreted as forgetfulness.

"Have you already followed up on that?"

"I made a few calls from home. After all, it's not as if I was dying," she said with a smile in her voice.

Roland still didn't like that sort of comment from such a young woman. When you're only in your twenties, you shouldn't be thinking about death, which of course was impossible in this job. Neither did he like the fact that she worked in her spare time and not at all when she was supposed to be on sick leave.

"I also found some old newspaper articles about the case. It's all very mysterious."

"Why do you say it's mysterious?"

"The sequence of events. The boy is found drowned in the lake. He is quickly identified as the neighbour's son and had been lying in the lake for many hours; he couldn't be rescued. The parents have a daughter, too. She wasn't with her little brother, as they thought. She had left him on his own. It couldn't have been easy for her when he was found dead. The parents are very religious. The journalist made a big deal out of talking about an east-facing cross between the trees in their garden, which they apparently prayed at to get closer to God."

"Sounds a bit extreme," Roland interrupted, mostly to show that he was still listening. His interest in the case had waned now that the murderous robbers were already in police custody, and he was reviewing the interpreter's translation of the interrogation once more. They couldn't spend time on a four-year-old case about a boy's tragic drowning accident now, but he had asked Isabella to investigate the circumstances, so . . .

"I think so, too, and maybe they weren't completely normal. They made a lot of cruel accusations against the neighbour, which couldn't be proven, and which were completely absurd. They claimed that—"

"It's probably very natural when a child dies like that," Roland interrupted again. "The parents want to find a cause and someone to blame. We'll take this further later—a fax is due in."

"Okay, that's probably more important. It seems like the usual squabble between neighbours, even though these disputes aren't always about a tree shading the other's garden or a glazed tile roof that blinds you in the sun."

# 28

The sun made the snow dazzle, so it hurt her eyes. Anne put on sunglasses, even though it felt weird when it wasn't summer. She turned left and continued along Nørrebrogade and further along Randersvej towards Trige. Something told her that the homeless man who had been found dead had something to do with the missing Rudolf. It was only her intuition, but it had rarely failed her. She had tried to call Benito again, but she was told he was unavailable. It was not even certain they'd done anything to identify Rudolf anyway. He had already been identified—as homeless.

A yellow city bus with an advertisement for the Jensens Bøfhus family restaurant at the back was ahead of her, blocking her view. Annoyed, she stayed behind it until she could turn right and further into the woods. She had no address but hoped to be able to find the house after seeing the picture that had been in the newspaper, despite the length of Trige Skovvej.

It was a long time before she stopped, reversed a bit, and turned into a courtyard with a giant Christmas tree. That was what she had been looking for. The tree. The bin was there, too. It had to be that house. The frosty snow creaked under her shoes when she stepped out of the car. She went up a pyramid-shaped staircase and rang. LAURA AND REINER GERTSEN was written on the sign above the bell. It took a while before she heard the door opening. Laura Gertsen seemed to be in the middle of baking; there was flour on an oversized black Weber barbecue apron that could have been her husband's. They were usually the ones who took charge of that activity. Their territory and all that. Anne imagined Adomas in front of the barbecue in the garden she'd always dreamed of and felt her cheeks warm. *Shit, Anne, you're turning into one of the petty bourgeois.* She realised the woman was staring strangely at her.

"Excuse me for interrupting. It's about the man who was found here yesterday."

"You're not from the police, are you?" the woman stated sceptically.

"No, I . . . I'm a journalist. I'm writing an article about the homeless in Aarhus, and I need some information."

The woman opened the door completely, but unwillingly—she couldn't hide it. Anne stepped in and smelled the freshly baked cakes. She unzipped her coat but didn't take it off completely to show that she wouldn't be disturbing the woman for very long.

"Is it okay if I just finish what I was doing? The dough has risen to where it should, so it has to be formed soon . . ." She began rolling some bread roll dough into a long sausage.

"Go ahead." Anne sat down on a chair at the kitchen table. *Aarhus Stiftstidende* was in front of her. She cast a sidelong glance at it. The front page only dealt with the home robbery and the murder; further down she spotted an article about three Lithuanians who had been arrested, but that one was still on the run and wanted all over the country and by Interpol. She swallowed a few times, trying to gather her thoughts about why she was there. Laura Gertsen wasn't very tall. About the same as herself. Anne judged her to be in her mid- to late fifties. Her hair was grey and cut in a nice, short modern hairstyle that gave it volume. Her eyes were hazel, and they looked worried. Of course, finding a strange dead man in your garden had also been a traumatic experience. She had begun to shape the dough pieces into bread rolls and placed them carefully next to each other on a lined baking sheet. Maybe baking was a kind of therapy. Or was baking just "in" again? She herself was not the domestic type. Where could she possibly have got it from?

"You did not know the homeless man? Did he just happen to find your yard?"

Laura turned her head and looked at her as if she had completely forgotten that she had let her in.

"Apparently so. We didn't know him. Maybe the lighted Christmas tree in the garden attracted him."

"From where?"

She shrugged. "Maybe he was from Fællesgården."

"Fællesgården?"

Laura sent her an inquisitive look. "The working community that the church's shelter offers the vulnerable who can't do a normal job." She said the latter with a slightly mocking undertone. Everyone had their prejudices, even if they claimed otherwise. Could Anne say she was completely untarnished?

"Where is Fællesgården?"

"Not far from here. Lergravvej. A little more than three kilometres."

"Still, though. Would he have walked three kilometres without shoes straight to your yard out of all of them?" She must have sounded a little too sceptical, for Laura looked at her angrily and opened the oven. A pleasant warmth hit Anne in the face.

"The police think he was going to hang himself in a tree somewhere in the forest, that it went wrong—at least from his point of view—and he ended up staggering into us, where he dropped dead." She put the baking sheet in the oven and set a timer that looked like a lime-green chicken egg.

"But why hang himself in a tree in the woods? He could have hanged himself somewhere warm—given that he was in possession of the rope," Anne mumbled, mostly to herself.

"He was probably drunk and might have taken drugs, too. So he didn't know what he was doing." She leaned her back up against the kitchen counter, crossed her arms, and stared at Anne with a look of impatience.

"Where's your husband?"

"At work. He's a bus driver. I'll be heading to work myself in a couple of hours, so . . ." She looked demonstratively at her watch.

"Yes. I need to get going myself." She would otherwise have liked to have heard Reiner Gertsen's version of events. She got up and zipped her coat. "Thanks for your help."

Laura accompanied her out into the hallway and watched her as she put on her boots and laced them.

"It amazes me that you don't know Fællesgården if you write about the homeless," she said with her arms still crossed.

"Which newspaper do you work for?"

Anne got up from a kneeling position and took her gloves out of her coat pocket while looking into a pair of very suspicious eyes.

"I work for the *Daily News*," she replied, opening the door. She assumed that Laura Gertsen knew as little about the closures of the local newspapers as she herself knew about homeless people's whereabouts.

She turned out of the courtyard with the beautiful Christmas tree and drove on along Trige Skovvej. The road she came out on was called Pannerupvej. Wasn't this where the home robbery had taken place? She turned in the opposite direction to the one she needed to get back to Randersvej. A little later, she saw the four farms that lay in a small cluster in the landscape surrounded by forest. A fifth was a bit secluded—that had to be the one that housed the collective. She drove past quietly; you couldn't see the yard where the murder had occurred. Why hadn't they just chosen the one closest to the road? She spotted a punk girl standing at a bus stop on the other side of the road; she seemed nearly breathless as she stomped angrily in the snow. When Anne caught sight of the back of the bus, she figured out what had happened. She made a quick U-turn, pulled in, and rolled down the side window.

"Are you heading into town?"

The girl nodded in surprise. She would fit in better there, was Anne's first thought. She seemed completely out of place in this rural setting. She recalled Stieg Larsson's hacker, Lisbeth Salander, from the film *The Girl with the Dragon Tattoo*, which she had seen in the cinema.

"Me, too. Hop in."

"Fucking bus. It never runs on bloody time," she hissed as she sat in and pulled her long legs clad in black knee-length boots with her. She slammed the door hard.

"Oh, I know," Anne said with a small smile, glancing in the rear-view mirror and over her shoulder as she pulled out from the bus stop.

"Are you from Copenhagen?" asked the girl with a look as if she herself were an alien species meeting a compatriot.

"Nørrebro—can't you hear it?"

"I'm from Copenhagen, too. Do you miss it? The city?"

"Not at all," Anne replied, genuinely meaning it. "Are you not thriving over here in Jutland?"

"It's boring. Nothing happens here. Can I smoke?" She lit the cigarette before asking.

"Of course. I don't think living out here sounds boring."

"You mean the murder?" Well, yeah, that was exciting, but it's been solved. It was some Eastern Europeans. We knew that already."

"You knew?"

"That's just the way they are."

"Eastern Europeans?"

"Yeah. Pretty much all of them."

Anne scowled at her to see if she really meant that claim, but she just stared out the side window with a sharply expressionless face.

"What's your name?"

"Bitten Mørk. And you?"

"Anne Larsen. Where are you going?"

"Hairdresser's—Ulla's on Åboulevarden."

"Are you a hairdresser?"

"A trainee. What are you doing?"

"I'm a journalist."

"Which newspaper?"

"The *Daily News*."

Bitten just nodded. Apparently, no one had any idea that their little local newspaper had passed away. Bitten could maybe be excused.

"Do you live in the collective?"

"How did you know that?"

"I guessed. I read about you in the paper."

"Oh, yeah, we've become quite the celebrities." There was a crooked smile that beautified her painted face and made the rings in her nose move. They looked like the ones Anne herself had once worn. She still had little scars.

"I honestly didn't know the farm was so far out when Brian, my boyfriend, wanted me to move here. There are some real weirdos living out here." She sighed after a couple minutes of silence and a few inhalations and exhalations that enveloped them in dense smoke. Anne rolled down her side window a little. Even though she herself was a smoker, this was still too much in a small Lada.

"Weird how?"

"Well, there's one neighbour—the ones who live next to the farm where the farmer was murdered—they have a ferocious killer dog and private forest that is fenced in, so no one can go in there. Strictly, strictly forbidden!"

"Why on Earth is it fenced in?"

Bitten dropped ash into the car's ashtray, which needed to be emptied.

"A few years ago, a boy drowned in the lake in there. There was a whole palaver, according to Brian, my boyfriend, who heard from Andreas, who started the collective—he's lived there since he was a child. The boy's parents went completely crazy and accused the people who own the dog of killing their son. Totally sick. They weren't normal, either. There's a cross down between the trees that they apparently pray to. Very religious, it's said. It gives you goosebumps."

Anne got them, too. She closed the window when Bitten finally stubbed out the cigarette.

"Sounds like an exciting neighbourhood." She smiled, stopping for a red light at Nørreport. Some pedestrians dashed across the pedestrian crossing; one woman pushed a pram in front of her. It was rare to make it across before the lights turned green again.

"It's a tad creepy. The boy who drowned lived on the farm where Albert was murdered. My boyfriend and I call it 'The Murder Farm.' The parents said the boy was murdered. But, like I said, they weren't exactly normal, either. And it was never solved."

# 29

So-called social losers—have they always existed? Or was it a new concept? One that emerged when humans became societal beings and there was no longer room for anyone who was different—despite *social* meaning *social conditions that take others into account* in his Danish lessons. He thought about all this as he sat in the car in front of the fashionable modern furniture and home furnishings boutique Tidens Møbler on Klostertorv, waiting for Irene. He'd promised to collect her from work as her car was in the garage, and anyway, they couldn't get any further with the murder case until the DNA analysis came back and the final perp was in their custody. Irene had gone in to buy a magazine holder that Rikke wanted for her birthday.

Some homeless people and drug addicts were standing under the bare trees in the light of the streetlamps. But not as many as in the summer. A few were holding beers that should have been hot tea or soup instead. All were close together to keep warm. As if they, too, were just waiting for the bus. But they were different. Not just outside the herd at the bus stop, but also outside the community. Or was it the rest of us who are, he thought further. Have we just misunderstood the meaning of life? Had they simply realised long ago that they couldn't be part of what was demanded nowadays?

The dead homeless man had begun to torment him now that the case of the home robbery had largely been solved. The fate of Verner Thybo affected him. Many people probably thought that the poor souls here at the church and all the other places around the city where they lived were the cause of their own misfortune, that they could just find a job and be "normal" if they chose to be. But everyone had a sad fate that had changed their lives. A bad childhood, illness, bankruptcy, or tragic deaths of loved ones, as was the case with Verner. But was it not the case that everyone else had failed—failed to provide the support they needed to get through their crisis? They probably hadn't asked for help, and so they were ignored in modern society, where no one was allowed to interfere unnecessarily. And what had happened to those Anne Larsen had talked about? They couldn't have just fallen off the face of the Earth. The words about police indifference were also still weighing on him. It was an unfair accusation; they treated everyone equally and had a good relationship with most. Neither did he like the fact that Anne was now in the process of investigating the mystery—he knew she was. And it was not the best environment to delve into with vigour. It was here on Klostertorv that a young student was brutally beaten to death beyond recognition one night in 1996. A homeless and crazed drug addict was charged with the murder.

"Bloody hell, that was expensive!" Irene groaned as she abruptly pulled open the door and jumped into the car with a bag that she tossed onto the back seat. "Some of the magazine holders cost almost three thousand kroner, so she won't be getting one. I bought some cushions that she wants instead."

Roland nodded without expression and cast a quick glance at the opposite pavement. A stark contrast to the luxury furniture of Tidens Møbler. How many of them over there had stood and looked dreamily at a twenty-thousand-kroner bed on display in the window?

Irene followed his gaze.

"If only there was more we could do for them." She sighed, fastening her seat belt. She was a social worker, and he knew she was doing what she could given the funds available.

"Having to stay out in these freezing temperatures is inhuman."

"They have to, the last drop-in centre closes at three. And the night services don't open until midnight. But that should soon change. The local councillor has promised them a twenty-four-hour drop-in centre."

Roland nodded doubtfully, looked behind him, and drove out of the car park.

"What about the drop-in centre on Jægergårdsgade—wasn't that renovated?"

"Centre Basen? Yeah, it's looking good with lighter colours on the walls and colourful oil cloths on the tables. It no longer looks like a pathetic pub. But they close at one, and so much has been cut from the budget that not many activities can be afforded."

Roland kept a close eye on the cars in front. The shops were closing, and the traffic was heavy. A long working day was over for many, and they were hurrying home to spend some quality time with the kids, cook, eat, watch TV, and sleep a few hours before a new working day began and it all started over again. The anguish of modern humans that social losers missed out on.

"You don't happen to know anything about a homeless man named Verner Thybo, do you?" he asked casually.

"Thybo? Nah, that name doesn't mean anything to me. Why do you ask?"

"You haven't heard of him? They found him dead in Trige with a rope around his neck."

"Oh yeah, they talk a lot about it at the office. He's been identified, then?" She sounded as if it wasn't something she thought they'd spent time on. "But it was a suicide, wasn't it?"

Roland shrugged. "Who knows? There are homeless people who disappear from the streets, and no one knows where they end up."

"Is this a case you're investigating?" An astonished tone again.

"No, 'we're' not. Anne Larsen is."

"The journalist? No, well, you told me she lost her job. So what does she have to do with it?"

"I don't really know, but that was why she rang late Thursday night."

"Is it something you're going to get involved in? I mean, it's not uncommon for socially disadvantaged people to take their own lives."

There was a new phrase. Socially disadvantaged. "Well, I doubt Kurt Olsen agrees. There are probably more important things to address, in his opinion. But if I know Anne Larsen, she'll find something. I just hope she looks out for herself. She's entering a world that's not exactly safe."

He turned on the radio, which was programmed to DR Klassisk. He couldn't stand pop music. It was the same thing over and over again. The station was in the middle of Sonata di Viole in D Major by Alessandro Stradella, and a happy smile spread across his face. He cast a sideways glance at Irene, who didn't care much for baroque music, but she was staring indifferently out the side window, lost in her own thoughts. The traffic was moving at a snail's pace. He listened to the violins and pictured the great halls of palaces with beautifully decorated high ceilings, statues in gold, columns in white and brown marble, and the ladies in colourful cascading dresses of silk.

Either way, the sound of the mobile phone didn't belong to that time when it broke through and forced him to turn down the music.

"We got him!" said DS Niels Nyborg with greater zeal in his voice than the violins. "He was bloody well here in Aarhus."

"The Lithuanian? How did we find him?"

"An anonymous tip, but we decided to follow up on it anyway—fortunately. Are you home yet?"

"Close. Have you brought him in?"

"It won't be long now, but you don't have to come in again. Kurt is here, and we'll deal with it."

Roland thanked him and hung up his handset. He took Irene's hand and gave it a hard squeeze.

"It'll all be over soon. We have him, so the family and neighbours can be left in peace. Let's celebrate that with a bottle of something good."

She reciprocated his squeeze and gave a relieved smile.

He turned into the garden and parked under the copper beech. The only place he had cleared the snow from.

# 30

The cold bit like little insects gnawing on his skin. Snow drifted down over the snow already present, making the scenery flicker before his eyes. His torch flashed back and forth in the darkness as he walked, but when he reached his destination, he turned it off and let the snow be his only light source. He knew the way. His footprints were covered from time to time. Lucky for him. He was walking in high snowdrifts and slipped several times. His hands were getting stiff from the cold despite his thick mittens.

His heart skipped a beat when he saw the red-orange glow ahead. He slowed down and moved as quietly as possible until he found his usual place and sank to his knees with a view to what he was hopeful to witness again. He pulled a plastic bag out of his pocket and placed it in the snow below his knees, so he didn't get too wet and cold. He had learned something.

They stood in the glow of the fire burning in the middle of the open space. The murmur sounded like a quiver in the cold air. Words that turned into ice crystals descended over him, making him shudder. That was why he came again and again. Why he couldn't stay away, despite the fact he'd often gone in vain. Hoped every time he would experience this. The thrill. The excitement. The mystery.

At last, it was happening. They lit the torches. He ducked involuntarily, even though he knew they couldn't possibly see him here. The dark silhouettes were distributed evenly and without any hint of uncertainty over who should stand where, so that they formed a circle. They began walking around until he eventually saw their torches as a ring of fire hovering between the tree trunks. They stopped and stood still around the fire. An eerie murmuring began again. They took turns to utter words he couldn't hear clearly. Some said more than others, and their voices were different. The horn he had seen last time was suddenly in someone's hands and was raised up to the sky. It shone in the glow of the fire. The person drank from it, said a few words, and passed it on. That is how they continued until everyone in the circle had drunk from the horn and said the same words. The silence of the night settled over the forest again. There was no clue that something was going on down in the clearing if you didn't know it. He waited a long time with his back leaning against a tree trunk. His eyelids began to get heavy. Movements in the dark ahead caused unrest in the group and woke him up. Something was going on. Something came out of the darkness and into the circle. He withdrew a little when he saw it in the glow of the fire and the torches, which had been set in the snow so they formed the circle. Its eyes shone with anxiety. It raised its head and tried to get away from the fire that frightened it. It wasn't bridled but had a rope around its neck, which it was being pulled by. It tried to rear but was held down with the rope that was tightened around its glistening neck. The smell of horse reached him. He got up onto his knees to see better and leaned against the tree trunk, but a shadow was standing in the way of his view. He couldn't see what was happening, but he heard the inhuman cry. A sound that cut through his brain, marrow, and bones so that he almost screamed aloud and gave away his presence. There was silence again, then loud cheers drowned out the scream still echoing in his head. The formation disbanded. Only the torches remained, forming the circle, a luminous ring of fire that melted the snow around it. Inside the fire there was activity, but he couldn't see what was happening. It looked as if they had thrown themselves at each other and were boxing. He wanted to get closer. Reveal himself and hear whether he could join in. His curiosity was roused. And his fear. Like when he was a boy and begged the others if he could join in their forbidden games. The smell of blood flowed through the frosty air like a warm, sweet stream that reached his nostrils and twisted itself further down his palate and to his stomach, where bile began to rise and burn his throat. In the light of the fire, he saw two blood-covered arms and hands rise above the group and up against the starry black sky, holding a chunk of bloody flesh—as if it were being handed to someone up there. Then, it was cast into the fire, and the smell of burned flesh mingled with the smell of fresh blood. He leaned forward and threw up into a bush, wiped his mouth with the back of his hand, and leaned up against the tree trunk with his eyes closed. He tried not to breathe until he had to gasp for air. But he gradually got used to the fumes. Now it became more appetising—roast meat, but still sweet to the smell. They sat in a circle around the fire and ate. It looked like a typical Danish Midsummer celebration with marshmallows. But he knew what they had on the spits. This was the third time he had witnessed the scenario. The first time, it was chickens that had left this life. The next was a pig. It hadn't affected him as strongly as now. Other times, the site had been empty. He had waited a long time but had gone home disappointed again. Who were they? It seemed like rituals. Devil worship? He shivered and froze when he heard something moving nearby and slowly turned his head. A fox had been attracted by the smell of blood. It approached cautiously. Its hunger in the food-forsaken frosty landscape had driven it closer to humans than usual.

# 31

The hand soap smelled faintly of green tea and bore a French label on a less than charming bottle that was as far removed from beautiful French design as possible. It mostly resembled a brown bottle of cough syrup. *Savon d'Usages* said the label. It was definitely one Pierre had brought back with him from his last trip home to the family. When it came to all that, he was pragmatic—no romantic floral scents or delicate pastel colours. Only when his wife did the shopping.

Kamilla smiled as she washed her hands and looked at her reflection in the gold-framed oval mirror hanging above the sink. She knew she should smile more. Maybe it would all fall into place now. She had met her father and half-brother. In her dream last night, she had seen Rasmus. He didn't cry about being alone in an unknown place like he did in all her many other dreams; he smiled, and his face had slowly changed into Mathias's. It was only a light, smooth transition, as their features were so similar. His nose had changed slightly, as Mathias's was a little more of a snub nose than Rasmus's had been, and his eyes sat a little closer. What did such a dream mean? What would a dream interpreter or a psychologist get out of it? She dried her hands; her eyes stared back at her from the mirror, frightened. Was she losing the memory of her son? Could she no longer remember him well and so was confusing him with Mathias? That was horrible! No, Mathias really did look like Rasmus. There was no doubt about that. She leaned in closer to the mirror and removed a bit of mascara that had spread under one eye. One of Pierre's regular clients was coming in for a meeting about an assignment in a little while, and as there would be both models and stills, Pierre wanted her to be there as well. She thought she'd already met all the customers given how busy they'd been up to Christmas. It was important to meet them, look at them, evaluate them. What style were they after—classic, modern, minimalist? That made it easier to work with them and get it right the first time. There was nothing deadlier than repeatedly missing the mark because you hadn't understood what the customer wanted.

When she came out into the hallway that divided the toilet and the meeting room, she heard voices coming from inside. The client had already arrived. But there was something about the voice that made her straighten. She stood still and listened. She knew it. Where had she last heard it? In the autumn, during the worst hurricane they'd had in a while, when she herself had asked him to come to Restaurant Egå Marina because she had intended to put all her hatred behind her. A realisation that sometimes you had to forgive even the unforgivable. Something that fate and her mother's passing had made her realise. But then she had seen the engagement ring on his finger, and everything had changed. He had moved on. He didn't need her forgiveness at all; his life hadn't stalled like hers because he had killed Rasmus. Negligent or not. He had proposed to her friend. To Majken of all people. Mostly, she wanted to turn around, go to the cloakroom, put on her coat, and drive home. But then she changed her mind. Straightened her back and fixed her jumper. She would show him that he wasn't the only one who had moved on.

They were already sitting at the table with two insulated coffee pots, stacks of white plastic cups, and dry cakes on a cardboard plate. And even though there were also cold cans of lemonade, the mood was mostly for the hot coffee. Pierre was pouring coffee for Danny Cramer, who was sitting with his back to the door, but she recognised his dark neck hair that formed little curls when it got wet.

"There you are! I didn't know where you'd got to!" exclaimed Pierre. "You haven't met our new photographer. Kamilla will be working with you on the stills," he continued, addressing Danny.

She held out her hand to him. His brown eyes lit up for a moment when he saw her. It was almost the same as when they'd first met each other almost three years ago. He opened his mouth to say something, but she interrupted him.

"Kamilla Holm," she introduced herself coolly, noting that he was still wearing the ring.

The expression in his eyes changed. Something teasing came into them. Yes, he *had* really moved on.

"Danny Cramer from Bureau-Step2." He smiled.

Kamilla sat down next to Pierre and set the pen ready on her pad. Pierre poured coffee for her. She felt Danny's questioning eyes on her, but if she revealed that she knew him, Pierre would keep drilling until he found out how, and she didn't want that. She hadn't even considered that Danny's advertising agency was a client of Studio Pierre; it wasn't far from his advertising agency on Badstuegade. Danny seemed to want to play along—thankfully. He pulled some drafts out of a black leather brief-case and laid them on the table.

"What my client wants is to have these burglar alarms presented in a catalogue. As you can see from the drafts, we need to shoot three models, and the rest will be stills."

"What have you thought of for the background?" she asked, drinking from the cup as she kept eye contact without blinking. It was about appearing professional, mostly for Pierre's sake.

"I'll leave that up to you. Something that sells."

"Do you even need to make sales material for alarms nowadays? People are desperate to buy them after all the home robberies, and especially now that one ended in a murder," said Pierre, casually reclining in the chair and drawing doodles on his pad. It seemed like they knew each other well. He was rarely so relaxed at client meetings.

"Yeah, I heard about it in the news—it was a scary outcome—and more alarms do sell when something like this happens of course. Journalists always blow it up."

Luckily, he didn't mention Anne, even though she knew it was her he was thinking of.

The rest of the meeting went as that kind of meeting usually does. The agreed on locations for the model shoots and backgrounds and direction for the stills. Danny handed the sketches to Pierre so they had them as a guide for formats and locations. Pierre took them into the photo studio, where the burglar alarms were lined up. They were left alone.

"Nice to see you, Kamilla," he said as he put on his coat. It smelled of his aftershave, and memories that scents often bring with them weighed heavily on her heart.

"But why don't we know each other?" he whispered.

Kamilla peeked into the studio. Pierre wasn't to be seen. "It's for the best. Pierre doesn't know anything about my past, and I would like it to stay that way."

He nodded and buttoned his coat. "How long have you been here? I had no idea you . . ."

"Only a few months."

"I've thought of you—when I heard that the *Daily News* closed. What's Anne doing?"

"The last I heard, she's looking for work."

Danny tied a knot in his scarf. "Tell her we need a copywriter. Would that be something for her?"

"Copywriter! Anne?" Kamilla couldn't help but smile. "If she can't sniff around in macabre murder scenes, then I don't think it's her cup of tea."

"You're probably right"—Danny smiled, too—"but she could do that in her spare time."

She was amazed at how easy it was to talk to him again. Given that the agenda was not to try to rectify the tragedies of the past.

"Well, I'll see you when the first shoots start. Pierre has promised to contact me when you're ready." He took longer than necessary to put on his gloves.

"I will," Pierre assured him, coming out of the photo studio. Danny shook hands with them both and disappeared into the darkness. She had to take a few deep breaths after the unexpected encounter.

"Does he *have* to be at the shoots?" she asked. "I mean, it's just burglar alarms." She felt short of breath just thinking of them working so closely together on such a time-consuming task, which it certainly would be.

"Danny was very explicit. The alarm company is a new customer at his agency, and he probably just wants to get it exactly how they agreed."

Kamilla nodded and gathered up the used cups in the meeting room. There was a single dry cake left. The obligatory one that was always left for some reason.

"He's a charming guy, Danny. Don't you think? A Zealander, you could probably hear?" Pierre started to tell her about how Danny had come to

Aarhus from a large advertising agency in Klampenborg, but Kamilla only half listened. She knew the story better than he did and was tempted to correct him a few times where he hyped it up a little, but she studied the elaborate sketches that Danny's ad agency had drawn up instead and realised that she was eating the dry cake even though she wasn't that hungry. She had a mouth full of cake when she picked up her phone, which was suddenly vibrating on the table to the tune of "I Want It That Way" by the Backstreet Boys, brutally interrupting Pierre. She had barely finished chewing before answering, and she swallowed a few times when she heard who it was.

"It's Mogens Arnskov. I'm to say hi from the happy couple and say thanks a million for the pictures. They were beautiful, and . . . well, I wanted to ask if we could meet? I'll be in Aarhus tomorrow. Could we get a cup of coffee?"

Kamilla laid the rest of the dry cake on the paper plate and wiped her hand on her jeans as she watched Pierre struggling with a photo lamp in his studio.

"Yeah, sure, I think I can make time for that tomorrow. When and where do you want to meet?"

# 32

It had been an uneasy night. He had twisted and turned, bathed in sweat, dreaming of a homeless man with a rope around his neck that had turned into dissolving corpses until Irene had woken him and, amid his confusion, told him that it was only three o'clock and that he should try to calm down a bit. They had been lying close together. He smelled her hair and had fallen asleep again. But then he'd dreamed of Salvatore, who dropped in a submachine gun salvo and dissolved in a lake of poisonous, steaming chemicals. Irene had woken him again, but this time it was because he had to get up and hadn't heard the alarm clock. He had talked to Giovanna the night before and was sure it was that conversation that had triggered the dream about Salvatore. He'd started school but came home late, claiming he had been with his friends. Giovanna believed her son, but Roland's fears were growing. It was rare that the Camorra gave up on a willing worker they could exploit.

Now he was mentally tired. He was sitting in his office chair over the newspaper and a cup of strong coffee when Chief Superintendent Kurt Olsen, intolerably perky for that time of day and with a smell of tobacco lingering on his clothes, came in and sat across from him, of course, with bad news.

"We received the results of the DNA analyses this morning. None of the Lithuanians are a match—nor is the driver the murderer."

Roland suddenly woke up. "That doesn't make sense. Did they double-check?"

"Several times. It's *not* them, Roland. But the driver says he can tell us who the cigarette smugglers are, so we've made a deal with him. If he tells us what he knows, he'll be let off."

Roland looked accusingly at his superior but didn't have the energy to protest strongly.

"After all, he was only a driver for the bank robbery in Kolding, and it's important we get hold of that smuggling gang," Kurt defended himself in a sharp voice.

Roland nodded, tired. Tired due to lack of sleep and tired from the thought that they had to start all over again now with solving the murder. "So, who the hell murdered Albert Hovgaard?" he mumbled into his coffee cup.

"We have to just start over. All leads have to be reviewed once more. There must be something you all overlooked. The murder weapon needs to be found, too."

Roland growled inside at his *you all overlooked* comment. That was how Olsen always expressed himself when it was negative. Otherwise, it was the royal we.

"There's nothing else for it. We have lots of leads, but what good is that?".

"Signe and Albert Hovgaard's entire family has been examined inside and out, haven't they?"

"Of course they have. All the way down to a new three-month-old great-grandchild. It's not any of them; everyone has a firm alibi. Most live far away, and they don't have much contact with each other. Families keep to themselves these days." Roland flipped through the papers and found something. "Only one son heard something about some neighbour disputes that Albert had mentioned at a family birthday."

Kurt Olsen tore the paper out of his hand. "Is that the report?"

Roland nodded, getting the dull feeling that they probably should have investigated the matter further. He himself had had the faint notion that something was going on between the neighbours that hadn't come to light, but the Eastern Europeans were the obvious choice—an open and shut case.

"And you have, of course, followed up on that and crossed it off?" Kurt Olsen questioned.

Roland's silence was answer enough. The Chief Superintendent handed the paper back after skimming through it. He got up and walked towards the door, where he turned and looked firmly at Roland. "Deal with this today. If a neighbour dispute is so serious that it leads to murder, one of them must have a burning desire to gossip. Do you know who you should talk to out there?"

Roland both nodded and shook his head. How was he supposed to know that? Anyone could be involved in that kind of conflict, and who would gossip about whom? He leaned back and stared blankly up at the ceiling once Olsen had left. And who said the dispute had anything to do with the murder anyway? Would they end up just wasting even more precious time? On the night of the murder, Ella Geisler had mentioned something about a fire in Signe and Albert Hovgaard's farmhouse. Was there something there? Could a neighbour be to blame for the fire? Was that where he should start digging? The newspapers were filled with bold headlines that the police were still at square one, which was making people feel even more insecure. He had better gather his team for a briefing and a little pep talk to keep spirits up, even though *he* was the one who needed it.

# 33

Adomas wasn't there when she returned to the apartment. She could smell him and missed him. If only nothing had happened! She lit a cigarette and tried to look out the window. Ice and snow had piled up on the pane outside. She opened and closed the window hard a few times until the ice came loose and fell onto the street below. She thought of her visit to Laura Gertsen and the newspaper on the table. If it was his friends who had been arrested, then it couldn't be them who had threatened him. She took a thoughtful puff of her cigarette. If it was in the newspaper on Monday, they had to have been arrested at some point on Friday or at the weekend; that was the only way the journalist could have got wind of it. That fact hurt. She found an ashtray and sat down at the coffee table with it in front of her. The police had put out an APB for another Lithuanian—in connection with a bank robbery in Kolding. Was it Adomas? She almost had to laugh at the thought. The apple didn't fall far from the tree. Unemployed and falling in love with a criminal—just like her mother. Annoyed, she got up and paced restlessly back and forth.

She hadn't seen her mother today, even though she'd been at the shelter. No one had heard of Rudolf. Was that who they'd found with a rope around his neck in the yard with the beautiful Christmas tree? Had he really tried to hang himself in the woods? She missed being able to discuss the story with the others. Britt, who usually never contributed anything useful, but who nevertheless sometimes waffled something that made sense. Kamilla with her common sense. Thygesen, who put her in place so she saw things from a different angle. Nicolaj—the quick student she had mentored—what had become of him?

She sat down again and flicked the ash off her cigarette. Bitten Mørk from the collective came to mind, too. She had stuffed the car's ashtray with butts, so Anne had finally been forced to empty it. What was that story about a drowned boy and a murder—maybe—that had never been solved? At the same farm where another murder had now happened? But it seemed too far-fetched to think the two things could be connected. The curiosity that had driven her to become a journalist stirred in her body as if it wanted to chase her out the door—out to solve the unsolved. She hadn't taken off her coat; she stubbed out the cigarette in the ashtray despite it having been only half smoked, put on her mittens, and went out the door again. It was time for her to take a look around the crime scene, and it wasn't far from Fællesgården—where she'd been planning to pay a visit anyway. If it was true that the homeless man came from there, they had to know him.

The country estate with red bricks and white-painted windowsills gave her chills. Not just because of the police's red-and-white-striped barrier tape and the yellow NO ENTRY! POLICE sign sealing the door, but because it was almost identical to her grandparents' farm in North Zealand. A childhood memory that made her feel nauseated. Her room there had been up in the dormer attic when she stayed with them for weeks on end while her stepfather was in prison and her mother couldn't handle all the kids she'd had with him.

The snow hung over the gutter as if it had leapt and been frozen in motion. Half the wall and garden were hidden by snowdrifts. If she went in and peered in through the windows, they would be able to tell she had been here. And what business did she have there? Where the bloody hell was the forest with the lake that had been mentioned? As she turned towards the property further down the road on the opposite side, she caught sight of the treetops behind it. She spotted the words *Organic Farming* on a gaudy wooden sign above the driveway. Everything was so quiet, as if the snow muffled every sound. As if life here on this road had come to a standstill when the home invaders left their mark on the small, safe community that usually kept to itself. She started walking down the road towards the forest and turned around to see the crime scene once again. From here, she saw the cross that the punk had mentioned, standing in between the trees of the property line. Behind, the yard with the dormer attic was almost covered in snow. Why had Signe and Albert Hovgaard not removed the cross when they'd moved in? Yes, it was well hidden, and maybe they didn't even go into that part of the garden. Maybe they were Christians? Or, they *were* for Albert.

Anne didn't get far into the forest when she came across a sign that, like the one from the police, prohibited all access. She hesitated, then walked around it and continued until she encountered a new obstacle—a two-metre-high wire fence. She followed it for a few metres but could see that it continued. She walked back, deep in thought. Wasn't that a slightly extreme reaction to a single accident? But you could do what you wanted in your own private forest. She had just made it around the sign when she spotted a man striding briskly towards her with a mottled muscular dog on a leash—or was he the one on the leash? The dog was certainly the one leading until the man pulled it back hard. It snarled ferociously at her.

"What are you doing here on private land?" He was a lot taller than her and well built. Or maybe it was just the big coat that made him look so huge. Or her own guilt that made her feel smaller. She involuntarily took a step back and stared in horror at the dog.

"I didn't know it was a private forest," she mumbled.

"Didn't know!" he thundered, pointing to the sign. "That's why we put that up."

"So, you own the forest?"

"I asked what you are doing here!"

He looked inquisitively at her, as if trying to figure out whether she was someone he should know.

"I'm a journalist. Anne Larsen—from the *Daily News.*"

"There's nothing for you here!" He gave the dog a little more leash, and the animal advanced quickly. She retreated further backwards, almost falling.

"What are you hiding in this forest?" She tried to look at him defiantly and to ignore the dog. Saliva dripped from its jaws down into the snow.

Vagn Mortensen's eyes became narrow under the edge of his grey wool hat. "Get out of here immediately; otherwise, I'll call the police! You are on private property!" The dog got a little more leash, and Anne held up her arms disarmingly in front of her.

"Fine, but then let me get around that beast," she whispered.

He pulled the dog back so that its claws left trailing tracks in the snow. She hesitantly walked around it and back out onto the road. He remained standing in front of the sign, following her with his eyes. As if on command, the dog began to bark, interspersed with threatening snarls. She turned her back to them and returned the same way she had come. Did Benito know anything about that forest and the drowning accident? Maybe she should have let that man call the police anyway. She could sense that something strange was going on here.

When she knew he could no longer see her, she turned and walked the opposite way from the road where the Lada was parked. Shortly afterwards, she was in the courtyard in front of the collective. Snow had only been cleared from the garage and out to the field road. In the yard, some of the drifts were so tall that they reached above her knees. She found a trail along the wall that had been formed by many footsteps that had trampled back and forth in the same place. Proof that humans are herd animals.

She rang the doorbell. Her mittens had become wet, and the frost was making her fingers stiff. A powerful-looking girl opened the door and looked at her questioningly.

"Is Bitten Mørk here?"

"Bitten? No, not now. She and Brian drove into town. Can I help you?"

"Maybe. I'm a journalist. Can I come in?"

The heat inside made her face and fingers tingle immediately.

"My name is Anita. Can I offer you something? Something hot, maybe? I was just about to make tea."

"That would be great."

"Who is it, Anita?" someone shouted from inside an adjoining living room.

"A journalist who knows Bitten!" answered Anita. "How do you really know her?" she asked, going out into an old country kitchen with beams in the ceiling. "Copenhagen?"

Anne followed her and told her about meeting the punk girl at the bus stop. Anita smiled.

"Typical Bitten. She's always late for that bus. Go in and sit down in the living room. Andreas and Linda are in there."

Anne greeted the couple sitting and reading on a light sofa. She felt really at home here, had even considered a collective when she moved to Aarhus, but couldn't find one that suited. You had to feel it deep in your stomach—like now.

Andreas immediately laid his book down on the coffee table. The title was *The Nordic Testament: The Walk of the Gods on Earth* by Vagn Lundbye. Volume One. In Danish. He offered a handshake.

"Am I disturbing you in the middle of your studies?" She smiled apologetically and reciprocated his handshake.

Linda looked up at her and laughed. "No, Andreas is just a mad Viking."

"Leave off! Just because that kind of thing interests me, you don't always have to—"

"There! See for yourself"—Linda laughed—"always on the warpath!"

Andreas explained that he was studying history, but that the Viking era had caught his interest and become a hobby. Linda shook her head slightly and put down her book, too: *Sports: Theory and Training.*

Anita came in with the tea and mugs and poured for all four of them. "What's so exciting about Vikings?" asked Anne, sniffing the tea. It smelled of elderflower and gave her a warm feeling inside of sun and summer.

"Nordic mythology and the gods are exciting on the whole. We can learn a lot from our ancestors, especially given the world we live in today. They would have made the sign of the cross because—"

"Do you really think they'd have made 'the sign of the cross,' those heathens?" Linda asked teasingly.

Andreas ignored her and continued. "Because for them, greed and avarice led to an immediate loss of honour, and honour meant a lot to a Viking. Generosity was their greatest virtue."

"What about the plundering, not to mention the human sacrifices? That can be compared to murder, can't it, or what?" It was clear that Andreas's girlfriend didn't share his noble view of the ancient Northmen.

Anita got up and went out into the kitchen. A door slammed somewhere. Anne figured she'd gone to the bathroom; she had turned so pale.

"They were at war, for fuck's sake! How do you think we behave in Iraq and Afghanistan!"

"Well, hopefully, more humanely."

Andreas seemed annoyed. "Sacrifices were part of their culture and faith. When they sacrificed and then consumed the flesh, they believed that it contained the power of the gods because it had been consecrated to them. Christians have the sacrament of the Eucharist, the bread and wine that either symbolise or have been transubstantiated into the body and blood of Christ. The Vikings lived in harmony with nature, and—"

"According to what Bjørn says, the wolf was exterminated in the Nordic countries in pre-Christian times because they hated wolves." Linda was in opposition yet again and quickly explained to Anne that Bjørn was one of the residents studying biology.

"It's true they hated wolves. The word *vargr* means wolf, but it was also used to refer to criminals. If you were called that, you were expelled and outlawed—an enemy. In Norse mythology, the giant wolf, Fenrir, is the epitome of the evil."

Anne listened in excitement as she sipped her tea that tasted of summer. She had completely forgotten what she had come for. "Isn't it just a theory that people were sacrificed? Nobody knows for sure?" she asked, feeling a shiver when Andreas nodded.

"Yes, they do actually. A nobleman's farm at Tissø on Zealand was excavated, and it gave good insight into the sacrificial acts. So has the sacrificial site at Slagelse, found where the Viking fort of Trelleborg was excavated in 1930, and which dates from around the year 980. Both human and animal skeletons were found there. The Vikings carried out a so-called blót. The word relates to the verb *blóta*, meaning to strengthen. They sacrificed to the gods to ensure fertility and growth. Human sacrifices were for particularly great prayers that were to reach all the way to Asgård, the world of the Aesir—the gods."

"Just think what that would have been like today—here during the financial crisis—heads would have rolled." Linda smiled as she scowled at Andreas, who was too busy to hear her teasing tone.

"There were four important blóts. In the spring, they sacrificed for fertility in the fields. In the summer, as a tribute to the sun. In the autumn, for a mild winter. And in the winter, for that sun to soon return. Weapons and warrior paraphernalia have been found in lakes, and archaeologists believe they were the weapons of the losers, who were sacrificed to the gods as thanks for the victory. Dead warriors were sacrificed, too. The Vikings believed that a man who died in battle ascended to Asgård with the gods as a warrior, while a man who died of old age or disease lying in his bed went to Hel—that is, hell."

"I heard that Danish Asatruar soldiers are wild about going to war for that very reason," Linda said thoughtfully. "And what difference is there really between that and Christianity? Heaven and hell? Or the Muslim faith, where a martyr goes up to seventy-two virgins?"

Andreas smiled. "Not so much. Christmas, Easter eggs, Midsummer, and the Danish *Fastelavn* all stem from heathen origins; we just don't think about it."

"Well, at least there's more food orgy and elves at Christmas than church attendance and hymns," Linda admitted.

"How did they do it? Beheading or what?" Anne didn't want to drop the subject, crime reporter as she was—or had been.

"You know the bog bodies Grauballe Man and Tollund Man, don't you? Well, Grauballe Man had his throat slit, and Tollund Man was found with a rope around his neck. They were both placed in bogs."

"But that wasn't the Vikings, was it?" Linda objected, pulling her legs up under her on the couch.

"No, the Viking Age didn't come until some years later, but the procedure was surely the same. No one can know for sure. It's the same with interpreting the old runes and scriptures—the few that exist. It was Christians who translated them, and as they didn't want to present too good a picture of the heathens, for good reason, you can't quite count on them being correctly translated. Just think of all the branches of contemporary Asatru—they each have their own way of interpreting their faith."

The words swirled around Anne's head.

"Are you okay, Anne?" she heard Linda's voice from far away.

She took a mouthful of tea and nodded. "I'm okay, it's just there were a lot of people who . . . actually, I came here because Bitten was talking about a boy who drowned in the lake in the woods down here. I'm, um— doing research for an article on unsolved accidents. Do you know anything about what happened?"

Linda looked at Andreas, who answered. "It's been a few years, but I remember well what happened to Marcus; it was terrible for the family."

"Bitten mentioned that the boy's parents didn't seem quite normal. Fanatically religious or something?"

"What would Bitten know about it?" Linda snorted.

"Maybe from Brian. He was asking me about it the other day," Andreas admitted.

"Why?" Linda looked at him over the mug.

"I've no idea, but I told him what I know."

"Which is?"

"What happened back when the forest was fenced in. There was a lot of mystery around it."

"Mystery how?" asked Anne, setting the mug down on the table. Her hand shook a little.

"The boy's parents claimed that something sinister was going on in the forest; something that had cost their son his life. But the police couldn't find any evidence of their allegation and closed the case as an accident. The family moved, and we never had anything to with them again."

# 34

Skejby Hospital, as it was still popularly called and probably still would be called even when people had finally got used to saying The New University Hospital or just DNU—not to be confused with the Danish Naturist Union—looked like anything other than a modern, well-run university hospital that was at the top of patient satisfaction surveys and was named the country's best hospital, due to the construction mess. But this is how the transition to becoming Denmark's largest superhospital of 232,000 square metres—current cost of about ten billion kroner—had to look, thought Roland, as he parked and pulled the handbrake. He felt lucky. Signe Hovgaard was finally able to have a longer conversation, and she had to have the answers to many of the questions he was ruminating on.

He found her with the assistance of a helpful nurse who didn't look particularly stressed. She was in a single ward because the traumatic experience had made her fearful of strangers. The nurse said that her jaw was broken, so Signe Hovgaard had been admitted to the Department of Dental, Oral, and Maxillofacial Surgery at Aarhus Hospital, but had now been transferred to Skejby, where she was waiting for an MRI scan.

She looked up at him nervously as the nurse opened the door and showed him inside.

"This is Detective Inspector Roland Benito from East Jutland Police. He would like to ask you a few questions." The nurse turned to him. "Signe can have a hard time speaking for long periods at a time, so I hope you show her some consideration."

Roland nodded. She closed the door behind him. He found a chair and sat down next to the bed. Signe Hovgaard was in her late fifties; it was hard to judge what she really looked like. Her hair was grey and frizzy. Her face was a mottled mask of yellow-green and violet-black marks, and one eye was completely closed. She looked worse than when he last saw her—that Monday night a week ago.

"First, my deepest sympathy," he began. It was hard to find the right words when a person had lost someone, and you knew that no words could help, and others could make it all much worse. "I have some questions as we suddenly find ourselves high and dry after questioning four Lithuanians, who—"

"I heard a little about it. My son keeps me informed. But I don't know if he tells me everything," said Signe strenuously. The jaw surgery was preventing her from opening her mouth normally.

"It turns out that the DNA doesn't match. They will, of course, be charged with burglary and theft, but we can't charge them with murder . . ." He fell silent when he saw her reaction. Tears ran from the swollen eye. "Can you tell me what happened that night?" He put a hand on her arm to calm her down but felt how her body jerked with fear when he touched her. She would be marked by this terrible experience for a long time yet. Maybe for the rest of her life.

"What do you want to know? I've told it so many times. The young men broke in and killed Albert. They probably thought I was dead, too."

"We need to know more so we can find the culprits," he said, thinking it sounded like a bad excuse for ruthless behaviour. "In addition to the weapons, we found a lot of stolen goods in their possession—from other thefts—so there's a good chance of getting the stolen valuables back." Even reassuring words seemed meaningless.

"You can keep the weapons!" she mumbled. "And we had nothing of value, anyway, so why us? We . . ." her voice cracked, and she went silent.

"Can you tell me what happened that night?"

"Albert was lying on the kitchen floor. I called him and shook him, but he didn't answer."

"Were the thieves gone by that time?"

She thought about it. "I think so. I couldn't hear them anymore. They made a lot of noise when they were searching through the house for money. I was unconscious for a while. I don't know how long."

"You didn't hear the fight?"

"There was a lot of noise. Albert wanted to stop them from entering the study."

"Why? Weapons?"

She nodded. The tears kept flowing, but her voice was firm now. "*Weapons,*" they shouted. First one of them shouted *Ginklai* and some other words. It sounded like Russian. They knew he had them; that much I did understand. I hated those guns." This last sentiment sounded bitter.

"So you didn't like the fact that Albert was a gunman."

She looked at him with her healthy eye, and it shone with fear. "I didn't like having weapons in the house. Look what it led to!"

"You think they came after them?"

"Yes, them or his gold medal. We have nothing else of value. He told all and sundry about his great results on the shooting range."

"How long were you with your neighbour? Do you remember?"

"No, it felt like an eternity. Should I have stayed with Albert?"

"You did the right thing. Don't doubt that." Guilt was often a consequence of a relative's death. He had seen it many times before.

"Do you know if Albert had enemies?"

"Albert had no enemies. He was a good man."

Roland heard the hesitation in her voice. Vagn Mortensen had said Albert was a tyrant, and Signe could confirm that. Was there anything she wasn't telling him? Could she have killed him herself before she ran over to the neighbour? A good opportunity to get rid of a violent husband.

"Your son mentioned something about some disputes with a neighbour. What is that about?"

"Disputes with a neighbour? No, I don't think we had any. Well no more than others. Why did he say that?"

"Could it have been Albert who disagreed with someone?"

"But wouldn't he have told me? I don't know. We get along well with the neighbours." She looked down at her hands lying on top of the duvet.

"Ella Geisler mentioned that your farm burned down once. What happened?"

"The fire? We had just moved in. Fire technicians investigated, and they thought it had been started on purpose, but the arsonist was never found. Fortunately, we were rescued. The fire engines came quickly, so someone must have called them."

"But the farm still burned down?"

"Not quite. The fire only managed to take part of the farmhouse."

She was getting tired, but there was too much he still needed answers to, and he had the feeling that she wasn't telling the whole truth.

"Do you know anything about the family from whom you bought the farm?"

"We . . . I only know them from the sale. They apparently moved far away. Something terrible happened to their little boy. He . . ." She fell silent again and twisted the corner of the hospital duvet as if it were an enemy she wanted to strangle.

Roland nodded.

"I know. He drowned in the lake. But do you know what really happened back then?"

"No, no one really talks about it. It was several years ago. And there's no access to the forest anymore, so it won't happen again. But Olga and Vagn know a lot more about it; it's their forest lake."

Roland nodded. "I've seen the cross in your garden. As far as I can understand, the family prayed outdoors to be closer to—Our Lord. It amazes me that they didn't take it with them. Or that you haven't removed it."

"I don't want it removed. Albert would . . . He . . ." She pursed her lips. "Well . . . I believe in God, and it would be a sin to remove it. They erected it for the boy. It was on that farm where he was born and raised. I thought it might protect us from everything else happening, too, but . . ." She started crying silently and used the duvet to dry her tears.

"Protect you from what?"

The door opened, and all at once, the nurse was standing next to him. "I think it's time to give the patient some peace. She's not able to talk too much yet. Maybe we can arrange for you to come back another day." She looked worriedly at Signe Hovgaard and took her hand.

Roland got up and said goodbye. "That may well be necessary," he said to the nurse before leaving.

* * *

He drove directly to Pannerupvej. Could a neighbour dispute really lead to such a brutal murder? He rang DS Mikkel Jensen, who was finally over his illness, and asked him to assist in interviewing all the neighbours once again. It would be good for him to get back to work again.

"We have to make sure to get DNA from everyone," he concluded, hanging up.

She was tinkering with the yellow Lada's engine behind the battered bonnet. He couldn't stop himself from parking and walking up behind her. "Having problems?"

She turned around immediately, startled at first, then she smiled—more surprised than he was.

"Hey, Benito! It's just this rust bucket of a car that won't start in the cold. Do you know anything about engines?"

"Absolutely nothing. I usually call for help."

"Did that, but they can't come for an hour because of all the drivers having problems at the moment."

"What are you doing out here? Dare I ask?"

She slammed the bonnet hard, turned to face him again, and smiled. "Just out for a walk in the beautiful winter landscape. That's not against the law, is it?"

"So why park here?" He glanced at Signe and Albert's farm. No one had walked in the snow in the garden, so she had not been up by the farmhouse after all.

"I'm not here for the robbery, if you can believe that."

"I don't believe anything. But then, what are you doing here?"

"I was just visiting my friend in the collective," she replied cheerfully. "Aren't you finished with the interviews out here? Didn't you arrest some Lithuanians?"

Roland fumed over her counter-question. She had a special journalist gene, which, it was a shame, had now been lost.

"You're a reporter—the press knows. It wasn't them. DNA proved it."

"It wasn't? None of them?"

She sounded relieved. How much did she have to do with the case anyway? He considered whether he should use her for something or whether the consequences would be too great. He abandoned the thought.

"Do you know something, Anne?"

"No, It's only Rudolf I'm interested in. I'm on my way to Fællesgården. They must know him. What else was he doing out here in the country?"

Another question he couldn't answer. "Is there anything new on him?" he asked casually, stomping snow off his boots.

"No, the only thing I found out is that his name wasn't Rudolf. His name was Verner."

# 35

Aarhus River ran January-grey in front of the café window. Only a few pedestrians walked by, huddled in their winter coats and looking ahead aloofly. This summer's Nyhavn atmosphere was gone. The tables and gas lamps were gone, and only the windows of Sct. Clemensborg, on the other side of the river, were illuminated.

Kamilla looked at the clock and wondered if he was lost. A fisherman who was used to the traffic at sea may have had trouble finding his way around a town, but then she remembered that he had lived in Horsens for a few years. She didn't know much more about him than what she had learned from the parish office and the Danish National Register that autumn. Her heart was pounding hard as if she were waiting for a date. She didn't have time for a long lunch today, so she was hoping he would show up soon. He should have been here ten minutes ago.

He arrived five minutes later, apologising profusely, hung his coat over the back of the chair, and asked what she wanted. He got two cups of coffee at the counter.

"Bloody hell! Twenty-six kroner for a cup of coffee—you can buy a whole bag of beans for that!" He set the cups on the table and sat down.

"Yes, cafés are expensive, but you're probably used to that in Bønnerup. The tourists pay there, too." Kamilla smiled. Her nervousness had almost disappeared when she saw him.

"I'm sorry I'm late. You don't have much time, do you? I parked in Magasin's car park and was stopped by a homeless man outside; I couldn't get away from him."

"What did he want?"

"He was trying to sell me a copy of one of those *Big Issue* newspapers. I bought one, but then he wanted to give me his whole life story, and I didn't have time for that, but it was hard to just leave. Poor man."

Kamilla studied him while he stirred sugar into his coffee. She was trying to see similarities to herself; there was something in his eyes.

He drank and smiled. "Well, the coffee's good." He put the cup down. "Does it surprise you that I wanted to meet you?"

"A little," she admitted, praying that the reason was the one she hoped for.

"I've been told to say hello from Alice and a huge hello from Mathias. And from Ida and Ole, too, but I said that. The pictures you took at their wedding were truly amazing."

"Thank you. It was pure luck; I'm not a model photographer. My boss tricked me into it."

"And thank goodness for that, otherwise I wouldn't have met you."

Kamilla wanted to confess who she was, but that's not how it should be revealed. She had no idea how he was going to react to such news.

"Are you happy working there? I understand you used to be a photographer for a newspaper."

"It's still so new, but I'm very happy there. I have no regrets, at least. I resigned from the newspaper. Press photos can be harsh—especially taking images at crime scenes."

"I can imagine." He hesitated.

*Now,* she thought. *Now, he's going to tell me that he has figured out who I am.*

"It's actually photos that I want to talk to you about. You took such beautiful pictures of the wedding, and it made me think about whether I could get you to take some of Mathias. Alice's birthday is in a few weeks, and I'd like to surprise her with them. Will you?"

"Photos? Yes—of course!" She swallowed the disappointment with a mouthful of coffee.

"I thought so. The second thing I came for is a little harder for me to ask. Mathias has talked a lot about you. It seems you got along really well with each other. So . . . would you be able to look after him one day? Alice and I are going on a trip, and we don't want to leave him alone for that long. We don't really trust Tanja anymore; she's let us down too many times. You could take the pictures that day, so Alice doesn't suspect anything."

Kamilla nodded a little too eagerly. Mathias had talked about her. "Yeah, of course. I'd love that. When?"

"It's on Friday. I can drop him off in the morning. Would it be okay for him to come with you to work? It'd be very exciting for him."

"No problem." Rasmus had also always been interested in her work and the camera, and she often missed his company and the many curious questions.

"He'll be delighted to hear that." Mogens drained his cup. "I'd better be getting home." He got up and put on his coat. Kamilla pulled hers on, too, wondering whether she should tell him, but it didn't feel right now that he was about to leave. Hopefully, there would be a better opportunity.

# 36

Anne had waited ages for the AA to show up so she could move on, and fortunately, it hadn't taken long for the car to start up again. Annoyingly, Benito had shown up in the meantime.

She drove back to town, thoughts swirling in her head. Yet again she had pretended to be a journalist from the *Daily News* and had been given a tour of Fællesgården. It was an admirable project with plenty of opportunities for both indoor and outdoor activities between nine and two every day and social community events all year round. A lovely garden with herb beds—she was told, because everything was hidden under the snow—and a mini lake with Muscovy ducks. The target group was benefits recipients who needed active retraining. She couldn't really see her mother working on a farm. Working at all. She tapped the ash off the cigarette into the empty ashtray.

The employee she had spoken to didn't know anything about the homeless man who had been found dead. It was rare for a homeless person from the shelter to come on the daily bus from Nørre Allé and Mejlgade; most participants came from a little further afield, usually had their own home, and were able to work for longer periods of time. "The bus doesn't go back to the town until half past two in the afternoon, so how were those who can't manage a whole day's work supposed to get back again?" she had asked. What the hell had Rudolf been doing all the way out here? It had seemed so obvious. When she told them why she was there, the helpful staff member called the Church Shelter's office and got the sparse information. Most homeless people went by nicknames. Luckily, they found Rudolf's real name, but they knew little about Verner Thybo, who hadn't shared much about his past. But now she knew his full name, and that improved her chances of finding information on him. He'd been implicated in a traffic accident a few years ago, and she had to be able to learn a little more about it. The woman had also told her about the Church Shelter's other work and the dangers homeless people were exposed to during the icy winter. Last December, two had frozen to death. One in Skagen. He was found in a basement shaft. And one in Horsens, who had been found at the railway station. Was that what happened? Did they die of the cold, but then where did they end up? She automatically stopped for the red light, but her thoughts drove on.

The danger to the alcoholic and drug addict on the street was to fall asleep in a snowdrift after drinking or getting a fix. Anne pressed the middle of the steering wheel a few times so the car horn beeped; the woman in the Peugeot in front hadn't realised the lights had changed to green. And on top of the problem with the cold, there was the issue of the number of beds in the shelters and hostels. Eastern Europeans and Roma had also begun seeking refuge, occupying a third of the available places. Of course there should be accommodation for everyone, the woman had said, but if the beds were being used as an alternative to a hotel room, action had to be taken. Anne hoped that wasn't what Adomas had done—and why should he when he could live with her?

She found a parking space near the library.

The smell of books made her suppress a sneeze. It was years since she'd been to a library, and the changes were noticeable. The digital world had intruded on flat-screen computers and large screens here, too. But luckily the bookshelves were still there—and the smell.

Time flew. She enjoyed the silence and heard only the occasional sound of pages being turned and the odd person sneezing or coughing discreetly.

On 2 August, two years back in the archive, she found the article about the car accident. A person's life could be drastically changed by a single misstep. A foot pressing too hard on the accelerator, and life was never the same again. Changed to life as a homeless person and to death with a rope around your neck. Maybe it really was suicide. Rudolf's case could be completely different to the others who had disappeared. He had probably just wanted to put an end to the suffering that alcohol couldn't eliminate. Now that she was here, she might as well search for details of the drowning accident involving the boy, Marcus. That was more difficult, but half an hour later she was sitting with a four-year-old newspaper article subtitled "Tragic drowning accident in forest lake in Trige" under the heading "Neighbour accused of murder." She read the article, shaking her head in disbelief. Bitten's account that the boy's parents weren't completely normal seemed to hold true. The police had also regarded the case as an accident. There were no signs of violence. Wouldn't all parents have a minor bout of insanity from losing their child? Kamilla had also had a bad time after Rasmus was killed. She had Danny as a scapegoat. Anne came to think of Andreas's stories about belief in Nordic gods. Was it really possible that . . . ?

She found a free computer and opened Internet Explorer, then Google. The search for *Asatru* yielded many hits. Organisations in Iceland, Sweden, and Norway. Some groups chose to stand outside an organisation and carry out their worship on their own or in small groups where they could decide for themselves, as there were no precise rules for how the faith or a blót should be performed, it said. The Elder Edda and the Younger Edda were the most important written sources for the basic elements of the faith, but the verses were open to interpretation. *Hávamál—The Sayings of Har, the High One*—which was part of the Elder Edda, and which was thought to be from the ninth century, was of great importance to most Asatruar. She searched for the name and found the verses that were described as Odin's speech to young Loddfáfnir, giving good advice on how to behave in the world. She couldn't make heads nor tails of them. The language was cryptic and was open to interpretation. It contained 164 verses; she skimmed through them quickly, but one jumped out at her.

*Cattle die, kindred die,*
*Every man is mortal:*
*But I know one thing that never dies*
*The glory of the great dead.*

How were you supposed to interpret a verse like that?

There was also something about Asatru that appealed to her—the belief in nature and the beings that live in it, and the belief in yourself;

that you must provide for your own happiness. That you weren't rewarded for being good or punished for being evil, which was the message of most religions—heaven or hell.

But no one really knew how the Vikings lived when it came down to it, and the fact that you could make your own interpretation of the belief in God and the rituals was what worried her. Could Marcus's parents be right in their outlandish claim?

She scrolled back and forth a bit and stopped at an article. The religious movement Forn Siðr had been approved by the church ministry as a community of faith a few years back. She clicked onto their website and went to the page *Rituals* and then *Blót rituals: Point 4. A sacrifice of some kind must be made.*

# 37

It had begun to thaw. Mist settled over the landscape, blurring the contours of the horizon.

Roland drummed the steering wheel with his fingertips partly to keep the rhythm of a sonata on the radio, partly to keep his fingers warm. He turned onto Pannerupvej and turned off the radio.

Did Anne really have a friend in the collective? She fitted into the category of unique personalities that the collective was characterised by so nicely, but he still couldn't imagine that coincidence. And Verner Thybo was the missing Rudolf, he had learned. He was curious to know what else she had discovered, but it wasn't really his place to contact her. Unless they opened a case into the missing homeless people. Chief Superintendent Olsen would never agree to that. Certainly not as long as there was a murder case to solve.

He parked in the courtyard at Olga and Vagn Mortensen's farm and popped a piece of chewing gum into his mouth while he waited for the killer dog. He kept an eye on the barn door, but it was as quiet as the grave. After a few minutes, he opened the door and stepped out into the snow.

Only Olga Mortensen was home, and for some reason, he felt it was a stroke of pure luck. If he could get anyone to divulge anything about neighbourhood strife, it was her—when Vagn's giant form and stinging cold gaze weren't watching over her, that was.

She opened the door immediately, as if waiting for someone else, and froze. "Vagn just went for a walk with Buster, so . . ." Her voice was already in defensive mode.

"That's fine, then the two of us can have a little chat." He smiled and was already inside. Buster! How could you give a monster that sweet name?

"I don't think I have anything more to say. And aren't the criminals already arrested? I read in the paper—"

"Unfortunately, none of the Lithuanians can be linked to the murder of Albert Hovgaard. And I managed to talk to Signe yesterday. She says hello," he lied.

Olga looked at him even more suspiciously. "How is she? She'll be all right, won't she?"

"She has a broken jaw, but the hospital says she'll be back on her feet again and be discharged soon." He sat down on the couch, and she sat across from him on the other side of a dark-stained coffee table with tiles in the middle and a pot with a resolute red poinsettia.

"You've lived here a long time, haven't you?"

Olga nodded.

"And you are happy to live out here?"

She nodded stiffly again.

"Do you get along with the neighbours?"

A pair of intelligent eyes glared at him. "Where are you going with that?"

Roland shrugged indifferently. "Just a friendly question."

"Yes, we get on fine with the neighbours; there's nothing to report there."

"Nothing with Albert Hovgaard, either? I got the impression the other day that your husband didn't care much for him."

"He doesn't always mean what he says. But of course not everyone has the same interests, so . . ."

"And what interests would they be?"

"That's just what it is. Some neighbours get along better than others, don't they?"

Roland nodded as he remembered the street parties on his suburban street in Højbjerg. "So, Albert not being well-liked has nothing to do with the competition?"

"Competition? You mean the pigs?" Olga laughed. "No, it's not that hard. Our pigs are free of heavy metals and pesticides, and their—"

"So, no competition at all?"

"Definitely not. We are also better known in the industry; we were here first."

"Yes, that's true. Before Albert and Signe Hovgaard, a family lived on the farm whose son drowned in your lake in the woods. That must have been a horrible experience."

Olga's smile died abruptly. She became even paler and clenched her hands in her lap. "It was horrible. But it is also inexcusable to let a boy walk around on his own in a forest with a lake. It was his sister who didn't look after him. She was a bit . . ."

Roland waited patiently. "A bit what?"

Olga pursed her lips tightly into a narrow line.

"Where does the daughter live now; do you know?"

Olga shrugged her narrow shoulders. "She moved with her parents."

"To Sweden?"

"Apparently, yes."

Roland turned his watch. For a moment, the rustle of the chain was the only sound in the living room, then Olga coughed and went out into the kitchen, where she blew her nose and came back with a piece of kitchen roll, which she clasped in her hand.

"Do you remember how old she was then?"

"The daughter?" she asked, not quite understanding, as if she had completely forgotten what they were talking about. "About fourteen or fifteen years old. But why is that important?"

"I don't know that it is," he admitted, not understanding himself why his thoughts kept revolving around the accident. Maybe because the bare treetops in the woods stood swaying in the wind against the steel-grey sky just outside the window. A flock of hungry, frozen rooks had symbolically occupied one tree, reminiscent of waiting black vultures. Scavengers, he thought. He shifted his gaze back to Olga.

"Would such an episode not cause a conflict between neighbours? I know serious allegations were made against you."

"Like I said, we have no problems with the neighbours. It's true, they made some strange accusations, but there was nothing to them."

Loud shouts and Buster's voracious snarling interrupted her; she got up nervously and went to the window. Roland automatically followed, and the sight of the two in the courtyard gave him a moment of nervous palpitations. Anne was shouting loudly, but Vagn was shouting louder. Roland couldn't hear the words as they were drowned out in the dog's aggressive contribution to the debate.

"Who is she? What are they arguing about?" Olga asked herself mostly. Roland was wondering that, too. What in the world did Anne have to do with Vagn Mortensen?

"I'll take care of it," he said, quickly putting on his coat. "But I expect to see you both at the police station tomorrow at nine o'clock for a DNA test."

"What does that mean? Vagn will never agree to that!"

Roland opened the door. "I would advise him to agree to it," he replied, staring at Vagn and Anne. Both were silent as he stepped out onto the stairs and closed the door. He almost cleared the steps in one leap.

"What are you doing here, Anne?" he asked after he had greeted Vagn briefly and glared at the dog.

"Do you know this woman? And what are *you* doing here?" Vagn said with a snarl. He caught sight of his wife in the window, evoking a worried expression on his face, which, in turn, was directed towards Roland.

He pointed angrily at Anne. "She comes here and accuses me of the most outrageous things. Here, on my own land. Is that not a violation of privacy?"

Anne was red in the face from the cold and rage and was about to say something, but Roland took her firmly by the arm.

"I think we should go now, Anne."

She forcefully pulled her arm free of his grip and trudged out of the courtyard with furious steps without uttering a word, passed under the wooden *From Farm to Fork* sign, and disappeared around the corner onto the road.

"See you tomorrow for a DNA test at the station. I agreed with your wife that you're to come in at nine o'clock." Roland nodded a short good-bye to Vagn Mortensen and ignored his inflamed comments on the invitation. If they refused to turn up, there wasn't much they could do about it given that there was no reason to summon them for a DNA test, but Roland still had faith in people's belief in authority and respect for the police, despite it having ebbed in recent years. He got into his car and drove, his insides churning with swelling agitation. Was Anne interfering in his investigation? He reached her further down the road and rolled down the side window. She strode on, fuming, pretending not to see or hear him. Her woolly hat was pulled all the way down over her ears and eyebrows, and her gaze was enraged and directed at the snowdrift in front of her feet.

"Been visiting friends in the collective again?" he asked with understated sarcasm, but she didn't answer. "Anne, stop! What were you doing with Vagn Mortensen?" He suddenly had to turn his attention to the road and swerved at Gunda and Thorkild's farm; he managed to straighten the car and keep it on the slippery road. He drove next to her again.

Finally, she turned her head and looked at him. "You have no idea what's going on!" she yelled.

"And do you? Do you, Anne? Bloody hell!" He had to brake completely when the road ended and the main road began. She walked over to her yellow Lada, which was parked by the roadside, stopped, and lit a cigarette. He saw it as an invitation. He parked and walked over to her with long steps. "Then tell me what the hell is going on! What do you know?" he said angrily. She leaned up against the car, looked at him and inhaled. The smell of the cigarette set his chewing muscles in motion; the chewing gum no longer tasted of liquorice.

"I'm certain that Olga and Vagn Mortensen are Asatruar—they believe in the Norse gods. Not only that. They are Asatruar extremists." There was still rage in her voice, but she tried to control it.

"Asatruar extremists? I've never heard the like!" He put his hand on his head. "Was that what you accused him of?"

"There are extremists in every faith," Anne lectured defiantly. "Why is it forbidden to go into that forest, well? He threw me out—again—when I wanted to go in and look around! Something's going on in there, and that's also what the drowned boy's parents were trying to make the police aware of back then, four years ago. Do you remember the episode?"

Roland smiled a little indulgently. She had apparently caught wind of the case and believed in the attempts of some mourning parents to justify a terrible accident. Only one thing bothered him—how often had she been wrong?

"It's a private forest, Anne. Private means—private."

"But can you not see there is something wrong? Why does Vagn react so violently to me wanting to look in his 'private' forest? What is he hiding in there?"

"Don't start, Anne." He shifted his weight to the other foot uneasily and spat the chewing gum into a snowdrift. "A boy drowned in there. Of course he wants to make sure it won't happen again."

"I'm telling you, something is wrong. I can feel it. The same Asatruar may be the ones abducting the homeless people. Nobody misses them or even declares them missing."

It sounded like she was tossing out random thoughts, without believing it herself, or as if it had suddenly hit her.

"Verner Thybo hanged himself. There is nothing mysterious in that. His fate is quite—"

"Oh, so you finally found out who Rudolf was!" She glared at him. "I know his fate, and yes, it was quite gruesome and possibly a suicide. But haven't you wondered what he was doing all the way out here, when he used to always stay in by the wall on Klostergade? He had a rope around his neck. Just like the Tollund Man."

Roland shook his head, genuinely worried. Perhaps idleness could drive a person to insanity, as someone once said. "He probably went to Fælles-gården," he suggested almost sympathetically.

"No, he didn't. They don't know him there."

They stood in silence for a while. He took out a new piece of nicotine gum from the packet in his coat pocket; she tried to stomp a half-thawed lump of snow to pieces. She succeeded. She threw her cigarette butt on top of it and stepped on it as well.

"We can't open a case, Anne!"

"It doesn't matter; I'll solve it myself." She opened the car door and got in behind the wheel.

"Take care of yourself," he managed to say before she slammed the door and backed out onto the road.

# 38

---

There weren't many customers at the checkout. She had shopped and waited in line, lost in her own thoughts. There was always something to plan in her head for the next day. That hadn't been the case at the paper. Murder and news happened spontaneously; they couldn't be planned—not by photographers at least.

She was putting her goods on the conveyor belt when she recognised the voice that said "Just that, thanks" to the young girl at the checkout. She pretended not to have seen her and discreetly turned her back as she took the next item out of the basket, but she was recognised.

"Kamilla! Hi—it's been ages!"

She turned around and tried to look surprised. "Majken!" Her hair shone red, more than Kamilla remembered. Her eyes shone, and so did the diamond on her engagement ring, which, Kamilla thought, Majken turned very ostentatiously towards her when she stuck her credit card back in her purse.

"How is it going, and how are you feeling? I heard the *Daily News* closed," Majken continued as she began putting her items into a bag while she watched Kamilla curiously.

Kamilla paid and started packing her bag, too. Apparently, Danny hadn't told Majken what she was doing now and how he'd met her and that they would soon be working together on a job for his advertising agency. "I work for an advertising photographer on Nørregade," she replied, grabbing her bag. They'd had so much to talk about once, but now it was like the words had dried up; they didn't flow so easily. Majken put gloves on and stroked her ring finger excessively again in the process. Kamilla really wanted to ask her directly why they hadn't got married yet or at least set a date.

"That sounds interesting. Maybe you could do something for Danny's advertising agency." Her voice trembled a little, but Kamilla ignored it and the question probably behind it.

"We have many clients, advertising agencies in particular. You never know." They started walking towards the exit. Kamilla noticed a twitch at the corner of Majken's mouth. She knew those twitches well; they surfaced whenever Majken didn't like something. Did she really have such little faith in Danny? She knew that Majken had never got over her sister marrying her boyfriend, who Majken had been with for years, and that she would never be able to forgive them for having a child together. Kamilla guessed that Majken had never seen her niece. That episode had ruined many of her romantic relationships because her jealousy had become completely pathological. It had reared its head during Kamilla's relationship with Danny when Majken thought he belonged to her. At that time, Kamilla hadn't known the significance of who he was. She felt nauseated and only wanted to get out of there quickly, into the cold air and take a deep breath. Rasmus had loved Majken; he called her auntie. They had tumbled, played, talked, and laughed together. How could Majken marry his killer? The bag felt terribly heavy even though there weren't many groceries in it.

"You know we're engaged, don't you?" asked Majken as they stepped out of the supermarket.

Kamilla stopped and turned to face her. "Yes, Danny told me." The reply came like a slap.

"Danny did! Did you talk? When?"

"It was a long time ago. Last year," she replied diplomatically. That was when she'd learned he had proposed to Majken. She didn't want to hurt Majken by telling her that they'd talked recently. Once upon a time they had been friends. Very close even. Majken had helped her through the divorce from Jan, when he'd left her for the much younger Nina and walked out on her and Rasmus. Kamilla wouldn't have managed the crisis and grief after Rasmus's death without Majken's support.

Majken stood still like a stone support with a shopping bag in each hand. She clenched the handles so hard that her leather gloves were completely stretched.

"Leave him be, won't you Kamilla? Remember, he's mine now!"

Her voice was small and completely without self-confidence, clinging to the last hope she thought she still had of a relationship and a marriage. A hope Kamilla herself had long given up. It had already happened after Jan left her. And definitely after what happened with Danny.

"Have you forgotten what Danny did? Or is it Rasmus you've forgotten?" The words couldn't be held back any longer.

"I have not forgotten Rasmus. I was very fond of your son, Kamilla. But Danny did his punishment, and he is not an evil man. It was a terrible accident."

"He was driving drunk after a reception!"

"Yes, but not so drunk that it affected his driving. The accident could have happened to anyone!" The uncertainty in her voice had turned into angry reproach.

"Maybe, maybe not. There are just some things a mother can never forgive. Of course you wouldn't know anything about that. But—yes, don't worry. I'll leave him be!" She turned her back on Majken and set off at a furious pace for the Suzuki in the car park.

# 39

An evening briefing had a completely different character to a morning one. The aroma of oregano from the takeaway pizzas filled the room, and several two-litre bottles of cola towered on the table like rockets in launch pads. The staff were both tired and invigorated, partly because the day was coming to an end and partly because Roland had unexpectedly called a meeting, which could mean a new development that could wrap up the case.

Roland did indeed have good news to announce to the attentive faces turned towards him as he sat down at the table and opened a bottle of Coke that emitted a reproachful hiss, like Irene would have done, too. Cola could damage sperm quality, it was said now, but what the hell, they weren't planning on having any more children.

"The Lithuanian driver provided such good information that we were able to arrest two Lithuanian men and two Danes for cigarette smuggling. The Danish National Cyber Crime Centre and SKAT, the Danish Revenue, already had a look at the organisation," he began, pouring the effervescent brown liquid that would soon give him heartburn into his glass. "The counterfeit cigarettes were smuggled from Lithuania to the Port of Aarhus in shipping containers with hidden sides. One of the Danes has long been under suspicion, so his mobile phone was bugged, but without much luck. Last night, they were caught red-handed after the information the driver gave us. The two Lithuanians are identical to those involved in the murder case." He drank the Coke.

Niels nodded contentedly. "So, they're getting what's coming to them anyway."

"Yes, but not for murder. As for the murder of Albert Hovgaard, we are now right back at square one again." Roland sighed.

DS Dan Vang had opened the pizza boxes so that the smell intensified and became almost unbearable. Roland's stomach started to rumble with hunger and carbonation; lunch had only been one quick open sandwich and a bottle of sparkling water in the canteen.

Isabella accepted the pizza slice that Dan handed her on a napkin. "Mikkel and I talked to the neighbours, but no one knows anything about a conflict. Or else they won't admit it. Did you get anything out of Olga and Vagn Mortensen?" she asked, looking at Roland and yawning over her slice of pizza.

"Not much. Did you get them all to show up for DNA tests?" Isabella nodded with her mouth full.

Mikkel answered. His eyes were still dull after his illness. "There were no problems with that. They said they were coming, and I hope they bloody well do. Forensics is ready for them. Why not just see which of them is missing a few teeth?" he added jokingly.

"Two molars, so a smile won't reveal the perp. It would have to be very wide to do that. No, we'll try the voluntary method first, while there are still no grounds for charging anyone."

"If they are charged, they can't refuse DNA testing," commented Vang, avoiding asking the question, although Roland was sure there would have been a big question mark after the words had they been written down. Vang was not the sharpest tool in the box, as they say. In every case, he'd managed to forget much of what he—hopefully—had learned during his education and training in the *Politiskole*.

"No, but we can't charge them when there is insufficient evidence," Roland replied. Finally, the pizza distribution made it to him. "We can really only wait for the tests and the DNA results, but in the meantime, we can look into another aspect. Isabella has looked into a bit already, but an episode today has made me think that maybe we should take a closer look."

"The drowned boy?" Isabella reasoned.

He nodded. "You're already on the case, so will you take it? If you can get in touch with the parents in Sweden, they might be able to give us some information."

Isabella nodded and took notes.

Roland chewed a bite of pizza while considering whether to tell his team about the encounter with Anne and her suspicion of extremist Vikings, but as he viewed the claim as highly unlikely in modern society, he let it lie.

"What does the old case have to do with the murder?" DS Kim Ansager wanted to know.

"You never know. Do you remember anything about it?" Roland suddenly recalled that Kim had been a police officer at the time, and something might ring a bell.

"Only a little. There was some talk about it because he was an innocent little boy, but it was an accident. The autopsy showed no signs of a crime, so the case wasn't investigated any further—as far as I remember."

"So you didn't hear anything about some—accusations?"

"No, the only talk was about how it destroyed the family, but that was it. I didn't know it was Vagn Mortensen's private forest lake he drowned in. But that has to be a coincidence."

"I think so, too," Roland admitted, "but there's no harm in following up on a lead." He welcomed the fact that the chief superintendent couldn't attend the briefing—Roland hadn't filled him in on the plan to investigate the circumstances surrounding the drowning accident. If a missing homeless man didn't merit a case in Kurt Olsen's eyes, a boy in a four-year-old drowning accident certainly wouldn't. Maybe it was a waste of time, but were they wasting time when they couldn't move on anyway?

"Isn't it better that we concentrate on the murder of Albert Hovgaard?" Niels asked cautiously. "Does Leander not have any idea what the murder weapon may be?"

Roland had sat for a long time studying the pictures of Albert's bruised body on the blackboard. Fortunately, he was sitting with his back to them now. The sight didn't sit well with a ham and cheese pizza with tomato sauce.

"His initial speculation was bare fists, but he ruled it out because of the imprints left by the blows. Plus, Albert's hands and knees were also crushed. Leander mentioned that the injuries could have been caused by repeated kicks from someone wearing hard shoes or boots. There was nothing to be found in the house or outside; any traces in the snow would have quickly revealed a hiding place. The techs were everywhere. It's easy enough to get rid of a murder weapon," he replied.

Irene wasn't home when he let himself into the villa in Højbjerg a few hours later. She was having dinner with the women from the social services office tonight. They were going into town, so he didn't know when she'd be home. Angolo met him with a wagging tail and happy barking. Roland knew he had better take the dog out for a quick pee before he took his coat off and went into the warmth. He didn't want to venture out into the cold again when Irene wasn't there to nag him.

The lighting on the suburban street was dim. The snowdrifts by the roadside had melted a little in the thaw and had run onto the pavement, where the freezing temperatures had transformed the water into a thin layer of clear ice that wasn't immediately noticeable until your feet went from under you. Many had ended up in Accident & Emergency as a result. Angolo raised a hind leg at a lamppost and drew a yellow line in the snowdrift behind, which was no longer white. Gravel and exhaust fumes had coloured the snow at the roadside brown and black. No more enchanting bright beauty of winter. Frequented by humans and animals alike, the romance had disappeared. Then again, it was easy to see Angolo's droppings in the dark because they lay in stark contrast to the still-white snow. He bent down and picked up the hot lump in his hand with the plastic bag over it, turned the bag over, and closed it. Roland's legs automatically followed at a quick pace, though he felt the rest of his body wasn't at all present. The cold bit his nose, ears, and cheeks. How long had Verner Thybo been walking around barefoot and in thin, tattered clothes? And wasn't Anne right that it *was* strange that he was so far from the city centre hostels and shelters? Not exactly the right weather conditions for a picnic—not even to hang yourself. He became aware of an oncoming pedestrian with a bandy-legged dog on a leash and pulled Angolo aside slightly. Angolo wasn't about to be sacrificed to one of those muscular dogs that could go on the attack against supposed threats on their turf, especially if their master didn't have enough power over them. He saw to his relief that it was only an elderly woman wearing a fur with a French bulldog who likely went by the term companion dog. When she had passed by, and they had said a polite and brief hello to each other with the implicit look and nod that dog owners gave each other, he wondered at the woman's appearance and the dog's breed reassuring him. Was there not both good and evil in all dogs, as there was in humans, too?

The living room was warm and comfortable after the cold evening walk. Angolo lay down on the couch beside him, enjoying the freedom of when Mum wasn't home. She didn't allow dogs on the sofa, and Angolo never lied there when she was home. Not even when she had gone to bed upstairs and Roland patted the seat next to him invitingly. Roland turned on the television and zapped from station to station without finding anything to watch. He was almost asleep in the unlit room when the phone rang. Aunt Giovanna sounded beside herself. Salvatore hadn't returned home after school. He hadn't answered his mobile, either, and she had found a lot of money in his room. Roland sighed and ran a hand down his face. He turned on the floor lamp and saw himself reflected in the windowpane, facing the darkness of the garden. A tired man, collapsed on the couch with a sleeping dog lying half over him. Giovanna cried, and as she continued sobbing, he felt the dreaded tingling crawl up the back of his neck. She had found a list in his room, too. A list with a lot of names and nicknames. They sounded like bosses. mafia bosses. Along with the money was a folded letter. Her voice shook so much that he barely understood the words when she read them aloud to him. When he hung up, they slowly began to translate into Danish in his brain. The man in the reflection in the windowpane had become even more pathetic to look at. He felt a throbbing sensation in his throat that grew into a large lump. His fears were justified. More than he had anticipated.

# 40

The wind increased in strength during the night. Relentlessly it crept like an insidious snake around every corner and into every nook and cranny, finding her and gnawing at her just when she thought she'd found shelter. If she wasn't so drunk and tired, she would stagger to the nearest hostel, but she didn't even know which direction to go right now. Aarhus was still difficult to find your way around on your own. She drank from the bottle again, believing that the burning sensation in her throat and chest gave warmth to the rest of her body. That the alcohol spread through her veins, dispelling the ice. She thought of Annie asleep in her soft bed or sitting in her cosy, warm apartment with its safe yellow light, like those she could see in many of the windows of the properties opposite. But she wouldn't bother her anymore. Wouldn't ask for forgiveness. She didn't deserve it. She was the one who had failed her daughter, not the other way around.

She tucked herself more into the space by the stairwell door, sniffed and wiped her nose on the sleeve of her coat, which had become dirty like the rest of the otherwise nice coat. The finest she had owned. With stiff, shaking fingers, she lit a cigarette she had bummed off Marie. Torsten was in his warm prison cell in Jyderup State Prison. To think that she could envy him. Not that he even knew what had happened to her over the past year. That she'd been put out on the street. In Nørrebro—the most dangerous place of all. So Aarhus was actually better. Safer. The gang wars hadn't reached here yet. The war on drugs on the streets of Copenhagen probably had to be fought first. It had taken her three days to reach Jutland hitch-hiking. Without the good coat that she'd found cheap at a flea market, she probably wouldn't have succeeded at all. The make-up had probably also helped in this feigned world, where neat clothes and a beautiful appearance were crucial to being a respected person. A thick, sweaty lorry driver with hair like a monk had even made advances. Had offered her money for sex, but she wouldn't sink so low. Drugs and prostitution were the very last resort, she had sworn to herself. But Annie wasn't to know anything about the dramatic downturn. She already had no faith in her mother, understandably. And she was doing so well for herself. She had a job, money, and an apartment with her own furniture. More than could be said for her stepsiblings—Torsten's offspring—whom she had spent more energy supporting than her own daughter. Annie had always seemed so strong, rebellious, independent, and unruly.

She smiled at the thought. Despite Anne's many protests against being sent to her grandma and grandad's farm, where Rose herself had grown up, it had been the best solution. That way Anne didn't have to cope with the whole flock of children when Rose was on her own with them, which she often was, as Torsten went on "holiday" a lot. And Annie had tackled her grandmother and grandfather far better than she herself could at that age. Or had she? What did she really know about how Annie felt about staying on the farm that she herself had been thrown out of because she was pregnant with her? The thought made her stare absently for a moment. Petrified by her lack of insight into her only daughter's life. But Annie had managed to get away, escape, find and develop an ability and skill that she could make a living from. She could write and communicate. Solve murders. Abilities she had never found in herself. She didn't know anything; that was what she had been told her entire life. But Annie had managed to break from that legacy, and she wasn't about to ruin it for her. Annie shouldn't hate her more than she already did.

The alcohol began to dull her mind. Everything became so distantly fairy-like. That was the world she wanted to stay in. If this is what it was to die, then she would let death come. Her eyes closed for a moment, but the dream came before sleep. Faraway and unreal. A warm hand touched her cheek. She beat it away at first, like an annoying mosquito, then it grabbed her shoulder and shook it gently. "Aren't you freezing?" The voice was distant. She opened her eyes, and an outline began to take shape in a fog.

"Aren't you freezing?" The voice sounded caring.

She nodded and became dizzy.

"If you come with me, I'll take you to a lovely place where you can have a hot, fragrant bath, food, and the finest whisky and cognac. Would you like to come?" The foggy figure took hold of her arm and helped her to her feet. Her legs were like jelly, and had she not leaned against the other person, she would have fallen. Protective arms around her frozen body led her, and she willingly followed. Now it was her turn to disappear. Maybe they were much better off there, wherever she was going now. They must have been, especially if it had heat, food, showers, and the finest alcohol. But Tove and Marie should be with her. She resisted and wanted to point out that they had to get them, too, but she was unable to say anything and was gently helped on. She wanted to go, to get better. They reached a dark place in the city where she hadn't been before. There was a nasty stench of rubbish. A backyard somewhere. The sound of a car door being opened. Shortly afterwards, she felt the car's heat and smell. Dusty fabric and leather from the seats. The heating system. She lay down on a soft back seat with blankets wrapped around her. She closed her eyes, and her body tingled as the cold was defeated.

Finally, she could sleep in peace.

# 41

W here were you last night?"

It wasn't meant to be nearly as reproachful as it sounded. She didn't want to come across like a petty bourgeois housewife blaming her husband for a trip to a pub with friends. Certainly not over breakfast rolls and coffee, which he himself had brought.

"I had to take care of the situation with my mates, you know." Adomas poured coffee for her in atonement. Or were the rolls the atonement?

"Have they been released again?"

"Released? What do you mean?"

Anne handed him the knife for the butter once she was finished.

"Don't lie to me anymore. I've read the papers. Aren't the Lithuanians arrested in the murder case your so-called friends?" She looked him straight in the eye and realised she couldn't really be angry with him. Yes, maybe, if Roland hadn't said that none of them could be the murderer. It was clear he was playing ignorant; she was hard to lie to.

"Okay, I lied. Anne, I was afraid you'd think the worst about me and throw me out. We haven't done anything illegal."

"Burglary *is* illegal."

"Yeah, yeah."

"But you were 'only' a driver for the bank robbery, weren't you?"

"Where are you getting this?"

"I have my contacts—in the police."

He squinted at her. "I thought you were a journalist."

"No. Not anymore. I'm unemployed." She stirred sugar into the coffee and wondered whether that status didn't actually suit her quite well, given the way things were at the moment. She had time to investigate the case of the Asatruar and find evidence she could slap on the desk in front of Benito. Triumphant. Of course triumphant.

"But you haven't answered. Where you were last night? With the police?"

He nodded. "I was helping them so they could stop the smugglers."

"Smugglers?!" She was completely out of the loop with what was happening in the underworld in general.

"Fake cigarettes. It was Valdas and Antanas, but they were only couriers. Not my friends. Now the police can catch the guys behind it."

"And you were able to walk away free?"

"My information for my freedom." He chewed and rinsed it down with coffee.

"Adomas, do you know what you did? You may be in great danger now. Do you think that will be forgiven? Snitching isn't a safe business."

"I'm no snitch!" he replied brutally. "And I'm never going back to Lithuania."

"But they can find you here!"

He shrugged indifferently.

She poured more coffee into her cup. "Do you really mean that—that you don't want to go back?"

"Yeah, I found a new job."

"You have? Where? Here in Jutland? On a building site?"

"No, there's not much of that at the moment. I got myself a paper round." He smiled and started laughing when she did.

"A paper round! Stay away from the newspaper industry, let me tell you!" She threatened warningly with a teaspoon.

"I can earn more doing that than with a good job in Lithuania."

Anne studied him as she drank from her cup. That was the attitude you should have. It doesn't matter what you do; it's just a means to an end. No prestige positions to brag about, so it sounded like you were bigger than you were. Maybe that was the path she should take. Take whatever work there was. Live from day to day. She reached across the table and caressed him on the cheek. His stubble, which had grown longer than usual and was beginning to soften, tickled her hand.

"Don't worry, I'll support you," he said teasingly.

She became quiet, staring down at her cup. Wasn't there something about being able to see the future in coffee? Or was it in coffee grounds?

"Adomas, it's not going to work between the two of us. You're my cousin."

"So what? I'm crazy about you!" He smiled boyishly, completely unconcerned about their familial relationship. And now she knew the answer to the question she had been asking herself so many times over the last few days—yes, you could absolutely fall in love with your cousin.

"We're family. Family members don't just become lovers. It's a mess." She put another half a bread roll on her plate and reached for the butter. It was like a Sunday morning, even though it was only Thursday.

"How's your mother?"

"We need to talk about this, Adomas."

"Why? The most important thing is that we love each other. Why don't you want to talk about your mother?"

"I've no idea. To answer your second question, I probably just don't care about my mother."

"Anne!"

"She feels the same way about me. If you knew how she just always—"

"I know she's let you down many times. But she hasn't exactly had it easy herself, you know. Your dad was killed when you were little, she couldn't get help anywhere, and your grandmother and grandfather didn't want to know about her or you."

"You seem to know more about my family than I do."

"It's about being interested, Anne."

"Okay, I just don't give two shakes of a lamb's tail about my mother." She got up and took her cup and the empty plates out to the kitchen sink, and she began to rinse them off. He came out with the rest and helped her. A hand stroked her arm as he reached for a washed glass to be dried. Next time, it roamed to her chest. Every fibre of her body trembled with desire for him. Another touch ended with a kiss and led them to the sofa. Anne smiled as he pulled her jumper off. No, she had not become a petty bourgeois housewife. She was still the same untameable Anne she had always been, and now she had finally found her opponent.

She ran her nails round in the black hairs on his chest while she counted the freckles on his pale skin. He was so perfect. Perfect in the right way.

Not "perfect" perfect. A freckle, a little spot, a birthmark—all the things that professional image processers removed when a model was to appear in a fashion magazine. He had all that. He was a real human being.

"Well, let's get back to the dishes," he whispered into her hair.

She lifted herself up onto her elbow and kissed him. There was barely enough room for the two of them on the narrow sofa. "Wow, this is so much better than working. Can't we just live like this forever?"

"Eat, love, and sleep. And why not really? But you love working, don't you? What else keeps you away for most of the day?" he asked.

She enjoyed the little touch of jealousy in his voice as if he feared she had someone else tucked away. She told him about the drowning accident in the forest lake and her suspicion that Asatruar had crossed way over the line and had something to do with the eerie accident.

He looked at her suspiciously and stroked a lock of hair away from her forehead.

"Do you believe that, Anne? Isn't that just too far-fetched?"

"Why does everyone say that?" she protested, remembering Roland's worried gaze.

"Everyone? Who else have you talked to about it?"

"Oh, nobody. I just voiced it to someone who didn't believe me, either. But I'm sure I'm right, and I'm going to prove it at any cost, even if they deny it . . ."

"Do you mean that you've contacted them? Anne, you need to stop this. Murder is a cruel accusation, and suppose you're right, then . . ."

She kissed him on the chin. "I *am* right! It's rare that I'm wrong. But don't worry, babe. I'm used to dealing with criminals." She sat up. He slowly ran a finger down her spine so that a pleasant shiver ran through her again. Then she put on her knickers and bra and pulled her jumper over her head. "So let's do the dishes!"

# 42

hope you can speed things up?"

"Turbo DNA testing, of course." Gert Schmidt nodded understandingly. "What about those who don't turn up. Can you charge them with something, if necessary, so we can . . . ?"

"One of them we can. Hash."

"The guy from the collective?"

Roland nodded. Gert sat down on the edge of his desk and skimmed through the report. His loud voice suited him. He looked like someone who had always had to speak loudly to be heard—and seen. He was small, smaller than Roland, with liver pâté–coloured hair that was almost the same colour as his skin, and he had bright, almost invisible eyebrows and pale light brown eyes that also blended in with the whole picture. His glasses encircled his eyes with round frames like John Lennon's. As far as Roland knew, he was also a big fan of Lennon's music. Of the Beatles in general. He was a skilled forensic technician and had quickly climbed the ladder to be head of the department. Younger than Roland, though by how many years, he wasn't sure. Even Gert's age was indeterminable.

He laid the report down on the table and folded his hands in his lap. "It was unfortunate that the DNA didn't match the Lithuanians—for us. But I can reassure you that if it is one of the neighbours who committed the murder, then he can't escape the DNA results."

"Or she," corrected Roland.

"Or she. There was also one woman who didn't want to be tested." He took the report and looked at it again. Bitten Mørk. Thorkild Hansen, Vagn Mortensen, and Brian Kjeldsen also refused. But that doesn't make them guilty since they are within their full rights to not want to hand over such an important part of themselves. The keystone of mankind."

"No, not even to help themselves. If they are innocent, the tests would rule them out."

"But it could also lead to them being charged for other things. Old, forgotten things they don't want to come to light."

"The press isn't making it any easier. Just look at the eerie murder case from New Year's Eve that our colleagues in the Central and West Jutland Police departments are dealing with. Who wants his picture on the front page of *Ekstra Bladet* and to be portrayed as a rapist and murderer and have his life destroyed long before he is convicted—or acquitted?" Roland replied.

"You're right. That kind of thing makes people afraid to come forward. You can quickly end up branded a murderer. In the old days, they were probably hanged from a tree, nowadays they're lynched on Facebook. What's worst?" Gert got up from the edge of his desk and sat down in his chair behind it. "Do you want a cup of coffee?"

"I'd prefer something stronger," Roland admitted.

"Is there anything stronger than *that* coffee?" Gert smiled crookedly as he picked up the insulated coffee pot on the table. He poured some out and handed Roland the mug. "So you got the cigarette smugglers?"

"Yes, thank God. But we also let a criminal go. Olsen made a deal with the driver, who fled the robbery at Jyske Bank in Kolding. He is free again."

Gert leaned back in his red leather office chair, which looked more like a comfortable armchair. Not like Roland's scratched version in worn black Oxford fabric. It spoke for itself: Schmidt's work was to whiz around and examine, not to loaf around in comfort in an office.

"Was it perhaps a smart move by Kurt? But a perp is a perp as they say, right? Were those cigarette smugglers worth that much?"

Roland swirled the coffee around in his plastic cup. It produced just as good "legs" and "tears" as his formidable and expensive red wine. "Time will tell. My feeling is that he might have been pressured a bit heavily by the Danish National Cyber Crime Centre."

"Of course, given that they had them in their sights. It was *their* big chance for a breakthrough. But to let a criminal go free. That doesn't seem like Olsen at all."

"No, he was an accomplice, and maybe our paths will cross again, but now we have his DNA at least."

"That we do!" Gert smiled proudly at his share in that fact. "And we also just have to rely on the superintendent's assessment."

"Mm."

"Anyway, I've also looked at the other little thing you asked me about." He put some pictures on the table. Roland leaned forward to get a better look. They were close-up images of the marks that the murder weapon had left on Albert Hovgaard's face.

"The depressions in the wounds are deeper in some places than others. We tried to find objects that could fit such a shape, but it's not easy. If we assume that it was something that was at the crime scene, then it's impossible to guess what it might be."

Roland drew one of the pictures towards himself and inspected it more closely in the white light from the snow coming in through the window. "How deep are the deepest?"

"About five millimetres."

"Five millimetres? That's not much. Was that really enough to kill?"

"It was the force of the blows that killed."

"Is it possible that it could be a pattern on an object?"

"It's not unthinkable, but do you have an idea?"

Roland put the picture back on the table and shook his head. "Have impressions been made? Maybe someone would recognise the pattern."

Schmidt smiled. "You watch too much *CSI* on TV, Roland. It's not that easy. The wounds have closed, so you can't just pour plaster in them and get an exact pattern."

Roland nodded, embarrassed. He had seen it being done on television. "So, we're looking for something of a certain weight and with a pattern where the highest point is about five millimetres."

"I don't know about the weight. Something light that swings with great force could cause the same damage as we see here." Gert pointed to a close-up. "But what's the motive? That's what you're working on now, too, isn't it?"

"Yes. It all sounded so damn easy, Gert. A home robbery committed by an Eastern European gang that got surprised by the residents and went on the attack."

Gert pushed the picture with his index finger. "But isn't it just a tad too violent in that case? Wouldn't the robbers just have knocked them out and disappeared as quickly as possible?"

"Yes, but it's not uncommon for Eastern European perps to be brutal. If they really were after the weapons, then they would have opened that cabinet, and if Albert Hovgaard tried to resist, then they may have panicked and acted based on that. That would make sense."

"Yes, it all sounds plausible. But that's not the case according to the evidence. Do you really think a conflict with a neighbour could end in murder? Who found him? Wasn't it his wife?"

"Yes, but she only *thought* he was dead at the time. He was lying on the floor and didn't answer when she called him and shook him. It was Ella and Finn Geisler, the closest neighbours who Signe ran to for safety, who were first on the scene. But by then he was dead." Roland looked at his watch. He had a meeting with Kurt Olsen in an hour but would like to have a little more time with Gert. Olsen was panicking over the case. The press was being very judgemental, and one interview after another with citizens dissatisfied with the efforts of the police filled the front pages of the papers.

"Has the victim's wife seen the pictures of her deceased husband?"

"No, for God's sake, she is obviously emotionally distraught. Seeing those photos would affect her too much. She's also the victim here."

"Did she say what she saw?"

"What do you mean, Gert?"

"I mean, is it conceivable that Albert Hovgaard didn't look like this at all when she found him? It amazes me that the forensic examination of her on the night of the murder didn't show blood underneath her feet. If she had stood by her battered husband, the blood would have been impossible for her to avoid."

"She ran barefoot into the snow over to the neighbour. I guess it must have—"

"Still, if she had stood in the middle of a pool of blood, snow wouldn't have been able to remove all of it. There were no footprints in the blood, either."

Roland hurried to take a piece of chewing gum. His hands needed something to do. He would like to have lit a cigarette.

"Haven't you stopped that yet?" Gert chuckled, nodding at the packet.

"No, now I have to break *this* habit," snapped Roland, not finding it at all funny.

Nothing was funny today. It wasn't only the murder case that was bothering him. He had talked to Giovanna this morning. Salvatore still hadn't come home, and Roland had felt a huge desire to grab the first flight to Naples. After all, it was his family, and he wasn't free from feeling guilty, either. But Irene had sent him to work and said she would keep in touch with Giovanna and let him know if there was any news. She felt guilty, too. It was she who had decided it was time for Salvatore to return home. And now . . .

"Burdens aren't something to get rid of; one overtakes the other. Apparently, we have to bear some," Gert comforted him, still smiling.

Roland got up. "I'll take these pictures here if that's okay?"

"Of course it is. So, you're going to follow up on it?"

"Definitely. It's an important detail that escaped our attention. If it is the case, we have a completely different situation."

He took the stairs down. Needed to move and stamp the frustration out of his body. There was something about Gert Schmidt's theory. Why hadn't he thought of it himself? Blinded by the obvious. But could he show Signe Hovgaard the terrible images? If she really hadn't seen her husband so banged up that night, it could tip her completely over the edge. And if she hadn't, it also meant that the murder had taken place after she left him to seek help from the neighbour. And how would it affect her to have that knowledge? He could hear the anxious trembling in her voice again when she asked him if she should have stayed with Albert. So how would she take it, knowing that yes, perhaps if she had stayed, he'd be alive now?

# 43

Her stomach rumbled from all the tea she had drunk in the collective. It had been rosehip tea this time, and it tasted good but was rather diuretic. She needed to go again already. It was so embarrassing to start by asking to use the toilet of a stranger and an Asatruar at that. What did a Viking's toilet look like? A hole in the ground? Ignorance was most often grounds for prejudice. But she would be there soon, so it was just a matter of holding it a bit longer.

Andreas knew more about Vikings than about Asatruar, but he knew Kasper, a student of religious studies at the university, and he had called him and organised for Anne to meet him and find out more.

At least the house at the address in Holme looked quite ordinary. There was smoke coming out of the chimney, so she figured there was a wood-burning stove or a fireplace—an open fire, perhaps? Was there straw on the floor? She smiled to herself. It probably wasn't that bad.

The young man who opened the door was also an ordinary student. Light shoulder-length hair and curious blue eyes. Knitted jumper and worn jeans. He smiled as they greeted and introduced themselves and showed her the door to the toilet. That was also quite ordinary, but very cold, as the window was slightly ajar.

"So, what is it that you'd like to know about us," Kasper asked after they had sat down and she had declined refreshments.

"I just want to hear a little bit about how you . . . live."

"If you are thinking of becoming an Asatruar, just sign up with the community you would like to be a member of. You have to vouch for the basis of our faith, and—"

"No, that's not why I'm here. Not at the moment anyway," she added to not sound prejudiced. The worn-out title of journalist was raised and polished again.

"Okay, but as you can see, there are no sun wheels on the wall or homespun wool kirtles." He laughed.

"Does that mean that you don't live like Vikings on a daily basis, but only come together at those blóts when you make a sacrifice?"

"It differs a lot. I can only speak for myself. I'd rather describe it as a view of life and the world than a faith."

"So you couldn't imagine there being extremist Asatruar?"

"How do you mean?"

"Well, for example, Asatruar who would sacrifice people as the Vikings' ultimate offering."

He laughed heartily while shaking his head. "That sounds pretty comical," he said when he finally stopped laughing. She felt her cheeks burn, and she was absolutely as hot in the head as she felt.

Kasper grew serious again but still had tears in his eyes after the outburst of laughter. "The only scary thing I know about Asatru is the unfortunate connection between Nazism and Norse mythology, which was created by Austrian nationalists. Right-wing extremists have always seen the Aryan human race—the proud, blond, Nordic Vikings—as superhuman in relation to non-Aryans, also called animal humans according to List, who are to be eliminated. Just think of Hitler."

"You mean racism?"

He nodded. "The Ku Klux Klan also uses the sun wheel as a symbol, and the swastika has been so thoroughly contaminated by the Nazis that we Asatruar can't really use it anymore. In the association's constitution, there's even a clause against racism, and unfortunately, it's there for a reason."

"But right-wing extremists can't just call themselves Asatruar, can they?"

"Some of them consider themselves that. But such interpretations of the Asatru are very far from ours, from the ancient sources and the handed-down sagas. They use mythology and religion to legitimise a narrow-minded racial theory and xenophobia. That's not the same as being proud of your cultural heritage and thriving with its practice. Unfortunately, it's too smooth a transition for some." He leaned back in his chair with a very worried look on his face. "Are you sure you don't want anything? I have homemade blackcurrant juice from the garden."

Anne glanced out into the snow-covered garden and smiled suspiciously.

"I freeze them and make the juice from the thawed berries."

"Okay, that sounds great."

"Now that it's so cold, I usually warm it."

He got up and went out into the kitchen. She looked around at his stuff as she wondered at the new information. Could Vagn Mortensen and the rest of the clan be Nazis or right-wing extremists? There was still a lot that didn't make sense. What did they want with homeless people? Most of them were part of the Aryan race, too. Did they regard them as *vargr*—wolves and criminals, fugitives and foes?

Kasper came back in with two glasses of steaming hot blackcurrant juice. She sipped it and praised him—it was not ordinary.

"There's no alcohol in it, is there?" she asked as she remembered that Vikings seemed to like that kind of thing.

"Not at all. Only honey, and that's homemade, too. Under the snow out there, there are both hives and a greenhouse. I try to be as self-sufficient as possible."

"There's a little Viking in you then." She laughed.

The hot drink made her cheeks flare even more. "Do you live alone?"

"No, my girlfriend lives here, too. She's a nurse and is at work."

"Is she into Asatru, too?"

"Not as ingrained as I am, but she participates in the occasional blót because she thinks it's nice and cosy."

"Nice and cosy?"

"Yep. Nice and cosy. It's about coming together for a common belief. The Old Norse culture interests me a lot. It's no coincidence that I'm studying religion. Asatru is definitely the one that best suits my outlook on life."

"How many do you think there are in Denmark?"

"There are no exact figures, as there are unknown groups around, but Forn Siðr—which is the largest association in Denmark—has over six hundred members."

"How and what do you sacrifice if it's not people?" She smiled as if she now also found it comical.

"Most Asatruar sacrifice outside, so they are at one with nature. A blót can also take place in your own garden. Some do it when they've baked bread, for instance, and want to give something back to nature."

He added by way of explanation, "So they sacrifice one loaf of bread in the garden when they have baked three."

"And the gods are completely satisfied with that—bread?"

"The gods are happy with everything. Some sacrifice jewellery or things they have made themselves." His hand danced out in the direction of a shelf housing several strange symbols carved in wood. They looked like runes and probably meant something.

"Did you make them yourself, too?"

"I did. Sometimes, of course, a chicken or a pig can be sacrificed, which we then eat spit-roasted over the fire with mead, but that's no worse than Danes roasting a pig in Mallorca."

Anne smiled at the comparison. She finished the warm juice and thanked him many times for the information. It hadn't confirmed her suspicions. Done the opposite actually. Maybe it was just too fanciful an accusation from a not-quite-normal family.

On the way home, she drove to the shelter on Mejlgade again. It had been a long time since she had seen her mother, and Anne didn't like the thought of her living on the streets anyway. Adomas was right. It was probably best that she lived with her daughter, and didn't you owe your mother that much? After all, she birthed you.

She found Tove sitting alone at a table, bent over a cup of coffee. She looked sick. Anne sat down at the table and asked about Marie and Rose. For a brief moment, Anne wasn't sure whether Tove knew who she was. She slowly shook her head and looked up at her wearily. It took a while before Anne saw in her dull eyes that she recognised her.

"Marie is sleeping somewhere with someone she knows. She has the flu. Your mother disappeared. They've taken her, too."

# 44

Anita locked herself in her room. If Andreas and Linda didn't realise soon that Brian and Bitten had to go, then she would leave, even if she hadn't carried out her plan. So many unexpected things had made her think twice about whether it was worth it. Bitten and Brian had been the only ones in the collective not to voluntarily submit to the DNA testing by the police—didn't that just show that they had something to hide? The test hadn't been that bad. Seriously! And now they were quarrelling loudly about it down in the living room, and it wasn't even Friday—that was tomorrow when it would all start over again.

She threw herself on the bed. The springs kept rocking long after she settled. She took a book from her bedside locker and tried to read. It was getting difficult to have enough calm to study, and wasn't that the whole idea of moving into a collective for students? A door was slammed hard downstairs. She put the book down and stared up at the ceiling. Tried to find sounds to listen to other than the argument. Had it been spring, the evening songs of the blackbirds and all the other little birds would surely have been able to drown it out. There were many birds in the area because of the forest. But now there were no sounds out there. Even they were frozen stiff. It was quiet downstairs, too, now. Thankfully. She hated fighting. Locking herself in her bedroom and pulling the duvet over her head so as not to hear wasn't an unfamiliar situation for her. But this time, she wasn't the reason for the loud shouting. She could not feel the unbearable guilt that had gnawed at her. She suddenly remembered that she had some chocolate in the drawer and struggled to sit up. She sighed when she got up to open the drawer. Marabou Daim, her favourite. She tore open the wrapping and inhaled the aroma of the chocolate. The scent made her mouth water. She shouldn't, but she needed it; she could lose weight later. For the summer. Bikini season, as the women's magazines called it. She was just about to take a bite when there was a knock on the door. Annoyed, she put the chocolate back in the drawer and pushed it in with her hip. A bottle of pills rattled as it rolled from one side to the other.

"Have you locked yourself in?" exclaimed Linda, respectfully standing on the right side of the doorstep. Their rooms were their domains. The place where they could always be at peace and have some privacy.

"You disappeared so suddenly, I just wanted to see if you were okay?"

"I *am*. I just hate those fights. Would you like to come for a moment?"

"May I?"

"Of course." Anita opened the door completely and let Linda in. Maybe this was the right time to talk to her about the proposed eviction so she could persuade Andreas in turn.

Linda went to the window and looked out into the darkness. "You have a good view from here. This was actually Andreas's room when he was a boy."

"Was it?" Anita sat down on the bed.

"You're happy here, aren't you?"

"Yes, of course I am. It's just Brian and Bitten. It's going to end badly if we don't . . ."

Linda turned to her and sat halfway up the windowsill. "Andreas and I have talked about it, but to put it bluntly, we can't really throw them both out, financially speaking."

"We can get two new people instead."

"We're not sure we can, Anita. Andreas is afraid that he's going to have to close the collective and sell the farm."

"How about renting out the horse boxes like you talked about?" suggested Anita persuasively.

"It takes time to find those kinds of renters. But let's see, maybe Andreas is right that the two of them will settle in. They haven't been here that long and are probably still getting used to life in the country, too. It was lucky that you adapted so quickly. You didn't grow up in the city, did you?"

"No . . . we moved a lot when I was a child. New schools all the time. But we always lived in the countryside. Maybe that's why I settled in so quickly." She tried to smile convincingly.

Linda jumped down from the windowsill in a smooth motion that only gymnasts can perform. You couldn't even hear her as she landed on the wooden floor.

"It's calm down there now. Everyone must have gone their separate ways, I think. It's getting late, too, and tomorrow is a new day we must get through before the weekend. I'm glad you're okay, Anita. Sleep well." She patted her lightly on the shoulder as she walked past. Anita got up and locked the door behind her. She started shaking at the thought of the chocolate and ate it way too fast. A two-hundred-and-fifty-gram king-size. Why didn't they make them in five hundred grams or larger—a kilo? She smiled at the thought and lay back on the bed with her book.

She must have fallen asleep and woken abruptly. The book lay on the floor. The clock showed it was just after midnight. She heard it again, the sound, and jumped up from the bed. From the window, she saw him walking down the road. She made a quick decision and hurried down the stairs, hastily throwing on a coat and boots. She grabbed her hat and gloves on the go and only pulled the hat down over her ears and put on the gloves when she was outside. It was time to hurry. Whatever he was doing at night might get Andreas and Linda to realise that she was right. There was no light to be seen in the windows of the conservatory, so Linda wasn't sitting out there and watching her leave. It wasn't long before she caught sight of Brian as a dark silhouette in front of her. Breathless, she slowed down her pace. He walked sluggishly, almost as if he were sleepwalking, and did not look back. She stopped as he disappeared into the woods. Her heart stood still, and her legs wouldn't listen. They felt like jelly. He lit a torch, and the cone of light disappeared between the trees. A deep breath, where she gathered all her willpower, made her legs listen again, but her breathing was fast, hyperventilating. She followed in his footsteps and stopped at the fence. Here, where it was joined, was an opening of about forty centimetres. Brian was so thin that by turning sideways, he could squeeze through; the footprints continued on the other side of the fence, and deep in between the trees, in the dark, she saw the flickering light from his torch. The fence was too high for her to climb over. Even if it had been lower, she would have been unable to lift her heavy body over it. Besides, she was wearing a long skirt, not exactly the most practical outfit. Something in that forest attracted Brian. She almost vomited when she thought about what it could be.

# 45

Did you promise him that today? Why in the world am I only hearing it now?" She could never have spoken to editor Ivan Thygesen like that, but Pierre just smiled and looked mischievously at Oliver as he adjusted the umbrella so the light was right when the models showed up for the shoot. They were expensive enough per hour as it was, so they weren't going to make the models wait too long because of that kind of detail. Pierre always thought of the clients' wallets.

"Wait now, who's the boss here?" he said with laughter in his voice.

Oliver was on his way out to a customer to photograph a furniture display. He had just finished packing the car and came in to pick up the last things, scratching his full red beard and looking questioningly at Kamilla. "And why shouldn't there be equality in our industry, too? They're calling for more female managers everywhere." He knocked on the doorframe a few times, smiled, and left.

"No doubt he'd prefer you as a boss," Pierre said, looking down at the viewfinder on his camera.

"I mean it, Pierre. You could have said yesterday. I'm sure you remember that my, my . . . nephew is coming today. You said so yourself that it was okay, and I have to take pictures of him, too."

Pierre straightened up with an annoyed expression on his face. "I did not know yesterday, Kamilla. Danny called me late last night, and as it fits nicely into your programme, I said yes. I am also sure that your nephew will think it's exciting to help photograph burglar alarms. When is he coming?"

"He'll be here soon." She looked at her watch. "When's Danny coming?"

"He said nine o'clock. He promised to bring bread rolls and Danishes." Pierre began photographing a mannequin that he was using as a stand-in for the models, again to keep track of the light before they arrived. Kamilla knew he didn't want to be disturbed when he was concentrating. She closed the door and went into her own studio, where the famous burglar alarms were ready. Butterflies were flying around her stomach as always before a big, demanding job, but this time there was some extra violent fluttering in between. Maybe it was good she had not known he was coming in, otherwise, she might not have come in today. In any case, she wanted to avoid having to spend an entire day with Danny, but she had to just think of it as a job and ignore who he was. *He's a completely ordinary client like all the others.* She repeated in her head several times so it became a mantra.

"I brought Danishes with me. And—Mathias."

She winced at the sound of his voice behind her and turned towards the door. He stood with a bakery bag in one hand and the other on Mathias's shoulder.

"Hello," Mathias said, a huge smile all over his face.

"Hey, Mathias . . . Do you know Danny?"

Mathias put his head back against Danny's coat and looked up at him confidently.

"I promised his father I'd take him up to you; it's all right . . ." Danny began.

"Mum and Dad were in a hurry to leave. They had to make a ferry," explained Mathias as his curious eyes now roamed around to all the exciting equipment in the semi-dark studio.

Kamilla put the camera on the tripod. "Do you know his dad then?" She wasn't going to look at him. See them together. Mathias came up to her and looked at the camera, squatted down, and looked directly into the lens.

"No, I met them outside as I was on my way up. They said he was coming to spend the day with you, and so we came up together."

Pierre had heard Danny's voice and came out of his studio. They went into the kitchen while talking, and she tried to catch her breath.

Couldn't Danny see that Mathias resembled the boy he killed that March night?

"I've really been looking forward to today. When are we going to take the pictures of me?" Mathias asked eagerly.

"We'll do that soon, but first you have to help me take some photos of these burglar alarms." She showed him the alarms and the drafts and explained what they were going to do. He smiled excitedly.

"Do we have time to photograph all of them?"

"I don't know how many we'll have time to photograph. But as many as we can."

"At least it's not school. I have today off."

"Yes, your dad said so."

Pierre came in and said hi. "So, this is your little helper. Would you like a roll and a Danish?"

"I just want to get this ready, so . . ."

"Come on, Kamilla. Danny bought breakfast bread for all of us. It takes no time at all to set up. Shouldn't she come to the kitchen with us and have something to eat?" he asked Mathias, who, of course, completely agreed.

For the rest of the day, she tried to avoid any close contact with Danny. Several times she smiled a little at his chat with Mathias behind her as she photographed and sent dazzling flashes across the dark room. He was good at talking to children, she had to admit. She watched them secretly when Danny explained to him like a teacher how they were going to use the photos she took. His engagement ring gleamed in the light. Did Majken know he was here?

Mathias was curious and involved, asked question after question, and wanted to try to "snap it," as he put it, which made both her and Danny laugh. He tried his hand at being a photographer and stood behind the camera in the same way that Rasmus had done. Legs slightly bent and shoulders pulled too high up. It wasn't just in the face that they looked like each other.

Pierre came in with big sandwiches for lunch and they took a break in the studio. They sat on the bar-stools that were usually kept for model photos, but they were being stored in her studio because there wasn't enough room in Pierre's today.

They ate without talking much. Only Mathias blabbered on about school, the trips with his dad on the fishing boat, the beach in the summer. Danny questioned him and listened with interest when he answered as if he were talking to an adult. Mathias spotted a tall, thin photo model on her way to Pierre and stretched his neck. Pierre, who went out to receive her, noticed it and asked Mathias if he would like to see a model shoot. Mathias jumped down from the high stool and disappeared excitedly into Pierre's studio. The silence became suffocating until Danny broke it. "I assume it's not sexy lingerie Pierre has to photograph. I doubt Mathias's parents would be happy to hear that."

"It's fur. But even it was lingerie, I don't think it would matter much. That kind of thing can be seen everywhere nowadays. You just have to look at some shop catalogues."

Danny smiled and nodded. "You're right." He drank some of his sparkling water. Do you really have siblings, Kamilla? I didn't know that. Pierre said Mathias is your nephew."

"I only said that to him so I'd be allowed to have Mathias here with me today. He's . . . the son of some friends."

"You could have had me fooled. He's a lot like you—the eyes and . . . You could easily be family."

She quickly wiped her fingers on a paper napkin. So, he could see the similarity. Not with Rasmus, of course. But with her.

He seemed to want to say more, but to her relief, Mathias came back. Taking pictures of fur wasn't so exciting anyway. They agreed that they probably only had time for a few more shots before the weekend. They could take the rest on Monday.

"And then it's your turn to be a model," she said to Mathias, changing the lens of her camera. Danny packed the burglar alarms they had finished with into a box. Mathias got a mirror and a comb and began to style his hair.

"You don't need to look *too* nice." Danny laughed. "You'll look like someone on their confirmation instead of a naughty kid." He tousled the well-groomed hair. "I was photographed for my mum once, too. She didn't think it looked like me in the picture at all because I'd styled myself too much." He had put on his coat.

"You're not going now, are you? Oh, stay, Danny, please!" pleaded Mathias.

"Danny is finished for the day, so I'm sure he wants to go home and start the weekend," said Kamilla.

"I'd actually very much like to stay and see you as a model, Mathias. I've nowhere else I need to be." He took off his coat again.

Kamilla looked down at the viewfinder in the camera as he tried to make eye contact.

# 46

———————

The results of the DNA tests still hadn't come. And they called it "Turbo!" Roland sat, trying to gather courage for the task he had imposed on himself. Kurt Olsen had praised the new turn in the case that otherwise appeared to be at a dead-end. Roland hadn't mentioned that it had actually been Gert Schmidt's idea. Sometimes you had to take the praise you got, even if it wasn't earned.

Signe Hovgaard had been discharged from the hospital and gone back to the farm. Her son was staying with her until she was more able to deal with things. If ever. The idea of whether it was worth fighting to defend your property had often surfaced in recent times. But wasn't it a natural human reflex? We defend those—and that—we love. Or, at least some do. Other people take and force their victims to choose whether they want to fight or leave it be. Maybe die because they chose option number one. And what is more precious than life?

He got up and put the pictures in the bag. If it was the case, as Gert had suggested, he would soon be forcing a survivor to relive her ordeal once again. And where did he himself stand in the investigation? If the perp turned out not to be one of the neighbours, then it was a random outsider. He consoled himself that the DNA samples would soon determine the case, unless the murderer was among those who had refused to participate in the testing, but they would have to cross that bridge when they came to it.

* * *

He stopped for red on the coastal road of Kystvejen. The cranes by the harbour stood like long-necked giraffes against the steel-grey sky, peering out over the sea. At some point, they would—according to the plans—be superseded by the so-called Lighthouse of 142 metres, making it Denmark's highest residential building surrounded by both homes and businesses built in wave architecture. Not to forget the chimneys and the foul smell of burned soy and grain from the agricultural company DLG Group, smoking upwards to the outer layers of the atmosphere, and where there were no rules for how much odour might bother the seagulls or the inhabitants on the upper floors. The financial crisis had stopped the construction project for a while, and it was now decided that it should run in two stages, the high-rise apartment block would be built in the final phase. The first stage was the lowest part, which contained a hotel and housing. The iceberg and the Z-house would also be part of the new modern port. Architecture of the future in glass and strange shapes; not at all to his taste. Where was the charm—the kind you found in the old brick houses? The plan to make the port area more attractive was indeed an excellent idea, but why did abstract and different-thinking architects have to test their projects here? He knew the answer well and followed the queue on the turning lane towards Nørreport when the light changed to green. A quarter of an hour later, he passed the Japanese Gardens on Randersvej, which he could hardly get Irene out of every single summer. What did it look like with snow?

Shortly afterwards, he drove onto the field road up towards Signe and Albert Hovgaard's country property. Diagonally to the right between two trees, the cross stood almost buried in snow. The symbol of another tragedy that had also happened here. Anne's claim made him smile a little. This time, she was really out of her depth, even though it was a bad choice of words in that regard. Editor Ivan Thygesen might have been able to put her in her place.

The police cordon was gone, and the door was no longer sealed. It was too late to do it all over again now anyway if it turned out that the murderer was to be found somewhere else entirely. The house had been scrubbed from top to bottom. One way to try to wash away what had happened.

It was the son, Erik Hovgaard, who opened the door. "Mum is resting right now. Coming back here has been traumatic for her."

Roland nodded understandingly and took off his boots on the mat in the hallway with its beautiful bright tiles. He dared not tread on them with boots full of salt and gravel.

"I made coffee. I thought you'd . . ." Erik went into the living room. It didn't look like the same one Roland had been in just over a week ago when he questioned Ella Geisler. It was tidy and neat; no broken glass and earth on the carpet or the presence of the white powder used by Forensics. Roland glanced into the study as he walked past the open door. The gun cabinet, the gold medal, and all the pictures of the smiling winner were gone. Only the desk remained, as if the plan was to use the room for another purpose now. He sat down in the chair with the chequered plaid. Erik brought in the coffee, handed him a cup, and also sat down. He looked tired. Tortured. Stooping and falling apart. A merciless way of losing your father. And the funeral couldn't take place until they released the body. Now it might drag on even longer. How could you find a way to move on before the funeral?

"Are you any closer to solving the murder? Now that it wasn't the blasted Lithuanians who murdered my father?" His grief and helplessness had turned into bitterness and hatred.

"Unfortunately, we don't have any suspects at the moment, and there are a few things we need to be sure of before we move on."

Erik Hovgaard nodded. He was the youngest son. Just turned thirty but looked about sixty. Roland found the pictures and laid them face down on the table. "Do you think your mother could face seeing some pictures from the crime scene . . . of your father?"

"What kind of pictures are these?" He was immediately on guard.

"Do you know what your father looked like when your mother found him in the kitchen that night? Has she talked about it?"

"Yes, he was dead! Could it be worse?"

"No, not much, but . . ." He drank from the cup to gain time to think about his words. "Was he his normal self to look at, or had he been beaten?"

"Mum hasn't said anything about him being beaten. What does that mean anyway?"

"It's very important. If your father wasn't beaten when your mother found him, then it means he was attacked later. That is, while she was with the neighbour getting help."

Erik looked at him uneasily and then at the photos with the reverse side up. He reached across the table and went to turn one over, but Roland quickly placed a hand on it. "If you want to see those pictures, I have to warn you that they . . . It's not a pretty sight. I wanted to show them to your mother, but if you know anything, we can spare her."

"What can you spare me?" Her voice was still a bit clipped because she couldn't use her jaw muscles normally yet. Signe Hovgaard was standing in the doorway of the living room, her blouse and skirt were wrinkled, and her hair was pressed flat on one side of her head.

Erik got up immediately and walked over to her, and he put a protective arm around her shoulders. "Mum, go in and lie down again. I'll talk to the detective. You need peace; they said so at the hospital."

"What can you spare me?" she repeated, having not moved her gaze from Roland. The bruised eye, now almost healed, was half open, like a week-old kitten with the same matte tinge in the eyes. She walked slowly to the table and sat down stiffly in the chair where her son had been sitting. He remained standing, resigned.

"Mrs. Hovgaard, we need to know how your husband looked when you found him. Can you describe him?"

She forced her thoughts back, frowned, and pursed her lips reluctantly to remember. They were dry and cracked and not sparkling red as in the wedding picture Roland had noticed on the shelves behind her.

"He looked like himself. But there was no life in him when I shook him. He . . ."

Roland waited.

"He seemed to have fainted. He was bleeding a little from the back of his head, probably from when he hit it on the floor . . . or because one of them had hit him . . ."

Roland shifted his gaze from the wedding picture and what there once had been and tried to look her in the eye. *Remain neutral.*

"So, he was not beaten in any way?"

"No, as I said, I thought he had fainted, and as Ella and Finn went to first aid in the autumn, I thought they could help . . ." She began to cry silently, her hands clasped in front of her mouth.

It moved her son out of his petrified position. He squatted down in front of her and grabbed her shaking shoulders, then he looked pleadingly at Roland. "Isn't that enough?"

Roland nodded and gathered up the photos. Signe Hovgaard shook herself free of her son's hands, her voice under control again. "I want to see those pictures!"

"No, Mum, leave it," warned Erik.

"I want to see those pictures," she repeated. "It's important for me to see them, otherwise, I will always imagine the worst."

The pictures were the worst she could imagine, but Roland had to be sure, too. He laid one of them in front of her on the table. She stared at it, turning her head slightly at an angle, like a hen, in order to see with her healthy eye. Her clasped hands almost disappeared into her mouth, holding back a scream.

"That was not what Albert looked like when you found him, was it?" Roland asked gently.

Her voice didn't obey. She shook her head instead and kept staring down at the table where the picture had lain, even after Roland had removed it and put it in the bag along with the others that he did not care to show her.

"Did you see him again when you came back?"

It took a long time before she answered. Her voice was almost inaudible. "No . . . it was just Finn. He went into the kitchen . . . Ella helped me into the bedroom, and a little later the police came . . ."

"Mum, come on, I'll take you into the bedroom so you can rest again." He sent Roland a warning look, forbidding him to ask more. Signe followed sluggishly as Erik grabbed her and helped her back to the bedroom. He closed the door behind him. They were in there for a while. Roland could hear a soft mumble as if the son were trying to reassure his mother. Sometimes he wished others could take over this part of the job. He emptied his cup and got up when Erik came out of the room and again closed the door gently behind him.

"There is just one more question. When you spoke to my colleagues last week, you mentioned something about a dispute with the neighbours that your father had mentioned to you. What was it about?"

Erik put his hands in his trouser pockets. He was also clearly upset by the sight of his father's bloody, unrecognisable face. He would have been hard to identify if he hadn't been found in his own home.

"Yes, that's right. He mentioned something was going on and that he was investigating it further. Apparently, it had been going on for a while, and Dad found something that would probably upset a few of the neighbours if it came to light."

"Did he mention what it was?"

"No. He told me on my birthday last summer. I think he must have had a little too much white wine." Erik smiled awkwardly.

"So it's not something you took very seriously?"

"No, I asked Mum, and she doesn't think there were any problems. Dad could see them in even small, insignificant things."

# 47

She remained sitting in the car with the radio on. AC/DC's "Black Ice" wasn't that easy to turn off.

Maybe this was where the Lithuanians had parked and monitored the farms. She fished in the bag of Malaco's Favorit Mix and stuffed a piece in her mouth without taking any notice of what it was. She kept an eye on the road between the farms. What was she trying to find? Maybe Tove was wrong, and her mother was sitting safely and warmly in a shelter somewhere. And why had that particular piece of information brought her out here in the country again? She took another sweet. The sugar helped a little, she convinced herself. Nothing was happening on the road. Covered in snow, the farms looked completely deserted. More snow had fallen last night. Almost five centimetres on top of what was already there. She could see some of the treetops in the woods. At the end of the nearest field road with poplars on each side, the rooftop of the farm where the murder had happened could just be seen. Signe and Albert Hovgaard's.

She had been waiting there for half an hour when she spotted a car slowly driving between the naked poplars and the piles of snow on either side of the road that a little tractor with a snowplough had made. She realised it was Roland Benito's car.

"Shit," she mumbled, chewing enthusiastically on a piece of liquorice as she contemplated flooring it and getting away quickly. The yellow Lada screamed its presence to all and sundry, practically luminescent in the white.

He could not help but see her. The car stopped when it was next to hers. He rolled down the side window and motioned for her to do the same.

"We can't keep meeting like this, Anne," he said without reproach. "Can you be at the station in an hour? I'd like to know what you know."

"I don't know anything. And . . . you still don't believe me."

"We'll see. See you in an hour."

He had already rolled up the side window again and driven off without hearing her refusal.

What harm could come from showing up? Get to see the police station from the inside. Roland's small, cramped office with stacks of papers and enjoy the canteen's strong coffee once again.

She was asked to wait. Meanwhile, she thought about how time was a strange concept. Usually it went so fast that you could barely keep up, but right now it felt long. Infinitely long. When she finally entered his office, he was buried in work as if he wasn't expecting her at all. He only looked up when she cleared her throat. When was the last time she'd been invited here? Not since the Doll Child murder. She tended to make her presence known unannounced.

"Take a chair, Anne." He poured coffee for her—also a new move on his part. She always had to ask for it or help herself.

"Unfortunately, I don't think I can help you with anything this time," she said as she sat down.

He handed her the mug. "Maybe I just need to talk to you a little." His smile was crooked. So he'd grown sharp, too. Maybe that's how he was to other members of the press. A side she had never seen in him before.

"May I ask what you were doing near the crime scene—again?"

"What were you doing?"

He looked at her angrily—now she recognised him. "We are in the process of solving a brutal murder, as you well know. But *you* have nothing to be doing out there. Are you still investigating the kidnapping?"

"Yes and no. Something strange is going on in that small, remote farming community."

"What, pray tell?" Roland raised his dark eyebrows with interest.

"There's a little too much of a connection between all the things that are happening. The murder of Albert Hovgaard, which was not committed by the Lithuanian gang—so who then? Rudolf's disappearance and that he is found dead nearby with a rope around his neck. The boy who drowned under mysterious circumstances in the lake on the same road?"

"Things can happen at random but still look like there's a connection. The boy drowned four years ago. How do you connect that to a murder that happened during a home invasion?"

Anne shrugged. "That is what I am trying to find out. Have you taken a closer look at the case involving the homeless?"

"The case with Verner Thybo is closed. Suicide. If other homeless people really have disappeared, then they are not being reported missing. So what do you want us to do? If more homeless people disappear, and it is reported, we will of course take it seriously, but right now we can't—"

"Rose Teresa Larsen has disappeared. My mother."

"*Your* mother?"

She nodded as tears welled in her eyes. Why did that have to happen right in front of Roland Benito? She told of her mother's unexpected visit, how she had thrown her out and later found her in the shelter on Mejlgade. She failed to mention her Lithuanian father and Adomas. They weren't part of the case.

"When was the last time you saw your mother?"

"Hmm, probably four or five days ago."

"And you're sure she's not gone off somewhere. Back to Copenhagen maybe?"

"I don't know," she admitted. "But I have the feeling that something is wrong. Mum and some other homeless women had begun to investigate what was going on. Maybe they got too close, and—"

"So you suspect someone of abducting them? Vagn Mortensen, perhaps?"

She nodded.

"Promise me you'll stay out of this, Anne. You sneaking around playing detective makes the investigation worse."

"So you also think there is a connection?"

"No, not at all, and that's exactly why you should let us deal with it!"

"Does that mean you're going to take the case now?"

"Do you want to report your mother missing?"

She nodded eagerly and had to remove something that tickled her cheek. It was wet.

"Then I will ask you to give us an accurate description of her—possibly a photo, too."

Anne's mother, imagine. Luckily, she hadn't mentioned Vikings or gods this time. He wouldn't have been able to take her seriously if she had. But the tears in her eyes had affected him. That tears had been in them at all. Not even when the stepfather had been close to killing her had he seen a single one. But who was she, the woman who was the mother of the indomitable Anne? Homeless, apparently.

He got up to go up to the canteen and get some food but was stopped by DS Kim Ansager before making it out of the department.

"We have received a missing person's report that we have to take seriously," Kim said eagerly.

"I know. Of course we'll take it seriously."

"You know? But I just got it." Kim's eyes shone with astonishment behind his glasses.

"Yes, Anne Larsen's mother, right?"

"Anne Larsen's mother? Has *she* disappeared, too?"

"Too? Who else?"

"Anita Andersen from the collective. Andreas Poulsen just called. They haven't seen her since Thursday night, when she locked herself in her room to get away from a quarrel between some of the residents."

# 48

They were looking through all the images on the computer screen. Kamilla knew more about editing in Photoshop than Danny did, even though he ran an advertising agency. He had people for that, he said in his defence.

"Your mum will be delighted with that picture," he said, looking over Kamilla's shoulder as she adjusted the contrast. Mathias hung over the back of the chair behind her and followed it all with a well-satisfied grin. She could smell him. A little sweaty after the day's many different experiences. Rasmus's scent. Danny's scent mingled with it. She had difficulty concentrating on the screen and was relieved when she heard Pierre talking to a man outside the studio. She recognised her father's voice, as did Mathias, who immediately ran out to him to tell him about his day.

"Well, I really should be getting home, too." Danny put on his coat.

"Yes, it's a long way to drive to Risskov when the roads are slippery," she said with her back to him.

"I'm not going to Risskov. Why do you think . . . Oh. No, I still live on Badstuegade, over the advertising agency, so it's not that far."

As long as he didn't think she was fishing for information. She wasn't interested in where he lived. Or when he intended to get married, for that matter.

Mogens Arnskov came into the studio and greeted Danny.

"Thanks for accompanying him this morning. We had a bit of a rush to make the ferry; we only made it because I didn't have to bring him," he said, hugging Mathias's shoulders.

"No problem. It was nice to get to know him."

Defiant, she tried to look Danny in the eye when he formally shook her hand before departing. But it didn't succeed for very long. He went.

"Dad, you need to see the pictures!" Mathias pulled Mogens over to the computer. He smiled at Kamilla and nodded contentedly.

"Mum is going to be thrilled with them. She's waiting in the car, so we better get going. You can send the pictures to me when they're ready—and your invoice, of course."

She nodded, disappointed. She had hoped to have the opportunity to be alone with him and Mathias for a moment; the day had gone so quickly. Too quickly. And Danny's participation had not been part of the plan. She shut down the computer, turned off the lights in the studio, and followed them out into the cloakroom. She put on her coat and shouted goodbye to Pierre. They went down the stairs and out into the street together, where all three of them, as though it had been agreed, pulled their collars well up around their ears and shook in the cold wind. Mathias complained that he was hungry, and Kamilla had to admit that there had been no time for anything other than a big sandwich for lunch. Mogens stated authoritatively that Mathias would have to wait until they got home, but that could take a little over an hour. Kamilla felt guilty about not taking better care of him.

"Don't you drive by Grenåvej?" she asked, continuing after Mogens nodded. "I live in Egå; you're welcome to come over and have some food if you don't have to hurry home. I have a cat," she said to Mathias to entice him further.

Mogens said they weren't in a hurry but that he'd better check with the boss in the car. After it was decided, Mathias shouted, "Yay!", "Yay!" Kamilla said they could just drive behind her.

On the way, she wondered what she had in the fridge. It had been a long time since she had been so impulsive as to invite guests without being sure of what she could offer them, but there was at least always rye bread and cold cuts.

Tarzan greeted them in the hallway, and Mathias immediately made contact with the cat, who was craving attention after a long day in solitude.

He didn't use the cat flap these days. The snow in the garden was far too cold and deep to venture out into.

She found some food in the fridge and beer and lemonade. Mathias was ravenous and ate eagerly. Afterwards, he sat on the sofa with Tarzan and played with him—the old, lazy, relaxed cat actually bothered to play.

"He's always wanted a cat," Alice said.

"Has he?"

"I think it's a shame for it to be alone so much. Despite children's eagerness to look after the desired pet, it's always the parents who have to take charge in the end."

Mathias protested and assured his mother that he would definitely take care of a cat if it looked like Tarzan, and then he asked Kamilla if he could call his cat the same.

"Forget it, you are not getting a cat!" said Mogens.

Alice's words were the same as those Kamilla had used against Rasmus. Words she had since regretted so much it almost hurt. She looked at Mathias. You think you will always have them, but . . .

"Who is the boy in the picture over there?" Alice asked, interrupting her thoughts. She got up and walked over and took a closer look at it. "It's incredible how he looks like Mathias. Have you seen that, Mogens?"

Mogens nodded. "Is he family?"

It took a while for her to pull herself together and tell them what had happened to Rasmus without mentioning Danny. She referred to him as the "motorist." As always, that kind of information turned a happy mood into a gloomy one where no one dared say anything. She wanted to tell Mogens that he was his grandson, but it seemed wrong to bring that up now—Alice and Mathias shouldn't be there when she revealed who she was. They sat in silence for a long time until Kamilla asked if anyone would like coffee and if Mathias would like another lemonade. She remembered she had some cookies, too.

The little party broke up an hour later. Mathias hugged both Tarzan and Kamilla and accompanied his mother out to the car. Mogens asked if he could borrow the toilet, excusing himself for having too much beer and coffee. He was in there for a while, so she took the cups off the table and put them in the dishwasher. She did not hear him coming, so the voice behind her, which suddenly sounded rough and different, startled her.

"Who are you? I demand to know who you are!"

She turned and saw anger in his eyes.

"What do you mean?"

"Follow me!" He took hold of her arm, hard like she was a naughty child, and dragged her out to the bathroom. He pointed to the washing machine, and only now did she remember that she had put the picture there when she was washing her jeans. The picture of the boy in the knitted jumper on the fishing cutter on Agger Strand. Her mother's brother, who had drowned and was never found.

"Where do you get that picture from? Tell me who you are!"

"It's a picture I found in my mother's Bible when I was emptying her apartment after her funeral last October," she replied hoarsely, not looking at him.

"Your mother! Who is your . . ."

He let her arm go, leaving a throbbing pain. That was not how she wanted to tell him. "My mother was Gloria. Gloria Svendsen when she was young. The boy in the picture is my uncle. He drowned when he was six years old because she and—"

"I know the story," he cut through. The anger in his eyes had been replaced by an expression she had never seen in any human before. He staggered as he moved backwards away from her and almost stumbled out the door.

"No, Dad. Don't go like that. I was going to tell you, but—"

He held his hands up in front of him and turned his head in a grimace as though he feared something was going to fall down on him. It was a rejection of the life he had left behind, and which had suddenly appeared from the gloomy darkness of the past in the form of a black-and-white picture on a washing machine. A rejection of her. He turned his back to her and left.

# 49

"January may be the coldest month in twenty-five years," said the radio news announcer. Roland certainly thought so; he couldn't remember when it had ever been so cold or there had been so much snow in Denmark before. A roof had collapsed under the weight of snow on a pigsty, but no pigs had been injured. He tuned it back to DR Klassisk. It was the same news reports as half an hour earlier. Nothing much new happened in little Denmark, either. That's why they had to repeat the news over and over again on both radio and television, where there absolutely had to be so many news broadcasts. But they could talk about the record low temperatures forever, and the relentless winter would apparently continue. There was a forecast of even more snow and ice.

Naples was thirteen degrees Celsius, Giovanna had said on the phone last night. There was no contact from Salvatore yet, but now the Carabinieri were on the case, and they were taking it very seriously. None of his father's old colleagues were left on the force, but everyone knew who Adriano Benito was. His picture hung in the local police station. Roland faintly recalled the picture that had previously hung in the living room just above a white bust of Our Lady until his mother decided that it should hang where it belonged. The black uniform, the neat cap, and the trousers with a red stripe down each leg. He was elegant. It was only from that image that Roland knew him. Faint memories might surface, but what did—or could—a four-year-old remember? Maybe it wasn't even the picture he remembered, but the image of a dad that his mother had described to him. Did the Camorra know who Salvatore was? Would there be a demand for ransom soon? Or were there completely different reasons for why the kid hadn't come home? A girl maybe? *L'amore?* He truly hoped so.

A salt spreader was taking its sweet time in front of him. "*Pazienza*," he said aloud to himself. Patience was the only criterion on the roads at the moment. The salt depots were being emptied, so they had to use coarse sand or gravel mixed with a little salt in many places. Denmark was never prepared for an icy winter. This salt spreader didn't seem to be relieving the shortage.

*Pazienza* was also the only thing he could have as far as Salvatore was concerned. Irene reassured him that there was no news. Though he hadn't told her everything. Not the part that made him guilty. But he needed to talk to someone. He thought about how close he was to Henry Leander's house and turned off at Kragelunds Allé. Of course it wasn't polite to arrive unannounced, but Leander had never minded before and tended to offer a whisky when he dropped by. However, they didn't get to see each other that often outside of working hours. But why not change that? The year wasn't so old that it was too late for new resolutions.

The house was built of yellow brick and always reminded him of Aarhus University—not as big of course, but still a considerable size for a detached house with a basement for Leander's "pets." There was light coming from the living room window, so luckily, he was home. Roland rang the doorbell and looked out over the garden with its snow and the icicles on the garage roof while he waited.

Leander looked puzzled. He was in casual home attire.

"Benito! That's a surprise!" For a moment it looked as if he wanted to slam the door in his face but then changed his mind. He glanced at his watch, surrendered with a small sigh, and opened the door to let Roland in. It smelled nicely spicy—not how it usually smelled in the forensic patholo-gist's home. Roland took off his coat and followed Leander into the living room. He couldn't help but stare at his backside in the tracksuit bottoms. Leander always wore a smock that hid it. *So, that's what it looks like.* There were two empty coffee cups and cognac glasses on the coffee table. A fire was lit in the fireplace, and the television was on a channel with perpetual food programmes.

He smiled in astonishment. "Do *you* watch that?"

"No, it's not really me, but . . . Sit down." He turned off the TV.

Roland sat down and looked at the cognac glass in front of him. There was lipstick on the edge. "I'm not disturbing you, am I?"

"No, well, I might as well come clean . . ."

A door opened somewhere nearby, and there was the sound of approaching bare feet on the parquet floor. Roland was not at all surprised to see her. The same could not be said for her.

"Benito! God!" Her hands flew up to her cheeks; she, too, seemed to want to turn around and disappear back to wherever she'd come from. She looked quickly at Henry and smiled as he nodded that it was okay. She offered Roland her hand by way of greeting and sat down in the chair next to him, close to the fireplace, which was emitting a pleasant dry warmth with the scent of birch-wood. She, too, was in leisure wear. A cream-coloured velour lounge suit that matched her hair, tighter than Leander's, and which clearly showed how much weight she had lost since he first saw her during the investigation of the Doll Child murder.

"I was already well aware," Roland revealed.

"How could you be? We've been so careful."

"He's Italian; they have a sense for that kind of thing," Leander replied, then turned to him. "Would you like a cognac?" Roland nodded, and so did Julie when asked if she wanted one more. "It's the weekend," Leander apologised as he poured. "And it doesn't need to be a secret anymore. Julie's divorce will be finalised soon, and then we're getting married."

"Cheers to that and congratulations!" Roland raised the glass.

"But what brings you by at this time?" asked Leander after they had taken a sip and tasted it in solemn silence.

"A sudden urge on the way home. I needed a man-to-man chat."

"I'll go then," said Julie without sounding offended or angry.

"No, you shouldn't. It might not be a bad idea to have a specialist in criminal profiling here."

"Sounds serious," she said.

Roland told them the whole story from the beginning about Salvatore's work for the "rubbish" mafia, where he and other fourteen- and fifteen-year-olds made a lot of money in jobs that would cost them their lives because of the chemical waste they had to deal with. He told them about his little holiday with them and how Aunt Giovanna had sent Salvatore to Denmark to get him away from the criminal environment in Naples, and about the showdown he'd had with his much younger cousin when Salvatore and Irene started getting on each other's nerves. "But now he has disappeared, and the Italian military police are looking for him. I have to admit that most of all, I want to go home and help them," he concluded, noting that he had unwittingly called Naples *home*.

"And you think it's the mafia that has him?" asked Julie.

"I'm afraid so."

"But Salvatore only helped them," Leander objected.

"Maybe I was wrong about him." Roland swirled the cognac around the bottom of the glass, and the colour changed from orange to caramel in the glow of the fire. "Giovanna went through his room and found a lot of money. His earnings from a dangerous job. She also found a list, and she thinks it's the names of mafia bosses that he's sniffed out during his work."

"Oh dear!" exclaimed Julie.

"Does that imply that his aim is to work for them? That he has, so to speak, been working undercover?" asked Leander. He reclined in the black leather chair with his hands folded around one knee, resembling an aristocratic count with his white handlebar moustache in all its glory and the cognac glass on the table in front of him.

"Maybe not all the time; I don't know. There are indications that he has been writing down the names for a long time, as there are so many, but perhaps not to reveal them."

"But why then?" Julie also sat with her glass, warming the contents in her hands.

"For contacts later—who knows? The thought of exposing them must have come from what I told him." He emptied the glass, put it on the table, and sighed. "I told him what a good Carabiniere his uncle had been and reminded him that La Camorra killed him. I also said that by working for the mafia he was mocking his family's great work of fighting the criminal organisation. What my father sacrificed his life for." He needed another cognac but wouldn't beg for it.

"And you think that made him want to follow in your father's footsteps?" Leander let go of his knee and leaned towards Roland.

"Probably not exactly by joining the force, but he wrote a letter to his mother. It was with the money. I don't remember what was written exactly, but it was something about his mother using the money if something happened to him, because he intended to expose the bosses so he could avenge the death of Adriano Benito."

"Your father?" asked Julie.

He nodded.

"So you feel guilty about what happened," she said quietly, laying a warm hand on his arm. Roland began to understand what Leander saw in her.

"Naturally. Had I not told him, he might not have had that thought, and perhaps he has now given the Camorra reason to . . ." It must have been the cognac that had relaxed his tear ducts. Or the exhaustion after a long day with lots of frustrations. He took out the handkerchief he always had in his pocket for the bereaved and wiped his eyes.

"You haven't done anything wrong, Roland. Maybe nothing has happened to him," comforted Leander, "but if he continues to work in that job, it will be certain death."

Julie nodded.

Roland stuffed the handkerchief back into his pocket and tried to smile and look relieved, but he was far from it.

For the next few hours, he sat with them in the pleasant, dry heat and enjoyed another cognac. They talked about Leander and Julie's relationship, the impending divorce, the difficulty of keeping everything a secret, and the relief that he now knew. Roland didn't regret dropping by when he got up to go home. He had called Irene earlier in the evening and told her he would probably be back late. Work. Julie remained seated in front of the fireplace; Leander followed him to the door. As he put on his coat, Leander stood twisting the tip of his moustache between two fingers. His white bushy eyebrows were raised, and his always attentive eyes, which had seen a bit of everything, followed Roland's movements.

"It was good you came, Roland. I thought it was about work, but it turned out to be a completely private issue. I was going to ring you early tomorrow anyway because I wanted to tell you something I discovered late today."

Roland looked at him uneasily.

"My substitute apparently took the slightly easy route on the autopsy of the homeless man. Young people, you know yourself. So I decided to look at him again as we still had him cooling. He did not die by suicide . . ."

Roland dropped his glove but didn't bend down to retrieve it until the forensic pathologist had finished speaking.

"There were faint traces of rope around both his wrists and ankles. He was tied down to something. Like a sacrificial animal."

# 50

It felt completely forbidden to be here after the meeting with Roland Benito at the police station. As long as he didn't turn up—but he probably wouldn't on a Saturday morning.

This time she had driven all the way up to the collective and parked out on the road in front. Snow had only been cleared from the garage to the road in the form of several repeating tyre tracks and whatever the undercarriage had taken with it, so she couldn't park in the courtyard. Not healthy for the old dark grey Volvo Estate. She could see into the garage where the door wasn't closed. It had snowed inside. The car had road salt on the wheels and far up the sides. They had to be home now for the weekend. She wanted to talk to Andreas again; he had to know more about the family who had lived on Signe and Albert Hovgaard's property, and maybe he knew where they had moved to after the death of the son.

"Oh, it's you," Linda said disappointedly as she opened the door.

"Are you waiting for someone?"

"No, but—"

"May I come in?"

They were gathered around the table in the kitchen and eating breakfast.

"No, we just thought it was the police with good news," Linda said as she sat down. She pulled out a chair for Anne.

"Or that Anita had come back," Andreas added, handing her a basket of bread rolls, but she had just eaten with Adomas.

"Where is she?"

"Gone. It's like she disappeared in the snow," said Bitten, who wasn't wearing make-up and looked completely vacant and pale in the face.

"She must have gone out Thursday night. I talked to her in her room that evening. She had locked herself in because we had got into an argument—she doesn't like that." Linda looked at Andreas worriedly.

Anne took off her backpack and set it against the wall next to two food bowls on the floor. They looked like water and dry food for a cat or a dog, but she saw no pets. "What were you arguing about—not that it has anything to do with me but . . ."

"It was because Bitten and I wouldn't take the fucking DNA test," Brian whispered. "But the police aren't getting their hands on a part of me for their own use in the future. My fucking DNA is my own!"

Bitten nodded approvingly, and Anne was inclined to do the same. She didn't trust the system enough to just hand over her genes and chromosomes to law enforcement, whatever the cost.

"But as you haven't done anything, it doesn't matter if they get it. Refusing implies you have a guilty conscience," protested Andreas, and Bjørn warned against starting up the quarrel again.

Anne pondered whether that could be the reason. Was she afraid of being caught for something if the police got her DNA?

"It's precisely because we are innocent that they shouldn't have it. You don't go around handing out your national identity number to all and sundry, do you?" Bitten shouted, knocking a cigarette out of its packet. She took a lighter out of the pocket of her tight short skirt and was about to flick it, when Linda cleared her throat loudly, lifted a finger towards her, and pointed outside. Bitten grumbled with the cigarette between her lips but got up and scowled at Linda before disappearing into the utility room.

"Has Anita been away since Thursday night?" asked Anne.

"Yeah, when she didn't come down for breakfast yesterday, I went up and knocked on her door, but she didn't open. She wasn't at her seminar, either."

"Has she not been to bed at all?"

"It looks as if she only lay on top of the covers. Her book was on the floor, as if she had dropped it or jumped out of bed."

"But why would she do that?"

"I have no idea," Linda replied. "She didn't say anything unusual when I spoke to her. She said goodnight when I left."

"And you've reported her missing, I understand?" Anne wasn't going to mention she had also reported her mother missing.

"Yes, but the police think that we should just give it some time, that she might be back soon. They experience that a lot with young people, they said. I thought you knew that since you came. As a journalist, I mean," Andreas said.

Anne nodded; she had completely forgotten that was what she was. "But that's not why I'm here now. I would like to hear whether you can tell me anything more about the family that lived out here before Signe and Albert Hovgaard moved in. You were neighbours. Did you play with the children? There was a sister, too, right? You don't happen to know where they moved to, do you?"

"So many questions! I don't know much more than what I told you last time. That they were very religious and strange. So you're not finished with your article?"

She quickly shook her head.

"They were much younger than me. I mostly played with kids the same age—and probably not with girls at all."

"How much younger were they?"

"I don't really remember. Was there maybe an eight- or nine-year difference between the sister and me? A little slip of a thing—that's how I remember her. She always looked like an apology for herself. Her brother, Marcus, was quicker."

"He was younger than her, wasn't he?"

"Yes, a lot. The sister had started school when he came along. They had tried to have another child for a long time because they wanted a boy. When they had given up, it suddenly happened. And it was a boy. The wished-for child. And then he drowns. Tragic and unfair."

"And do you know where the family moved to?"

"To Sweden, I think."

The cat came in with Bitten. She stank of cigarette smoke. It was a grey-striped domestic cat that was missing the top of its tail. Many farm cats caught their tails in the combine, she remembered from her stays in the country. It ran to the food bowl without noticing all the people sitting at the table. Bitten almost stepped on it as she sat down on her chair.

"Shit, it's freezing! Why would Anita go out on a night that was even colder?" she said, shaking her shoulders and pulling them all the way up to her ears, her face scrunched up.

"Maybe she has a boyfriend somewhere we don't know anything about. She's probably just out to get herself a little—"

"Shut up, Brian! And why do you go out at night?!" The words came angrily from Linda. Afterwards, the corners of her mouth twitched when it dawned on her she had said something wrong.

Brian's vulgar smile died. He glared at her. "What the fuck do you mean?"

Linda's cheeks turned red; her voice trembled a little when she answered. "I've seen you walk at night . . . several times. After midnight. What do *you* do? Are you going out to get a little . . . hmm?" She glanced at Bitten.

Brian jumped up from the chair so it almost fell on the cat, who was fleeing in panic. "Are you spying on me, bitch?" he shouted, which brought Andreas to his feet.

"Do not call Linda a bitch, or . . . !"

They faced each other like two snorting bucks in heat, until Linda grabbed Andreas's arm and pulled him down onto the chair again.

"He did not mean it like that, my love."

"But you didn't answer," Andreas snarled, not moving his gaze from Brian.

"Brian has always gone on night-time hikes," Bitten said. "No need to wonder about where he goes."

"How do you know he's not meeting another girl?" asked Bjørn, who had followed the scene with disgust in his eyes.

"I just know," Bitten replied, smiling at Brian.

"Did you go out on Thursday night, too?" asked Anne.

Brian's gaze moved towards her in a way that made her skin crawl.

"No, I didn't go anywhere," he replied.

# 51

In the centre of town, it was hard to see that nearly eight centimetres of snow had fallen over the weekend. Here was only slush. Brown slush reminiscent of melted dark brown sugar. His boots slipped around in it as he walked across the police station car park. It drifted down from the roof, and the wind stung his ears. The thermometer showed minus ten degrees Celsius this morning, and with a wind speed of seven metres per second, it corresponded to a "wind-chill effect"—as it was cleverly called—of about minus twenty-five degrees Celsius. Brabrand Lake was frozen, so you could cross it to and from Stavtrup. It had been years since that had last happened. He ran the last stretch to come into the warmth quicker.

Leander's words about the homeless man had been ruminating in his head since Friday night. *Like a sacrificial animal,* he had said. Why did he have to use that phrase? It had helped a little to talk to him and Julie about Salvatore's fate. No one seemed to believe that anything had happened to the boy. But they didn't have his knowledge of the nature and malevolence of the mafia—confirmed in the *Corriere del Mezzogiorno*—which he always bought when on holiday in Naples, mostly for the sport section.

He took the lift up. The team was gathered in the briefing room, chatting away, and they did not stop because he entered. They did, however, when Kurt Olsen arrived.

"The murder case has taken a new turn," began Roland. "After a conversation with Signe Hovgaard, we have a new lead." He paused to

judge whether they were all listening. Only DS Vang was more preoccupied with the snowdrift from the roof outside the window, but he
looked intently at Roland when he cleared his throat and continued.
"Albert Hovgaard was not beaten when his wife ran to the neighbour
for help; we must, therefore, *keep in mind* that he may not have been
dead at that time. Signe thought he was only unconscious and ran for
help to revive him."

"Why don't people learn first aid?" Mikkel commented emphatically.

"The murder happened between two o'clock and a quarter past two
according to Signe Hovgaard's statement, though she is unsure. But as Ella
and Finn Geisler are saying the same time, plus or minus a few minutes, we
have to assume it's around then."

"What does pathology have to say to that?" asked Kurt Olsen, who was
tilting his pen back and forth between two fingers. He was always impatient, especially when under pressure.

"As they were already unsure about the exact time of death, they
haven't been able to deny that the murder happened later in the night
than they noted in the report."

"But then that doesn't exclude the Lithuanians—they might have
returned," Dan reminded them.

"You're right, but the DNA tests exclude them, so we're not spending
any more time on them." Roland rummaged through his papers.

"The DNA results are due this afternoon; I just talked to Forensics a
few minutes ago." Roland looked over at the chief superintendent and nodded, smiling. Finally good news from the Turbo case.

"Anything else?" He let his gaze wander over the small group.

"I managed to track down the boy's family in Sweden, and I talked
to the father yesterday afternoon, or at least I tried to. They aren't very
happy with the police after their experience when Marcus drowned, so
they weren't willing to tell us anything. Certainly not when it was in connection with the fact that we wanted to reopen the case, and . . ."

Roland was just about to shush Isabella. Chief Superintendent Olsen
hadn't yet been informed of the turn in the investigation, and now the
emerging red patches on the chief's throat clearly indicated what lay in
wait for them.

"What case is that?" Kurt stared at Isabella, who looked pleadingly at
Roland. He tried to look Olsen in the eye as he quickly turned his angry

gaze on him. "A drowned boy! What has that got to do with the murder of Albert Hovgaard?"

Roland tried to explain, but he could hear how contrived it sounded.

"And you seriously think there is a connection to the old drowning accident? I remember it well. That family went way too far. No one believed the allegations. The boy drowned of natural causes. There is no doubt about that at all."

"We can't progress any further with it anyway, as no one wants to talk to us, and—"

"No, but you have spent time on it and without consulting me!" Kurt Olsen interrupted angrily and still bristling, took a bite of the roll, spreading crumbs around him and down on the floor.

"I'm the bloody detective inspector on the investigation, and I thought it was relevant, but now it has been investigated, and it yielded no result. So, it was not a waste!" Roland defended himself and forced his voice to calm down.

Olsen fumed, but his neck slowly regained its normal skin colour as he brushed the irritating crumbs off his shirt and trousers.

"As it stands now, we have to wait for the DNA tests. It is almost certain that only one of the neighbours had the opportunity to commit the murder in such a short space of time. One who knew that Albert Hovgaard was lying helpless on the floor and seized the opportunity—for some reason."

"What about Finn Geisler? He went out into the kitchen while his wife followed Signe Hovgaard into the bedroom," said Kim.

"He is definitely under suspicion, but he submitted his DNA. Would he do that if he was guilty? He was also the one who called us that night," Roland reasoned.

"It doesn't have to be a sign of his innocence," reprimanded Kurt Olsen firmly. Roland knew the chief superintendent would have it in for him all day. He breathed heavily before tackling the next point—Leander's discovery about the homeless man.

"Now you are once again blending several cases; if it is about the murder of a homeless person, others will have to deal with it. Pass the case on to Morten Holsted."

Roland knew the response already, so he only nodded and didn't look at Kurt Olsen. But Morten Holsted of all people? How would the young detective in the nice silk shirt and fashionable trousers with creases be able to understand the situation of the homeless and fight for their case?

"But we have two missing persons that seem to stand out. First, Rose Teresa Larsen, who is also homeless, and then Anita Andersen, who disappeared from the collective. Can we just completely rule out that the cases are somehow linked to each other?"

Kurt Olsen shook his head quietly. "A home robbery must be investigated as a home robbery."

"Has the Canine Unit not been out to the area?" asked Niels, openly trying to back up his boss.

"Yes, but the new snowfall and the drifting snow meant they had to give up. There are no leads to follow." Roland straightened his back and informed them instead about what he had been told about the murder weapon. Then he asked those who had been at the crime scene to try to think about whether they could remember anything that could inflict that kind of damage.

"A piece of jewellery?" suggested Dan, and Roland looked at him in astonishment. As did everyone else, not least Kurt Olsen, who had often asked him to fire the incompetent young man, which hadn't happened due to the lack of officers. For once, he had said something sensible.

"A ring maybe?" Mikkel grabbed the chance to get a share in the credit.

"A ring," Roland repeated, feeling all the way down to the pit of his stomach that that was the answer. A ring that had been sitting on the hand that had struck.

# 52

Adomas had protested loudly as she packed a small bag of biscuits and a bottle of water, determined to get what she had set out for no matter what he thought of it. She had shouted at him that she would be back tonight before slamming the door and racing down the stairs and out into the icy morning. The Lada had protested almost as loudly as her boyfriend, but now the "Yellow Lightning" had warmed up, and she had enjoyed the rush that came with surfacing from the darkness of a tunnel and out into the dazzling light. Out to life. A little while later, she was driving on the bridge with slush on both sides again, screeching hungry seagulls in the sky and Sweden's white coast in front of her. Of course the Swedes had snow, too. But here the sun was shining. She found her sunglasses in the glove compartment. Her mobile phone was in there, too, flashing about missed calls, probably from Adomas, but she wasn't in the mood for arguing with him anymore and slammed the door to the glove compartment hard. Bloody hell, it only took just over four hours to drive over here—she'd be home again before he'd even started to think about dinner. But she knew what was wrong. He would rather she spent time finding her mother, and it was impossible to explain to him that this was exactly what she was trying to do. It was sheer luck that the boy's family hadn't moved to the depths of northern Sweden. Then she probably wouldn't have hopped in the car. The farm they had bought was in Hörby municipality in Scania, more precisely Äspinge. It had taken time to find them, but during her search, she had come across a relative on Zealand, an aunt of the mother, it turned out. An old woman who provided her with the right information without asking too many questions herself.

She had to stop at the border and pay before she could drive on into Sweden.

She turned off the motorway and shortly afterwards pulled in to stretch her back and legs. Enjoy the view. Draw the cold air all the way down into her lungs. The landscape was similar to Denmark's, but somehow it was more open here. It was easier to breathe. Against nature's purity, she lit a cigarette, inhaled, and wondered what she had got herself into. A buzzard hung over the landscape with outstretched wings as if shielding something from the sun. If a mouse appeared on the white landscape, it was doomed. The bird seemed larger than those she had seen at home. Maybe there were more mice in Sweden. She stubbed the cigarette butt into the snow and drove on.

It was a largely agricultural area with sparsely located properties. The family had apparently settled down far out in the country again. From the colour of many of the farms she drove past, she could see where the term *Swedish red* originated.

However, the home she stopped in front of when the GPS told her she had arrived was a pale yellow wooden house. She looked at it before getting out of the car and had to smile a little as it reminded her of Pippi Longstocking's house. But her expression was serious when she pressed the doorbell a few times and waited. Here from the steps she could see that behind the wooden house was an old stable building in the traditional red colour; only the farmhouse was new and yellow.

She had called last night and arranged to come, so it was no surprise. She had said she was a Danish journalist writing about unsolved cases and wanted to hear if they would like to give an interview. She had expected to get a rejection, but that had not been the case. She was very welcome, they had said. It was the boy's father who opened the door. He was still marked by the grief that must be the hardest in the world to bear—the loss of a child. She had thought the same when she wrote about Gitte's murder in the Doll Child Case, which was the result of a sick person's evilness. Someone to punish and blame. In this case, it was an accident—or was it?

She followed him inside. The living room was warm with cosy Swedish décor and a pleasant faint aroma of freshly cut wood. Over a sideboard hung a cross, and under it lay the Bible.

The boy's mother was standing in the kitchen, which smelled of coffee. Anne was delighted that so much good was said about Sweden. The woman turned around and held out a hand after drying it on a tea towel.

"I'm Ulla. Welcome."

"Thank you. Anne Larsen."

"You're from Copenhagen?"

She nodded.

"Which newspaper are you with?" asked the man.

"The *Daily News*. Local paper in Aarhus."

Anne looked around the room. The ceiling was wood, too, and the windows were traditional curved farmhouse-style.

"I can certainly understand why you chose Sweden. It's beautiful here. How did you find such a great property?"

"Aksel has Swedish roots, so it was natural that we should live here. We wanted to be as far away from Jutland as possible, and his family helped us buy this place. But come and sit down and have a cup of coffee. There's cake, too. It was a long drive; you must be hungry."

Anne took off her backpack and coat and sat down at the set table next to Ulla. She was wrapped tightly in a thick patterned jumper with a polo neck. Her hair reached to her shoulders and was blond, a little messy. Her eyes were more vivid than her husband's, but there was a dark shadow deep in them, too, from that time. Grief that never disappeared. Something that gnawed at you.

"You, too, Aksel!" she said urgently.

He sat down stiffly and stared absently at the stream from the coffee pot as she poured the liquid into his cup.

"We are both so happy that you want to take up the case again. It would help us a lot to get to know what happened. Especially for our daughter's sake," she continued.

"It must have been terrible for her. She was supposed to be looking after her brother, wasn't she?"

The woman looked at her husband, but his gaze quickly found a point outside the window to concentrated on. His eyes were shiny.

"Yes, but she met a school friend and forgot about her brother. It can happen at that age." She looked at him again. Reproachful.

"So, you don't think it was an accident?" Anne tasted the coffee but didn't find it much different from the Danish.

"Many strange things happened that we didn't understand."

Aksel suddenly looked at Ulla. "Maybe we just didn't *want* to understand."

"What?"

"We never got along with the neighbours," said Ulla. "When we moved in, we could feel that we weren't welcome. They had something in common that we could not be a part of."

"What?" Anne repeated.

"Take a slice of cake." She handed the dish to her and then to her husband, who also took a slice of Swedish spice cake that smelled of cardamom and cinnamon.

"That's what we never learned. Or didn't want to understand," said Aksel. "But she tried. And it drove her mad."

"Who, your daughter?"

"Yes, she became more and more peculiar after the accident. She was riddled with guilt, of course, and you . . . We did not make it easier for her, either." She said that to Aksel and then looked at Anne. "We quarrelled a lot—we were in shock and grieving, and it was hard not to blame her for us losing Marcus. She had promised that she'd . . ." Her lower lip trembled, but she continued as if she didn't notice it. "We did not see what was coming until it was too late."

Anne gazed intently at Aksel as his wife looked down at the table and tried to calm her quivering chin. He stared back without neither blinking nor seeing. "She was hospitalised. Something snapped in her." His voice sounded like a moan.

"Hospitalised? Where?"

"In Risskov. Adolescent Psychiatric Centre."

Anne fell silent. This wasn't exactly what she had expected. They had, so to speak, lost their daughter, too. She glanced around at walls, cupboards, and bookshelves to find pictures of the children, but there were none. No pictures at all.

Ulla pulled herself together and straightened her back. "That's why it's so important to find out what happened. We have prayed to God that something would happen. The police rejected us. More like mocked us. It also sounded strange to us, too, but now that so many other strange things have happened, why not? But they didn't believe her, and they didn't investigate properly whether there was anything to it."

"It—what?" Anne wanted Ulla to say it herself.

"What our daughter claimed to have discovered."

"So it was your daughter who said Marcus was . . . murdered?"

"I think she made it up so she wouldn't feel so guilty," Ulla said quietly. "It's only natural. She was just fourteen at the time."

"So you didn't believe her, either?"

"She said she had evidence hidden in a chest. But no one believed her. It all sounded too far-fetched, and then she was admitted to hospital."

"What evidence do you think she had?"

"She didn't say."

"And you never found the chest?" Anne sat stiffly on the chair, barely able to breathe.

"No, and she was in no state to tell us about it. She was given so much medicine that we could barely talk to her." Aksel wiped his eyes and again found something to look at outside in the dazzling white light.

"Then we moved. Maybe we didn't bring it with us, Aksel. Maybe it's still in the attic." She tried questioningly to catch his eye, but in vain.

"May I visit her? Maybe I can talk to her."

A little smile without joy formed on Aksel's narrow, bluish lips. "She isn't hospitalised anymore. She was discharged about six months ago. I really hope she is better. She found a place to live. We're just very surprised that she stayed there instead of moving to our home here in Sweden." He shook his head.

Ulla absently crumbled the last of the cake on her plate. "No, Aksel, we do not understand that, but she is eighteen, so we can't make decisions about her life anymore. She won't allow us to anyway. Now she is taking her revenge on us." She glanced up at the black cross on the wall. "Maybe there's a meaning to her choosing to live there. Maybe it's a way to move forward. She has always been a special girl who has followed her own path."

Aksel nodded. They sat in silence, each having disappeared into their own world.

Anne cleared her throat. "Would you tell me where she lives?"

Ulla lifted her head and looked at her husband's closed face.

"She lives in a collective not far from where we lived back then. Close to the lake where her brother drowned."

# 53

The mobile phone kept playing music and vibrating in her coat pocket, persistent and demanding, but she didn't answer it. Partly out of principle—she never used it while driving—partly because she didn't want to talk to anyone, no matter who it was.

Danny's words were still going round in her head, and she was annoyed that they made her feel anything. A lot of feelings actually. When they had taken the last photos, he had asked what was wrong, why she was so silent. She had answered evasively and knew full well that she had been quite closed off all day. Had been thinking of her father. Would she ever see him again? And Mathias—how could she get by without him? Danny had looked worriedly at her with the dark eyes she had fallen for once and had asked directly if working with him for two days had tormented her that much. And then he had begun to talk about it. The accident. Rasmus. Said he'd never had the chance to tell her what happened that night four years ago when he lost control of the car and hit him on the bike path. She didn't want to hear it but couldn't avoid it as she took the camera off the tripod and packed it away. She couldn't forgive him, even though she could see that what he had done tormented him, even though he still laid flowers on Rasmus's grave, even though he still loved her. Those were the words that kept whirling in her head. She had looked at his ring, and he had seen it. Majken was so full of hatred and jealousy for her family that it was hard to live with, not just for herself, he had said. *Of course, if I really loved her, I would but . . .*

Luckily, Pierre had entered the studio, and she had taken the opportunity to put an end to it. She kept seeing Danny's eyes as they had looked at her before closing the door and walking away. "Forget him," she mumbled to herself, turning on the radio. The phone made a noise again, and she turned up the volume louder.

The traffic on Grenåvej was heavy, and she had to stop at the barrier when the train arrived. Good, it was working; there had been level-crossing failures before with catastrophic consequences.

The neighbour had cleared the snow in her yard. He was retired and had nothing better to do, so it was no problem, he had said when she protested the first time he had done it. She drove into the garage and had just let herself into the warmth when the phone rang again. She looked at the display and saw a number she didn't know and answered as she pulled off her coat.

"Kamilla Holm," she said annoyed.

There was silence for a while. "It's Mogens. Mogens Arnskov; we need to talk."

She sat down on the nearest chair still with one arm in her coat sleeve.

"Hi! Are you the one who has called so many times? I'm sorry, I was driving and—"

"Are you at home now? I'm on my way, so I can be there in ten minutes. Does it suit?"

"Yeah."

He hung up before her. She stared absently at Tarzan, who was crouched by his food bowls and drinking water. He had sounded strange, her father. She got up quickly, took off her coat and hung it up on the coat-rack, then found two mugs and made coffee. Her heart was pounding in her throat. He knew who she was and wanted to talk to her, so it could only mean that he . . .

She was practically standing and waiting at the door when he rang the bell. Didn't know if she should smile but decided not to when she opened the door. He didn't smile, either. Stayed on the steps until she asked him to come in. He didn't take off his coat and sat down at the dining table.

"I made coffee . . ." She put mugs on the table and poured. Waited. He avoided looking her in the eye. Drank the coffee. She wanted to ask him to take his coat off. Stay a little. She sat down opposite him.

"I'm sorry that I didn't say anything but . . ." she began when the silence became oppressive.

He didn't look like himself. His stubble was grey, and his eyes had a tormented expression. "I should have guessed it myself. You look like her."

"Did you know she was expecting me?"

He looked down at the table again. "Yes, I knew. Her family threw her out because of it."

"Grandma and Grandpa were very religious. I didn't know them, but so I have been told."

He wasn't listening, just staring into the cup.

"I followed Gloria to Horsens when she ran away. She had apparently seen an ad for a job there, but then she met another man. I managed to talk to her before she got married, but she told me that she'd had an abortion and that she didn't want to see me again. Abortion was God's punishment, she said."

"So you didn't know I was born, and then you moved to Bønnerup?"

"I didn't want to go back to Agger. I wasn't welcome there. To have got such a young girl pregnant isn't viewed well in the area. And with what else happened . . ." He looked away and swallowed a lump. Kamilla put her hand on his arm. He looked at it quickly but didn't move his arm.

"We forgot him. It all happened so suddenly. It was a lovely evening; the sun turned the sea orange-red at sunset. We kissed, we . . . I really loved her. Gloria. Her brother was sitting at the railing with a little fishing net. He wanted to be a fisherman like his father." His eyes that were surrounded by fine wrinkles from the harsh wind at sea shone with horror. "Suddenly he was gone. It was Gloria who realised. On instinct, she suddenly tore herself out of my arms and looked towards the railing. We called him, and I dived in to look, but I couldn't see him, and the undercurrent was so strong that I would have drowned if . . . Your mother was hysterical of course, but we came ashore, and she had to run home to tell them what had happened. But it was only later that it all began. Drowning accidents happen often in fishing villages—a natural part of life—and Gloria hadn't told the whole truth. But she had to when she started getting morning sickness, and when it could be seen, and not least when the doctor told her parents that their young daughter was in trouble—she was still only a child herself."

"But when she told you she'd had an abortion, couldn't you still see that she was expecting me?"

"She wore a large coat. And, of course, I believed her."

Kamilla didn't reveal how changed his beloved Gloria had become with time, an enclosed, bitter, and hateful woman. He raised his head and stared at the bookshelf. "So that's why your son looks so much like our Mathias. I'm his grandfather."

She smiled. "Yes, and Mathias is my half-brother. Just when I thought I had no family, then . . ."

Mogens gently pulled his arm back and stood up. He stood with his back to her by the patio door, looking out into the garden, where the snow-covered bushes stood like white ghosts.

"Alice and Mathias must never hear about this. It's going to have to be a secret between you and me."

"But . . ."

He turned around. "You have to . . . no—you *must* promise me that it will never come out that I am your father!"

"So you do not want to be associated with me? I thought . . ." Anger fought with disappointment.

"It's not that, Kamilla. There's much more to it."

"Like what?" The lump in her throat grew.

"It's best you don't know. Believe me."

She watched him as he walked out into the hallway. He turned in the doorway before going out. His eyes had the same expression as when he'd arrived.

"I'm sorry, Kamilla. But that's the way it has to be."

She wanted to run out and hug him. Feel her father's arms around her, but he was gone before she could get up. The cold he had let in was the only thing she could feel.

# 54

S orry," Isabella said, entering his office. "I didn't know that Kurt Olsen didn't know."

Roland shook his head. The morning briefing hadn't gone as well as he'd hoped. Not the afternoon briefing, either. The DNA analyses had come back and none of them matched the perp's. So they had another problem. Either it was a random stranger out of his mind, or it was one of the four who had refused to be tested. Bitten Mørk was so small and slender—could she strike with such force? And what about the boyfriend? On drugs perhaps. They were both types to wear an atypical, patterned ring—if that is what had left the marks on the victim.

"It's fine, Isabella. I hope you have good news. How is the search going?"

"There's still no trace of the young girl from the collective. How long do we have to wait before sending out the helicopters? If she's walking around in the cold, then . . ." Isabella cast a worried look out the window where beautiful icicles had formed deadly awls after the thaw and new frost. Roland had thought about getting them removed before they fell and drilled their way through some unlucky person's skull in the car park.

"We'll wait and see with her. Rose Teresa Larsen?"

"Mikkel and Kim were making inquiries around hostels and shelters; I've been to the places they hang out, and many homeless people have been questioned, but no one has seen hide nor hair of her. Neither are they happy to talk to us. How can it be that those we could help the most detest us?"

"Some homeless people have to survive by turning to crime, burglary, and such like. The drug addicts, in particular, disappear around the corner when they see us."

"Yes, I understand. But it's about helping them. Someone seems to have it in for them."

"If those missing turn out to have been murdered, yes. But we don't know. Have you heard from Holsted?"

"No, but do you think he would want to tell us? It doesn't concern our case."

"No, of course not." Roland took the case file and handed it to Isabella. "You'd better give that to him, too. It does seem to concern his."

"The drowning accident?"

"Yes, if the boy was sacrificed to the gods, and the homeless people are being, too." He suppressed a small smile.

Isabella accepted the file but couldn't hide her smile as she left and closed the door behind her. It was probably only Anne Larsen who had jumped on that story.

Isabella was barely out the door before the phone rang and he had Gert Schmidt's voice piercing his ear.

"You got the results of the DNA test, didn't you?"

"Yes, thank you, but what good is it if there is no match?"

"True, true. Unfortunately, there's nothing new on the rope. We haven't been able to trace where it may have been bought yet, so—"

"The rope?"

"The rope that was around the homeless man's neck," Gert explained.

"Well, that information isn't to come to me anymore. The case of the homeless man is no longer mine. DI Morten Holsted has taken it over." Roland caught himself tilting the pen between two fingers like Kurt Olsen had done to express his annoyance throughout the morning briefing; impatience was spreading.

"Okay, I guess you also have enough to do with the home robbery."

"Yes, now we're back at square one."

"There is something I think you should look at. We ran all the DNA profiles through the system. It's routine, you know. Cold cases can suddenly be given new life. There is a suspicious coincidence between DNA from one of the people tested and another old case."

Roland put down the pen and took a sip of lukewarm coffee. His heart started beating faster, and it wasn't due only to the high caffeine content of the black liquid.

"About three years ago, Signe and Albert Hovgaard's property burned down; I suppose you're familiar with that?"

"Yes."

"You haven't looked into that fire again?"

"No, not really; what about it? It was three years ago. I only know that the arsonist wasn't found—it happens from time to time," he said, sounding like Olsen.

"Indeed, but DNA was found at the site where the fire inspector thought the fire had been started with petrol at the time. They found a plastic can near the hearth. It had contained petrol, and DNA in the form of blood was found under the handle. It was believed that the arsonist had cut themselves on the can."

"But the perp was never found . . ."

"No, there was no match in the DNA register, and as there were no suspects to test, the case had to be dropped as unsolved."

"Gert, can I ask you to get to the point? Who are you alluding to here? Have we suddenly found the arsonist?"

"It can't be said with certainty, but as I said, DNA matches one of those tested."

"Well then, it's guaranteed to be our murderer, too. There's nothing unnatural about drawing the conclusion that the same person who tried to burn the Hovgaard family inside their home has now killed Albert Hovgaard. Who is it?"

"Family relationships are in themselves suspicious. The strange thing is that the person in question no longer lived there when the fire was started, as far as we know, because no one knew she had returned."

"She?"

"Yes, *she*. It's made no less suspicious by the fact that now she is missing."

# 55

---

She closed her eyes as the hot streams from the shower hit her face. Her groin was still burning. Adomas had woken her up in the middle of the night, not shaking or calling her awake, but with soft, warm lips sliding across her body from her shoulder blades, down her spine towards her lower back, and on. She had been lying with her back to his stomach. Spooning. Initially, she had thought it was a dream and maybe still thought it was. If not for the fact that she could still feel him. The warmth and the pleasant pain he had left in her. It no longer felt like incest when they made love. He wasn't her cousin. He was her boyfriend, and now she was pretty sure she was really in love. That cold interior had thawed, and the thought of Torsten's hands no longer prevented her from enjoying another man's touch. He hadn't ruined everything in her life after all. She smiled and listened to the splash of water against the tiles and the greedy gargle of the drain trying to keep up. Adomas's welcome when she returned late last night had almost made her forget the conversation in the cosy wooden Swedish house. She had thought about driving directly to the collective, but it had been too late. The ice-rink roads had made the trip home slower and more difficult than expected. Long queues on the motorway after an accident had meant delays for hours. She had almost gone doolally from being stuck there without being able to do anything. Felt the road rage surface. But Adomas had been waiting for her with food—and wine. He had been there to share the excitement and experiences with her. Listened and offered advice. He had made her relax, and she had asked herself what she had done before he came into her life. Let the anger build up, that was what she had done. But now she was no longer alone, and it gave her a nice calm. His advice had been to sleep and not think about it until the next day. And then he had given her something else to think about.

She turned off the shower and wiped the water from her face with both hands before grabbing the towel, rubbing the condensation off the mirror, and drying herself. She looked at her body. The small pert breasts. The tattoo of the fish, the logo the religious sect had demanded of all its members, was almost gone, faded by steadfast rubbing with salt. The flat white stomach with a single ring in the belly-button, the only piercing she had left in; it hung slightly over a narrow and tightly shaved black triangle. Her eyes slid back to her face, which was red after the hot shower, making the scar on her eyebrow even clearer. Adomas loved this scarred body. Did it make it more beautiful? This is what it looked like. She brushed her teeth and went back to the bedroom. The air felt icy cold after the hot, humid bathroom. It was still dark out, and the frost on the pane grew clearer against the black background. She hurriedly got dressed. Adomas's chest swelled and sank rhythmically in a deep sleep. She didn't have the heart to wake him and gently closed the door to the bedroom behind her.

What was she to do now? How would she make progress? Benito needed to know who Marcus's sister was. Why hadn't she said it herself? What was she really doing back there again, and was she completely better now? Inpatients fled all the time from closed wards; maybe she was . . .

Lost in her own thoughts, she made coffee. Pure routine. It was six in the morning, but she hadn't been able to sleep any longer. There was too much she had to do, but now that she was up, she didn't know where to start—and what could she do at this hour of the morning anyway? She turned on her mobile as she ate. It had been off since getting on her nerves too much in the traffic on the motorway. Most of the calls were from Adomas. There was a single message, too. But he hadn't been plaguing her to turn around and come home as she had thought; he wasn't reproaching her. He'd only promised to stay up and wait for her. Cook. Buy some wine. He missed her. She looked towards the door of the bedroom and wanted to go in and embrace him, but then she wouldn't get anything done today. She flipped through the phone menu and eventually deleted the calls. Without fully realizing, she was looking at a picture message. It was a dark picture, so it was hard to decipher. She took the phone over to the lamp and turned the display to catch the light, but she could see nothing but darkness, and something that might have been a fire somewhere in the middle. She clicked on to the next picture, which was a little clearer. It looked like fire forming a circle. Next was the full moon, faintly visible between bare branches. Treetops? The last were close-ups of snow around a burned-down campfire. That's what it looked like, but they had been taken closer, and a flash had been used, so they were much clearer. She didn't recognise the phone number. She was just about to delete them. It all seemed like a sick joke. Maybe from one of her old mates in Copenhagen, who always slagged her off about becoming a crime reporter and cooperating with the police. Until now, it had always been in good fun, but this . . . She took a closer look at the last picture. There was something in the snow. She zoomed in and was in no doubt about what she was seeing. It was big bones and blood. Lots of dark-red solidified blood.

# 56

___

There was someone near her. The sound of fabric moving, breathing, and footsteps.

She shook her head at the sounds and tried to catch a glimpse of her surroundings, but the blindfold was tied so tightly over her eyes that she couldn't force her eyelids open, and she even doubted whether it was a cloth she could see through anyway. In turn, the back of her head throbbed even more violently from the movement. She no longer had any sense of whether it was night or day, or where she was for that matter. It smelled like an old house that had been vacant for a long time, and moisture, fungus, and mould had long since taken over. She struggled to ask who they were and what they wanted with her. Clenched her teeth and listened to them pace impatiently back and forth on the floor in front of her. She wasn't the only one being held here. She'd heard something last night in the room next door. Someone complaining. It sounded like a woman.

Suddenly she doubted whether she was alone again. It was so quiet. No smell other than of mould and rot. She waited until she was sure and then tried to get the rope off again by rubbing it hard against the back of the chair like she had done for most of the night without knowing if it was helping. She was tied to the backrest. There were ropes around her ankles, too, and each leg was tied tightly to a leg of the chair, so she couldn't get up. And it was cold here. Freezing cold. It came in across the floor; her feet were frozen stiff. Was she to freeze to death? She moved restlessly on the chair and rubbed the rope even harder. Her strength was about to run out, but it was impossible to sleep, not without help. She couldn't stay seated here; in time she would manage to snap the rope against the rough wooden chair. They would look for her in the collective, wouldn't they? Yes, they would. When their servant and maid had disappeared. They'd report it to the police. The thought comforted her a little, and she allowed herself a little smile and a sigh of relief.

"You may stop that; you'll never break it." The voice was close, and it startled her.

"What were you sniffing around in a private area for?"

She pursed her lips and didn't say anything. There was something familiar about the voice, but she couldn't place it. There was silence for a long time, and again she thought they had left her alone, but dared not believe it. The silence and the cold made her uncomfortable. She felt nauseated and came to the thought that she hadn't had food since Thursday night when she had eaten with the others in the collective. Before the argument had broken out. The advantage of that was that she hadn't needed the toilet yet, but what if she did? Once in a while, she felt pressure in her bladder, but she had always managed to hold it back until the feeling disappeared.

The sound of a door being locked—or unlocked. Was she alone now? She suddenly felt the danger; it lay almost in the cold like a dank fog. Why had she followed Brian, and who had spotted her, knocked her out, and dragged her here? There had to be tracks in the snow. The police would quickly find her. But how many days had passed? How much snow had fallen? Maybe Brian had heard or seen something, or maybe he knew what had happened to her and would come soon to help her. Brian of all people.

After half an hour, she realised that she really was alone. She shook from the cold, and she could no longer resist the pressure on her bladder. The heat spread down her thighs and made her skirt wet. The smell of urine mingled with the smell of wet wood. The humiliation provoked hysterical tears.

# 57

The seagulls sought far inland in the fight to stay alive. They circled in flocks over apartment blocks with outdoor bins and quickly dived for crusts of bread and other edible waste. And seagulls took everything. They weren't so unusual a sight at the police station, which lay close to the Port of Aarhus. Some of the large birds often sat on the cornice just outside his window, looking inside. Frozen. Getting some warmth from the draughty window, which in turn made him freeze. They circled around out there while Anne got some coffee. He again turned his gaze to the pictures she had printed from her phone. It was hard to see what she was getting at. But there was not much doubt about the ones with blood and bones in the snow, even if he wasn't a forensic pathologist. But it couldn't be human bones, so he refused to believe it.

She came back and sat down. Pale, yet with a warmer glow in her eyes than she usually had. Maybe not having to get up early in the morning and show up for work did a person good. That she had come to him before doing something stupid was also a new development.

"Those pictures are certainly suspicious, but as I said before, it's no longer my case."

"Which case do you mean?" She drank greedily from the coffee mug.

"The case of the homeless people."

"Who said it's about them?"

"Is that not what you're suggesting? That the pictures were taken in Vagn Mortensen's forest and are proof that blood is being shed there. Sacrifices?"

"I didn't say anything about that. I'm only coming to the police because I received some mysterious images on my mobile from an unknown number and I hoped you could help me track down who sent them. Isn't that what you do if someone is sent pictures of a crime?"

"Crime? Yes, we can trace who sent the pictures to you. There are several options depending on the nature of the case."

"But it was an anonymous number."

"It doesn't mean anything. We can get a court order for the phone number, so we can see who contacted you."

"What if it was a prepaid phone card?"

"That would make it more difficult, but it doesn't stop us from finding the sender. We just get the IMEI number of the phone used for the prepaid card. But we only do that kind of thing for very serious crimes. That you've been sent some dark pictures of a bonfire and the moon isn't crucial enough. So you believe it's the kidnapper and murderer who sent you these pictures?"

"Who else?"

He shook his head. "Unfortunately, Anne, it's not enough evidence for further investigation."

She did not like the answer; he saw it clearly. But as always, she had something up her sleeve.

"I went to Sweden and talked to Marcus's parents," she said.

He straightened up in the chair. She had succeeded where Isabella had drawn a blank. "What did you get out of them?"

"It's not your case; you've just told me."

"No, but . . ." He looked towards the door to make sure it was closed and Kurt Olsen wasn't standing there. "But we tried to contact them ourselves. They wouldn't talk to us."

"Of course not. You didn't treat them very well then. I have to ask you for the name of the person who took over the case. Because I'm sure you realise it's the same case?"

"You mean the same case as the missing homeless people?"

"Yes."

"We haven't realised anything, Anne. That boy accidentally drowned. All the old investigations and forensic reports say so."

"Perhaps."

She, too, watched the gulls, and the almost unnoticeable ripple of a smile at the corner of her mouth irritated him.

"Do I really have to beg you to tell me what the parents told you?"

"And you'll take over the case from your colleague?"

"Of course not. I'm not *allowed* to take it, according to my superior, but you'll certainly still tell me."

"Fair enough. They told me who the boy's sister is, that she returned to the area, and why."

"Is that all? We already know about Anita Andersen from the collective."

The answer shocked the former journalist. Now it was Roland's turn to smile unnoticed.

"Are you doing anything to find her? It can't be a coincidence that she's disappeared now, too. She knows something!"

"Don't worry, Anne. We are working hard on the case. If you hadn't arrived here declaring you have crucial information, then I myself would be hard at work. And then you come up with something I can't do anything about." He gathered the printed pictures and handed them to her. "His name is Morten Holsted."

"Who?"

"The detective inspector you need to talk to." He got up and took his jacket from the back of the chair.

"Roland, you can't be serious. I trust only you, and this is about my mother . . ."

"I'm sorry, Anne. Do you now think your mother has something to do with this, too? As you can probably see, I'm busy with other more important cases than sacrificing Asatruar, old, solved drowning accidents, and maybe kidnapped homeless people. We have to find a killer."

She remained seated. "It's guaranteed there are more people involved— a whole flock. Do you also know that Anita was researching it and that it drove her crazy that no one believed her? She was admitted to Risskov. She had the evidence hidden in a chest."

He stopped at the door. Had a hard time not caring. Morten Holsted's case or not. He turned around. "What evidence?"

"Of her little brother being murdered."

"What is it?"

"Her parents don't quite know."

"And why didn't she come forward with it?"

"Because the family moved when she was admitted. They couldn't forget that she had left her little brother to look after himself. In fact, they left her on her own in a closed ward doped up to the eyeballs. No doubt who they loved most of their two children. Clearly, she broke down. They think the forgotten chest was in the attic." She scratched a stain off her jeans. "Maybe it burned when the pyromaniac acted."

He sat down. "You mean the attic on the property where Albert Hovgaard was murdered?"

"Exactly! Can't you see how it all makes sense?"

"Not quite."

"Perhaps Albert Hovgaard found the chest and threatened to reveal the deeds of the Asatruar. Maybe they were the ones who tried to burn down the farm—if they knew there was evidence. Maybe they even arranged the home robbery, and—"

"Stop, Anne! It doesn't make sense! The Lithuanians confessed to the burglary and the assault on both Signe Hovgaard and her husband. Moreover, a DNA match has shown that it was Anita who started the fire at her childhood home." He shouldn't be telling her. That sort of information shouldn't just be shared with the public. But he didn't regret it when he saw the surprised expression on her face.

"I don't believe it. They didn't live there then—it must have happened while she was hospitalised. And why would she do it?"

"As you yourself said, she has been overlooked her entire life and not least after her brother's death, for which she was even blamed. The childhood home with her brother's cross in the garden had to be obliterated."

Anne laughed hoarsely. "Now I don't believe you."

"Do you have other suggestions?" He leaned back with his hands behind his neck, waiting for what she would now come up with. She sat thinking for a long time. Trying to find answers in her coffee mug.

"Where was the DNA found?"

"On the *can* with the petrol that was used to ignite the fire. Blood. She cut herself on the handle."

"So it was a petrol can that was on the property?"

He nodded.

"What's to say that didn't happen before the arson attack. She lived there all her life. Maybe she cut herself on the can when she used it once."

Roland had had that thought himself—if only it didn't all bloody well fit so well together. She could easily be the perp, that is, except for the new information that she had been hospitalised. He made a note to investigate when exactly that was.

There was a knock on the door, and Isabella came in. She gave Anne a snooty look. "Sorry to disturb you. I didn't know you had a visitor."

"It's okay, Isabella. Anne is about to leave. DI Morten Holsted," he repeated and nodded kindly towards the door. She made a dissatisfied grimace, drank the last of the coffee, got up, and picked up her backpack.

"Promise me you'll contact me when you find my mother." She turned her back on him and left without closing the door.

"Has her mother disappeared, too?" asked Isabella, sitting down on the chair Anne had just vacated. She threw Anne's empty plastic mug in his bin.

"Rose Teresa Larsen is her mother."

"The homeless woman? Oh dear." Isabella looked towards the door as if to make sure Anne had gone. She spotted the prints. "What are they?"

"Oh blast. She forgot them," he said annoyed, thinking that it was probably on purpose. "They're pictures that were sent to her mobile. Would you mind giving them to Holsted, too?"

"How do you know it's his case? What has that got to do with the homeless people?"

"Who knows? It's all getting so confusing. Anne believes that all three cases have something to do with each other." Roland sighed as he got up.

"The home robbery and the murder of Albert Hovgaard, Anita Andersen and the disappearance of the homeless people, and the drowning accident four years ago?"

"And her mother's 'abduction,'" he added.

"Does she really think fanatical Asatruar are behind it all? That's not possible." Isabella smiled and looked up at him, searching for his opinion.

"The home robbery can be kept separate. As usual, she has some fairly outlandish theories, but . . . I'm doubtful, too. Anyway, it looked like *you* had something important."

"Yes, someone from the collective rang. They found some tablets in a drawer in Anita's room. Benzodiazepines. Valium. She must be very sick; they didn't know that in the collective. Linda Carlsen read about the pills on the internet. They're for panic disorder and agitation in severe cases.

She has been taking them for a long time. After weeks of use, you become addicted."

"So she's addicted to those pills?"

Isabella nodded. "Definitely."

"Which means she didn't leave home voluntarily without them. What happens if she doesn't get them?"

"Dizziness, insomnia, restlessness, anxiety, tremors, and hypersensitivity to light, sound, and touch. Eventually cramps, spasms, or convulsions. But it takes some time before it reaches that stage."

"But do we have that time?" Roland put on his coat and left.

# 58

Aarhus could boast profusely of hospitals with great honours. More than one here had been named the country's best psychiatric hospital by *Dagens Medicin* magazine. The buildings always reminded him of Brideshead for some reason. They lay in a bluish haze, big, beautiful, and striped, at the end of Skovagervej, so no one could get further. The Child and Adolescent Psychiatric Centre, which he was to visit, had been ranked number one for the second year in a row. But it was sad that such a department was needed at all. Mental illness had always existed, all the way back to when it was believed that the sick were possessed by the devil and the only cure was exorcism, but the number of children with depression, suicidal thoughts, eating disorders, and other "new" behavioural disorders should not exist in modern society. Or was it precisely the modern society that bore all the blame? He had discussed it with Leander at the Institute of Forensic Medicine while they had been reviewing the entire forensic content of the murder case. He had needed it to get things clear in his head, but now he felt only more confused. Leander believed it was due to the greater focus on mental illness than before that made it seem like the situation was worsening. And it wasn't just the Danish situation being discussed. "The fact is that today we have to take a position on everything that happens in the entire world and not just what happens to our neighbour, who by the way does not interest us much anymore because everything else is more exciting," he added.

And so they were back to the usual culprits—the media, the press, the journalists.

He drove to the left at the roundabout onto Harald Selmers Vej and shortly afterwards into the car park in front of CAPC, to which the department's name was abbreviated. He was expected and was led to the head of the department. Her office was bright and friendly, and she smiled warmly. Her hair was shoulder-length and had modern grey highlights. There were smile lines at her eyes and around her lips, the latter of which had been refreshed with a faint rose colour. She offered him some coffee, and their chat started with what everyone was talking about—the weather and the impossible state of the roads. When would winter end?

"Anita Andersen," she said, running her mouse over a blue mat with a summery image of a boy eating an ice cream cone. Her son maybe. Irene had made a mouse pad for him with a photo of the "police dog" Angolo, but it was in the drawer in his office. She clicked on a link. He couldn't see what she was doing behind the screen, but he gradually recognised the sound. The little *tick*.

"I remember her well. She had a very hard time after she was committed." She retrieved a pair of glasses from the drawer and peered more closely at the screen. "That was three and a half years ago. Half a year after her brother drowned. She felt guilty and had tried to take her own life."

"How?" Roland asked in surprise, thinking of the smiling well-built girl with the happy eyes from the collective. He hadn't taken off his coat and was sweating from the sun baking in through the window that he was sitting next to. Outside, he could see the buildings where young people were trying to deal with their various psychoses, probably primarily with the aid of medication.

"Tablets. She was first admitted to the Centre for Suicide Prevention, from which she was quickly discharged. She only tried once."

"Did she go home then?"

"Yes, she went home, but it didn't last long. A few months later she was committed again; she was admitted to the closed ward but was transferred to the open one after six months. She seemed to be improving."

"And then patients may go where they want?"

She nodded. "It's not a prison, and the best thing for the sick young people is for everyday life to be as ordinary as possible. After, of course, professional assessment and management that they are taking their medication. They are not just left to fend for themselves."

"But hadn't her parents moved to Sweden by then?"

"Yes, I was actually surprised that they moved. But as they said, Sweden wasn't Timbuktu. They just had to get away from the farm and the lake where their son had drowned. Can you blame them? It was their way of moving on. And they came often and visited her in the beginning. But that was when she had been most ill and was on a lot of medication. Patients are often quite dull when the medicine is new to them, so . . ."

"So, then maybe they didn't come that often?"

"No, they didn't, but they blamed her for their son's death. I'm sure you know the story?"

"Yes, perhaps it's a natural reaction?"

"Grief manifests itself in many ways. Some need someone to blame to be able to process it. You probably know it from your job. A culprit must be found and punished—and if so, no one else is guilty . . ."

Roland nodded.

"Naturally, I spoke to them about it and pressured them see a crisis psychologist. Some of Anita's problems were just self-recrimination, so it was no help that they blamed her, too. They may not have said it directly, but you could see it in their eyes and body language. They were very Christian, but in their case, even God couldn't help, and true human nature took over. It's not that easy to forgive."

Roland knew what she meant. It was a matter of forgiving oneself. Salvatore dominated his thoughts constantly. He shouldn't have said what he did; he shouldn't have sent him home already. Why had he waited to talk to him until he was provoked by it? Was the fear of the mafia so deep that he did not even dare to talk—or think—about it?

"Perhaps you know what I am talking about?" the head of the department interrupted his thoughts.

"When was Anita moved to the open ward? Can you see that?" he asked, circumventing her question.

She used the mouse again. "Six months after her second admission."

Roland did some quick mental arithmetic. It was true. By the time the fire was lit, Anita had been able to go wherever she wanted.

"But may I ask why the police are suddenly so interested in Anita Andersen?"

"You haven't heard that she is missing?"

"No, I must admit that I don't have much time to follow the news. That's awful. Has something happened to her, or what is it about?"

"Pyromania. Would that be like her?"

"Pyromania? That is a rare disorder. It is categorised under personality disorder. It was not one of Anita's disorders. Her psychosis came from grief, guilt, and very low self-esteem."

"We often see pyromania in young people who are bored and want to ignite a little life on the street," he replied. The many fires set in Gjellerup were one example.

"That's not pyromania, that's arson, which is something else. It's not Anita at all. How is it connected to her?"

"We'll leave it there then." Roland got up and thanked her for the coffee. She shook hands without getting up and smiled again.

He left without being much the wiser on Anita Andersen's state of mind. Now it was a matter of finding her.

# 59

She was sure it was night. The sounds told her. The tawny owl. She listened again, waiting. Yes, that's what it was. She had listened to the same sound at night as a child, and the same sound could be heard in her room in the collective. Marcus had been afraid of the sound. It hooted the most during the breeding season, and he had always come into her room to sleep with her. He believed it was a ghost; she had reassured him that it wasn't and had talked him to sleep with long tales of the owl. Now its hoot had become a symbol of what they had had together on those many nights. Their secret. He didn't dare go into their parents' room as their dad didn't want a big child in the bed and they would only have made fun of his anxiety anyway. But she did not. She understood him. Had been horrified by the sound, too, when she was his age, and had also been turned away at her parents' bedroom door. One May night, they had sneaked out hand in hand and had gone after the sound. They had found where it sat in the big oak tree out by the road. After seeing it, he hadn't been so scared, but he still came into her room at night when it hooted; she always waited for him. Was it sitting in the same tree now? Was she somewhere quite near to where they had stood with each other, holding hands and looking at the bird's dark eyes in the moonlight? The sound was closer than in the collective. Had they really not hidden her better than that?

She had completely forgotten to work with the rope and started sluggishly again, despite how much her shoulders hurt from the movement back and forth, and it dawned on her that it was hopeless. She had been alone for a long time. What were they waiting for? Sometimes she didn't know what was what; darkness was all she saw. Her dizziness had increased. If she had not been tied to the chair, she would have fallen off it. The stench of urine was probably nauseating, but she had got used to it now. To the cold, too. She no longer shook. She had just become limp and passive, and every movement was without energy as if her body knew she had to conserve it. When the owl hooted, she rested her arms and listened. Many owls had died in this ruthless winter. The mice had scurried under the snow or were dead, and when many of the small birds that they also lived on succumbed to the cold, there was no food. Marcus would have cried at the thought of it. She froze when she heard crying. It sounded as if a wall was muffling the sound.

"Hello! Is somebody there?"

The crying stopped.

"Who are you?" she shouted, as loud as she dared to avoid attracting the attention of anyone else. Only an incomprehensible mumbling reached her ears behind the blindfold, but she had perceived from which direction it was coming and moved the chair towards it by wiggling it back and forth. It creaked, and she knew her weight wasn't good for the movements of a flimsy wooden chair, but she kept rocking it back and forth, moving sideways slowly. A chair leg broke with a crunching sound, and when she landed on the floor, she hit her hip so hard that she screamed aloud. The floor was cold and there was a draft along the floorboards. The voice behind the wall said something again, but she still couldn't hear what; her ears were buzzing. She tried to gather her strength. Turned around cautiously. Broken wood from the chair bore into her thigh, the pain brought some movement back. She discovered that her arms were free. The rope was still there, but she was no longer tied to the chair. She kicked with her legs and heard wood land somewhere in front of her. Now her legs were free, too. Why hadn't she thought of doing that before? Just smash the chair. She came up to sitting and began to shuffle along until she bumped against the wall. With her back to it, she pushed herself up to standing, staggering on stiff legs, and suddenly the suppressed stomach contents came; she couldn't do anything to stop it. Pure bile that burned her throat and splashed onto the floor. She leaned her head back against the wall and got used to standing upright again.

"Is somebody there?" she asked into the wall as the discomfort subsided. But no one answered. She heard a door unlock nearby and, a little afterwards, voices.

"Fuck, it stinks in here!"

"Fuck, it's foul! You need a dip in cold water, don't you?"

She began crying silently as they grabbed her arms and pulled her with them. There was no more strength left to resist.

# 60

---

It would have felt comical and ridiculous that they were sitting there if they both hadn't been so taken aback. Anne had the feeling that something was going to happen tonight. An owl was hooting nearby, otherwise, there were no sounds. The moon shone, and the trees cast long shadows in the snow. She crawled further down into her coat and hid her chin in her scarf.

Adomas was practically lying down on the passenger seat next to her with his legs bent up against the glove compartment and his collar pulled far up over his ears to where his hat reached. His eyes peered towards the country road and the forest. She squinted at him without turning her head.

"Is this what you were waiting for?"

"What? What do you mean?" He kept staring out the window, his voice sounding tired.

"That night. You were here, weren't you?"

"No, I said wasn't."

"You didn't ask which property was robbed. Why not?"

"Because it doesn't interest me."

"Because you already know which one?"

"Stop, I wasn't here."

"I know you didn't kill him. Your DNA proved that, but you were here, weren't you? You were the getaway driver who sat out here waiting."

"I told you I wasn't here and don't know anything about it, so drop it, Anne."

She took a piece of chewing gum. "Okay, we'll drop it."

"So, what are *we* really waiting for?"

"I don't really know. But if those pictures weren't meant to scare me, then maybe they were meant to enlighten me about something. Someone who wants to help me find my mum maybe."

"And what does us sitting here freezing our arses off in a car on a deserted country road have to do with her? We could be lying on the couch at home and having fun."

She pointed up at the sky. "That."

"What? The moon?" He put his head back against the headrest and stared up at it. His eyes shone in the darkness.

"Yes, the moon. The pictures may have been taken after a blót happened, and those with the moon in them might have been to tell me when the next blót is to take place. A full moon blót is something special for Asatruar."

"And?"

"And—it's a full moon tonight."

"Does that mean we have to sit here and stare at the moon all night?"

"No, of course not. We need to keep an eye on the road and see if anyone goes down into the woods. If this small farming community really has come together for a shared macabre faith, then they'd have to go out onto the road to get down into the forest."

"And if they're already down there now?"

Anne bit her lip and thought about it. "If we have to wait here too much longer, we'll go down and look."

"But you say you can't get in there."

"Then we'll have to cut a hole in the fence. I brought a pair of bolt-cutters with me." She nodded towards the back seat.

"You surprise me every day, Anne. Where the hell did you get a pair of bolt-cutters from?" He laughed softly as he sank further into his coat.

They sat for a long time looking at the moon. She laid her head against his shoulder and enjoyed that he was with her even though she had been against it in the beginning. Was her mother really somewhere inside the dark forest, and was she soon to be murdered—sacrificed? Benito was right that it sounded too crazy, but so many terrible things had happened that credibility was at breaking point. She closed her eyes and let her imagination run wild, though it did not reassure her. Adomas moved uneasily.

"Someone's coming down the road. He's seen us."

Anne sat up quickly.

"Maybe they got security guards after the home robbery; the police can't do that much. But he looks more like the Michelin Man."

The figure came closer, and Anne smiled, relieved. "It's just Brian. He lives in the collective."

"Maybe he's one of *them?*"

Brian knocked on the window, Anne rolled it down, immediately filling the car with subzero air.

"So you got my pictures?"

"It was *you* who sent them. What do you know, Brian?"

"More than you want to know." He looked at Adomas. "Who's he?"

"He's my cous— my boyfriend. He's okay."

Adomas glared just as hostilely at Brian, who cast a quick glance towards the back seat. "Follow me, then you won't need the bolt-cutters." Being smiley suited him even if it was forced.

They stepped out onto the ice and followed Brian. When they passed the No Trespassing sign, she thought of Vagn Mortensen and the muscular dog. Their tracks in the snow were covered, so it looked as if the sign was working and no one had been inside the forest.

"Come on, I know a shortcut here."

Thorn bushes ripped their clothes, and she grabbed Adomas's arm several times to avoid falling into the snowdrifts that were hard in the crusty frost. It crunched under their boots, and she wondered whether they were making too much noise, but Brian went on as if he knew the way. He stopped at the fence and pulled it out. "You're both so skinny, you can easily get through here, too." He laughed.

"How often have you been here?" she whispered.

He did not answer.

Silently, they walked after him. No light was needed—the moon shone brightly, reflecting the snow. Anne's legs were starting to cramp, and she dared whisper to Brian again. "How far is it? I had no idea the forest was so big."

"We'll be there soon. It's certainly not small, and the fence is broken further up in the forest, too, where it joins Trige Forest."

"It ends at Trige Skovvej," mumbled Anne, nodding. It was all falling into place now.

As they approached a clearing, Brian slowed down a bit. Suddenly, he stopped. "It's here. They haven't arrived yet." He lay plastic bags out in the snow. "Pull up a chair. We'll have to share. We should almost be buying tickets for the performance."

"And what performance is it exactly we're about to see?" Adomas sounded a little panicky; she wasn't feeling too good herself because she had an idea of what they were about to see or rather—stop.

They sat down. The cold immediately penetrated the plastic and their trousers, but they didn't get wet.

"Do you know who they are?"

"No, I've never seen their faces. It's always too dark."

"Where is the lake?"

"It's further down in the clearing, by those trees there, where the moon is shining through now. I thought that as a journalist researching what's going on in this forest, you'd be interested in seeing this."

"Thanks," she contented herself with saying, her conscience pricked. Although little white lies were everyday events for most people, no one really liked lying. That was probably why it was hard to look at people when you lied.

"It's not just that," Adomas said before she could stop him. "They have Anne's mother."

She looked at him angrily. Brian looked at her incomprehensibly.

"Have you seen the—uh, victims?" she asked.

 Brian nodded and stared again excitedly down towards the clearing.

"People, too?"

He laughed quietly. "No, are you mad?! Only a pig and a few chickens. The worst thing I've seen was a horse."

"Fuck." Adomas groaned.

"Have you witnessed a full moon blót?"

He did not manage to answer because Adomas grabbed her thigh and squeezed hard. "Shh, something's happening."

The flock came almost silently in the snow. Each bore a torch in their hands as they moved into a circle formation. A bonfire was lit in the middle, the smell of burning wood reaching them along with a longing for the fire and the warmth. Anne began to shake, and Adomas put an arm around her shoulders and pulled her to him. His heart was pounding.

"Where do they usually keep the victims?" she whispered, not moving her eyes from the performance.

"The horse was led into the circle with a rope around its neck," Brian replied in a trembling voice.

"That means they have a storeroom or something nearby." She tried to get up, Adomas pulled her down again desperately.

"Stay here!"

"I have to look."

"Do it tomorrow."

"Tomorrow will be too late."

"Then I'll go."

"It's best I go alone. It's less conspicuous." He pulled her down one more time as she tried to get up again.

"Am I going to regret letting you come?" she whispered, annoyed.

Brian's teeth shone in a smile. "Let the ladies decide—it's always easiest. Mine would rather see pictures of this; they turn her on." He laughed obscenely. Anne used Adomas's disbelieving gawk to get to her feet and jog in between the nearest bushes and duck down behind them. She had to go down to that lake. The Vikings hid their victims in lakes, the bogs of today.

She sneaked behind the séance, hidden by tree trunks and bushes, and could hear them praising the gods. It had begun with a resounding "Hail Odin" that they kept repeating. She caught sight of the lake. By the shore lay a small boat—it was frozen—stuck in the ice. There were a few nets in it. Could you fish here? Was that what had attracted Marcus? The fish? She moved closer and discovered the hole made in the ice. Not a little hole for pulling a fish up, rather a larger one so something big could be dropped in. The ice was probably about twelve centimetres thick; the hole had been made with a saw. Hyperventilating, she scouted around the area. There were many footprints leading further in between the trees. Something had been dragged through the snow, but the moon wasn't shining as brightly anymore; a cloud had slid in front of it. She looked up and was relieved that the cloud was small, and it wouldn't take long for nature's night light to shine again. Where were the traces of blood? Covered by snow? Removed? Of course they cleaned up after each blót. It could have been ages since Brian had taken those pictures. She sat down on the edge of the rowboat and waited. The moonlight slowly returned, and the tracks in the snow became clear again. She got up and followed them. The voices were now only an eerie whisper between the trees.

The wooden shed was suddenly ahead of her. The tracks stopped at the door. It wasn't locked. She pushed it open. The room was dark, so she left the door open to orient herself and spotted a torch lying on a sort of packing table. She turned it on. The first thing the cone of light hit was a large empty wooden box with a lid, then another. They seemed to be hastily made coffins. Snow had drifted in onto the cement floor, and the tracks continued further in. They sat in the corner of the shed, leaning against the wall. Their hands and feet were bound, and they appeared to be already dead. But could you sacrifice dead things to the gods? Wouldn't that provoke their anger? She ran to them and shook their lifeless bodies. Their skin was icy cold, but there was a pulse in each of them.

"Mum, wake up! Wake up now! Anita, can you hear me?"

She froze when she heard ice crunch outside. A dark shadow fell over the cement floor. She quickly turned off the torch and held her breath. Adrenaline pumped around her body. She was ready to defend herself and hugged the shaft of the torch.

"Hurry up, Anne. They're getting to the main attraction," said Adomas.

"Adomas," she sobbed, and her breathing began again with a loud gasp. "I could have fucking killed you! They're both here. Help me get them out of here."

Adomas squatted in horror in front of Rose and pulled up one of her eyelids. "She's been drugged—look at her pupils. They probably both have. Come on!" He lifted her slender mother up into his arms. "The two of us will have to take the other one." He carried Rose out of the shed and laid her gently in the snow out back. Together, they pulled Anita around there, too.

"It's bloody well impractical to weigh so much." Anne groaned. "How are we going to get her out of here?"

"I've no idea, but we have to hurry."

Anne dug the mobile phone out of her pocket and had to take off her gloves. She found Roland Benito's number, called, and listened impatiently. "Roland! It's Anne. You have to get to the forest now! It's urgent!"

Adomas stood again with her mother in his arms, and she wished she could do the same with Anita. She grabbed her arm with one hand and squeezed the phone to her ear with the other. The heat of rage and desperation rose in her cheeks. "Morten Holsted! No, I damn well won't! You'll come now and do not come alone! They are about to be dragged into a forest lake!" It would have sounded loud if there had been no crying in her anger. She hung up. "Come on, it's urgent!"

"Isn't it better to wait for the police?"

Anne looked back. They weren't far from the lake and the clearing where the ritual was taking place. "Who knows if they'll even come. They don't believe me. We'd better get away from here."

Adomas grabbed Anita's other arm and they dragged her between them through the snow like a sleigh. Rose draped lifelessly over his shoulder. They were hidden by the shed, but how long would it be before their tracks were found?

# 61

----

After the long and dramatic conversation with Giovanna on the phone, he couldn't sleep. The police had still found no trace of Salvatore, and Giovanna had accused them of not wanting or daring to do anything. But Roland knew the reaction. The police were easy scapegoats.

He got up carefully so as not to wake Irene and was happy for the dog's company in the kitchen, where he poured the last drop of the evening's red wine into a glass and sat down at the kitchen table. Angolo laid his head on Roland's thigh and looked up at him sadly. He patted him on the head. "Where's our Salvatore? He should have stayed with us so you could take care of him." Angolo whined quietly as if he understood what Roland was saying, Roland had to wipe his eyes. He drank from the glass without tasting the contents. The taste of guilt was bitter and surpassed all others.

Anita Andersen. Was that how she had felt since her brother drowned? How could you live like that? Of course, she had also tried to put an end to it all, but how psychotic was she really? Committed, the warden of Risskov had said. So hospitalised against her will and a lot of tablets to dull her senses, but did that kind of thing really go on nowadays if it wasn't justified? What if someone just wanted her out of the way? That seemed to only happen in Hollywood spy movies.

The moon shone out from between the bare branches of the copper beech outside the window. He looked down at Angolo's wet snout and whispered the words; the dog's ears shot up into a vertical position.

"How about two of us go for a little wee and tire ourselves out?" His voice was husky.

Angolo wagged his tail as Roland put his coat on over his pyjamas knowing he would freeze out there, but a physical pain might remove the inner one.

There was no wind, so it didn't seem as bitterly cold as the other nights had been. Angolo hurried to the nearest lamppost. Benito waited patiently and looked at the moon. The same moon was shining down somewhere on Salvatore, too. The night was so quiet. The muffled sound of the phone in his coat pocket reached him slowly. He had forgotten to take it out when he'd got home. The nightly calls were not his favourite. He took it and listened to Anne's tearful voice. She hadn't yet understood that he had nothing to do with the homeless people case. He reminded her who to contact, but then she grew rude and commanding and then had hung up on him. But something was wrong, that much he got. He went to the next lamppost with Angolo and let him sniff around. Far from all, he used a bag. He found Morten Holsted's number in the meantime. An eternity passed before his colleague responded with a sleepy voice.

"Roland Benito here. Sorry to wake you up so late, Morten, but I have something you need to look at in the missing homeless people's case."

"What case?"

"The homeless people. Has Isabella not given you the file? Olsen demanded that you take over."

"Roland, for God's sake, it's the middle of the night."

"I know it's the middle of the bloody night. Most crimes happen during the night. You have to get yourself to the private forest on Pannerupvej. Anne Larsen has—"

"Anne Larsen! The unemployed journalist? She's probably bored. Yeah, Olsen mentioned something about that case. He called it ludicrous."

"Ludicrous! Is it so ludicrous that homeless people are being abducted and perhaps murdered? Shouldn't they be protected like all their other fellow citizens?"

"Yes, Roland. Of course they should. Tell me, are you drunk?"

"Drunk! No . . . damn it! Does that mean that no one is dealing with the case?"

"Not me at least. And now I want to sleep, we have a drug raid early tomorrow morning. I've only got a few hours' sleep left. Goodnight, Benito." He, too, hung up.

"Bloody hell!" He pulled Angolo back inside against the dog's will, pushed him into the hall, took off Angolo's collar, and patted him apologetically on the head. Then he grabbed his car keys on the dresser.

# 62

They had been walking for an eternity, or so it felt. Anita's weight had put Anne's arm to sleep, and she suggested to Adomas that they change places. He set her mother down in the snow and shook her lightly, patting her gently on the cheeks.

"I think she's waking up. Rose, are you there?" Her mother's eyelids flickered. She tried to open her eyes. Narrow cracks blinked at them.

"Mum! Oh, thank God!" She patted her on the cheek as well.

"They may have just given them enough drugs so they'd still wake up for the main event. It's probably supposed to happen soon."

"Where am I?" muttered her mother, collapsing. Adomas shook her to consciousness again. Anne looked down at Anita.

"Why isn't *she* waking?"

"Maybe she's more susceptible than your mother."

"It would be nice if she were the one to come round first."

Suddenly, her mother threw up. Adomas kept her hair away from her face in the meantime.

"That's good—then whatever they gave her will come out."

Anne looked back. Their footprints and the deep mark from dragging Anita's heavy body lay behind them for as far as she could see. They might as well have lit their path.

"They'll find us in no time; we need to get going."

Rose was silent, but she was able to stand on her feet. Anne supported her. "Would you be able to carry Anita? It'd be better if we didn't have to drag her through the snow."

Adomas grumbled but tried to lift the girl. Sweat sprouted from his forehead, his thighs were heavy and uncertain, and his legs shook underneath him. But adrenaline was good fuel. They went faster now, and the tracks they left behind weren't as conspicuous.

Adomas moaned and set Anita down, supporting her, when they reached the fence.

"Brian said there was a hole somewhere else that would lead us into Trige Forest. But it's obviously not here." Anne leaned her mother up against the fence. "It'll probably be quicker if I find where it is on my own first and then come back for you."

"Which way are you going to go? If you have to go all the way around the forest, then we'll be discovered in the time it takes you to find it and come back."

"Okay." She hitched up her mother again. "Let's try going this way."

They walked along the fence. There was forest on the other side, too, but Vagn Mortensen's private one stopped here. Then she heard someone behind her. The crusty snow crunched with each step.

"Hurry up," she whispered behind Adomas, who was walking in front with Anita hanging limply over one shoulder. Fortunately, the moonlight had disappeared. Dark clouds had taken over the sky. The meteorologists had promised more snow during the night. It would probably fall soon. The footsteps behind her came closer, and she began to realise that it would be impossible to escape a trap behind the fence. She supported her mother and used the fence to keep her upright. Anne suppressed a scream as someone grabbed her arm and pulled her back. She turned around, struck into the air, and hit a face with great force.

"Ow! Fuck, you little . . ."

She struck again and again and didn't stop until Adomas shouted, "Stop, Anne! It's Brian!"

She forced her arms to stop and looked up at the face, which took shape in the dark. His nose was bleeding, but he was smiling. "You're a bit of a wildcat." He looked almost enviously at Adomas, which only increased her rage.

"What the hell do you think you're doing, sneaking up on me like that? I thought you were . . . Where are they?" She was about to cry hysterically.

"The police have arrived; it looks like the show is over. Who's that you're dragging around?"

"The victims. They would have done it again tonight, Brian. They've done it before with the homeless man. He was found with a rope around his neck. He escaped from here and found his way out through Trige Skov."

Brian's smile died. "Are you trying to find the hole in the fence? That would have taken you a long time—it's the other way. But come on. The police want to talk to you."

"With me? Is it Roland Benito?"

"Yeah, the Italian. You can follow your own tracks back. You were easy to find. I'm going to head back to the collective."

There were throngs of people by the lake. Some officers were talking to a small crowd by the fire. Roland was standing with Olga and Vagn Mortensen. Anne heard Vagn say that it was an innocent blót, which according to him was not illegal. He fell silent abruptly when he caught sight of her. She was supporting her mother, and Adomas was carrying Anita. Roland turned to them.

"You can say what you want, but you would have killed them and thrown them into the lake. What went wrong with Rudolf? And what was in the wooden chests in the shed?" She barged into Vagn Mortensen, not even looking at Roland, who was calling for an ambulance.

"What shed are you talking about?" he asked after the short conversation as he put the phone back in his pocket. He directed the flock to come with him as she showed the way. Adomas was left with Rose and Anita and some officers to wait for the ambulance.

They gathered in the shed.

"This is our storeroom," said Vagn. "We mostly use it in the summer."

"Yeah right. Storeroom!" snarled Anne.

"Is there no light here?" asked Roland. Shortly afterwards, a solitary blinding light bulb illuminated on the ceiling, forming long dark shadows across the empty boxes and giving them a ghostly air.

An officer, whom she recognised as DS Mikkel Jensen, took a closer look at the wooden chests. "Do you store fruit in these boxes here?"

Nobody answered.

"Forensics are on their way," Roland said to Mikkel and then stared at Vagn Mortensen. "You are right that a blót is not illegal, but murder is."

"Murder! No one here has murdered anyone."

Roland laid a hand on Anne's shoulder to hold her back. She would have gone straight for Vagn Mortensen's jugular like his killer dog had been close to doing to her.

"If there are victims here, Anne, where are they?" Roland's voice was still tainted with scepticism.

"Try the lake. I'm sure there are a lot of skeletons in there." she said, looking up at him. Only now did she notice he was wearing nightclothes under his coat. Striped pyjama bottoms were tucked into his boots.

"They killed Albert Hovgaard, too. I'm sure of it!"

Vagn stared malevolently at her. Then he smiled, scratched his beard, and looked at the detective with an indignant shake of his head. "It's hard to prove such an insane claim."

"Yes, without technical evidence, it is. There are, as you know, a few people here who refused to submit a voluntary DNA sample. But perhaps that ring you're waving about is enough." He nodded to Mikkel, who walked over and removed the ring from the big man's finger despite Vagn's attempts to prevent it. Mikkel held it up against the light bulb almost as though in triumph. Anne stared at it. She'd seen something similar on the internet when she'd read about the Vikings. It was a silver chieftain's ring. You could buy copies in the National Museum of Denmark's shop. It was a large and heavy ring divided into four high-relief sections that were sure to symbolise something. She wondered why Benito was interested in it.

"The boy, Marcus. Was he . . . ?" Mikkel Jensen couldn't bring himself to say the word, and his eyes on Vagn were filled with disgust.

"We didn't do anything to that boy. His sister should have looked after him so he didn't go down to the lake. That's what happens when there is a strange intrusion." Olga Mortensen's voice was dark and hoarse. She was hidden in the group and didn't make herself visible.

"I see; a strange intrusion. Was that what happened in Signe and Albert Hovgaard's home that night? First, a bunch of Eastern Europeans, and then you came and finished off their work? Is that how it happened?" asked Roland. When no one answered, he nodded to Mikkel and another officer, who led them all out of the shed and to the police station for questioning. The sound of ambulances disturbed the night. The owl was silent.

Roland put a hand on Anne's back and pushed her gently forward. "Take your mother to the hospital. We'll talk tomorrow."

She had tears in her eyes again. "Thank you, Roland. Thank you for believing me."

"Who says I do?"

She walked towards the ambulance, then she turned around. "You should either go home and change your clothes or go to bed again."

# 63

----

An aloof Ella Geisler was the first to speak. She admitted to having kept Signe in the bedroom while her husband and neighbours Thorkild and Vagn were in the kitchen with Albert, who had been beaten by the Eastern Europeans and needed help.

"But it wasn't exactly help that he got, was it?" said Roland with a patience he had to force. None of the men mentioned had confessed to anything, and the interrogations had been long and hard since the early morning, without yielding any result. He was exhausted, and if they had not lied to the Aboriginal woman and claimed that one of the others had said that she was involved, they wouldn't have got anything out of her, either. But he could sense that she wanted to reveal the terrible truth. As a rule, he found the weakest link in a bunch of suspects. Some had a harder time concealing that kind of thing than others—and that usually shone through.

"But let's take it all from the beginning. Signe Hovgaard wakes you up in the middle of the night and tells you that they have had a burglary. You and your husband follow her back and find Albert lying on the kitchen floor. What happened then?" He poured more water into her glass, and she took a mouthful before she started talking, looking down at the table. She hadn't looked him in the eye at any point. Mikkel sat with folded arms next to him.

"Albert has always threatened to report us to the police . . ."

She looked uncertainly at him, and he nodded in encouragement to continue.

"I took Signe into the bedroom and got a cloth to wash her face. In the bathroom, I heard Finn talking on the phone, and I looked out into the kitchen before going back to the bedroom. Albert was regaining consciousness, and I asked Finn if it was the police he had called. He replied that it was Thorkild and Vagn he had talked to and that they were on their way, for this was our chance to talk some sense into Albert. Then he led me back to the bedroom."

"Did you hear the fight in the kitchen?" Mikkel asked, leaning towards her.

"No, I closed the door so that Signe wouldn't hear the conversation. She doesn't know anything; it was only Albert. He claimed to have found something in an old box in the attic."

"What had he found?"

She shrugged. "Some pictures, I think."

"How many Asatruar are you?" asked Roland, fearing the answer.

"There's only us."

"Only us? You on the three farms? Are you the only woman?"

"No, Olga is a member, too, but not Gunda. She knows, of course, that Thorkild is a believer and accepts it, but she has never participated. There are five of us. Initially, we joined a faith community. That was how it all started, but it wasn't at all like we imagined. The gods demanded more."

"So you broke away from the community and established your own little sect?"

"It's not a sect!"

"Do your children know anything about this?" Mikkel asked.

"In time, Dorthe and Sam will become believers, too, but they aren't ready yet." Ella smiled a little, but quickly grew serious again when she saw their faces.

"So Finn summons Thorkild Hansen and Vagn Mortensen. What about his wife, Olga? Did she also take part?"

"No, she was asleep. Vagn got away without waking her. She gets nervous often, so—"

"So she knows what her husband has done?"

"Yes. Yes, of course she knows. She helped the homeless people to a better life, too."

"You have not helped anyone! You're common murderers. Crazy bastards!" Mikkel rushed up from the chair. Roland knew his limit was about to be exceeded. He had seen it coming and wished he had taken Isabella into the interrogation instead of sending her to the hospital. Mikkel left, slamming the door hard behind him, but there was nothing more to do now. Ella refused to say anymore. Roland was familiar with Mikkel's temper—it occasionally surpassed his own—but he wondered at this reaction. He was fuming; this was behaviour that a trained officer like DS Mikkel Jensen shouldn't show. It would warrant a reprimand.

Isabella was waiting in his office.

"Did they confess?" she asked.

"Ella Geisler opened up a little, right up until . . . We didn't get anything out of the others."

"Right up until what?"

"Nothing. Did you talk to Anita?"

"Yes, she had a credible explanation for how her blood had got on the petrol can. That night she had taken the bus out to her childhood home to pray at her brother's cross in the garden. She did that once in a while. She didn't know whether the new owners had removed it. But then she caught sight of someone with the petrol can about to set fire to the barn. She surprised him and tried to wrestle the can from him, cutting herself on the handle in the process. She succeeded, and the arsonist escaped. She immediately called the fire brigade from her mobile."

"So, she was the one who prevented the fire from becoming more extensive. But why did she not report him?"

"She doesn't know who it was—he was wearing a hoodie and fled quickly. And she said that the police didn't believe her anyway. She was a psychiatric patient at the time—who would have believed her?"

Roland nodded bitterly. Credibility was always at stake.

"Why did she return and move into the collective so close to where her brother died?"

"When she was discharged, she needed to get to the truth. Most of all, she wanted her parents to believe her. I didn't ask directly, but it sounded as if it was her plan to find out if the chest was still in the attic."

"So the home robbery got in her way?"

"You could say that."

"But what was she doing in the private forest in the middle of the night?"

"Following Brian Kjeldsen, who had apparently also noticed the mysterious goings-on."

"So, maybe he was the one who sent those pictures to Anne. Did he know who Anita really was?"

"I don't think so. There was no one who could recognise her—not even Andreas, who had known her as a child. Back then she was fair-haired, small, and slender, but she's far from that now."

"But she was discovered, and Brian wasn't."

"She said that Brian was able to squeeze through a hole in the fence but that she had to go back, and on the way out of the forest, she was knocked down and woke up in an old house, which may have been the back room of Vagn Mortensen's farm shop."

"We'll check that out."

"Yes, Niels went over there."

They sat in silence for a moment.

"But do you really think Marcus was murdered and thrown into the lake to make it look like a drowning accident?"

"A child? No, I doubt it. Forensic details would have been uncovered if it had been a murder."

"How could they kill people like that? I just don't understand. Do they really believe so much in the Norse gods that they . . . ?"

"It seems they believed that while benefiting themselves with the blessings of the gods, they were also giving the homeless people a better life. Maybe they really did for a short time."

"Yes, until they needed them. Maybe it's an honour to be given to the gods? So, the motive for Albert Hovgaard's murder was that he was going to unmask them. That's sick. Will they be psychologically examined?" Isabella had the same expression on her face as her boyfriend had when he'd abruptly left the interrogation.

"Definitely. The ring has been sent for analysis—I'm sure it was on the perp's hand—so when the results come back, there won't be much to deny." Roland had a hard time finding satisfaction, there was too much still nagging at him.

"Which of them is missing two molars?" Isabella continued.

"Thorkild Hansen."

"Imagine, the journalist was right about extremist Asatruar being behind it. That they were also behind the murder of Albert Hovgaard was impossible to predict, so if she hadn't—"

"How is her mother?" interrupted Roland.

"She's feeling better but is having withdrawal symptoms. I hope they send her to rehab, so—"

This time it was the phone that interrupted her. Roland received a short message. He put on his coat. "I have to go out to the forest lake. They've found something out there."

The lake looked so different in sunlight compared to the moonlight. Now it lay in all its bright beauty surrounded by tall, bare trees and dazzling white. The ice had been broken and scattered along the shore in big flakes. On a large tarpaulin spread over the snow, some skeletal remains had been laid out. A pair of dark skulls seeing the light of day after a long stay in the water. The Bog Case from the autumn popped into his memory, but these skeletons had been stripped of everything, and so they weren't nearly as macabre to look at. It was a textbook illustration of what skulls looked like. On a stretcher lay a corpse. The appearance told him it was a homeless man. The rope was still around his neck. He hadn't been as lucky as Verner Thybo, who had escaped. If anyone who saw him could call him lucky.

"How many does that make it?"

"We've found two or three. We don't think there are more. But the bones need to be sorted and identified. Some of them are from animals. The biggest is from a horse."

"A horse!? And the man on the stretcher? When did that happen?"

"It's difficult to judge due to the freezing temperatures, but the hanging may have taken place about two weeks ago. It probably took place there." Leander pointed to a tree at the end of the lake; a technician was examining it for evidence. Roland narrowed his eyes in the bright light and tried to imagine the séance on a dark night. Then the image of the lake on a hot summer's day came to mind. It had to be beautiful. Pigs trotting about and rooting in the ground by the lake shore, drinking the water . . . "From farm to fork."

"Call me when you know more," he told Leander and left.

* * *

Outside the woods, people had gathered behind the police cordon. A journalist tried to ask him a question, but he quickly dismissed it without hearing it and got into his car. Again, he thought it was strange not to see Anne Larsen's dark head in the crowd.

# 64

Anne laid her head against his shoulder and felt the T-shirt's soft cotton fabric against her cheek, inhaling his scent and closing her eyes. This is how every night should be from now on, she decided. No more dangerous missions that could prevent moments like this. His arm lay protectively around her, and she sighed comfortably. *Family is a good thing.* She gave a sly little smile. Maybe her relationship with her mother would change now, too. Then she only needed to find a good job, and life would be perfect.

They had seen the news on TV, and it was hard to understand that they had been involved in the crime that everyone would now be talking about for a while.

"It's incomprehensible," Adomas said.

"I hope people don't start holding it against Asatruar. It's a few bad eggs. Asatru is actually beautiful."

"Is it? Do you think your mother thinks so, too?" Adomas pulled her closer to him and kissed her neck.

"I don't think she's fully aware of what has happened. Anita is, though. She keeps saying that Marcus didn't drown, but there's no evidence of that."

"What kind of evidence did she have in the chest?"

"She had seen them by the lake one evening and had taken pictures like the ones Brian sent me. But something suggests the chest was burned, so Albert didn't have anything on them anyway, but, of course they didn't know that."

"But it's not proof that they did anything to her brother."

"No, but you don't know . . ."

Adomas's mobile cut her off. He looked at the display and got up quickly. She looked at him worriedly as he walked into the bedroom and answered. He spoke Lithuanian, and she decided she wanted to learn that language. She *should* learn it. It was the second time since she'd come home from the hospital after visiting her mother that his phone had rung. He stood by the window, looking out as he spoke. First in a calm voice, then more excitedly. Just like last time. She half continued to watch a nature documentary on sharks on Discovery before he came back and sat down with her.

"Who rang? Your family?" It was her family, too, so she probably had a right to know what they had talked about. He didn't answer and got two cans of beer from the fridge. He handed her one and sat down again. The can was cold in her hand, and she didn't know if it was that or Adomas's eyes that made her freeze. They opened the beers and drank. She lay down on him again and looked up at his face.

"Aren't you going to tell me who it was?" Your wife maybe?" She smiled so he could see she meant it jokingly.

"I have to go."

She straightened up and set the beer on the coffee table. "What do you mean by *go*? To Lithuania? Has anything happened at home?"

"I can't say any more, Anne." He emptied the beer can in one gulp and put it down.

"But you promised you wouldn't go back. You . . ."

He got up and went back into the bedroom, where he found his bag.

"Tell me what the fuck is going on! Where are you going?"

He didn't answer. Shirts, jumpers, and trousers were thrown into the bag, then he got his toiletry bag from the bathroom. It dawned on her that he meant it seriously. He placed the bag on the floor by the door and came over to her, squatted down in front of her, and took her face between his hands. Kissed her. In a way that suggested it would be a very long time before they would get to do it again.

"I'm doing this for you. As soon as I can, I'll call you."

She couldn't find the words. Not even a feeling. Was she upset? Angry?

"I'm coming with you. I can pack a bag quickly." She wanted to get up, but he pushed her back onto the couch.

"You can't come. Maybe later, but not now."

"Tell me where the fuck you're going!"

"I'll ring you." He put on his coat, grabbed his bag, and left before she could find a way to prevent it. She heard his footsteps disappearing down the stairs, got up stiffly, and walked to the window. Watched him come out the front door and go to a waiting car. He really did it—had left her here. The anger turned into a tight lump in her throat. To tears that she held back. She watched the red taillights until the car turned the corner at the traffic lights and disappeared. It was dark and deserted again down on the road. She wanted to turn around, but then the headlights on another parked car turned on, and it slowly pulled out from the kerb and drove the same way. A black estate car. When it drove under the streetlight, she squinted and focused. It had Lithuanian plates. Her blood froze. She ran to get her coat and found her phone in the pocket. Pressed Adomas's number so fast that at the first attempt she hit the little keys incorrectly. She went to the window again while waiting for his voice. The street was empty, cold and frozen, just like she felt inside. It took a while before a metallic female voice announced that there was currently no connection to the dialled number. She sat down heavily with her mobile in her hand and stared at the television screen where the sharks were tearing apart their prey under-water, staining it red with blood.

# 65

Roland remained seated in the car under the copper beech after turning off the engine. The darkness was about to subside. A lone blackbird sat puffed up on the bird table, where it had found shelter from the wind and frost.

There wasn't the same relief at the solving of a case that he usually felt. Chief Superintendent Olsen hadn't seemed as chipper as was customary after a successful case. He had apologised for not believing the expounding as Roland had presented it to him, but had also stated that Marcus Andersen had drowned, so there should be no more digging into that. Roland couldn't blame him for his doubts. Even he had had a hard time believing Anne Larsen. But it only went to show that completely outlandish theories shouldn't be rejected, either. Motives and methods of murder were constantly evolving along with new cultures and beliefs in society.

He got out of the car and stood for a moment, looking at the house in the middle of slowly falling snowflakes that hit his face and melted. There was a dim light in the kitchen window, as if only the lamp in the cooker hood was on. Irene was probably sitting in the living room and watching TV. Salvatore's snowman had turned into a creepy creature after the last thaw. Angolo had peed a yellow zigzag stripe up it. He pulled himself together and went up the steps. Wondered why something was holding him back.

There was no life in the house when he let himself in. Not even Angolo met him like he most often did. He took off his coat, scarf, and gloves and went out into the kitchen with all his senses on guard. Something was wrong.

Irene was sitting practically in the dark at the kitchen table with a kitchen roll in front of her. She lifted a tear-soaked face and looked at him. He read her eyes, and his heart froze. In the open door to the bedroom, he saw the suitcases ready. The tickets were on the table. He stared at them and then at Irene.

"They . . . They found Salvatore?"

She nodded, not having to say anything.

He sat down on the chair opposite her. She took his hand and squeezed it hard.

# ACKNOWLEDGEMENTS

*A Strange Intrusion* takes place in Aarhus and the surrounding area like my two previous detective stories *Dead in the Skip* and *Death on Demand*. If you try to find the farms, the forest, and the lake on Pannerupvej in Trige, you will actually find something similar. But this is not intentional—all characters are fictional—though most of that fiction has been spiced with real events.

The research work is the greatest part of writing a novel. Many questions arise along the way that the internet alone cannot answer. I have again this year been overwhelmed by all the help I have received when I have asked, and I would like to take this opportunity to thank everyone for sharing their time and knowledge so actively. Many thanks to:

Chief Superintendent for Organised Crime at East Jutland Police Jens Peter Andersen.

An Asatru who shared information on the everyday life of Asatruar despite my eerie interpretation. However, they preferred to remain anonymous, which, of course, I understand and respect.

René Dybdal Pedersen, PhD, external associate professor and development consultant, Faculty of Theology, Aarhus University, for information on the Asatru and insight into his own book *I Lysets Tjeneste* [*In the Service of Light*—available in Danish only] about new religious and spiritual groups in Denmark.

And thank you to Else Lindhardt, night services of Kirkens Korshær charity for her help with information about working with the homeless in

Aarhus, shelters, and other services. It's a huge job that Kirkens Korshær does on a completely voluntary basis.

Thank you, too, to my friend Margit, who read the manuscript through with critical eyes and always supported me with encouragement and help when something wasn't quite right.

Not least, thank you to all my readers for accepting *Death on Demand* as much as *Dead in the Skip*. I hope *A Strange Intrusion* will also be read by many.

A very special thanks to the publishing director, Susanne Jespersen, Forlaget DarkLights, for wanting to continue our collaboration even though I chose to go my own way. Thank you for your understanding and help with editing and proofreading.

Inger Gammelgaard Madsen, 2010

# ABOUT THE AUTHOR

Inger Gammelgaard Madsen is a prolific Danish crime writer best known for her Rolando Benito detective series. Ever fascinated by police work and forensics, crime fiction was a natural fit for Madsen when, after working for some time as a graphic designer, she decided to return to her first love: writing. She is also the author of the Mason Teilmann series, which has been published in four languages.

www.ingramcontent.com/pod-product-compliance
Lightning Source LLC
Chambersburg PA
CBHW031249120726
47906CB00003B/665